P9-DHA-369

Praise for *Sugar*

"*Sugar* by Deirdre Riordan Hall is one of those books that sneaks up and hits you in the gut with its powerful truth. *Sugar* is not easy to read. Between the nearly pornographic description of food and the cruel slanders of those who are supposed to love her, this novel will take you down the dark path Sugar is walking. But as she sees a light at the end of the tunnel, you will be reminded of hope and the importance of loving yourself first and foremost."

—Hypable

"*Sugar* is about a teenage girl who seeks solace in the sugary, greasy foods she both craves and despises . . . Yet Sugar summons the strength to find her own inner beauty, and it's not a size zero. Her triumph is heartbreaking and triumphant."

—*Denver Post Pages*

"Sugar's character has depth, and her unhappiness and determination to conquer it are realistically portrayed. Readers will sympathize with Sugar and understand her struggle to reach her full potential."

—*Publishers Weekly*

DISCARD

PEARL

Also by Deirdre Riordan Hall

Sugar

To the Sea

Surfaced

In the Desert

Mirrored

On the Mountain

Kindled

PEARL

DEIRDRE RIORDAN HALL

SKYSCAPE

SKYSCAPE

This is a work of fiction. Names, characters, organizations, places, events, and incidents are either products of the author's imagination or are used fictitiously.

Text copyright © 2016 by Deirdre Riordan Hall.
All rights reserved.

No part of this book may be reproduced, or stored in a retrieval system, or transmitted in any form or by any means, electronic, mechanical, photocopying, recording, or otherwise, without express written permission of the publisher.

Published by Skyscape, New York.
www.apub.com

Amazon, the Amazon logo, and Skyscape are trademarks of Amazon.com, Inc., or its affiliates.

ISBN 10: 1503948587 (paperback)
ISBN 13: 9781503948587 (paperback)
ISBN-10: 1503953092 (hardcover)
ISBN-13: 9781503953093 (hardcover)

Cover design by Shasti O'Leary-Soudant

Printed in the United States of America.

Dedicated to my sister, MDS, xo.
And to all my sisters everywhere, you are loved.

"No, I do not weep at the world—I'm too busy sharpening my oyster knife."

—*Zora Neale Hurston*

Chapter 1

The sweltering days of late summer make me yearn for a great escape, but all I have to hang on to is this so-called life. With the start of school in a few weeks, at least there will be art class to distract me. For now, I'm standing outside Darren's—my mother's boyfriend—apartment door, dreading what's on the other side, wishing to paint myself out of this picture.

The key I received last March, when we moved in, cuts into my palm. My legs are as useless as cooked noodles, and my stomach twists in its usual knot, telling me *don't go in*. The nausea particular to this situation worsens as Janet, my mom, shouts, her voice carrying through the thin plaster. The timbre reveals that she's been using. I resent my watch for keeping slow time—I don't know why I wear it. It indicates it isn't yet midday. She probably hasn't even slept.

A door slams inside the apartment. I count to ten and then slip the key in the lock, hoping to sneak into my room.

The toxic smell of burning plastic bites my nose. Today on the menu, crack. With the utmost delicacy, I close the door behind me. As I turn around my mother stands opposite me, in the doorway to her room. Blue-gray smoke billows out from behind her.

It isn't that I'm startled or scared or spooked. It's something else, and it's heavy, like dread.

"Where the hell have you been?" she barks.

"Just went out to get something to eat," I reply cautiously. One wrong word will send her down a rabbit hole of paranoia and hysteria.

Darren appears behind her and places his hands on her bony waist and his nose in the crook of her neck—it looks like a mossy place to be. Unsteadily, she elbows him off as if he's a needy stray unworthy of her attention.

He pushes by her to the kitchen and gets a beer out of the fridge. The only thing I can say for Darren is he pays his electricity bill. The power company turned off the service in the place we lived last winter with a group of burned AA dropouts. I'm lucky I still have my toes.

My mother stalks over to me. When I meet her eyes, they're darker than they should be. Her once-long, perfectly straight hair tangles into a matted nest. A clip hangs in the back, suggesting she had it up earlier.

How much earlier?

When I'd slipped out, I didn't dare check to see if they were home. Maybe they'd been partying somewhere else all night and just returned. She doesn't get VIP treatment anymore, but the low-dwelling addicts she associates with consider it an honor to slum it with the formerly great Janet Jaeger, queen of the guitar, the melodic growl, and rock and roll. Or so she thought. Where there was once fame and fortune, now there remains the rough gravel of her undoing, causing friction and blisters to wear me thin in some places and leave calluses in others.

Experience promises that this will be a long day.

"I just came back to grab—"

I can't think of what to say as she puts her clammy hands on each of my shoulders. I need to think of my exit strategy and quick. But my body, already riddled with nerves, bails out, shuts down, gonzo, just as it always does.

What's it going to be this time?

My mouth is dry.

What kind of nonsense will she say?

My mind clouds.

Is this addiction or insanity? The line between the two seems narrow.

She brings me over to the tatty couch.

What new theft of my mother's personality will she reveal?

When my mother is high, she has a series of tics or, like an unskilled poker player, tells, varying slightly from drug to drug, indicating to my knowing eyes and ears that she's been using.

Her body tremors. But to my semi-relief, docile Janet presents herself; it's the ascension in the rickety cart on the roller coaster before the plunge. I want to let go, but all I know how to do is hold on tight.

"Let's listen to *Pearl*." She isn't talking about listening to me but to the Janis Joplin album, my namesake. Joplin is a classic Janet Jaeger move. Her eyes shutter as "Move Over" comes out of the torn cloth covering the speakers. Her soundless lips move in time with the lyrics.

Darren grabs another beer and quietly nips back to their bedroom. *Crap.* She won't be pleased if he takes a hit without her.

She opens her eyes. Her lips twitch. "I first heard Janis at a party in—it was—"

I recite the well-worn monologue in my head.

"I can't—" She's more spaced out than usual.

"At the party after the Shrapnels show at the Starlight, in Texas, Mom?"

This reminder puts her back in the worn groove of the story. I just want to get the ordeal over with.

"Someone passed me a hit, and when I inhaled Janis's music was there, like her ghost had come back and she was singing just for me. I said, 'Hey, what's this?' Some asshole told me all about Janis Joplin, like he had written her biography. Probably did. And I realized I'm Jan too, *Jan*is, *Jan*et, *the* Janet Jaeger, JJ. I wanted to marry that album." Her voice trails off, and her breath slows.

I want to press my ear against her chest to make sure her heart is still warm, still beating, but I'm frozen.

"And what about the Shrapnels? How could we measure up to that fierce voice of hers? That sweet as honey-wine sound . . ." my mom says, drifting, reminiscing.

I wish I were anywhere but here. I'd take the Starlight back in the nineties, the humid streets; I'd even settle for nowhere, wherever that is.

She goes on. "Then that guy, with eyes like yours, said, 'You were great. You rocked the joint. Wish I could play like that. You're an animal.' Those were the days, Pearl. Wish you could have met him. Nah, I don't. But there was nothing like hearing those songs that first time. Janis was fuckin' alive with rock and roll, but now you carry on her legacy. You carry the name, Pearl." She tries to approximate a meaningful smile but looks deranged.

I have no interest in carrying on anyone's legacy, not Janis's, or Janet's, for that matter. I sense she's hinting about my father but know better than to ask.

She slumps back on the couch, her eyes halfway closed. I want to get away, away from the tired, old story and away from the stranger who is my mother.

Suddenly she sits up. "Darren," she says. White spit showers the slivered glass coffee table. "Darren," she calls louder. "Where the hell is he?" Moments before she'd looked like she might have passed out in reverie, but like a rabid coyote, she clambers to her feet. "Where did he go?" she shouts at me accusingly.

The apartment boasts six hundred square feet of valuable Manhattan real estate, and a quick scan reveals he isn't in the closet that passes for my bedroom. The bathroom door hangs open and dark, narrowing the possibilities down to only one other room.

My mother jiggles the doorknob to their bedroom. "If you used the rest of our shit, I'm going to—" She doesn't finish because the flimsy door bursts open, emitting another puff of menacing smoke.

"You're goin' to what?" Darren asks, shirtless and sinewy.

"Where is it, Darren?"

A fiendish smile peels back his lips. "Up in smoke, bitch." He laughs.

With that, she lunges feebly at him. Glass smashes. I shudder. They disappear for a moment before my mother emerges from the room, still dressed in nothing more than a ratty T-shirt under a faux-fur vest, and underwear. The magnetic fascination she once wore so well vanishes like smoke.

She snatches his wallet from the counter and hustles to the front door. She trips over an empty case of beer, a blanket, and some guitar cables—items carelessly discarded in the littered apartment. I curse myself for not leaving when she went into the bedroom.

Darren trips over an extension cord but catches JJ's ankle as she unlatches the chain lock. She falls to her knees. I cower on the couch. This is their fight. I've tried intervening in the past, but with a slap to the face, my mother made it clear that I should stay out of it.

"Where the hell do you think you're going?" he asks her, though it is less a question and more a warning.

"What do you think you're doing, using all our shit?" she says.

"My shit," he corrects.

"I went and got it."

"I paid for it," he counters.

She tries to wriggle out of his grasp, but unable to, she stands on one foot and with the other pushes down, hard, on his hand.

"Damn it, JJ. I need my fucking fingers." He jerks her ankle, struggling to get to his feet. "Give me my wallet."

"Give me the money to get more," my mother pleads, the fire dying in her voice.

"No," he says.

"Are you holding out on me?"

They scrabble against the dirty linoleum. A coatrack falls. I close my eyes. I hear a smack of skin on skin, probably my mother's hand meeting Darren's cheek, the former being the champion of the slap. I pull my knees into my chest. Janet squeals. A dull thud follows. I put my hands over my ears. Unable to leave because they still block the front door, I scurry to my room; snap up the latest issue of *Vogue* blocking the doorway, the glossy cover scorched by drug paraphernalia—no doubt JJ's doing—and shut myself in.

Through the thin wall, the fighting continues to the sound track of *Pearl*. "A Woman Left Lonely" plays, underlining exactly how I feel. A door slams, telling me they're back in their room.

I take out my journal and the cheap watercolors I got at a ninety-nine-cent store on Sixth Avenue. As I bring the brush to the paper, I let the liquid colors carry me away like a river of tears.

I consider running away from the madness. It wouldn't be the first time. I live in a frenzied cycle where my mother hits rock bottom, then inevitably gets clean and promises sobriety, and I stick around if only to look after her and make sure nothing happens.

Where would I go?

I practically already live on the streets, so that's not much of a leap. Becoming a ward of the state is as unappealing as licking an ashtray. My uncle Gary and his family live in a prestigious neighborhood just outside the city, and last I checked he wanted nothing to do with his sister and, by extension, me. Especially after he discovered she sold the car he'd bought her and received notice that we'd been evicted from the condo he'd rented for us, which messed up his credit. After my grandfather and then grandmother passed away years ago, he'd stepped in, but even then, JJ was beyond help. It's as though she took the notorious destruction of hotel rooms and stages to an extreme and went ahead and bashed and smashed everything else in her life.

My uncle doesn't know Janet hasn't touched a guitar for years, practically since I was born. She had me around the time when her band left the charts, when junkies traded CDs for cash, and when the sonic landscape as she'd known it became a digital blur. I was like a punctuation mark, the end.

For a while, my uncle believed his sister was a successful musician who'd fallen on hard times, and excused her behavior with a tight-lipped shake of the head. After a long string of deceptions, he caught her in a weak, hole-filled lie in her already-deep trench of fabrications. The final straw was when she stole and sold my late grandmother's rare and treasured print of *Watermelons* by the famed artist Frida Kahlo. It had been left to my uncle, but was always the centerpiece of my grandparents' home—an oasis in the mire of dysfunction. The painting, not their household.

The quarterly royalty check my mom receives is the only thing, aside from boyfriends and handouts, that keeps us going. She's reduced the small inheritance she received from her parents to ashes, but she doesn't know that yet. I opened the statement when it came in the mail recently, and the little zero under *account balance* made me fear we'll disappear into a black hole, supernova out of this world into a void, into nothing, oblivion. There is nowhere for us to go.

Lying on my bed, I look up at the framed poster of the Shrapnels on my wall. The three women pose haughtily around a military tank. In tight pants and tall boots that reach her knees, Nell, the drummer, straddles the cannon. She hit drugs and alcohol hard and ended up dying almost a decade ago. Sandra, the bassist's, long feathered hair falls past her bare shoulders. She wears a tube top that exposes her midriff. She did OK. After rehab, she became a real estate agent somewhere in the Southwest. Then there's my mother, the singer, the guitarist, the performer, and the addict, standing atop the tank, wearing a fringed miniskirt and a torn-up T-shirt. She's smirking at the camera.

Looking at this shot of her, taken when she was a handful of years older than me, is like looking in a mirror. We have the same stick-straight blond hair, only I have bangs and very thick eyebrows that

9

somehow grow darker than my hair. We share defined cheekbones and full lips, along with a smirk. I only hope that this reflection is all that I've inherited from her.

Sometimes I wish I'd known her then. I'm not sure when her life as I know it, one of addiction and poverty, crystallized, but she hangs on to her glory days with a death grip.

The wall adjacent to my mother and Darren's bedroom quakes, yet the earth, somehow, is still. She's the earthquake, the wrecking ball, the walking disaster.

The signed and framed Shrapnels poster drops to the floor, balances for a moment on the edge of the baseboard, then falls forward, shattering the glass. My tacked-up poster of Frida Kahlo, wearing agony and beauty in the same subtle smile, remains affixed to the wall. I hear a crack followed by a cry of pain from beyond my small room. The front door slams, and moments later, my door opens.

Chapter 2

Sweat and tears intermingle on my mother's face, and a cut bleeds slowly from the side of her eye.

"Pearl, we gotta get out of here."

I've heard this before. We've had to leave abruptly from other situations: lousy boyfriends, landlords she owed rent to, roommates she'd stolen from, and the police.

As the stream of blood reaches her T-shirt, she clutches her side. Her face crumples in agony. "I think I have a broken rib. He hit me with his guitar."

Everything about this is wrong. I want to wish it all away—go somewhere simple, clean, and faraway, like Antarctica. I'd prefer the cold to the fevered flush of fear running through me. I get to my feet and grab a pair of stretch pants from the floor. I help her into them. As she leans on me, we slowly make our way to the door. In the hall, she falls against the door frame of the bathroom.

"Come on, Mom, let's go." She probably needs an ambulance, but who knows how much crack—and whatever else—she has in her system, so I dare not get the police involved. We've gone that route, and I don't want to see her arrested again.

"Wait. Get my purse and some clothing. Pack me a bag. No, never mind. I'll do it," she says hoarsely. She gets to her hands and knees and crawls back to her room.

"Mom, come on, let's just go. I can come back for whatever you need later." I grip my hands together, my fingers blanching as I hold on tight.

"I have to get a few things," she whimpers.

"I'll get them. Tell me what you need," I say insistently, my vision starting to blur.

She shakes her head, continuing. She wants to get the crack pipe and other drug paraphernalia she has hidden in her room. This scenario is uncomfortably familiar.

I shift from foot to foot. My stomach clenches with anxiety. *What if Darren comes back?*

Part of me fears what other damage he might do, but the bitter part is that if he comes back with drugs, she'll do them instead of getting medical attention.

"Mom, let's go."

She must have used the bed to pull herself up and stand, because she emerges, staggering on her feet, dragging a duffel bag. "Why don't you grab some clothes too?"

I scoot past her and stuff a couple of outfits, underwear, and *Vogue* into my backpack. I scrounged whatever I could this past month, saving every penny, even the ones I found on the ground, to get the latest issue, my lone extravagance. "Ready?" I say when I step back into the hall.

She nods. Step-by-step, we make our way down two of the three flights. She droops on the top of the last one.

"Do you have any money?" she asks.

"No," I answer honestly. I tried getting a job, but no luck. I complain that I have a young face, and well-meaning adults assure me that when I get older, I'll be thankful. It doesn't help me now. I inherited my mother's youthful look, the one she had before drugs and alcohol took their toll. But I'm already taller than her, five seven to her five three, my father's genes. I'm slender, but that probably has more to do with the scarcity of a hot meal than anything else. She occasionally reminds me I have my father's gray eyes and his height, like my DNA insults her.

She mumbles something about going to the bank, but all she'll find are overdraft fees and denied credit. I'm afraid to tell her.

"Go out to the street. See if you recognize anyone. Tell them I need to see them," she orders me.

I bound down the stairs. It takes my eyes a moment to adjust as I emerge into the bright summer sun. I look up and down the sidewalk. A homeless guy perches on top of a newspaper box, and a kid rides by on a bike. Finding someone my mother knows is a sketchy task. I retreat inside.

"I didn't see anyone."

"Pearl, I need to get out of here." Her cheek rests against the grimy wall, and the gash on the other side still bleeds, staining her yellow T-shirt crimson around the shoulder. "Go across the street to the apartment with the Christmas wreath on the door. Knock six times." She lifts her knuckles and beats them, weakly, on the floor. "Ask for Pauline."

The building across the street houses a pimp and an assortment of women who emerge, raccoon-like, around dusk. I've met Pauline, long limbed, with scars on her arms that she doesn't try to hide. My mother has gone over there a few times and returned with fifty, and sometimes a hundred, bucks.

I knock as directed. Vinyl blinds part, and a pair of bloodshot eyes appear. The door opens a crack. I seize the opportunity.

"I'm looking for Pauline. My mom, across the street, needs to see her. It's urgent."

The door opens just enough to let me slip through into a dark foyer. Something like cinnamon hangs in the air, but mostly I smell cigarettes and defeat.

A woman about my mom's age, wearing a silk robe, leads me back to the kitchen.

"Midge. Says she's lookin' for Pauline. Somethin' about her mother across the street."

A giant of a man sits at the kitchen table, playing solitaire. He looks up at me and licks his lips. "Whatcha looking for, sweetheart?"

I swallow hard. Leave it to my mother to put me in this situation. I draw a breath. "Janet, across the street, Pauline's friend, she just needs her help real quick." I sense that if I bring any word of trouble to the table, they'll escort me to the door.

Midge looks at me full on, his eyes simultaneously hungry and concerned. Finally, he jerks his head toward the lady who answered the door. She gives me a sharp look before exiting.

"Pauline will be right with you," he says gruffly before returning to his game.

With the toe of my boot, I trace the lines between the tiles on the floor like a maze, trying to find a way out of feeling vulnerable and helpless.

I hear Pauline's smoky voice from down the hall before she appears. She greets me with her arms opened wide. Even though we've only met a few times, a long embrace is her customary greeting.

As we exit the shady building, Pauline asks, "You still collecting those magazines?"

I nod.

"I'll be sure to save some for you. Sometimes the girls leave them in the house."

I hope I'm not still hanging around here by the time the next issue comes out.

I jaywalk through traffic, filling Pauline in on what happened. I worry Darren may have returned.

When Pauline pushes open the door to the building, my mother is where I left her, but with her eyes closed. At first, I fear she fainted, but she's probably been up at least twenty-four hours, if not longer. Pauline, gentle as ever, strokes my mother's leg to wake her up. For a vague instant, I picture Pauline tending babies or the elderly. She doesn't belong in this harsh life.

"Pauline," my mom says, brightening.

"Hiya, JJ, how ya doin'?" she coos softly.

"Been better."

"Well, come on," Pauline says, wrapping her arms underneath my mother's to help her up.

"Where we going?" Pauline asks, but before my mother answers, Pauline suggests, "How about the Constance House up on Riverside?"

I get the sense she's done this before. Constance House is a battered women's shelter—a place I doubt will abide my mother's lifestyle—and as such, I expect Janet to protest, but apparently Pauline's caring manner is all the convincing she needs.

"Pearl, you have a towel or something? She can't go in a cab like this. She needs shoes too."

I run upstairs. Each step reminds me that Darren might be back any second. I grab a pair of flip-flops and look in the bathroom cabinet for a towel. There aren't any clean, so I pull a worn pillowcase off the bed and race back down to meet them outside.

"Thatta girl. Thanks," Pauline says as she helps my mother into the flip-flops. Janet's eyes are nearly closed as she leans heavily against Pauline's shoulder.

It's times like these I'd also like to give myself over to Pauline's capable hands, the hands of a mother, sister, caretaker. Instead, she hails a cab and hands me a twenty.

"Look after her, Pearl," she says before I close the cab door. That's what I've been trying to do, but how can she expect a kid to look after a grown woman when neither one knows how to take care of herself?

The cab drops us off on a side street in front of an anonymous brick building. A woman with tight curls confidently helps us inside. I flash to a magazine clipping of my mother holding her hand up to the camera as she emerged from a limo, back when the Shrapnels were big. It was rock star glitz and glamour. Now it's just grit.

I suppose sightings of Janet are about as significant as spotting a yeti. She dropped off the rock scene years ago, but the public doesn't know my uncle bought her out so she'd keep quiet when he decided to step into the political spotlight. If nothing else, Uncle Gary doesn't want anything to tarnish his upstanding good-old-boy reputation. I imagine she knows about a few skeletons in his custom-built closet. He should have known his money, the condo, and the car had an expiration date.

The lady who helped us out of the car examines my mother's wounds, and the two of them disappear to another room. If she recognizes JJ, she doesn't say as much. When I was younger, fans would stop JJ, asking for an autograph, but in the last ten years, it seems she's slipped from everyone's minds, including her own.

I sit in a stiff chair like the kind in hospital waiting rooms, twisting a wisp of my hair around my finger. A sign on the wall explains in English and Spanish that domestic violence is unacceptable. There's a number to call for help at the bottom. A phone rings somewhere in the background.

The lady returns with a clipboard. "Don't worry. Your mom is going to be OK."

I know that without her telling me. Janet is always OK, fine, or all right, but never any more than that and most of the time a lot less.

"I asked her a few questions, but she's resting, and I was wondering if you could try finishing. She indicated that she wanted help and to stay here with us, but first we need to know some things. Can you help?"

I nod, aware that answering very carefully means the difference between having a place to stay tonight and ending up out on the street.

After confirming some basic background information, she asks me what transpired. "This will be kept in the strictest confidence, between you and me."

I've heard that line before. Nothing's actually confidential, but my stomach growls, reminding me all I've eaten today is a dry bagel. Where there's a bed, there's bread.

It wasn't always like this. I can't begin to understand why JJ traded in her old life for a starving, groveling half-life.

After the intake interview, the woman leads me to a dining room. I dig into a bowl of watery soup and sliced white bread. I nervously squish it between my fingers and roll it back into dough.

Beyond the kitchen, a talk show plays dully from a community room. On the screen, a well-meaning doctor tries to convince a young mother to use birth control as audience members chime in. Some sound sympathetic, others accusatory. During a commercial break, there's an ad for an exposé show on the latest celebrity scandal. I wasn't sheltered from the media storm when the Shrapnels imploded, Nell died, and my mother burned through money, boyfriends, and people, leaving herself with nothing, but I was too young to understand it fully. I hope there aren't too many casualties in the wake of whatever crime the latest starlet has committed. The drama usually ends in tragedy.

By the curtained window, a pair of twins and a toddler play with shabby toys, their mother's eyes glued to the ancient wood-paneled TV set.

I settle on the couch and reach into my backpack for something to occupy myself. I dig for my notebook with the heart stamped on the cover and a pen, but the notebook isn't there. In my haste earlier, I must have forgotten it. My hand rests on the once-glossy, now-scarred copy of *Vogue*. Burn marks scorch the gown the model wears like a calla lily. I've been collecting issues of *Vogue*, US and foreign editions, vintage and new alike, for as long as I can remember. The perfumed advertisements, the shiny images, the tropical backdrops . . . They promise another kind of life, an escape from this one I'm barely hanging on to. As I flip to the first page, I become a stowaway on a glamorous yacht bound for distant lands; I withdraw into the visual fiction, hiding from what will surely be a long ride, and leave everything else just a memory.

Chapter 3

After a few days, Janet and I graduate to a homeless shelter. The counselors there urge her to get help. In the past, she'd smile and comply, everyone involved confident their particular method of assistance would pull her clear from self-destruction. This time, through drags of the cigarette continually between her lips, she smiles and cackles like we should all be grateful to be graced with her charming presence.

Despite our thighs pressing side-by-side on the bench, the brush of her arm against mine, and her smoky breath, she seems further away than usual.

"I can take care of us, Pearl," she tells me while she flips through my magazine. "I'm going to the bank—gonna get us out of here."

I want to tell her she can hardly take care of herself, so how does *us* figure in, but instead I take a deep breath, having held on to the empty nothingness of the bank account through our flight from Darren's. "About that."

Her head whips in my direction; her lips pull back in a snarl. "You didn't spend it, did you?"

"No, of course not," I say, rooting through my bag for the statement. I hold it out to her. "You did." My words are a whisper, but the truth hangs in the air between us, charred like the blue-gray haze that's been clouding her head for months.

She swipes it out of my hand and glances at it. Her glare turns to me. "This is bullshit. I didn't sign up for this." And by *this*, she means *us*. "If I didn't have to—"

I crumble, a sand castle washing away, and stop listening to the veiled speech about how I'm a burden, how she used to have stylists and be on TV. She's inflamed, but doesn't finish reflecting on how good things were. Instead, she stamps out of the shared, narrow cubby containing a bench, a bunk bed, and our few possessions. I pick up the bank statement and rip it to pieces. I hope she went to talk to someone about applying for the work program, government assistance, anything that demonstrates she's willing to help *us*.

A sign hangs by the exit, written in bold: *No drinking, no alcohol, no drugs, no fighting.* Below that are the words: *10:00 p.m. curfew. No exceptions.* Then, as the door slams shut, I wonder which rule she's going to break.

If anyone at the shelter has recognized the famed JJ of the Shrapnels, they haven't mentioned it. Lately, I don't recognize her. But I want to find my way back into her arms, even if they were never very snug around me to begin with. We used to be closer, her more of a mother and less of a ghost. I wish for us to have our own apartment, with a tiny kitchen and a stocked fridge. I'd have a shelf for all my issues of *Vogue*; she'd have a closet filled with designer clothing, a wall lined with plaques and awards for my designs and art. We'd dance together in the living room, singing at the top of our lungs. I wouldn't mind the parties, the people crashed on the couch and floor, because every morning I'd snuggle in next to my mom, assured by her heart beating next to mine.

She doesn't return for mealtime, and the bunk below remains empty as the minutes tick down to curfew and I drift to sleep, afraid that this building filled with snoring and farting, shifting mattresses, failed dreams, and calamity is my ultimate nowhere.

My chest and throat and face and eyes burn like I've breathed fire, like I've swallowed bullets, like I've combusted. Maybe I have. My head and body throb. Yes, I have a pulse. I hear beeping, screaming, and smell fire and smoke. I should get up, run, find fresh air, but I can't move. I am heavy, molten, disintegrated. I'm also thirsty.

Time is an indistinguishable thread. With great effort I blink open my eyes. There's a mask over my nose and mouth. A white curtain with brown and blue stripes surrounds me. A bleached blanket drapes over my body. I wiggle my toes. Thank God. I lift my arm to take the mask from my face and see tubes running from my hand to an IV.

What happened? Shoes squeak by on the other side of the curtain. There are murmuring, distant voices.

"Hello?" I call, lifting my head slightly, but my voice is huskier than usual. My entire body burns, stings, aches. I drop my head back and close my eyes.

Sometime later, a nurse holds my wrist, refreshing the IV. "Hi, sleepyhead," she says sweetly.

"Hello?" I say, more of a question than a greeting. "What happened? Why am I here?" I hardly recognize my voice.

Her expression is conciliatory, like we've reached the last page of a story that doesn't have a happy ending but she knows that I'm a child and won't want to hear it. "There was a fire. At the shelter on Avenue D. You were very, very lucky."

Her words come to me slowly, in pieces, as if she's communicating in the private language of dream-filled sleep instead of English.

"There was a fire?"

She nods, adjusting the bandage. "Does that feel OK?" she asks, smoothing her thumb over the tape holding the IV in place.

Nothing feels OK.

"Where's my mom?"

Her expression moves past charitable to a kind of hardness I don't know how to interpret. "The good news is I think you'll be able to leave tomorrow."

"Where's my mom?" I say, urging my voice above a hoarse whisper.

The curtain parts as the nurse leaves. On one side, my mother stands with a hand on her hip, her hair stringy and her eyes vacant. Her fingers flit and twitch with impatience. On the other side, my uncle, a formidable figure in a slate-colored suit, has his arms across his chest. His lips purse together like he's holding back the kind of verbal grenades he's known for as a higher-up on a government legal team.

"Pearl," my mother says. "I got a spot at the rehab center." She says this like it's a jail sentence. From the stormy expression on Uncle Gary's face, I think it is. She's familiar with both.

Her voice grates against what feels like edges inside my aching head. "Your uncle Gary wants to send you to a special school." She says his name with disdain, as if I'm more related to him than she is. This gets my attention. "He says you're leaving in a week. Don't go, Pearl. You can stay with one of your friends or something. Or I can talk to someone . . . I'll be out in thirty days, and we'll get an apartment. I'm going to stick to the program this time, promise."

"What happened?" I ask again.

Uncle Gary's silence is louder than the nicotine-stained growl of JJ's voice.

"It was an accident. I promise. I was just—it was an accident."

Uncle Gary doesn't dignify her with eye contact, but instead he stares at me, his eyes filled with something other than sympathy. "Janet, explain to your daughter, to the press, to me how starting a fire at a homeless shelter and almost burning it down was an accident. Explain why you ran to me, practically confessing, hoping I'd clear your name. Explain why you left Pearl in the building."

"I couldn't wake her up. She's always been a heavy sleeper."

I look into her eyes, comprehension rushing toward me this time. "I wasn't thinking," she says.

"No, you weren't thinking, because you never do. Because you were high. Because you're a filthy addict. A selfish—" His face is in flames.

I've stopped listening, the rush of facts burning in my head. I almost died. In a fire, possibly along with tons of other people, because JJ was getting high. My body aches. My eyes, throat, chest, and parts that I don't have names for, the places where love and hope live, sear.

I want to roll over, roll away. Instead, I close my eyes.

I wake up to a doctor at the foot of my bed.

"Morning, Pearl. I make it a point not to ask patients how they're doing. I already know you're in a lot of pain. But it's a good thing there weren't any burns. The damage from the smoke inhalation should resolve before long. Thankfully, the fella on the next bunk got you out of there quickly."

It's like there's smoke and flame in my head. I can't remember anything other than a dream where I was sailing through the air, landing with a bump on a hard surface, my wings tattered and feathers like ash.

"I don't remember," I say, my voice slightly less harsh than it was the day before.

The doctor sighs and sits down next to me, pulling a folded newspaper out from under his arm. He sets it down, along with my chart. His skin looks like he once saw more sun. The stark lighting highlights the dark shadows under his eyes. He glances at the paper. "You were lucky, and even more so that you have an uncle like Gary Jaeger."

I have no idea how my uncle is synonymous with being lucky. All I know is that he's cold, distant, and unpleasant. Or, according to my mother, *an asshole she'd rather never see again.*

The doctor clasps his hands and gets to his feet. I'm not sure if that was supposed to be an assuring moment, but a hundred questions scatter me in as many directions, yet I'm firmly rooted to this bed.

"Get as much rest as you can. The medicine has been helping. You'll be fine before you know it. Your uncle will be here this evening to bring you home. Good luck, Pearl." He whisks away, leaving the inky paper next to me on the white blanket.

Home. I don't have one of those. I guess my backpack, clothes, magazine, and everything that wasn't at Darren's went up in smoke.

I doze until dusk turns my sterile surroundings into shadows. I imagine my mother at my side, brushing my hair out of my face and telling me everything is going to be OK. I want to hear it from her and, for once, believe her.

I pick up the newspaper, folded to the article about the Avenue D fire. I skim the words, not wanting them to make sense.

After curfew a resident spotted suspicious activity in the lavatory. A short time later a fire broke out, displacing seventy-five homeless men, women, and children.

My eyes land on the final sentences: *Authorities believe the blaze began after a temporary resident of the Avenue D Homeless Shelter used an open flame, forbidden at the facility, while in the course of drug use. The suspect is believed to be a former musician, fallen on hard times, staying there with her teenage daughter.*

It's like I'm turning a corner, taking it slightly too fast, but there aren't any brakes, no stopping, no denying the message printed in black and white. There's a sudden distance between Janet and me. At the same time, there's a kind of absurdity in this situation. For years, I tried desperately and feebly to piece together a quilt to keep us warm, connecting bits of our tattered reality. Now I not only see but acutely feel how threadbare and hopeless it is.

I move into a spare bedroom at my uncle Gary and aunt Beverly's condo that reminds me of a hotel—the upscale kind with gilded frames, Louis XVI decor, and appropriated heirlooms. It would make a great set for a *Vogue* spread. The last time I stayed with them, my cousins were still home and they lived in a city penthouse.

JJ's here too, a cranky, petulant houseguest. At first, I confine myself to my room, and either anger or shame keeps her at a relative distance. However, Janet's pleading, whenever her brother makes an appearance, over the course of the next days does nothing to help my perma-headache. The pills dull the pain until her growl from another room grows louder. I stagger to my feet.

Janet, dressed like a cross between a Barbie and a clown, wears a pair of heels beneath bruised legs and a skimpy dress that hangs off her shoulder. She looks as out of place as I feel. Her complexion is rugged, like she hasn't slept in days. She probably hasn't. I part my lips to say something, but nothing comes out of my mouth or hers. I return to my room.

In the two days she waits for her slot at rehab, she and my uncle duke it out in a verbal assault that could rival a world war. Her lyricism translates well in debate, and she has a rebuttal for every single one of my uncle's justified claims. I gather his top concern is not having his public image tarnished by her delinquency. He'd all but made the bad press disappear years ago, saving his profile in the government from going up in flames along with her fame. With tight lips, Uncle Gary usually keeps control over his temper, but Janet has the unique ability to push even the strongest, most disciplined, steely people over the edge.

I pull the couch pillow over my head, but their words, or maybe just the truth, reach me nonetheless.

"I have no doubt you're beyond saving, Janet. The writing has been on the wall for years, but I won't let you drag my family into this."

"Since when has Pearl been your family? She's mine."

"You're only thinking about yourself and the government financing you receive from checking off the *child* box on the welfare application."

"Bullshit. You wouldn't understand. Pearl means everything to me."

"I do, in fact, understand, and their names are Erica and Logan. If you haven't noticed, they have a roof over their heads, food in their stomachs, and are both going to top universities."

"That's always the bottom line for you—success, prestige, money. You pimp your kids out so you can get a few more notches in your belt. Valedictorian, Notre Dame, law degree. Blah, blah, blah. We're all prostitutes; some of us just wear our heels better." She smirks like she's won.

"No, Janet, that's called being a caring, stable parent."

She doesn't give up, going for low blows and fabrications, throwing her fists at his chest. The final straw is when she shouts, "You can't take my daughter away."

He storms out. I try to ignore the fact that it was her doing that almost took me away permanently.

In the haze of pills to dull my physical pain, her protests sound like an echo. She spots me retreating down the hall.

"Pearl, there you are. You can't leave me. He's sending you to that school your cousins went to. You can't leave me," she repeats.

"I don't really think this is a choice," I say evenly.

"Please, Pearl, stay."

"Where?" I ask dumbly.

She grovels and whines as if it isn't her fault we're going in different directions. We resided at a homeless shelter that she set on fire. Now she waits for a vacancy at a drug rehab facility, and then who knows, jail? Kids and pets aren't welcome at detox centers or in prison cells. There isn't room for me in her life.

"Pearl, if you go . . . I can't live without you. Please . . ." Her pleading tugs at my heart as she tugs on my hands. Tears fill her eyes.

I look away. The room tilts and shifts. A cough rattles my chest.

"Pearl. Please don't go. Thirty days isn't long. Then it'll be over. We'll figure it out. Maybe we can move or maybe—Pearl, I won't survive without you." Her croon, trying to pull me back into her web, morphs into a growling threat.

The orchids on the table in the foyer, the lamps, the sectional, the walls, and the rugs snap into glassy focus.

"You don't get to say that to me. I almost died. Me. Because of you." I wrest my hands from her grip and slam my bedroom door, anger and sadness mixing like salt and water as tears spill from my eyes.

It amuses me, in a melancholy kind of way, that the adults in my life—rich Uncle Gary and my aunt—have finally decided it would be best to remove me from the failing situation that is Janet's inability to be a parent. Teachers at school and other adults say life isn't fair. I want to throw this fact at her like mud.

After two long days, she's finally quiet. Resigned. I assume she's only remained at Uncle Gary's out of necessity. Aunt Beverly certainly doesn't want her, or me, here. However, unlike JJ, I'm quiet. Even though I'm starting to feel better, I can hardly talk anyway; my throat, jaw, and eyes are perpetually too close to tears. I'm not sure I'd even know what to say.

"I'm leaving," JJ says flatly, standing in the doorway to my room. "In an hour."

I nod or shrug. I thread a loose string from my shirt around my finger—I found it in the drawer across the room. The designer label suggests it is my cousin Erica's. I gaze at my feet.

"Say something, Pearl." Her voice softens to the memory of a lullaby.

I swallow. My mind is foggy. Emotions stack between us like dominos. I'm not sure which direction they're going to fall. I should know better; history has taught me a powerful lesson in the force that is Janet Jaeger.

In the absence of my reply, she turns on me. She glares, and her lips crease into a scowl. "You're just like your father," she spits.

I want to ask her about him, find out what about me is like him. *Why didn't they work? Where is he?* But that is a conversation for another time, and anyway, she's told me often enough that he's not worth remembering, and if I'm so much like him, I guess that means me too.

"No, I'm just like me," I whisper, but she doesn't hear me as she rustles in her purse and pulls out a pack of cigarettes.

"One more before they take everything away from me," she says with disgust, glancing at me, putting the filter between her lips.

When she flicks her lighter, the flame blooming from the opening, words suddenly burn on my tongue. "You always think it's you against the world. This life, you made it. It's you against you. That's what this is, y'know, your own doing. No one made you start taking drugs, or be in a band, or do anything you've done. No one made you have me or start that fire. You made all these choices. Your life is hard because you made it that way."

I'm breathing heavily as the last words tumble out of me, but she doesn't flinch.

"That's the problem, Pearl." She goes outside to the patio, and we don't say good-bye.

Chapter 4

Uncle Gary waits impatiently for me outside Darren's apartment. Perhaps he's hoping to shake the city out of me. He doesn't realize a girl like me doesn't belong in a preppy private school.

Before I add a selection of *Vogues* from my collection to my small stack of books at the bottom of the cardboard box, I let the familiar pages of an issue from the 1930s fall open. My eyes catch a vivid spread about the artist Frida Kahlo. The same one who painted my grandmother's beloved *Watermelons*. If anyone ever asks me who my fashion icon is, I answer, Frida. Although she is better known for her paintings, her aesthetic shouts, *Run fast and run far, unless you're fearless. Unless you're courageous.* I'm not, but I'd like to be. That's why I look at her through the safety of seventy-five years of preserved monochromatic imagery. However, I feel as if her dark eyes follow me from the poster on the wall, evaluating whether I'm ready to lift my chin and meet her gaze.

I run my finger along the drape of her flowing skirt in the magazine. She poses in the desert; her expression suggests home. She experienced ceaseless pain; it's there, in her eyes, reflecting mine, and yet she holds herself like royalty. Funny how *painting* and *pain* seem to share the same root words. Frida created beauty from what hurt her the most.

I close the magazine with a slippery feeling inside. It's easier to ignore what hurts. I slide it in the box, along with a couple of keepsakes, including a stuffed bear my dad won for me at Coney Island. I was too young to remember him or the trip.

After clearing shards of glass from the broken frame of my Shrapnels poster, I roll it up and place it lengthwise in my suitcase. I add the poster of Frida too. The small room echoes with nights I long to forget as I pick up a couple of shirts and some mismatched socks off the threadbare rug and stuff them, along with my other clothing, in the tattered suitcase.

I pack my few art supplies. I'd managed to get into an advanced art class my sophomore year, not an easy feat given my spotty attendance record. I try to imagine what the art department at Uncle Gary's school will be like. Probably fussy and regimented. I toss my journal with the heart on the cover in last.

I slip into my mother and Darren's room and slide the closet door open as quietly as possible. A few metal hangers dangle from the rod, and at the back, I spot the dress JJ wore to the Grammys. It's the only remaining item from her once-abundant collection of designer clothing. The gown matches the color of the little gramophone award the Shrapnels didn't win that night. She's shredded or sold everything related to her music career—guitars, equipment, rare and rough copies of albums, clothes, dignity—except this, a rendition of what she perceived to be her ultimate failure.

When I was little, I'd try on her dresses and heels, parading around the house, asking her to take photos of me so I could see if I looked just like her. I wanted to be her. I would get lost in the folds of fabric, the scent of her perfume lingering there, and disappear to festive nights, lights flashing like flickering stars.

Now it's all gone. And she's gone. Sometimes, it's like I cling to my magazines and sketches, hoping to resurrect my icon, my heroine, my mother. Other times, they are a buffer between me and the world, like

I'm bleeding graphite onto the page, trying to get every last ounce of JJ out of my system.

I take the dress from the closet, along with fragments of hope that our life could still be different.

I carry my luggage through the dingy apartment to the door. Darren watches TV listlessly. He should be Janet's ex, after the two broken ribs and six stitches beside her eye. Somehow, that didn't happen. She said he'll be waiting for her when she's out of rehab, but this time they're not going to live together. I quickly write a note, sensing she's more likely to get it here than at my aunt and uncle's house.

Mom,

I packed everything up. If you find any more of my stuff, set it aside and I'll get it when I come back for Thanksgiving. Wish me luck and you too.

Love, Pearl

I take the scrawled good-bye from the counter, amid empty beer cans, an overflowing ashtray, and insignificant clutter, afraid she won't see it there, and post it on the fridge. *Love, Pearl.* It's easier to communicate with her through the scratch of pen on paper than to say things to her in person. She's quick on the defensive and has given me verbal whiplash more than once.

"This building ought to be condemned," Uncle Gary mutters when I exit to the hall. He irritably jingles the keys in his pocket. When the hired car honks outside, he takes the box from my arms. I trundle down the stairs behind him with my suitcase and backpack.

On the sidewalk, Uncle Gary awkwardly squeezes my shoulder. Maybe he worries a hug might infect him with whatever makes me undesirable.

"Stay out of trouble," he says as I get into the black sedan.

As the car speeds out of New York City, in the wake of my lonely departure, I whisper good-bye to all the people I didn't get to see again. So long to the boy who hung out at the falafel place, filling notebooks with sketches—he'd sometimes show me his work, but I was too shy to share mine. Adios to the guy at the deli who gave me free coffee on Sunday mornings. Bye to the kids at the clubs downtown, the lady at the thrift shop who offered me the senior discount, and the librarians who were kind enough to waive my late fees. Thank you to the person who carried me out of the encroaching fire, away from peril.

I've always wanted to leave, prayed for a way out, but now that the time has come, I'm not sure about the terms or the destination. I don't believe the end of nearly two decades of living with the recklessness and uncertainty that define Janet Jaeger has reached its conclusion. I'm sure my uncle will see his error and return me like an overdue book, or the students and faculty will see I don't belong and send me packing, and then life will resume its natural chaos.

As the car quietly motors north, the tightly packed buildings give way to sparse trees and open sky. For a brief instant, I feel like the blackbird that flies above the guardrail in the slipstream of a tractor trailer. It keeps pace with the sedan for a distance, then flies toward the clouds. Freedom. But it's a trick. I'm sure. I don't trust it.

I think back to all the limos and cabs early on, then later bus and subway rides, the hitchhiking, and the squalid places my mother dragged me, all within the relative twenty-three square miles that make up Manhattan. We rarely left the city. Then the memory of the last ride together, courtesy of Pauline, screams back into my mind, leaving me nervous all over again.

The sullen girl inside, loyal to JJ and prone to recklessness, campaigns against me going to boarding school. *She said she won't make it without me. She needs me. I won't fit in. I won't keep up. I won't have friends. The walls won't be able to contain me.*

When the car pulls off the main road and onto a quaint tree-lined street, gratitude hushes the doubt. Relief flicks away the alternatives, such as a center for homeless teens or worse, a foster home.

A painted wooden sign surrounded by flowers—whose names I don't know—welcomes me to the Laurel Hill Preparatory School campus. The sedan comes to a stop. I recall my impromptu interview, just days ago, with one of Aunt Beverly's former classmates, also on the board of alumni and a generous benefactor.

I'd put on my most convincing smile. I knew how to charm the matronly woman into believing the boarding school would be lucky to have me. I've learned to wear the mask that convinces people that despite my circumstances I'm well adapted and deserving of their help. I think it might be a primal survival technique. Ask Darwin. Acing the interview, along with the purse strings my aunt and uncle pulled, got me a seat in the junior-year class at Laurel Hill, a boarding school for promising young men and women.

The driver graciously opens the sedan's door and helps me gather my things. He nods at me before driving away, and now, truly, I'm on my own. I take a deep breath of the fresh, rural air and wonder if I've come home.

As I stare at an ivy-clad brick building, golden in the late-afternoon summer sunlight, there's a shift inside as though beliefs are rearranging themselves, making room for possibilities, for deeper breaths and wider views. My life *could* be different. But it rivals a sharp sense of betrayal, leaving behind all that Manhattan represents, namely my mother. I tuck these thoughts away and glance down at the letter of welcome guiding me toward my dorm assignment.

I clumsily carry my box in one arm and the suitcase in the other hand. For once in my life, the knots in my stomach have nothing to do with JJ. Still, the shadows of the past linger like wisps of smoke. I cough.

Etched in granite, the name *Vivian Brookwood* spans the top of the threshold as I enter the girls' dormitory. A woman with graying hair greets me. Her name tag says *Connie, Head of Dorm*. Seated next to her, *Terran, Senior Dorm Assistant* scans me from head to toe, her eyes narrowing.

"Welcome, welcome," Connie says, passing me a pink Sharpie and a name tag. "Please write your name and graduating year."

I glance over my shoulder one more time, just to be certain Janet isn't sneaking up behind me, ready to tear me from this sanctuary and back into her life. Only a mousy girl stands in the doorway, waiting for her dad and a handful of luggage.

"Welcome to Viv Brooks"—Terran pauses to read my name tag— "Pearl. You're in room twenty-two. Just down that hall, up the stairs, and then take a right," she says, pointing. "Do your parents need any help bringing your things in?"

"Oh, no, this is everything."

Terran's smile is the opposite of friendly and understanding.

I may as well have entered the dream where I'm in a classroom naked and everyone turns to point. It's the hush before the laughter. With those five words, it's as if I sealed my reputation at Laurel Hill Prep—at least with the girls who matter. I had a chance to build a new identity, and I blew it before I could conjure a story that colored me favorably.

"I see," Terran says measuredly.

Connie gives me a thin smile.

They know. But they can't know. No one can know. Uncle Gary put out the proverbial fire before it spread too far.

"Well then, when you're all settled in, students and"—Connie clears her throat—"parents are mingling in the common room, just that way." She follows up with a bouncy-nervous laugh.

I grab the Sharpie, scribble out *Pearl*, and replace it with *PJ*. More fitting. Yes, I'm the girl with no parents to hug her warmly as they wish her well. I lack anything that resembles a hug or a kiss. I just got a kick, all the way from New York, here.

Alone, I find my way to room twenty-two.

My roommate arranges shiny things on top of her bureau, while her mother, in a cream, gold, and indigo *salwar kameez*, a modern version of traditional Indian dress, makes the bed. Her father, hands clasped behind his back, paces, appraising his surroundings. The mother turns as I plop my things on the vacant bed.

"Hello, you must be Pearl Jaeger. It's very nice to meet you." She sweeps her hand across the room. "This is Mr. Rajasekhara. I'm Mrs. Rajasekhara, and this is our daughter, Charmindy." Her tongue dances over the letters in a way that makes me want to listen to her tell a story and have her tuck me in.

Silver clips pull Charmindy's hair back on either side of her head. She wears straight-leg pants and a lavender cardigan. Her eyebrows twitch as she looks me over.

My cutoffs, boots, and flannel shirt tied in the front scream *outsider*. Thankfully, my aunt took me to get my hair trimmed, so at least from the neck up I fit in. Apparently, as far as my aunt and uncle are concerned, that was enough. *Vogue* fashion spreads prepared me for this, but I don't have *Vogue* money, and Uncle Gary didn't include a clothing expense account in the boarding school bundle.

"We weren't expecting Charmindy to have a roommate, but we're so glad to know she won't be on her own."

I nod and smile politely, not sure what else to say, so I unzip my suitcase upon the bare mattress. I slowly unpack. After the Rajasekharas leave, I unroll the Shrapnels poster and pause, looking carefully at my mother, before sticking it above my bed. I tack Frida up by my bureau.

I wander out to the hallway, wondering where to find sheets and a blanket. Charmindy has a brand-new set, in pale yellow gingham, with a matching comforter and sham.

On my way to the common room, I pass scores of girls unpacking their coordinating linens and chatting with their parents and friends. I don't feel free anymore. Lack of preparation and family cloisters me into a little box labeled *loser*.

My heart yearns for a "normal" family, the kind with a house, a dog, and a couple of stable parents who remember to send bedsheets to boarding school. I'd even settle for divorce, with visitation on the weekends. Instead, I have a mother who seeks drugs before her kid, an absent father who, according to Janet, was a deadbeat, and a great big chasm in my chest that fissures deeper with every tinkle of laughter, every word of encouragement, and every smile exchanged between the families in the common room.

I haven't eaten since this morning and swipe a finger sandwich from a platter on a folding table before escaping outside. I lean against a maple tree and nibble at the tuna and cheese. I don't belong in the dorm with its formidable brick and stately trim, the elbow patches and cardigans, or the laughter and ease.

In the distance, two guys and a girl, dressed mostly in black, parade across the sweeping lawn toward the woods. I know the movements of creatures like them. They're going to smoke or do something forbidden on campus. One by one, they disappear into the cover of the leaves. Ballsy—the place still crawls with parents. I root myself to the tree. I have no plans of going back inside, no plans of moving, ever. Nor do I want to stay where I don't belong. Or worse, get kicked out. I'm stuck, feeling the tug and pull of the familiar and the extraordinary.

Chapter 5

As the sun lowers, the shadowy stamps of leaves dapple my bare legs. Groups of students and parents make their way to the dining hall. Dinner. A bed and food. Uncle Gary gave me a free pass. He sternly told me all I need to do is go to class, get good grades, not cause any trouble, and he'll handle the tuition.

Going to school has never been a problem. It offered a break from the crazy that inhabits my mother. I learned that as long as I pay attention in school, the work comes easily. I'm no stranger to trouble, but I don't seek it—it finds me. I've learned when to rock the boat and when to hold steady. So if one plus one equals food and shelter, at least for the next two years until I graduate, I'll do the math, the science, and the English lit. I'll do whatever it takes to keep it together.

With an aching growl from my stomach, I follow the stream of students and their parents to the dining hall. I imagine for a moment I belong to a mother and father walking arm in arm, sister to their son wearing pleated trousers.

At an otherwise empty table in the corner, I twirl pasta around my fork, savor slices of garlic bread, string beans, and some kind of exotic Italian salad. I added a scoop of mashed potatoes because I could. I smile, thinking about a time I snuck into *Oliver!* on Broadway. I'd joined an unsuspecting field trip group from a far-flung New England town, maybe this very one.

For an hour, I belonged to the assembly in the springy, red-cushioned chairs, watching the play. Just after the scene where Oliver stuffed himself with gruel, an usher discovered me and threw me out onto the snowy street. As much now as then, I know I don't belong.

The thought that the whole charade will come apart any second churns my insides even as I fill my stomach, washing it all down with chocolate milk.

A tray clatters beside me on the wooden table. A girl, with jet-black braids twisted on either side of her head and burgundy lips, and two boys form a semicircle around me. One has a faux-hawk and a pair of earrings, the other, dark blond hair that falls below his ears. He wears distressed denim and a flannel shirt like mine. They settle into the remaining chairs.

"Hey," the girl says. "New here?" The tone of her voice is as intimidating as her scrutiny.

"Yup," I say after swallowing a mouthful.

"I'm Sorel and this is Pepper and Grant," she says, pointing at the faux-hawked guy and the one with long hair.

"What's up?" asks Pepper boldly by way of greeting.

Grant just nods in my direction.

"I'm P—PJ," I say. If I were going to have the right kinds of friends, I would've had to arrive at Laurel Hill with more than a suitcase and a grubby box of sad memories. If I'm going to have any friends at all, my name can't be Pearl.

Pepper stares at my chest. I look down, notice the scribbled name tag, and tear it off like a Band-Aid.

"Cool. What dorm are you in?" Sorel asks.

"Viv Brooks," I say, using Terran's abbreviated version.

"Sweet. Me too. Ground floor. Senior. You?"

"Uh, second floor. Junior."

"Nice," Pepper says. "Sorel's been here since freshman year, but me and Grant are juniors too. I came as a sophomore. I got kicked out of the day school I went to, so my parents cracked down and sent me here. It's not so bad. You smoke?" he asks, pushing his half-uneaten food away.

"Yeah, sure," I lie, licking a spoonful of pudding. I've smoked, but it isn't a regular thing. I'm more of a cigarette tourist.

Sorel and Pepper take up conversation about some people I don't know. It's as if they've already forgotten about me. I sense Grant eyeing me curiously, but when I look at him, he intently studies the green beans on his plate.

"Boys, PJ and I are going to go have an after-dinner mint," Sorel says, winking at me. "Wanna join?"

In the fading evening light, we make our way across the lawn to the woods where I saw the three of them disappear earlier.

Tromping through wild tangles of underbrush, likely grown up over the path during the summer, we emerge into a small clearing encircled by a couple of overturned logs, with a huge boulder in the center. Sorel lights up first and passes her Bic to Pepper. After she exhales, Pepper has his lips on hers, and soon they're making out.

Grant leans on the boulder and takes out a pack of American Spirits, flips the lid, and offers one to me. His eyes match the color of the twilight sky, a deep blue.

"So where are you from?" I ask.

"Scotland," he answers. His voice is slightly deep, sleepy, and strangely soothing.

I tilt my head. "You don't have an accent," I say hesitantly. He hasn't said much, but I would have noticed one.

"No, and you don't have a New York accent," he counters.

"How'd you know I came from New York?"

"My car was behind your car. Plates. I saw you getting out. Lucky guess," he says carelessly.

"Oh." His sweet shyness and mystery, divided by a measure of recklessness, draw me out of the JJ-and-Pearl fog I've been in all day. I want to hear more about Scotland and luck.

He takes my unlit cigarette from between my fingers, brushing my hand. He lights it off the end of his. Ignoring the moaning coming from the shadowy edge of the woods, I try to think of something interesting to say, but my attention is on the two fingers that grazed mine. There's an unusual bubbling and fizzing in the space between my chest and head.

"Have you been here since your freshman year too?" Apparently, that's the best I can do.

Grant nods. "That, and two years of boarding school for the middle grades, effectively erased my accent. My dad shipped me off, out of sight, out of mind. I see him once a year at Christmas."

Maybe I'm not the only almost-orphan at Laurel Hill Prep. "What about the summer?" I ask.

"Summer school," he says bleakly. "But not next summer." Grant takes a long drag. His eyes smile, but not his lips.

"What's your story?" he asks.

Where to start? What do I want him to know? My secrets are mostly safe, buried deep under the streets of Manhattan. I could make up anything or leave out select bits of information, but the truth, the one I'm trying so hard to keep, swishes and froths. I swallow.

"My mom was uh . . . Things got messed up. And my dad took off, so she raised me. Sorta. That's her story. I don't know what my story is."

I don't need to impress Grant, but I've been a passenger on my mother's train wreck for so long I don't know what else to say. I don't know how to answer the question honestly. The summation of my life this far is a jigsaw puzzle of misguided and haphazard living. I've mostly avoided having a life, opinions, or emotions. It was enough just to get through the days and long nights.

Grant stamps out his cigarette. "By the looks of you, you were raised by wolves."

My laugh surprises me when it comes out like a howl.

He bites his lower lip. His gaze holds steady with mine, as if the descending night gives us courage.

Leaves crunch, and Sorel appears, rosy cheeked.

"We better get back," she orders.

I put my cigarette out—JJ would flip if she saw me waste one.

After we cross the lawn, Pepper gives Sorel one last wet kiss. "See you later," Sorel says coyly.

Grant's eyes twinkle in the low lantern light that illuminates the path, and then, with a small smile, he strides away.

Before Sorel and I enter the dorm, she pulls me into an alcove. She spritzes perfume on us and gives me a stick of gum.

"Smoking: prohibited; boys in your room: a big no-no; drinking—" She shakes her head. "Stay below the radar and you'll graduate. Get into trouble and, depending on the crime, it's either suspension or the old boot out the door. I've survived three years here and plan to complete my fourth, so don't do anything stupid. Got it?"

I check in for the night and creep upstairs to my room and am surprised to find it empty. Charmindy has a couple of framed photo collages of friends and family already hung on the wall. A thick coffee-table book sits on her desk. *The Life and Work of Amrita Sher-Gil.* I flip a few pages; the self-portraits of the artist look uncannily like Frida Kahlo. I run my finger over the polished edge of Charmindy's wooden jewelry box and the equestrian trophies on her bureau.

All her clothing hangs, pressed and color coded, on her side of the closet. On my side, some shirts and a faded gray sweatshirt hang limply next to my mother's salvaged Grammy gown. Not that I have an occasion to wear it, but I lament how over the years, she sold garments gifted to her by the collections of Calvin Klein, John Galliano, and Jean Paul Gaultier, just to name a few. It was all hawked for a fix, rarely for rent, and even less commonly for food.

At the foot of my bed, three large boxes form a pyramid, with my name penned on them in marker. The return address reads *New York*. I tear the packing tape off the first one and pull out a couple of pillows, a warm, sage-colored blanket, and a set of crisp, white sheets. The second box contains two pairs of pajamas, though the legs look a little on the short side, and a bag of socks and underwear, granny panties, but I don't care—they're clean—along with toothpaste and a toothbrush, face wash, a package of soap, some hair elastics, and ChapStick.

On top of the third box a short note, written in my cousin Erica's looping handwriting, says, *From Uncle Gary, Aunt Beverly, Logan, and Erica.* Beneath, there are a couple of bags of clothing. The shirts, slacks, and skirts spell *preppy* and aren't my first choice, but with a few adjustments, I'll make do. Awash with gratitude, I tuck the card away, ignoring the likelihood that, despite the names printed on the card, it was all Erica's doing.

While I make my bed, Charmindy comes in and slumps into the chair in front of her desk, opening the book of paintings and photos. She rests her head in her hands, sniffling.

I stuff the pillow into the pillowcase, toss it on the bed, and step toward her. "Charmindy, are you OK?" I ask softly. I want to give her shoulder a squeeze, but I'm not sure what roommate etiquette is, since we've only just met.

She discreetly wipes her eyes, but doesn't look up from the book. "Yes, I'm fine. Preparing for another year." Her voice is crisp and to the point.

"How long have you been at Laurel Hill?"

"I arrived as a freshman." She twists her long, dark hair and clips it back, and then she meets me with sharp eyes. "If you'd like to know, I will be graduating cum laude and high honors. I will have early admission to any number of Ivy League schools, and I will become a doctor or something similarly honorable and well paying to impress and satisfy my family. Trophies, awards, and letters of recommendation are available upon request."

The words on my lips are *That sucks*, but they stay put, obediently retreating to my tongue, because more than anything, she intimidates me. Aside from being incredibly smart—obvious from all the accolades she recited, not to mention the awards and trophies her mother placed on her side of the room—the dark pools of her eyes, her long hair, and her refined features make her seem like she knows exactly what she's doing, who she is, and, more importantly, why—causing me to come up clueless when I ask myself the same questions.

I'm about to say something inane, but instead pull my chair next to her and ask about the artist in the book. She shakes her head, but then stops when her eyes land on the Frida Kahlo poster. She looks at me, perhaps assessing whether I'm a kindred spirit or if our kindred spirits are kindred spirits; they do look remarkably alike, and from what I saw in the book, their artistic aesthetic was similar. She flips open the pages.

"Amrita preferred watercolor. Portraits. Pushing the limits of what was acceptable for a woman of her time. She was without apology for who she was. She didn't yield to the pressures, she was just herself."

Charmindy mesmerizes me with stories about her favorite artist, about painting, and I'm about to ask her what art means to her, when a knock sounds on the door. Connie, the head of dorm, appears and asks how we've settled in.

Charmindy's cheeks quickly lose their pinkish hue from her impassioned description of Amrita and her work as she responds politely.

Connie nods like she's listening, except I've learned that being present in the room and hearing what someone says aren't the same. "Tomorrow we have a dorm-wide icebreaker at eight a.m., followed by the Head of School Welcoming Ceremony, and then peer group and sports sign-ups in the afternoon. Best get off to bed, ladies. Lights-out."

Chapter 6

I wake from a sound sleep to birds chirping and sun streaming through the window, like a perfect scene out of a fairy tale. I get up and settle on a combination of the outfits my cousin sent, a slate skirt with a thin red belt, topped with a navy-and-white-striped sweater, but I pull my denim jacket over it and my hair back into a ponytail, my straight blond bangs grazing my thick eyebrows. The head-of-school thing sounded important, but I already feel far out of my league. I swipe on my favorite matte red lipstick. The tube says it's called Diva. I snagged it from JJ and save it for special occasions.

I endure the icebreaker, meeting the rest of the girls in my dorm, and attend the assembly, where the entire school, including the faculty, represents a well-dressed Polo ad or something equally untouchable. I inhale the fresh feeling on campus, wealth and potential—like anything could happen by virtue of power, connections, bottomless bank accounts, and old money. Except Sorel, Pepper, and Grant stand off to the side, like a trio of renegades ready to cause an uprising.

After lunch, I sneak off with Sorel, at her insistence, for a smoke. I mindlessly take a drag, willing myself not to cough.

"So what brings you here, City Girl?" she asks.

"How'd you know I was from—"

She cuts me off with a big smile spreading across her burgundy-stained lips. "Grant told me. Or rather, I asked him what you guys talked about last night."

"When did you have a chance to talk to him? We've been in the same room and then the auditorium practically all day."

Her grin is mischievous. "Snuck to Pepper's dorm after lights-out. He and Grant share. After you're here for a year you can put in a roommate request. An arrangement easily made since Grant and Pepper won't snitch on each other."

"You snuck out, really?" That seems like a quick ticket to expulsion and something on the top of her list of no-nos.

"Like I said, you can do what you want, just don't get caught," Sorel says, puffing smoke out of her nose. "Since I've known Grant he's always been kind of quiet. Except when you get beer in him." She laughs privately. "He hasn't had a girlfriend in a while. Don't get me wrong, he's not innocent. He's hooked up." She pauses, like she knows the punch line to a joke but I haven't heard it yet, and then adds, "A lot."

My cheeks flush.

She doesn't spare my embarrassment but looks directly at me with inquiring eyes. "Just in case you wanted to know. We can go over there together, anytime, any night, you just say the word."

Grant's blue eyes pop into my mind, but I didn't come all this way only to end up kicked out and homeless again. I haven't even been at Laurel Hill for twenty-four hours. I need to get back to campus and hang around with someone more savory, like Charmindy.

Sitting haughtily on the giant rock like it's a throne, with a cigarette in hand, Sorel reminds me of JJ, ever eager to dabble in the forbidden. The difference is Sorel's protected from the consequences by her parents' money. She takes a drag on the cigarette and exhales a large plume as if daring anyone to usurp her.

"I better get back."

Sorel shrugs. "Suit yourself."

Without giving in to any more of Sorel's proposed distractions, I fall into the rhythm of life at Laurel Hill: attending classes, studying, and selecting the cross-country team for my athletic requirement. When we do warm-up laps on the track, I spot Grant at soccer practice, weaving the ball between cones and shooting goals.

To keep myself out of trouble's way, and because Charmindy often frets about how involvement in activities adds polish to college applications, I join the graphic design club, meeting weekly. I learn how to use computer software, along with creating visuals for various programs and events on campus. I prefer my sketch pad and pens, but it serves its purpose.

Forever fascinated by fashion but not having much in the way of a budget for clothing, I've made do with pieces I'd sneak from my mother's previously impressive collection, free items picked up at churches and community aid groups, and the occasional vintage splurge. Oftentimes I've sifted through boxes of donated items only to uncover a single T-shirt or skirt that's usable. Once I scored a faux leopard print jacket that rocked, but those finds are rare. Maybe it was necessity that forced me to figure out how to use a thread and needle. I'd use what fabric I could find; taking it apart and putting it back together was a way to dream up what I might someday be able to create. I'm not particularly skilled at sewing, but imagining the fit of fabric against my skin, the way some clothes tell a story without using words, the place where edginess and elegance meet in leather and lace, and how it invites me out of this world and into another, helped me disappear from reality for a little while.

Over a month after school starts, when the sky turns sleepy, with the clouds spreading out like a down comforter, Grant transfers into my precalculus class. I see him every day, in the dining hall and around campus. Now that we're in a class together, an altogether different window opens, revealing how carefully he listens to Mr. Meshcheryakov, Grant's patience as he explains to me, again, quadratics, and that he isn't all jokes and debate, like when he's with Pepper and Sorel.

I look at him the way an artist studies values and composition, lighting and contrasts. When the teacher asks a question about the upper limit of a sequence, I'm caught daydreaming about his ruffled bedhead, the way his shoulders hunker over his desk as he works, and how one ankle twists beneath the other under his chair. Focusing on understanding what Mr. Meshcheryakov says, with his thick Russian accent, requires every bit of my attention. I miss the answer and have to redo the entire page. If I were solving for Pearl plus Grant, I'd find he's exquisitely flawed and I'm cautious, afraid, damaged . . . the common denominator that we're both kind of shy . . . end of the equation.

On Halloween, Sorel corners me in the hallway of the history building. "Whatcha been doin', City Girl? Study, study, study?"

I shrug. Lately, Charmindy and I are companionable nerds, our conversations rarely veering away from classes and only occasionally delving into art. The one time she mentioned anything remotely saucy was to ask if it was weird that this guy Brett, who hangs around with some of the girls in Viv Brooks, always shows up after her AP Chem class and walks her back to the dorm. Apparently, she sputtered something nonsensical at him, and judging by the three shades of red she turned while relaying the story, she isn't entirely an academic automaton.

Sorel snorts. "Tonight's Halloween. We're going to the woods to drink, want in?"

I look around for witnesses. I shrug again.

"It'll be spooky," she says, clawing the air with her fingernails, chipped with black polish.

"Yeah, sure," I say, uncertain if answering *no* is an option.

That night, Sorel swoops into my room, dressed from head to toe in black, which pretty much has become her typical attire as the first two months have passed. She parts her lips in her trademark grin, revealing vampire teeth—and not the fake, cheesy plastic ones.

She roots through my stuff, trying on bracelets and tossing them back on my bureau. She pops a piece of Charmindy's gum in her mouth. She points at the Shrapnels poster over my bed. "Who's that? Never heard of them."

"Just an old band."

She gets a closer look and then points. "That chick looks kinda like you."

I close my eyes, bracing myself for confession time, but when Sorel turns around and the image of my mother comes into focus, I simply shrug. Unless she recognizes JJ from one of those "Where are they now" shows, Sorel doesn't make the connection, and I don't need to help her along.

"They were popular in the nineties," I say, pointing. "She played guitar and sang for the music industry's grunge-goddess sensation *the Shrapnels*. They got big playing festivals, touring the world, and were huge in Europe—totally feminist with tits-in-your-face action," I say for Sorel's benefit. "They had a few hits, really popular with college radio. One of the original girl bands. But I guess their hearts weren't in it, or maybe the next big thing replaced them." Though it probably just came down to addiction.

"Totally obscure. Pepper's way into all these random bands. Signed and everything," she says, tapping the scribbled autographs. "Wait, did they do that song 'Rotten'?" Sorel asks, singing a few lyrics.

"Yup, and 'Potholes in My Heart,' 'Guerilla,' 'Make It or Fake It' . . ." I answer, listing a few more off with a tired and relieved sigh that my secret still seems relatively safe.

After another moment studying the poster, her eyes flit to Frida. "Dress warmly," she orders, riffling through the clothing on my side of the closet. She holds up the dazzling gold dress from my mom's Grammy night and makes a gagging face. "The woods are cold, and this is hideous," she says, letting the dress slip off the hanger and onto the floor. I'm about to pick it up and explain that it's couture, but as she exits, she steps right on it, but then again, so did my mother. It's a miracle she didn't sell it. My chest tightens. Maybe it doesn't matter.

I follow Sorel outside to the lawn. The smoke from the fire at the shelter memorized the contours of my lungs, and a dry cough issues from my chest.

As we walk toward the woods, the bottom of the full moon grazes the tops of the pine trees, illuminating their pointy peaks in the distance. It's like a backdrop for a Halloween play or the opening scene of a horror movie.

"You didn't strike me as the studious type, PJ. Pepper and I placed bets that you would've been at least suspended by now, but I suppose not everyone's who they seem." She gives me an uncertain look that I brush off as the woods close behind us like a door.

"What better thing to do on Halloween than party with your friends, right?" She looks back at me with a crazed glint in her eye. "Screw the school-sponsored parties in the student center. They're lame," she says as if daring me to disagree.

I don't care if she doubts me. I don't need to prove that I'm hardcore, having seen and done things that she probably only fantasizes about in a warped, wannabe, alterna kind of way. Since arriving at Laurel Hill, when people ask me about myself, everything that comes to mind has to do with Janet, Janet, Janet. *I'm* not sure who *I* am, which is of far greater concern than others wondering who I am.

Our feet crunch along the stiff corridor of weeds that leads to the clearing.

"Trick or treat," Sorel calls.

Pepper sits atop the rock, with a glow stick casting eerie green light around his face. Grant materializes from the shadows.

"Hey, ladies," Pepper says. He pulls out a bottle of tequila and passes it to Sorel.

Grant lights a cigarette, and for a moment, he glows in the light of the match, but softly, like an invitation for warmth.

Sorel pushes the bottle into my hands, studying me.

I don't hesitate and tilt it to my mouth. "Happy Halloween," I say after the liquid burns my throat.

Pepper lights a sparkler and passes it to Sorel. The two dance around the clearing, creating trails of light. Grant smokes quietly, as if inhabiting his own world. After I take another chug, I settle on a log and amuse myself by penning a love letter to alcohol against the dark tapestry of sky. After too many late nights partying with friends, and morning hangovers that made me feel like a lollipop plucked from the floor—sticky and hairy—I told myself I wouldn't drink anymore.

This is just an interlude.

Pepper and Sorel run out of sparklers. The bottle of tequila rounds the circle as Pepper weaves a creepy story about a hitchhiker and a bride. The leaves rustle with the mood of the tale. I find myself closer to Grant and am extremely aware that the arms of our jackets touch. If I squint my eyes, I almost think I can see high-voltage purple-white lines striking the space between us like lightning between clouds. Or fizz from the sparklers.

When Pepper concludes his story, he and Sorel disappear to make out, leaving Grant and me with the bottle of tequila. Whether because of nerves or its promise to keep us warm, we quickly empty it. Our voices chatter with the cold and nervousness. The trees sway even though the wind has died down.

"When was the last time you went trick-or-treating?" I ask Grant after we've cataloged our favorite movies.

"Don't remember. At the boarding school before here, we just had a party. But—"

"What? Tell me."

"Nah, never mind." He smirks.

"No really, what?" I ask. A giggle escapes. *Thanks, tequila.* "Come on," I say, banishing the giddiness.

After a few more rounds of me begging like a dope, he leans against the rock, softening. "Promise not to laugh?"

I nod. "Promise." The word carries the weight of something more, of what hides in the night.

"Last time I dressed up I went as a hot dog." He looks sheepish.

"A Hallo-ween-ie" I say, laughing and breaking my promise. The tequila makes the joke funnier than it is.

Grant offers a chuckle as if he's forgiven me already. "How about you?"

The alcohol helps me plow through my self-consciousness. "Last time I went out, I dressed up like Frida Kahlo," I say, going on about how I don't admire any fashion icons but real people who wear clothing as an art form, whose hearts are literally on their sleeves. "I can't wrap my head around her, and yet in a way I see something of myself in her art, how she created beauty from her pain. She translated what ached inside of her into a visual shock or an evocative representation, so the person on the other side of the canvas felt what she felt. She—"

I've lost track of what I'm saying; it's like the trees echo my voice. The dim outlines of the trunks, lined up like matchsticks, spin faster and faster as the tequila twirls me to the beat of my own music. As each disorganized thought crosses my lips into words, I lean closer to Grant, his eyes dark in the forest light. For a moment I fear he sees too much of me, like all my dusky secrets are about to spill out and be made visible and bold, like Frida. I'm not ready for that kind of exposure.

The tequila suddenly betrays me. I lurch and then throw up in the woods behind where we sit. My head slowly clears as embarrassment crushes me.

"I'm sorry." I wipe my mouth. That wasn't cool. "I gotta go."

I stumble down the path out of the woods and to the dorm, bypassing the common room where I hear the canned screams from a movie. I shower, washing away the evidence of my recklessness, and hope to forget the night.

Chapter 7

A note to go to the administration building appears, taped to my door, penned in Connie's script. I don't know how getting kicked out works, but the wires and cords that hold me to the earth warp and wiggle as I contend with the tequila hangover. I am not ready for classes or being vertical or landing wherever it is they send homeless private school failures. I brush my teeth twice, the mint toothpaste yielding to the sharp taste of tequila, lingering in my throat.

As I follow the path to the building, the blur of Halloween night haunts me. I berate myself for drinking too much and for making a fool of myself in front of Grant.

I struggle to pull open the heavy wooden door, nearly closing it on my shoulder and backpack with a foreboding feeling like I missed a sign that said, *Turn back, you're about to get your ass handed to you.* A susurrant hum comes from the depths of the building, like in a church or water flowing over rocks in a brook, like futures are made and broken here. Then a phone rings, startling me.

"Yes," asks the woman with a tight black bun streaked with silver, seated behind an oak desk.

"I received a note to come down here this morning." I show it to her.

"Ah, yes, Justine Baptiste, your advisor. I'll let her know you're here."

The beginning of relief washes through me as I take a seat on the edge of a plush chair. I've learned to be cautious around people with titles and secretaries. Because Uncle Gary and Aunt Beverly enrolled me late, I didn't get to choose my classes, so perhaps she wants to meet me and see how the semester is going. Wishful thinking.

"You must be Pearl," says a tall woman, extending her hand. Braids twine together at the back of her head and reach down to her waist.

"Pearl, PJ, yeah," I say, looking down at my chest as if the name tag from the first day is still there.

I follow her down the corridor to an office with a desk, table, and filing cabinets piled with papers, pamphlets, and books. Looking down on the papery mess is an oil painting of a woman, her gaze even, her lips pursed; bold blocks of color surround her, a village perhaps.

Justine follows my line of vision and smiles. "My grandmother painted that portrait of my mother and her sisters, back in Haiti," she says, pointing. She sighs as she settles in her chair and folds her arms across her chest. "I understand you were enrolled last-minute?"

"Yeah, I um—"

"You must be exceptional," she says, the word lengthening on her tongue.

"Actually, no. I was—"

She holds up her hand. "When I found out I had a last-minute advisee, without a transcript, I thought it best not to ask questions. Don't get me wrong, I'm all for asking questions, but—" She nods as if she knows it's better I keep my story to myself. "Your transcript finally came in on Friday, and I was able to apply your science credits. So, unless you really enjoy biology, you can switch out to fulfill another requirement or an elective. We didn't have any humanities or art classes left open when I created your schedule, but there have been a few openings since then."

"In what?"

"Well, there's Econ, Psych 101, and an art class. Painting IV. Rasmus Shale," Justine says, cocking an eyebrow in my direction.

I shrug mildly. "OK."

She glances at her computer and then swivels the monitor toward me. "I see here you have numerous art credits under your belt, so you have permission for that level class, if you're interested."

"Definitely. I mean, I draw mostly, but I love painting too."

"How much do you love painting?" she asks measuredly.

"A lot. I love art," I say, uncertain where she's driving the conversation.

"This class sees a lot of withdrawals. There's a reason for that, but OK. Painting IV it is." She taps away at the computer. "Rasmus Shale," she repeats. "Trial by fire, as they say." She locks me in her gaze, and then her lips spread into a thin smile. "I'm sure you'll do fine."

That wasn't much of a vote of confidence, but I take my newly printed schedule and exit.

"Nice to meet you, Pearl, and good luck, you might need it."

Unfortunately, I do need the good luck, because I'm five minutes late for first period, which used to be bio, with an ancient teacher who forgave tardiness because the clock in the classroom was slow and she couldn't see it, but now my schedule directs me to the art building, on the opposite end of campus.

I walk up the three flights of stairs to the top level. The floorboards creak beneath my feet, and the dust motes, always written so poetically, dance in a shaft of light. The door at the very end of the hall hangs halfway open, and a man's accented voice booms.

"You will not waste my time or materials. You will worship this canvas, this brush, and these colors as if they are the only means by which you will be fed, clothed, and sheltered."

When I push the door all the way open, I watch as he takes the canvas from a student's easel and tosses it on a table. I edge into the room. The floor creaks, and he turns sharply in my direction, then stalks over to me.

I brace myself.

"Who are you?" He has a broad forehead and white hair swept back, in need of a trim. His bearded face, the hair going white at the roots, conceals any suggestion he knows how to smile. He's tall, purposeful in his movements, like a great beast that requires a lot of energy to move, but his tongue is fast, sharp.

"I'm Pearl Jaeger." I clear my throat. "PJ. My advisor found I already had science credits, so she said—"

He puts his hand up to silence me. "I do not care. If you want to take this class, you will show me why you are here." He gestures around the room. "Find an available easel. We are doing still life. Get to work."

There are a half dozen available easels to the six already occupied. A dark-haired figure stands at the other end of the room. I walk cautiously toward her.

"Charmindy?" I ask, surprised to discover my roommate, queen of AP classes, is in the art studio.

"Sh," she says, almost below a whisper. "Can't talk now."

"Quiet," the teacher bellows. "When you are in here, you are working. I will only say it one more time. Embody the canvas, the brush, the oil, the lines and curves. There is no separation."

I study Charmindy's vessel of flowers and the way she's captured the light exactly as it is in the image tacked to the top of her easel. On a table in the middle of the room a shallow box contains more photos and clippings of famous still life paintings. I select one with a bowl of fruit and gather paints and other supplies before I get started. Just as I'm about to touch brush to canvas, a hand grips mine tightly. Gray eyes, the color of the sky in winter, bore into mine.

"You do not sketch first?" he asks, surprised.

"Oh, was I supposed to?" I ask, my hand still suspended in his. The evidence of years of painting has fossilized underneath the line of his fingernails.

"No. It is not allowed," he answers, not taking his eyes off mine. "Continue."

I sense Charmindy watching us, but as he releases my hand, she's intent on her canvas.

I step back, just to be sure my assessment of the light, shadows, and highlights was accurate, before I apply thin spheres of paint to the canvas, forming the base of the fruit. I continue, adding layers and dimensions, losing myself in the motion of creating stillness. Instead of a chime or bell, like in the other buildings, Shale barks at us when the class is over.

I hustle to clean up my space and then dart out of the classroom, not wanting to be late for my next class or endure any more of Shale's wrath. I try to catch up with Charmindy, but she's already gone.

Instead, Sorel catches up with me, claiming she's cutting class. "Come with. Woods. Smokes."

The workload, compared to public school, has me so busy I hardly have time to sneak off with Sorel. She assures me I'll get used to it and will eventually have time to *not* get into trouble, her way of saying go to the woods, smoke, or sneak to her boyfriend's dorm at night, along with whatever other rules she breaks. With her, it's just a game to see how far she can push the limits. For me, it's a matter of not being kicked out and landing on the street.

"You look like you could use one," she prods after I tell her no.

"I just transferred into an art class. Painting IV."

"Tell me you don't have Shale."

"I have Sh—"

"Badass. But you need a cigarette. I didn't survive Painting I. He's known around here as the Norwegian Nightmare."

I start to follow her, but then spot Charmindy outside Cullen Hall, the mathematics building. "I have to go. Catch up with you later." I know I'll see Charmindy back at Viv Brooks, but I'm shell-shocked from Shale's class and need info.

"Charmindy," I call.

She stops on the steps.

"Can't be late. I know what you're going to ask me, and I promise I'll tell you later." Then she disappears through the door.

Each week I write my mother letters, pouring my insides out, describing Charmindy, Sorel, and Grant, the minutiae of days, answering questions I wish she'd ask. Normal questions, like *how are you*, to inquiries about the secret garden of my heart. Today I describe Rasmus Shale, the frontier of his eyes like everything they've seen can only be expressed through oil on canvas. I tell her he terrified and ignited me in equal measure. Something about that classroom, his hardcore reaction to that poor kid and his canvas, his inquisition when I didn't sketch first, and the latent poetry of paint makes me want to go back tomorrow.

I sign my name at the bottom of this latest letter just as Charmindy enters and collapses on the bed, her bag still strapped across her shoulder. "Can you wake me up next June? No, scratch that, in two Junes. No, wait; I have eight years of higher education after graduation. Just wake me up when you start to see gray hairs, OK?"

"Only if you tell me why I didn't know you took a painting class." I stuff the letter in an envelope, doubtful I'll hear back from JJ.

"Because I'm a glutton for punishment." She sits up, planting both feet on the floor. "Obviously I love painting, and he's the best."

"Never heard of him."

"That's because you focus more on fashion and sketching and less on the oil painting community. He's a rock star. A guru, a legend."

"Then why does he teach at a private school in the middle of nowhere?"

"That's what everyone wants to know. Tragedy? Delinquency? Angry ex-wife? I have no idea. No one does. But he believes enough in his students to stick around. At least that's what I tell myself."

"Do your parents know?"

Her eyes grow wide. "No. No way. Painting is my silent rebellion. They see my progress reports and grades, but I, um, I arranged it, as a special favor with my advisor and the art department, to keep it off the copy sent to them. I know it's wrong, but that class is the only thing I have that's for *me*. I started last year, taking art because I couldn't cope with the pressure. I needed an outlet."

"Yeah, but odd choice if you're looking to relieve stress, if it's true that Shale is tough—"

Charmindy lets out a laugh that borders on crazy, and her eyebrow lifts in question. "Tough? Brutal, vicious, honest. But if I'm going to go through all the trouble of concealing an art class, I'm going to take the best one available. When I found out who he was, basically this famous outlaw painter, I couldn't say no."

"What's he done?"

She flips on her laptop. "What hasn't he done? He started with skies, these crazy Norwegian winter storm clouds. It was intense. Then figures. There's this entire catalog of beautiful men and women, they're demure and lovely, but also somehow carry the ferocity of those skies he knew so well. Then there was a period with nothing, though I doubt someone like him stopped painting. Then out of nowhere, a painting, black on canvas, appeared. It's called *The Starless Night*. Then after that . . ." She leans back as gorgeous images rendered in thick lines tapering to thin, blending, moving, shifting my perspective of this stoic man, appear on the computer screen. "Then after that it's like everything blew up, like he created the cosmos anew."

I scroll down to find his latest works. In each successive painting it's like fire gives way to feathers to fish to ocean and sky. There aren't words to describe it, other than awe.

"See, told you. He's—there are no words," she echoes.

"No words," I repeat, wishing I could clear my schedule and spend twenty-four/seven working with Shale, because I want to paint that wordless feeling, permanently, into my life.

Chapter 8

Days before break, Uncle Gary informs me Janet will remain in rehab, canceling my visit to New York for Thanksgiving.

I decline Sorel's invitation to her house for the holiday. She insists her parents won't mind, but when she and I sneak off for a last smoke before vacation, she says, "It's better you don't come anyway. Sheila and Blake are such asses." Her eyes are heavy, like something weighs on her mind, but she quickly changes the subject. "While I'm home I'll try to bring back some more booze. Halloween was epic."

I wonder if Grant told her about my not-so-epic moment. I've been avoiding him as much as possible, breezing through lunch and dinner if we're at the same table in the dining hall, which is almost guaranteed. Although I might want to deny it, when we're in the room together, the air ionizes, stirring up the molecules of what could be.

As polished sedans and passenger vans carry students home and to the airport, I stay on campus with a small collection of international students, including Charmindy. The American History teacher has us to his period home for dinner and engages us in discussion about the origins of our great nation.

That night Charmindy and I hatch a plan to go to the studio the next day to work on the still life assignment. Earlier in the week, we'd arrived in class and everyone's canvases were missing. Shale told us we disgraced and disappointed him and ordered everyone to start over.

The next day, Black Friday, while shoppers feverishly fill their carts and bags with electronics and other sale-priced merchandise, during the early hours, I get ready to go to the studio. When I return from the bathroom, Charmindy moans in her bed.

"I think some of the clams Hodges served off his early American menu disagreed with me."

"I told you not to eat them. Shellfish, not good," I say, shaking my head.

"I was being polite."

"What can I get you?" I ask.

She suddenly sits up, her face the color of the asparagus also on the table last night. Tangled in the bedsheets, she stumbles past me and out the door. I go to the basement where there's a soda machine, get a can of ginger ale, and nab some crackers from the kitchenette on the first floor. I leave these items by Charmindy's bed.

As I slip through the dorm, if I didn't know better, I'd think this was a regular morning and everyone was still asleep in bed. Only Connie sleeps off yesterday's meal, having stayed behind, allowing us to remain in the dorm, because her family lives far away in one of the Dakotas.

The door to the studio is ajar when I get there, and the scent of turpentine nips my already chilly nose. The room is still, the high windows diffusing the light. I get a new canvas and mix my paints, optioning this time to start on the fruit bowl, a mixture of blue gray that reminds me of smoke or, looking up from my palette, Shale's eyes.

"What are you doing here?" he asks abruptly.

"Painting."

"On your vacation?" He clasps his hands behind his back and straightens.

"Yeah. Charmindy was coming too, but she's sick in bed. Bad clams." I dab the brush in the paint and, without another word, begin blocking in the bowl, then adding volume by focusing on the movement of light across the rim. I forget Shale stands at my shoulder until he clears his throat.

"Where did you learn this?"

"I, uh, Mrs. Salucci, my art teacher freshman and sophomore year, books, the Internet. I draw, though, mostly, sketches, fashion design."

"No." He shakes his head. "You didn't learn this from those places. You learned it because you are disciplined, because you practice, because you got up at dawn on a Friday morning and came here when you could have been sleeping in."

I wonder why he's here.

I resume painting in companionable silence until my stomach grumbles. I ignore it, finding the silky press of the brush soothing, wiping away the last months of madness in clearly defined lines, giving shape to oranges, grapes, and plums.

The sun lowers in the November sky, and my stomach now clenches with hunger, making the fruit taking shape look delicious. I step back, admiring my work, an exact replica of the image tacked to the top of my easel.

"Pretty good so far, huh?" I say, nearly forgetting Shale is in the room, standing at my shoulder. He must be as starved as I am.

"It's perfect." He makes a tsking noise and picks up the canvas, assessing it. "Perfection is overrated. It is a lie." Then he breaks it over his knee, the wooden frame splintering. "No. Nope. Nope. Nope."

I stand back, my eyes widening with shock, then narrowing with anger. "Why did you do that?"

"You think it's good. It goes in the trash. We do not become attached to our work."

"But you said we are the same as the canvas, the paint, the brush. How could I not become attached?" I say, my voice rising.

He leans toward me. "Because when you are attached you hold back. There's still this much separation between you and your work," he says, pinching his fingers an inch apart. "There is no difference."

"But that was just an exercise. You said last week that we have to learn the rules, replicate the masters who made the mistakes first, paving the way for us. If I were painting my own piece, something I'd thought up, then, I would pour everything into it. You said yourself that it was perfect. I don't understand."

"I want what's beyond perfection." With that, he sweeps away, and my tears smatter the wrecked canvas at my feet.

Everyone returns to campus tripped out on tryptophan except for Mr. Meshcheryakov. The sub who takes his place writes her name on the whiteboard, *Mrs. Dittly*. Grant pulls up next to my desk when she assigns us to work as partners. My month-long embarrassment trickles away in the comfort of his cerulean eyes, like the promise of a clear blue sky.

"Sorry if I was weird on Halloween," I say at last, belatedly breaking the seal on my silence on the subject that had been eating away at me.

He shakes his head. "No worries. I did you a favor and didn't tell Sorel. She would have had fun with that one."

I give him a questioning look.

"Sorel's OK, she's just the mama hen. I suppose she thinks Pepper and I are her chicks or something. She can be territorial."

"If that's the case, it seems like she wants me to earn my position in the pecking order, at least when we're around you guys. Other times she's as sweet as the fudge she gobbles when she can't break free for a cigarette."

He laughs. "What I do think is weird is that it seems like you've been avoiding—"

But Mrs. Dittly shushes us as she explains our assignment. While Grant and I work through a page full of numbers that blur between black and battleship, ash and gunmetal, our hands brush, sending a zing through me. Creases form between his eyebrows, just visible beneath his slouchy knit hat, as he works at a long equation. I would like to sketch or paint him. I try to take a photo in my memory, the way he bites his inner lip when he's focusing, the way his lips part when he looks up at me, his angles and symmetry.

After that, I find myself in the woods more often, hoping Grant will join us in the roost. During boisterous mealtimes, we sit at the corner table, some combination of Sorel, Pepper, Grant, and me, passionately discussing the injustices in the world or debating our favorite bands.

One afternoon, the sky is as moody as most of the students before exams. Sorel rushes off about a call she has to make. Pepper, lost without her, shambles away at her heels, leaving Grant and me alone in the clearing.

Grant stares at his cigarette like he doesn't know why he'd put something like that to his lips when there might be something better. He flicks it away and steps closer. The forest lights up with the electricity of us as I meet him halfway. We're standing shoulder to shoulder, a mere arm's length away.

"Thanksgiving," I try again, ready to inquire about his holiday and desperate not to be so keenly aware of how glossy my lips are and how his part in amusement or with a question.

He shakes his head. "Tell me two truths and one lie," he says boldly. "Don't tell me which is which. I have to guess."

I shift and rub my hands together and then stuff them in my pockets.

"You can tell a lot about a person based off the stories they tell themselves."

"Yeah. Uh, OK. I was raised by wolves. My birthday is next month, and my favorite fruit is apples."

"True, true, false. You seem more like a cherry kind of girl."

If my cheeks weren't already pink from the cold, dry air, I'd have blushed. "You got it. Your turn."

He links his pinkie in mine and leads me over to sit on the rock. "My brother is one of my best friends. I'm shit at card games and"—he turns in my direction, gazing into my gray eyes—"I'm looking at my favorite color."

I turn his words over in my mind; the blush replaced with warmth, radiating from my chest, north, south, east, and west. "True, true, true."

"You got it. I couldn't, I wouldn't lie to you. Not to anyone. Can't do it. Except, occasionally to the faculty if I'm somewhere I'm not supposed to be." He looks toward the path leading back to campus.

"We better head back. Don't want you to have to break that rule," I say.

Despite my occasional violations of school rules, I'm prepared academically when we arrive at the holiday homestretch, the last few weeks leading up to exams, followed by Christmas vacation.

I'm on my third attempt at the still life in Shale's class. I told Charmindy what happened after Thanksgiving, but she didn't seem surprised.

He paces around the classroom, casually throwing out comments that seize even the strongest egos. "Too thick, there, that line," he barks at Charmindy, whose line isn't thick, not really.

"What is this, a doodle? A child could do better than this. You are no longer children," he practically shouts at a boy with green paint in his hair. "I didn't wake up today to be disappointed," he hollers to all of us.

I try to keep my hand steady but feel as though he's breaking me down. I tremble when he passes, afraid he's going to swipe my canvas from my easel and toss it out the window.

Thankfully, there aren't any more still life casualties, but I'm the last student in the classroom during free studio hours. It's still open season. He sits on a stool in the corner, under a reading light. Every now and then, he says "Hmm" as he peruses a thick book.

I add a final layer of color to intensify the three-dimensional aspect of the fruit, then put my brush down. I don't know if I'm done with the painting, but I feel done. Without looking, I close my eyes, back away, and clean my materials.

When I return from the washroom to get my bag, the shape of Shale's silhouette takes form in front of my easel. His broad shoulders stiffen at the creaking sound from the floor as I approach. He turns to me.

"Are you done?" he asks. "Are you handing this in to me?"

I'm afraid to answer. He's a live wire. I say the most honest thing. "It feels done."

"You do not paint to win my approval, Pearl. There is no gold star awarded in this class. I rarely write comments on your grading sheets. I don't do recommendations."

I want to know what he does do, aside from tearing everyone's confidence to shreds. I nod, because anything else will come out wrong. Instead, I want to ask him questions, fill canvases with the answers. I want to know about *The Starless Night* and what came before and after. How he makes the dried pigments mixed with oil explode from the canvas in some places and, elsewhere, downy and soft, like a nap.

"Then you are the first one done with your still life. Until vacation, you will replicate this. Exactly. Then I never want to see you do a still life again, at least not someone else's. If you take a sudden fancy to bowls of fruit and vases of flowers, then by all means. This was merely an exercise. Do you understand?"

I don't.

"When you return from holiday, you will do a self-portrait. I want to see who you are."

That night, I daze out the window into the windy night; the white twinkle lights festooning campus glitter through my window. I reflect on how, historically, the holiday season often resulted in disaster. If my mom and I spent it with family, the copious consumption of holiday cocktails inevitably led to fighting. If we spent it alone, I'd listen to the lock click on her doorknob as she ducked into her room to get high. Not very merry. Another time I taped paper snowflakes to the windows. I wanted a white Christmas. In a drunken fury, Janet smashed one, shouting how she hated snow.

I doodle a broken window and then rub my finger over the scar on my hand from when I picked up the glass. Maybe this year I can paint myself into a different scene. Part of me misses my mom. But I can't identify exactly what about her I miss. I became so accustomed to looking after her and making sure she didn't go too far off the rails; without her to occupy me, part of me feels idle and mismatched with pieces of confusion. I peer over my shoulder, into the warm glow of my dorm room. I also have high grades, a growing portfolio of paintings and fashion designs, and what I might call a few friends.

Chapter 9

One evening, as we walk to the dining hall, Charmindy says, "Break cannot come soon enough, but sometimes I wonder what would happen if I couldn't finish this insane amount of work assigned these last weeks before vacation."

I imagine her world ending and have a peek at mine. Sorel left campus for a family function, and Grant has a soccer banquet. As to Pepper's whereabouts, I have no clue, probably in bed with a video game, leaving my sole remaining friend, Charmindy.

"I suppose you could create a hypothesis and find out," I suggest.

"I would never. Where are you going for break?" she asks.

"Not sure yet. You?" I answer with honest uncertainty.

She offers excruciating details on the long flight back to India, a wedding, and all the family she's obligated to visit. My mind rudely wanders away.

Charmindy and I get along well enough, but other than her quiet interest in art, we actually don't have much in common. She's on the edge of the alpha girls, as we called them at my old school. As her roommate, I skirt the periphery, but they don't accept me, and I sense gossip crackles whenever I leave a room, especially if Terran happens to be in it. Since that first day, the sneer that dissolves into a puckered smile whenever I look in her direction makes me certain she doesn't like me.

Most of the girls here, Charmindy included, come from parents with money. They had their names down at Laurel Hill—or at least *private school* penciled in—when they were born, like my cousins, Erica and Logan. They have new cars waiting for them at home and exotic trips planned abroad. If I didn't know better, I'd think we live on different planets. And I don't want them to know about my native terrain.

Charmindy's friend Aubrey, plus Terran, Brett, and a few others, joins us at a table in the dining hall. Aubrey promptly spills a delicate forkful of marinara sauce all over her Burberry merino-wool sweater.

"Some soda water will probably get it out," I offer, standing up to go fill a cup.

"Don't be silly," she huffs and rolls her eyes. "I'll just order a new one when I get back to my dorm."

I'm definitely from Venus or some other distant world. Even if I couldn't get the stain out, I would strategically cover it with a pin or repurpose it, removing the sleeves for a vest or something creative.

"If you're just going to throw it out—" I start, but she interrupts, saving me from embarrassing myself.

"Of course I'll toss it in the holiday clothing-drive box," she says, meaning the one in the student center. "I'm sure some poor person can get the sauce out. They probably won't even care," she adds as if I'm not some poor person.

As the girls talk about what they're hoping to get for Christmas, I catch Charmindy eyeing me in apology. And I catch Brett eyeing her with interest.

"What?" Terran asks, glancing between the three of us.

Charmindy shakes her head as if to say it was nothing.

Terran turns to me. "I saw the look you gave her. What was that about?"

I shrug. "Nothing," I answer. I've been the new girl enough times to know to keep my head low and avoid being noticed, at risk of people finding out about my home life. It's better kept a secret, especially the not-home life I recently left in flames. I think about how I still haven't heard from my mom. I tell myself the polite deceit that no news is good news.

Terran jars me from my thoughts. "No, I don't think it was nothing. I saw you," she accuses me. Her eyes flit to Brett more than once.

"I wasn't looking. Honest."

Her eyes narrow, and her lip lifts in a sneer. "PJ, do you think—" She points between Brett and me and then starts laughing.

I play with a prickly, artificial holly leaf glued onto the centerpiece of the table, and I recall the numerous times my mom had gone to rehab and how afterward, ranging anywhere from half a year to a month, she'd stay off drugs, illegal drugs anyway. She takes a range of prescriptions for obscure pain, anxiety, and depression. I can hardly keep them straight, which means she certainly doesn't follow the directions on the bottles. But then again, the more medicated, the easier to avoid looking too closely at the mess she's made of her life. Comfortably numb. Sometimes I think I understand the desire too well.

I rise to bring my tray to the dishwasher and to leave this scene that I sense is about to unravel.

Terran abruptly stands up and stops me when I'm just out of earshot of the table. "If you think there's the possibility of anything going on between Brett and you, you're crazy. And if you think I'm going to let you get away with whatever pathetic fantasies you have running through your little mind, you are mistaken. Why don't you go back to sitting at the loser table, Pearl *Jaeger*?"

I prickle at the sight of her devilish smile telling me she knows more than I want her to.

Mid-December brings bone-biting cold. I wake to a thin dusting of snow on the morning of my birthday. After precal, Grant slips an envelope in my hand as I stuff the thick textbook into my backpack.

"Sorel told me," he confesses as I open it.

I look down at the folded blue paper. On the front, it reads *Let's not talk. Let's not be friends.*

I open it, and on the inside, it says *Let's just . . .*

Below is a print of two people embracing, their lips tight together so it's almost impossible to tell where one begins and the other ends. Their hair tangles like curling vines.

On the bottom it says,

Happy Birthday.

Yours,

Grant.

When I look up, Grant has disappeared, but the words on the card bypass my mind and shoot dangerously toward my heart.

That night, Charmindy and some of the other girls in the dorm make me a huge tray of brownies, which we all devour in the common room before Terran, the dorm assistant, reminds us it's nearly lights-out. She looks at me pointedly with pursed lips, as if I'm to blame for having a birthday, for being born.

Part of me wants to bask in the celebration, but Terran's expression brings the sharp memory that over the years my birthday has only received sporadic acknowledgment, dimming the moment like blown-out candles. I pad up to my room. In the dark, I screen memories of birthdays past, when Janet didn't remember until the last minute, stomping out happy sentiment.

I wipe my eyes and click on my reading light. With colored pencils, I sketch a dress consisting of previous birthday gifts from my mother: candles, an old cassette tape, a box of animal crackers, a calendar with puppies, and a spiral-bound notebook and crayons. It doesn't translate well onto paper, and I crumple it up. I slip the card from Grant safely between two blank pages and feel it there, warm, an invitation.

Sorel catches me brushing the bits of brownie from my teeth in the bathroom. My spit is chocolatey.

"Happy birthday. We're both seventeen. Woo-hoo," she says sardonically. "I have a present in mind, but it'll have to wait until we can escape for a weekend off campus. For now, come down to my room at eleven thirty and don't get caught." Before I can protest, she sweeps out of the bathroom.

I tuck into bed at 11:05, tossing about whether to sneak down to Sorel's room or stay put. By now, I know that many of the girls turn their lights back on after lights-out, and late-night visits within the dorm aren't uncommon. It isn't a huge deal, I tell myself. She probably wants to hang out. Then I worry about her roommate, Lucy. *Will she be asleep? What if she tells?*

I bargain with myself that if I fall asleep, I'll just shrug it off in the morning and apologize to Sorel with the truth. Obviously, I can't set an alarm.

The minutes tick by. At 11:15, I'm still wide-awake. Charmindy breathes deeply from across the room.

I try recalling Grant's expression when he passed the card to me, but the commotion in the classroom as we packed up and my own surprise obscures it. *Let's not talk. Let's not be friends. Let's just . . .* Sorel mentioned he'd fooled around with many girls. Maybe he has a stack of those cards, ready and waiting, his way of proposing the idea instead of waiting awkwardly for the right moment. Although we've shared plenty of those: in Mr. Meshcheryakov's math class, the dining hall, the woods . . .

The glowing numbers of the digital clock flick to 11:25.

Sorel claims to sneak out to Pepper's dorm a few times a week, going on her second year. She has the hickeys to prove it. She's never been in trouble. Whatever she has planned will be fine.

At 11:28, I slide back the covers and place my bare feet on the cold wooden floor. I stand motionless, making sure I haven't disturbed Charmindy, then pad over to the door, turn the knob slowly, and exit.

I quickly formulate an excuse in case Connie catches me in the hall. I have to use the bathroom. Duh. I drank too much soda at my party and need the toilet. When I pass the bathroom and move to the stairs, I create a second plan; I'll claim to have forgotten something in the common room.

Fortunately, or maybe unfortunately, I can't decide, I don't need any excuses, because in moments I stand in Sorel's room. Lucy snoozes on the top bunk, and Sorel leans against the wall, with a book light illuminating the pages of a thick novel. Maybe she just wants to hang out and talk Tolstoy. My jitters dissipate.

"I didn't think you'd actually come," she says, not looking up from her book.

"What about Lucy?"

"What about Lucy?" she echoes. She slams the book closed and levels me with a glare. "Listen, she's part of the Korean Connection; don't think I'd just have some lousy roommate that's going to rat me out. Lucy and her friends work harder than anyone else at this school. If they want to let loose on the weekends, far be it from me to say a word, but I'll do a public service and aid and abet them on their occasional exodus from the campus by providing inebriating beverages. And sometimes I score pills so they can pull all-nighters before exams to study and then others so they can sleep afterward. I just look the other way, and so does she. Lucy's all right. Trust me."

I don't want to know any more. Experience has taught me the less I know about sketchy dealings the better.

"But"—she looks me up and down—"I won't have Grant see you wearing your pj's, PJ. I should have been specific when I said what we were doing; as if you couldn't have figured it out." Her eyes roll ghoulishly in the low light. She stalks to her closet and pulls out a sweatshirt and jeans. "Put these on," she orders.

I stand dumbly, unmoving. *I can't be caught. I can't be caught.* It becomes a mantra.

"Come on, we don't have all night. What size shoe do you wear?"

Holding her clothing lamely in my hands, I shift from foot to foot. "Sorel, I don't know if this is a good idea."

"Just chill. It's your birthday. I thought you were from NYC. When I met you, it looked like you'd seen some shit. Rough around the edges. Not like the rest of the pampered girls here. Let's live a little."

Up until my time at Laurel Hill, I did do what I wanted when I wanted. I didn't have a curfew or lights-out. I came and went as I pleased, with the exception of when JJ, on mind-altering substances, ensnared me. I haven't thought much about what it means to live with rules. I just accept them as part of the room-and-board package here at Laurel Hill. Losing those two simple necessities terrifies me. Nevertheless, under Sorel's demanding stare, I pull the jeans over my pajamas. She gives me a withering look.

"It's flippin' cold out," I say defensively.

She shakes her head. "Shoes. What size?"

"Eight and a half," I answer.

"Sasquatch."

"Shut up. What size do you wear?" I retort.

"Nine," she says with defiance in her voice.

"Sasquatch, is that the best you can do?"

She tries not to laugh. "Come on, they'll be waiting."

I slide my feet easily into the fleece lining of Sorel's oversized boots. She wordlessly guides me out her window and onto the bulkhead to the basement that acts like a ramp.

"I chose this room for the easy exit. Senior privilege. We have to be quiet and steer clear of the lights on the motion detectors."

The first instruction is obvious, the second causes me to worry, but she navigates easily enough.

I catch sight of the moon between the spindly branches of the naked trees, and my shoulders relax. I spent so many nights roaming the streets of New York, if only to avoid the scene at home. I take a drink of the still air.

Sorel smiles. "What you needed, right?" she asks.

"Yeah."

"Want to throw rocks at the security trucks from the bushes?" she dares me.

"Nah."

I still don't know her story, but it doesn't approximate mine. She came from a family, with a mom and dad. I get the feeling there's some tension there, along with rules to break and expectations to flout. Unless Sorel really gets herself into trouble, I imagine she'll graduate from college and have a successful career. What she does at Laurel Hill is merely a game to her, and tonight, apparently, I'm her pawn.

Chapter 10

We arrive at the boys' dorm beneath a checkerboard of windows. Within a minute, one on the ground floor, two from the right, slides open. Pepper's pale face appears in the darkness, and he lets a rope ladder down.

"He brought that from his tree house back home," Sorel says with a rare giggle. It's clear she wears the pants in the relationship. In the same petulant way she let my mother's dress slip to the floor, she orders him to get her more ketchup, carry her backpack, and act at her disposal.

Sorel puts her foot on the bottom rung, but before pulling herself up, she turns around and whispers, "Grant's waiting for the birthday girl."

The combination of the faint smell of cigarette smoke wafting from Sorel's sweatshirt that I'm wearing along with her dirty socks from the dorm room makes me feel most unlike myself.

What if I act like an idiot?

What if we're caught?

What am I doing here?

After drawing the shades, Pepper flips on a night-light, which casts light dimly in their cookie-cutter dorm room. Around the corner of a bureau jutting out, forming a partition wall, Grant sits on his bed, under a reading light attached to his headboard. The folded newspaper he holds suggests he's doing a crossword puzzle. Before I know it, Sorel and Pepper are all over each other, leaving me on my own.

"Hey," Grant says sleepily. I slink closer to his bed as he pushes himself to the edge. "Happy birthday." He gets to his feet and bites his lip.

I bite mine. "Thanks. The card—" I whisper. I'm not sure if the ticking I hear is a clock or my heart.

Grant glances down shyly, as if it was easier to put his desires into words, on paper, than it is to say what he wants out loud.

"Do you take printmaking with Pepper?" I say to diffuse my discomfort.

"Yeah. It's cool. I'm not super arty, but as Pepper would say, the teacher is chill. Doesn't mind if we're late, that kind of thing. You have Shale, huh?"

"Yep. Pretty much the opposite of laid-back."

"Hardcore."

"Hardcore," I repeat.

"So, do you paint, draw? What goes on in the art tower?" Grant asks with a laugh.

I can't even muster a smile. "You mean art dungeon. Humiliation, yelling, disgust . . ."

"He's as bad as they say?"

"Worse."

"You should do printing."

"Then I'd see what you make before you can surprise me. The birthday card," I say, helping him along, bringing us back to what we both want.

"Yeah," he says, looking up from his hands.

"So, what are you waiting for?" I ask.

He leans in, and our lips press together. The little planets that make up my personal inner universe stop spinning. I think of the sizzle of the sparklers back on Halloween. This is like fireworks, filling the starless night, blanketing the little planets, lighting up the universe.

We linger, the warmth radiating from our skin magnetic, before we pull apart.

"First time sneaking out?" he asks, sitting on his bed.

"Sorta." I lower myself down next to him, the mattress giving softly. My heart twitters.

"She's over here at least three nights a week." His expression puckers as if he's eaten a lemon, like he's heard too much out of the two of them for his liking. "But I'm glad *you* came," he says, meeting my eyes.

In his, I see so much blue, a fathomless sky, an endless ocean.

"Thanks. I mean, me too." Ugh. My tongue ties around the things I want: Grant and not to be expelled. Part of me keeps wondering when we'll go back to Viv Brooks, even though we just got here. I want to slip between the crisp sheets of my hard-won bed and wake up tomorrow as if I haven't given myself the opportunity to be kicked out. Then I remind myself that I'm with Sorel and somehow she's managed to avoid trouble. Yet each creak of the old building settling or gust of wind from outside makes me flinch.

Grant shifts on the bed, leaning so close his edges get blurry. He takes my head in his hands, pulling my lips toward his, and we kiss again, erasing my worry, fulfilling my craving.

When we pull apart, he tucks a wisp of my hair behind my ear, studying me as though realizing I'm a piece to his puzzle. He hesitates for a fraction of a breath, as if wanting another confirmation of how perfectly our lips fit together, but instead he reclines along the short side of his bed, his knees bent and feet on the floor. He cradles his head in his hands like a hammock. His shirt creeps up, revealing the sliver of skin above the slim waist of his jeans. I debate whether to join him. I could easily just lean back, and we'd both be lying on his bed. Together. I inhale sharply. If someone discovers us, expulsion for sure. His fingertips gently test out the top of my hand, then find their counterparts, and they twine together. I lie down on my side, bringing my knees up between the two of us.

"I don't want to be friends. I don't want to talk," he says, echoing his card. I wonder if he's really an artist, just modest. "It makes things complicated. But your voice, it's like music, a husky melody. Tell me something. Anything. Talk to me about New York City," he says, turning his head toward me, but the words don't come. Instead, he kisses me and kisses me and kisses me until the fireworks become stars.

I wish I had my sketchbook. If I'd known what tonight was, the dress would be off the shoulder, with shining threads in silver and copper, amethyst and indigo. Safely wearing this dress in my imagination, a memory appears.

One sleepless night, while I was curled up in an armchair in a squat, a condemned building my uncle would volunteer to bulldoze, my mother, in another room, did lines of coke or, from the smell of it, smoked it. As I rested my head on the wings of the chair, I peered between crumbled brick at the lights layering the city. Part of me wanted to get up and go, leave that mess behind me, but then I considered where. Instead, I just sat there.

After a time, my eyes got heavy, blurring, and I realized that when a person doesn't have a proper home, one with a roof and four walls, preferably heat and electricity, and a family in that place to love them, a broader place becomes home, in my case Manhattan. I know the streets, the stores, the restaurants, and the museums like the lines drawn on my own hand. Only I often was on the outside looking in but always, always under a blanket of stars.

I don't say this aloud and wonder if this whole night is a dream, but my eyes flutter open—

"Where'd you go?" Grant asks, and when my eyes meet his, I smile.

"I'm right here," I say, relieved memories are only abstract recordings of history, nothing more. And right now, I'm making new ones.

He nips my lip, kisses my neck, and I forget the streets and stale memories. I don't care about being friends or talking; I just want to do *this*, forever.

As our lips tire, Grant moves slower, sleepily. His hand still holds mine, and we remain that way, warm and interlaced, until I hear my name.

"We've got to get back. Now," Sorel demands.

My eyes fly open, and for one groggy instant, I forget where I am. "Sorry, I must have—"

She cuts me off. "Come on."

I glance at Grant, his face peacefully asleep, filling me with longing to stay there, get under the covers, even. Instead, I bungle through the window, and we jog back to our dorm, the early morning sky, heather and oatmeal, easing awake along the horizon.

"We all fell asleep. Cardinal rule of sneaking out, never fall asleep. Hurry up," she says.

I stumble through the following day with exhaustion as my constant companion. Shale is unforgiving and instructs me in my still life by standing over my shoulder as I paint. It's nerve-racking, and the inquisitive looks from my classmates make me wonder if he's done this to everyone and at some point he's going to startle me, causing me to smear paint across the canvas or do some other horrible thing to embarrass me and test my patience.

By the evening, my steps are heavy and my head swims in the peculiar twilight that happens just before sleep. The only thing keeping me upright as I do homework is the stolen moment on Grant's bed, our lips outlining constellations and distant galaxies.

Chapter 11

Later that evening final-exam preparation transforms me into Charmindy's twin and study buddy. She explains a memorizing technique involving encoding, storage, and retrieval.

"I'm overwhelming you, aren't I?" she asks when my eyes dip toward closed.

"I'm just tired," I say with a yawn.

Her sharp eyes land on my mouth. I hope she didn't wake up and find my bed empty.

"Tea?" she asks, warming up her hot pot. She continues to impart intense study tips, including color-coded highlighting with coordinating sticky notes, repetition, and lots of nudges to keep me awake.

Over the course of exam week, Sorel badgers me about going to the woods. After our nighttime escapade, she practically begs me to go back with her each day, but I've managed to come up with a reasonable excuse—namely sleep—each time. It isn't that I don't want to see Grant again, and I'm not a Goody Two-shoes, but I've pledged these two years to school. I don't want to give up meals and warm showers. Plus I don't mind learning; I like it, even. The teachers here are passionate about educating, collaborating, and, as is the case with Shale, detonating. As time widens the crater between my old life and new, the alternative has me replenishing my sticky note supply at the school store.

On the last day of Painting IV before the break, Shale isn't pacing his track along the creaky wooden floor when class starts. Expecting him to breeze through the door at any moment, we all promptly begin to put the finishing touches on our paintings. Except Charmindy. She stares at her canvas, her head tilted, dazed. She can't organize or color code her way through this final.

I glance over my shoulder at the banner printed above Shale's desk. *Creativity takes courage. —Henri Matisse.* Charmindy hasn't moved out of her comfort zone. I go to the paint station and take squirts of bittersweet, tangerine, and cadmium. I pass them to her, pointing at the underside of some of her flowers. Her eyes light up, understanding the shadows need gradation.

In the doorway, Shale clears his throat. I turn back to my canvas, my fourth rendition of the same image. I don't ever want to see a bowl of fruit again. He stalks over to Charmindy's easel and surveys her work. He grunts and turns to the next person in the ring of easels lining the perimeter of the room. He dismisses each student after he accepts their work, some less kindly than others, until I'm the only person remaining.

He doesn't even look at my painting, but leans against the workbench opposite and folds his arms in front of his chest. I don't detect a smile beneath his beard, but amusement plays along the lines around his eyes. "Pearl Jaeger. What color is your blood?"

I don't answer.

"What shade? Where are you on the spectrum?"

I remain quiet under his scrutiny, because I don't have an answer and can't bring myself to lie.

"Is paint your medium?"

I look out the window, the tops of trees bathed in the golden honey of morning. "No, usually I sketch, but I love painting. It's great. My favorite artist is Frida . . . I mean—" My words mush like hash, and by the flat expression in his gray eyes, I can tell he doesn't believe what I'm saying. I try again.

"I sketch because most days I'm afraid to commit to something as solid and permanent as oil, but—"

"A painter can add layers, hide mistakes or secrets under more paint. They're still there."

"Well, I'm here to paint, honestly."

"Are you?" He grunts. "The solution is the skill in adding only what is necessary, creating a balance between sketching and painting." He takes up a brush, and I sense that if the rest of the students were here, they'd gawk at him. Then he throws the brush down as if with disgust. "You may not help other students in this class, not even friends. Painting IV is about independence. However, I haven't had a student follow through with three, much less four, renditions of a still life, ever. And I've been doing this a long time." He braces his hands on the table. "So, what are you made of, tell me?"

"Half broken dreams, the other half, I'm not sure yet," I say.

"No, not broken," he says with what I think is tenderness in his voice. "Not yet."

His eyes gleam, verging toward platinum. I hastily gather up my bag and coat.

"Every day, over holiday, make sure you have a brush, a pen, or some implement in your hand, creating, without fail. The only way to get better is to do the work, daily. There are no shortcuts. Not many people realize that."

"Is that an assignment?" I ask.

"No. That's an order."

I exit the building at the same time as Brett—apparently, Terran's claimed him as her territory. We're walking at the same pace, so it would be awkward, not to mention rude, if we didn't acknowledge each other.

"Almost done?" I ask.

"Yep," he answers. "You?"

"Charmindy schooled me in the fine art of successful studying. For once I think I've got this."

His cheeks tint pink. "You're roommates, right?" he asks. But I know he knows, because it's been mentioned at the dining hall table when I sit with Charmindy's crowd. "Is she going back to India for break?" He also knows the answer to this question.

"Yeah."

"Um, so this might sound horrible, but I, um, does she already have like a boyfriend, or like—I don't know exactly how it works."

My forehead forms lines parallel to my eyebrows as I grimace at him.

"I know that sounded super ignorant. I just didn't want to ask her and offend. Do you know what I mean?"

"You're asking if she's single? Available? You could have just said that."

"I'm sorry. I walked her back to her dorm once, and I felt like she didn't want me there. It's hard to explain. I've hung out at her table, around the dorm. I don't really know how to get her attention."

I interrupt. "In a word, she's fierce. So, the short answer is yes, she's single. The long answer, unless you're interested in spending ridiculous amounts of time in the library, studying, and would consider that quality time together, you don't have a chance. She's married to scholarship—"

His face matches his red North Face jacket. Down the sidewalk, I spot Terran, wearing a matching coat, but hers is in teal. As she nears, I feel the burn of her glare, and her bare hands form fists.

"But Charmindy is one of the coolest people I know. You should give it a shot," I say quickly, with a reassuring smile. As I cross the lawn to my next class, I wave good-bye to Brett, shouting, "Good luck, lover boy."

By the end of the day, my brain feels like a Ping-Pong ball as it bounces from subject to subject. Sorel finds me zoning out in the library, returning some books from a research essay.

"You look like you need a break. I was just on my way to meet Pepper and Grant," she says enticingly.

As we enter the glade, with sparse leaves and muted by shades of brown, Pepper holds the remainder of what might be a cigarette but smells like marijuana up to his lips. He coughs fitfully, trying to speak. "Uh, sorry, babe. I just finished it. I didn't know you were coming. Grant's on his way too."

Sorel glares at him in a way that reminds me of my mother, a hungry animal, starved for something that drugs or attention won't satisfy, no matter how much she smokes or how outrageously she acts. I feel myself shrink, wishing to blend in with the leaves on the dirty ground.

By way of explanation, Sorel barks, "Pepper and I split a couple of ounces when I went home for Thanksgiving, and he hasn't been doing a very good job sharing." She flies at him, her hands reaching into pockets and under his vest as she searches for more pot. Unlike my mother and Darren, they play fight; he tickles her, she giggles, and as far as they're concerned, I disappear.

A pack of cigarettes falls out of Pepper's vest, and I seize it, lighting one up. One drag and the long ream of tension wound tight inside me from studying and repeating brushstrokes disperses, much like the remaining oak leaves flittering off the branches above. I take a few more puffs, starting to cough. My throat hasn't been the same since the fire.

Sorel rolls another joint. "Victorious!" she proclaims, holding it up. "Gimme the light, PJ."

I toss it to her, and soon the familiar, herby smell of marijuana dominates the cigarette smoke. As she pulls the joint from her lips, Pepper makes for it, but Sorel brushes his arm away. "Ladies first," she says, passing it to me.

I take one practiced hit and pass it back to her.

"Not your first time, eh?" Pepper asks.

"She's a city girl, stupid. Of course she's smoked pot," Sorel says, instantly asserting her provisional version of respect for me.

"Nope, not my first time," I say, exhaling, feeling more relaxed.

I've found myself in countless situations where marijuana held court as the centerpiece of conversation and activity, and in some circles, at least it seemed, taking a hit or ten was the sole purpose for getting out of bed.

"Stoked classes are almost over. Glad you and Grant are done with that art class? What was it, card making for dummies, for the lovelorn?" Sorel glances at me. I don't flinch at her words.

However, Pepper does. "No, it was printmaking, and if you want to transfer in next semester, I can talk to the teacher."

She answers with a plume of smoke directed toward him, and then they proceed to gnaw on each other's faces and leave me with the joint and a pack of memories that drift back to me through smoke and haze. My lungs burn and blister, but my insides quickly mellow, dulling the remnants of pain.

The sound of Sorel and Pepper's laughter, and my own, involuntarily issuing forth at something inconsequential in my memory, rolls over on itself just when Grant shows up. He smirks at me and motions with his hand. "Pass the fresh J this way."

When nothing more remains than a fragment of white rolling paper, the four of us laugh at Pepper's elaborate plan to grow weed in the clearing, harvesting it to fund an M&M candy dispensary on campus.

"In every color. I call orange," he says.

"Dibs on blue," Grant says with a laugh.

Sorel rolls her eyes.

With nothing to occupy their hands or lips, Sorel and Pepper make out again. Grant and I move away, taking a seat on top of the boulder in the center, our backs to the couple.

"I didn't expect to find you here," he says.

"Blame Sorel," I say, meaning she dragged me.

"How'd you do in precal?" Grant asks, imitating our teacher's thick accent. I almost fall off the rock, laughing, and grab his arm to keep from plummeting to the hard earth.

"Gotcha," he says as he pulls me closer to him.

The momentum of him catching me propels my face just inches from his, and our eyes meet for one heart-stopping second. My pulse records the unfolding instant as time slows. I gaze at the pale freckles splattered like paint across his nose, then travel down to his full lips. A tiny scar marks the space between his bottom lip and chin. I wonder where it came from. I feel his breath tickling my skin, the scent of mint and pine. Our eyes meet again, and before I can stop it, I let loose more peals of laughter.

"I don't want to admit it, but I like that sound."

"I thought you liked my voice."

"That too. I'm going to break the no-talking rule. Holiday plans?"

"I didn't know that was a rule," I say, remembering how he asked me to tell him about New York City that stolen night in his dorm and how we talk fairly regularly, but usually it's in Sorel and Pepper's company. In fact, we're rarely alone, at least not without them in close proximity.

"I meant it when I said I don't want to be friends—or anything else," he adds almost as an afterthought. "But I can't help it; I want to hear you. Tell me your plans, tell me anything." His voice pitches toward agony, like it physically pains him to bear my silence.

I shrug, baffled and tired of the question about vacation, of the whole idea, hoping maybe by not committing, a better option will arise. "My uncle's condo down in Florida," I say, having received instruction to go there instead of meeting my mother in New York.

But the rules Grant has imposed burden me more than vacation. At first, I thought it was romantic, but now I'm just baffled.

"I've read that card you gave me going on a hundred times. I don't get it. It didn't occur to me that we weren't friends or what it means not to be friends or more than friends." I tilt my head as though the explanation is in his expression. When he doesn't answer, I add, "But you can't get away with kissing me or asking to hear my voice, never mind our great dining hall debates, and not consider me a friend."

"Like I said, it gets complicated. It *is* complicated."

I shake my head, not buying it. "Believe me, I know complicated, and you"—I wag my finger between us—"this seems straightforward."

"Trust me. It isn't."

Undeterred, I say, "Where are you going for vacation, O vexing one?"

"Scotland," Grant says, mimicking my lack of enthusiasm about the prospect of Florida.

"I'd rather go there."

"Ever been?" he asks.

"Not even close," I say drearily.

"There's always someday," he says expectantly.

Chapter 12

My uncle meets me with a thin smile as I emerge into the bright Florida day. After I slip off my jacket and sweatshirt, the razor-like sunlight feels as if it cuts my skin.

"Pearl, nice to see you," Aunt Beverly says, glancing up from her compact after fixing her lipstick. Her awkward hug makes me think the words are more convention than sincerity.

My cousin Erica's hug makes me think of koalas.

My uncle's grumblings about traffic are in tune with my ambivalence about the upcoming weeks.

Seeing this branch of the Jaeger Corporation reminds me they were essentially absent until, of course, my mother's uncensored activity threatened a media blowout. I wonder if JJ succeeded in, once more, parlaying bad press on my uncle's dreams of political office. I make it a rule not to read anything other than *Vogue* and whatever my teachers assign me.

The word *resentment* volleys into my mind, punctuated by my aunt's nearly constant thinly veiled criticisms. "Your clothes are just, so . . . *unique*, Pearl; have you considered a haircut; what about joining the school senate—when your uncle was your age—" she says in rapid succession.

"Mom, Pearl and I are going shopping. You remember what boarding school was like. It isn't as if there's a mall on campus," Erica says without sarcasm. "The school store certainly doesn't carry clothing, unless you count spirit tees and athletic gear."

I rerun the disaster of the Christmas my mom and I spent with them years back. The tree toppled to the ground, the roast burned, and my uncle ended up with a glass of scotch tossed in his face. Classic Janet.

Perhaps this year everything will be amiable, my mom will be sober, and beneath the tree, there will be shiny packages filled with rainbows, unicorns, and darling bunnies for each of us to unwrap.

When the Cadillac pulls into the high-end condominium development—where my aunt and uncle will go when he retires, although from what I gather she spends the winters here—it looks like we've entered a grandiose Lego set. The identical buildings, a bland color that may have once been coral, now bleached by the sun, stand nondescript from one to the next. Sure, there's lush greenery and opulent fountains, but it's a place for retirees, who, escaping the cold northern winters, convinced themselves they could endure the hot, humid Floridian summers. Really, they just traded heating for air-conditioning. The only redeeming thing is the proximity of the azure ocean.

"How is school?" my uncle dutifully asks.

I fill them in with sparse details about my dorm, roommate, classes, and cross-country. Of course, I omit smoking, drinking, and Grant. As the words issue forth, I sound like a normal teenager, not one with a murky past, a cracked-out mother, and a fractured sense of self. I learned about that concept in a therapy group I attended a couple of years ago.

"We sent your mother her ticket. She'll be arriving on Christmas Eve. I bet you're excited to see her." My aunt speaks flatly.

I change her statement into a question and ask myself if I am excited. My *yes* comes out at a whisper.

"And do tell us, how's the cough? It seemed you were well on your way to recovery at the beginning of September. What a tragedy. Did you know that, along with a generous endowment to Laurel Hill this fall, your uncle and I funded the restoration of the shelter? Did your mother mention that?" Her smile seethes.

"Actually, I haven't heard from her."

As I unpack in the spare bedroom, the polished tile cool beneath my feet, I accidently knock over a framed photo of my grandparents with Gary, and Janet—around age twelve. I stare into her then-clear eyes. Sometimes I want to blame my grandparents for my life, but they're both dead. What did they do to my mother to make her nuts, helpless, and hopeless? Or what didn't they do for her? I can come up with a quick list of things JJ hasn't done for me. I wonder what it would look like if she and I compared notes.

Later that day, as promised, my cousin and I go shopping. We talk about Laurel Hill—she graduated last year—and swap stories about some of the teachers. I mention Shale, but she just shivers and says she never took art classes. I almost forget I'm Janet's daughter and instead feel like I'm just Erica's cousin.

When we walk into the air-conditioned mall, she flashes her dad's credit card. "I know he seems uptight, but it's just that his job is really demanding. People always say CEOs, lawyers, people who make money have it so easy, but the level of stress he's under, it's like he's contractually obligated to have a heart attack." She doesn't say anything about how much he hates his sister and, therefore, me. "He wants us to have a good Christmas. And by *good Christmas* I mean let's go shopping." Her lips curl up, and despite Uncle Gary's sad attempt to express his affection for his daughter with plastic, I'm all for having what she calls a good Christmas.

Erica insists I pick out a few outfits and get some Christmas gifts for my mom and the rest of the family. As I tote our bags to the car, she hands me a hundred-dollar bill.

"This is just extra, for when you go back to school, in case you need anything." I dimly recall my grandmother slipping my mom bills and wonder how quickly they disappeared up her nose.

"Thanks, Erica, but you don't have to," I say courteously.

"Consider it part of your present," she says, but the pity I've braced myself for isn't there; instead I find a kindhearted smile.

On Christmas Eve, my uncle pulls out the artificial tree as my aunt pours herself lunch: a glass of rosé. She detours down memory lane, describing the various ornaments my cousins made as children.

My uncle retreats to his home office, mentioning a follow-up call he needs to make, while my aunt's emptying glass ferries her further into her own world.

Late that afternoon, we pile into the Cadillac to go to the airport to meet Janet and Logan, the latter coming in from Indiana, where he goes to Notre Dame.

Checking the monitor, we see that the flights are on time. They greet Logan with a big hug. I get an oblivious hug from him—he probably hasn't followed the Janet saga from afar. As we wait, my stomach binds into the familiar knots of uneasy anticipation that have been forming for as long as I can remember. *Will she be sober? Will she be high? Will she be coherent?*

Passengers dressed in New York black—leather, puffers, and peacoats—disembark. I look for the shock of blond hair that identifies my mother, but she doesn't appear. A parade of baby strollers comes off the Jetway last, and she isn't among them.

"I bet she fell asleep," Erica says, offering a reasonable excuse.

"Yeah, maybe," I say softly.

"She said the halfway house is noisy day and night. This is probably the first time she's had peace and quiet," my uncle says snidely as the families with crying babies move out of earshot.

The pieces neatly fall together. Janet slipped up again. She isn't coming. However, I indulge the fantasy that history isn't repeating itself and inquire about the passenger in seat 24-B, Janet Jaeger.

"I'm sorry," the frazzled employee says as she scans the computer screen. "She wasn't on the flight. It looks like the ticket was transferred to O'Hare."

"That's strange. Why would she go there?" Erica asks naively as we walk away from the desk.

"She sold the ticket, Erica," I say, surprising myself with my candor. I'm usually good about going along with the excuses or making up some of my own. However, that scenario is tired, pinpointing what has bothered me over the last couple of days.

I gaze up at the tiled ceiling to gather patience for my mother and this situation. I want to shake her. Tell anyone who will listen to wake up and smell the coffee, wine, crack, or whatever gets them out of bed in the morning. I wish I knew which was easier, denial or oblivion, because right now I'm so desperate not to feel so far beyond disappointed that I discover a thick layer of disgust that threatens to unhinge me.

Heavily, I look at the small cast who plays my family. "She's not coming," I say simply. "Let's go."

I want someone to go get her, to run to her. Save her. Do whatever they need to do. Race the two thousand miles to New York, steal a motorcycle, or travel back in time to whenever that critical point was when they stopped caring. If they ever did. I just want us to love her, for goodness sake, and loving her doesn't mean giving her money or excuses. Loving her means—but I don't know what it means. Whatever it is, she makes it very difficult.

When we return to the high-rise in paradise, I retreat to the guest room and slowly wrap the gifts I picked out for my aunt, uncle, and cousins. I wind the scarf I bought for Janet around my neck. Through the wall, Logan boasts loudly about his semester and the brotherhood on campus.

As for Janet, it's unlikely she'll be welcomed back to the halfway house if she did, in fact, break the rules. She always screws up. After I put a few gifts under the tree, I ask my aunt and uncle if they'll call around to try to find her, but my request is not met with enthusiasm. Nonetheless, I overhear Aunt Beverly on the phone, inquiring and then hissing as she relays to my uncle that JJ cashed in the ticket and he should *just let it go.*

I curl the ribbon on top of the chair massager I got for Uncle Gary—to help relieve his stress. My finger catches on the blade of the scissors and starts bleeding.

In the guest bathroom, all I find are Q-tips, an emery board, and various outdated balms and ointments. I wrap a tissue around the cut and go to my aunt and uncle's bathroom.

In the back, among half the stock of a drugstore, a box of Band-Aids peeks out. As I shift aside containers promising relief from a host of ailments, my hand lands on a bottle of painkillers. I read the label. *Do not take with alcohol.* Which I know, at least in my mother's language, means *do* take with alcohol. *May cause drowsiness,* reads the second warning. Perfect. I recall the crumbling borders of reality during my hospitalization after the fire. Sleep would be a quick exit from this vacation. I pop the lid and swallow two of the chalky white tablets with water from the tap. *Oblivion.*

I set the rest of the wrapped packages under the tree and go help in the kitchen, while my uncle zones in on a squawking news show. I'm electric with the promise that in about twenty minutes, I'll be floating away from reality.

I go to the kitchen and help my aunt arrange crudités on a platter, which seems pointless. Then, noticing the glass of white wine on the counter, next to a nearly empty bottle of my aunt's favorite, I think maybe we'll all be in our own little worlds before long. When Aunt Beverly adjourns to ask Uncle Gary if he'd like eggnog, I chug the wine directly from the bottle, then pour some into my cup of the thick, festive drink.

Shortly after, the substance in my veins feels sluggish and my eyes droop. I finish setting the table and lie down on a cushioned lounge chair on the lanai, what Aunt Beverly calls the screened-in patio.

As if on one of the wispy clouds that drift by the setting sun, I glide back to New York City. Back to strangers' beds, mattresses without sheets, walls with peeling paint, drafty windows, and abandoned dreams.

I see a clone of my mother seated in the corner of the room with a needle in her arm, and then passed out on a moldy bathroom floor. Another image of her floats by, while a female officer reads her rights. I see her eyes bugging wide with paranoia as she checks closets and under beds for a threat only known to her warped mind. Later, there's her face, screwed up in fits of detoxing agony. As a backdrop I hear her laughing, always laughing. She seems to laugh at herself and everyone else like the most rebellious of children, as if to say, *I don't give a shit.*

This is not the escape I'd hoped for. But then, as her laughter fades, I float farther north to a room that smells faintly of smoke and dirty socks, a bed of pine, and clean sheets. I look into Grant's eyes. He holds my hand, and we linger there, together, joined, then I lean over his bed and heave. Only instead of a wood floor, I stare at tile and realize I've just puked all over the lanai. I snap to and stumble to my feet to get a towel.

"Not feeling good?" my aunt says when she sees what happened.

"Maybe it was the eggnog," I mumble.

"We've all had it. Seemed fine."

Denial.

I carry out the following days with the pills, but avoid the eggnog and wine. I read *Vogue* or sketch elaborate designs on a sketchbook in my mind. Each time, I float away from my body to the chorus *I never want to not feel this way.* There's no fight inside or around me. The cocktail of fear and disgust that pierces my mind freezes, and nothing matters.

Erica and Logan return to New York to meet up with friends for New Year's. My good-bye with Erica is the only time I allow myself to be lucid. She leaves me with some clothes and extras from Christmas, including moisturizers, hair products, and a refill of my favorite shade of matte red lipstick.

As the humid mornings and stormy afternoons pass until my return to Laurel Hill, I find Grant's image occupying my thoughts, and my mother just a dim silhouette in my mind.

"Pearl," my aunt calls.

The lanai has become my sanctuary from my uptight aunt and uncle. The thick air does me the favor of keeping me prone.

"Pearl," she repeats.

The pills assist with me not caring whether or not I answer. I don't bother lifting my head or opening my eyes. I have daily fantasies about Grant's hand on my back in the clearing, our lips meeting for a kiss, and more. I long to feel his breath on my bare neck and his fingers on my skin.

"Pearl."

A shadow blocks the bricks of sunlight formed behind my closed lids. I blink open my eyes.

"It's time to go to the airport."

For a moment, I'm hopeful, like Janet realized she was looking at the map upside down and finally found her way here.

"We don't want you to miss your flight," my aunt says.

I snap to sitting, both of us thankful it's finally time for me to leave.

As a sedan returns me to placid Laurel Hill, I feel something of my former obedient-schoolgirl self returning. While staying with my aunt and uncle, I felt shackled and filled with resentment. I couldn't quite be me, yet it was like they even held the not-me against me with their criticisms and looks of disapproval, as if I were JJ.

All I want to do is kick and scream my way out of their deep mine of anger veiled as criticism. At Laurel Hill, even though no one truly knows my past, no one blames me for it either. The sole responsibility of the adults around me is to prepare me for the future, and that is what they do. No covert insults, no denial. The rest is up to me. I wonder how long it will take for my internal landscape to shift, now that my outward one is populated by rolling hills that disappear into the horizon, trees that brush the watercolor-blue sky, and smiles from passersby instead of sneers. It feels good to be back.

Chapter 13

After returning to Viv Brooks, I'm stashing the pills I took from my aunt and uncle's copious medicine cabinet with the remaining prescription from the fire, when I hear Charmindy approaching with a cheerful hello to someone in the hallway.

"How was vacation?" She doesn't wait for me to answer, and I don't offer one. "I brought you some clothes. I thought you could work some of your design magic on them," she says, carting in her luggage.

It's impossible not to notice how few things I own. Charmindy is being charitable, but it could easily have been insulting. However, I'm used to seconds and am nearly as happy with them as I would be with brand-new swaths of untouched fabric—though that has yet to happen. My visions for fiber grandeur remain on the page alone. I'm not even really good at sewing. Vintage is my favorite, because the stitching and embellishments tell the story of the previous wearer.

"Thanks," I say, tucking the bag in my closet. "How was your time back home?" I try again, my interest the only thing I have to offer her.

Her expression passes through disappointment and lands on a version of unpleasant, but she doesn't have time to answer, because Sorel bursts into the room, eager to fill me in on her trip to Seattle. Casting an irritated glance in Sorel's direction, Charmindy busies herself with unpacking.

"The people there are so chill. And, seriously, the coffee rocks, and don't get me started on the bands and the parties . . ." She goes on to describe the city like it's the best place in the world, Disneyland for hip and jaded youths. "All the schools I applied to are out there. You have to promise to visit."

"Sure," I say, uncertain if that will ever happen.

Her story gets more and more elaborate, and the slight tint to her skin suggests she saw some sun. I don't know much about the Pacific Northwest in December, but wonder if her itinerary also included a tropical getaway. I don't get the sense her parents appreciate her interests and doubt they would have sent her to Seattle for long, but I indulge her, only half listening.

I avoid divulging how I fantasized about Grant, anesthetized myself against my aunt and uncle's false cheer over the holiday, and failed to pick up a brush, pen, or other artistic tool, as Shale instructed, the entire holiday.

As classes resume, I dutifully recalibrate to having responsibilities and meeting expectations. I replenish Charmindy's colorful sticky note supply and pledge study hours to her. However, like misdirected luggage, everything I learned last term in math, I lost somewhere between Laurel Hill and Florida. Maybe my mom is on a baggage carousel in a lonely midwestern town, holding fast to my understanding of polynomials and leading coefficients and waiting for someone to send her home.

In the next days, an insistent storm paints the campus with a pristine blanket of snow. I sketch versions of my self-portrait but wrinkle them into snowballs and toss them to the floor. Shale would be proud.

There still hasn't been any word from my mom. I've dialed a few contact numbers I have, using the dorm phone, but I either was hung up on or received a message saying the number was no longer in service.

I'd hoped my uncle would get me a cell phone for Christmas, but the pajama set and student planner are still in my suitcase.

Disappointed, I rest my head on top of my sketchbook. An image of JJ, a replica of me, after she'd gotten out of rehab, dips and floats into my mind. She was golden that day. I flip to a new page, eager to capture the memory before it flutters away.

Halfway done, I sit up and run my hands over my face.

Charmindy throws the door open, her expression a mixture of gusty and delighted. "Guess what?" she asks.

"You figured out a way to scan your class notes directly into your brain," I say.

"That would be awesome, but no, Brett asked me out." She collapses onto her bed.

I'm not sure if she means this with the giddy glee of a typical sixteen-year-old or with the excitement of just having finished a math marathon.

"We were at the library and then went for a walk down by the pond and he kissed me and then asked if I wanted to, well, be with him," she says all in one breath. "I didn't see that coming."

"I did . . . all the way from him walking you to the dorm, from the art building, and in the dining hall, and—"

She puts her hand up to stop me. "He called me over holiday break. In India." She rolls over to face me. "Pearl, at the risk of sounding slightly more mature than I am, I have AP-level classes, student government, debate, cello, Students for Seniors, field hockey, theater . . . my parents. There isn't time for a boy."

My thoughts quickly yield to Grant and boyfriends. As though reading from a spreadsheet, Charmindy details the pros and cons of the hypothetical guy who may or may not have the credentials approved of by Mr. and Mrs. Rajasekhara. The various guys I've done more than hang around with over the years appear one by one in my mind.

There was Nathan and then Brody, whose lives were pretty much identical to mine, which made for a challenge, because we'd try to one-up each other with dreadful stories. Then there was Anthony, whose mother always enticed me into her kitchen with the scent of garlic and basil. None of them ever took me on a walk down by a pond or officially asked me to be his girlfriend. With each of those boys, we just fell in with each other, but not in love with each other. Our relationships lacked romance and fire. I was never taken on a date, unless I count sneaking into clubs. I may have grown up in a strange limbo between privilege and poverty and been given a shoddy sense of direction, but I've gleaned an idea of how relationships work. I've yet to claim that experience for my own, but I was never in love with any of the boys I dated. We were just convenient for each other, a warm body, a friend to cause trouble with, a kiss and a tell. And what's Grant? He doesn't want to be friends, but he acts like one. He doesn't want to talk, yet he asks to hear my voice.

Charmindy flits around the room, gathering her robe and her tote of toiletries to take to the shower, while singing, "I'm going out with Brett Fairfax."

Smiling at her sweet innocence, I'm just turning back to my sketch pad when I hear Terran shouting in the hall. Charmindy flies back into our room and flings herself on the bed, this time facedown.

I sit next to her. "What happened, Char?"

She sobs into her comforter, one terry cloth slipper dangling from her foot, the other halfway across the room. She turns her face so she can talk.

"Terran totally just yelled at me, saying Brett only asked me out to make her jealous. She said I'd better back off or else. He asked *me*, PJ. He asked me, the brainy girl from halfway across the world who has only talked to boys during class. A girl who'd never been kissed, no less asked out."

After a few hiccupping sniffles, she says, "We kissed. It felt so real and a little wet, but still. He didn't say anything about *her*." She eyes the door as if Terran might barge in. "I mean, I've seen them walking from classes together and sometimes at the table in the dining hall. If I knew they were together or serious, I wouldn't have kissed him back. I thought they were just friends." She groans.

I think back to Terran's stares and the warning in the dining hall, along with the stink eye when Brett and I walked together from the art building. "I bet Terran just heard about it and is mad it wasn't her. Jealous, y'know? Brett probably really likes you. Don't worry about her," I say, trying to be comforting.

"You should have seen her, PJ. She looked crazy, like she was going to tear my hair out or spit fire."

"I *heard* her," I say quietly. In fact, since my first encounter with Terran, I have done my best to avoid her. I can smell crazy a mile away, having been born and bred into it. The brand of crazy I'm accustomed to often doesn't wear shoes and has missing teeth or a gold grill, but Terran hides her brand of crazy neatly behind a perfect smile. I know enough to keep a safe distance.

"What am I going to do?" Charmindy asks, rolling over and pressing herself up onto her forearms.

"I'm not sure. Maybe talk to Brett about it? You'll know if he's sincere. I get the feeling Terran probably had a crush on him and he didn't return the interest," I say carefully. "It seems like she tends to get really involved in things, like *a lot*."

Charmindy sits up and gives me a hug. She feels tiny in my arms, like a baby bird.

"I'll go down to the showers with you. If she gives you any more trouble, I'll be there." I gather my toiletries. Lacking a fluffy robe, I grab my towel.

When we enter the bathroom, sure enough, Terran stands before the mirror, blowing out her ash-blond hair. Turning off the blow-dryer, she glares at Charmindy and then me, through the mirror. She slowly turns around. Using her wooden hairbrush as a pointer, she hisses at Charmindy, "I told you to stay away from me and to stay away from Brett. This is my dorm, my school, and he is *mine*."

Terran found Charmindy's weak spot, the chink in her armor. She hardly bats an eyelash at her extra class load and the intense pressure her family puts on her to achieve, but as the tip of the brush comes close to her nose, she cowers, uncertain in the land of boys and relationships.

I start to say lightly, "Listen, Terran, Charmindy doesn't mean anything by it. She didn't know that you and Brett—"

Terran rounds on me. "You stay the hell out of this, bitch." Her eyes narrow. "I found out all about you and where you come from, one of the perks of being the student liaison to the dean. Speaking of which, why don't you tell Charmindy here why no one dropped you off? Or showed up for parents' weekend? Where was it you went for Christmas again? Does she know? How about your parents, Pearl Jaeger? Tell us all about them." Her words fly at me like knives.

My breath comes sharply through my nose. My fists tighten. My vision takes on a reddish hue. I feel Charmindy's eyes on me, growing wide. I have been in a few fights with bullies. I'm scrappy and unafraid when the survival instinct kicks in. I catch a glimpse of myself, wild, in the mirror behind her. The reflection is too familiar, too much like JJ. I exhale and lower my hackles. I take a deep breath.

"Nothing to say?" Terran spits.

I bite the inside of my cheek.

"You'll be sorry," she says as she sweeps out to the hall. I distinctly feel like I will.

Without another word, Charmindy and I quietly take our showers. I let the steaming water burn away my anger.

Of course, everything Terran said is true. It isn't the first time someone has loaded my past and present and fired away, using them as ammunition. In elementary school, I'd been insulted plenty because I wore the same thing to school three days in a row and my unbrushed hair smelled like cigarettes. I endured taunts because no one came to school plays or open houses. When my mother did appear, her erratic behavior was enough to peg me as the weird girl. It's a fact of academic life: the weird girl is picked on, at least in my experience. I changed schools frequently, forcing me to learn how to combat the teasing. Either I made myself as small and invisible as possible or, as my mother told me, as long as they threw the first punch, I fought back.

This situation is different. We all live at school and in the dorm together. We're all nearly adults. This fight really belongs to Charmindy and Terran or, if I'm being rational about it, just to Terran.

I don't want to provoke her. I've used the tactic of inconspicuousness to avoid trouble. She has the faculty in her pocket, which she makes perfectly clear, first with Connie, then at the all-school assemblies where she puts on skits about peer-health education, through her activities, and by being on the dean's advisory committee—the student liaison or whatever. She leads the debate team and captains volleyball. She is Laurel Hill's all-star golden girl. I don't want to be on the wrong side of her, any more than the conventions of high school naturally dictate.

Once safely back in our dorm room, when we're snug under our blankets and the lights are out, I say, "Hey, Charmindy, Terran puts the *ass* in dorm *ass*istant." Our shared laughter distances me from my growing anxiety and invites the feeling of what it would be like if Grant asked me out down by the pond.

Chapter 14

As the first frigid months of the new year wear on, everyone comes down from the high of holiday vacation. The teachers lose their luster as distraction and disinterest vie for our attention. The sand and salt spread on the sidewalks and the resulting slush reflect the general mood. Except for Shale. His eyes are brighter, his beard trimmed, and it appears he's pulled out his favorite Nordic knitwear. Despite this, to say he isn't pleased that I haven't started my self-portrait would be an understatement. He's livid, possibly ready to throw me from the third-floor window.

"You say today, you will get out the paint. No. Nothing. Dry canvas. You are stalling. I want to see who you are, Pearl. The assignment is self-portrait. Do not waste time in this class. Do not blow smoke in my ass."

Despite the usually reserved demeanor of the students in the class, this elicits a snicker.

I try, and fail, to tuck away a smile. "Actually, sir, it's 'do not blow smoke *up* my ass.' Not *in*. Or, in this instance, up *your* ass. No smoke in anyone's asses," I clarify.

His eyes bore into mine, icicles, ice daggers. I turn back to the blank canvas, and, as I've been doing for weeks, I stare, waiting for the form to take shape, but all I see is my mother there, whether my eyes are opened or closed.

On our way to the dining hall, Charmindy says, "That was legendary. Seriously, in the history of Shale's tenure here, no one, and I mean no one, has ever responded to him like that. I've investigated. Never mind the fact that he's never said a single word to me, nor I him, I can't believe . . . well, Pearl, I think he likes you. Not in a weird old-teacher, young-student, *Lolita* kind of way, but like a prodigy."

But her words drift away with the snow. I have enough problems on my hands, practically failing precal, despite the fact that my roommate is, in fact, a math, science, and English genius and could help me; my crush on Grant; my missing mother; and how my toes are permanently frozen.

Out of the blustery day and in the bustling dining hall, I inch away from Charmindy and toward Grant, ready to warm myself in the glow of his quiet presence. I sit with him, Sorel, and Pepper during lunch.

"I'm going to a party this weekend. Who's in?" Sorel asks. She doesn't even bother to look at me. I've declined enough offers for her to assume it's a pass.

"I have band rehearsal for the winter concert," Pepper answers.

"You're such a dweeb. I thought you said you were going to quit playing."

His cheeks blossom pink. "My advisor said it will look good on college apps."

"So you listened to him? Major dorkville, dude. I guess that just leaves you and me, Grant," she says with a smirk that neither Pepper nor I miss.

I sense Grant's eyes flitting toward me. I should ask him if he wants to study with me; he could help me with math or do whatever it is guys and girls at boarding school do when they're together if they're not friends and if they don't talk. The birthday card was merely a poetic gesture, a way for him to say let's kiss without having to actually use the words, but everything he doesn't want to do breathes between us like a living entity. Sorel hinted he'd been with a bunch of girls—maybe he was hurt, cheated on, or otherwise burned. I don't know, and he won't say.

Across the room, Charmindy sits at a table with Brett. They've been hanging out often, despite Terran's warning. I should ask her what they do together, but I'm afraid to mention the card and Grant's singular interest in kissing, because that might make me sound like a pushover. In Manhattan, I could come up with a riot of things to do, but living in this frozen tundra with umpteen rules about where we can be together and when leaves my mind as blank as the canvas of snow on the broad lawn in front of Viv Brooks.

⁓ ⊙ ⁓

When little red hearts and doily decor crop up around campus, I wonder who'd be willing to have an anti–Valentine's Day party with me. We could smash a heart-shaped piñata filled with chocolate, create our own badass messages for candy hearts, and make sure everyone knows Cupid can suck it.

I haven't seen much of Grant. The chilly winter days, the freezing nights, or his ambiguity have made the card and the kissing both confusing and, now, irritating.

As I imagine the broken-heart decorations we could make, I realize I don't really know anyone not in a couple. Charmindy and her friends, all with dates, prepare for the Valentine's dance at the student center. I fantasize about Grant asking me to go with him.

That evening, Charmindy fusses over what to wear, while I consider reading some Edgar Allan Poe. Although it would be nice, for once, to have a reason to get dressed up, for someone to wait for me at the foot of the stairs, to share in the laughter and romance of the night.

Never mind, the piñata would be much cooler.

I wander to the common room, where I find Sorel with a feed bag of popcorn, watching a rerun of *Buffy*.

"Where've you been, PJ? What's going on? You too cool for school?" she asks pointedly.

She knows where I've been. What she's really asking is why I haven't been hanging around with her and sneaking off to the woods for a smoke. Misery loves company or something like that. The cold and cigarettes are painful reminders that my lungs almost burst months ago, when my mother nearly killed me, along with a roomful of people.

There are the Charmindys and there are the Sorels of the world. Even though I somehow have a genetic predisposition for the Sorels, in other words, the misfits, the liars, and the thieves, part of me wants to join the ranks of the good girls, the respectable and successful girls. In other words, the girls who have dates on Valentine's Day.

"Not going to the dance, huh?" she teases.

I take a handful of her popcorn. "Nope. You?" I consider elaborating on my anti–V Day ideas.

Instead of answering, she laughs loudly along with a quippy comment made on the TV. When it goes to commercial, she says, "You don't want to see Pepper dance. But we're going to meet up later. Party tonight. You should come. I bet Grant would like to see you." She wears her usual mischievous grin cut with a snide upturn of her lip. "Or do you have to study?"

I should know better than to provide her with an excuse to strut around with this insider knowledge, but I ask, "What's up with him? Grant, I mean. What's his story?"

Her smile is ten degrees of sly. She can't subdue her satisfaction. "He hasn't told you?"

I understand this is her mother hen way of trying to undermine my connection to him. I reply with a penetrating, hypnotic, steady gaze. My eyes are dry, and they burn, but I don't let up until she caves.

"He's been with a bunch of girls. They were helpless when he showed up with the remnants of his sexy accent. He never got serious, though, except once. He was a player in indie-guy clothing. Taking names, kissing lips, breaking hearts. You've been warned."

If this is true, maybe I'll burn the card.

When I return to my room, Charmindy has left only a spritz of floral perfume in her wake. I take notes for a history presentation, but questions unrelated to the Cold War fill my head. *Why don't I have a Valentine's date? Why am I undesirable?* I'm not horrible looking. My mother wasn't in the Shrapnels because of her outstanding talent or her winning personality. She didn't regularly have boyfriends half her age by accident. Maybe that was drug related, but they spent nearly as much time fooling around as they did taking hits. Although she'd let herself go, she had been gorgeous.

I'm not hideous. When I look in the long mirror on the back of the door, by some miracle, relatively straight teeth appear beneath my smile. My eyes are bright, and underneath I'm mostly a good person. I don't see *pretty*, but I'm passable.

Then again, my mother always said my cheeks were too big and that I walked funny. I don't like how veiny my hands are. I refuse to pluck my eyebrows. My voice sounds scratchy, like I've perpetually just woken up, even worse now after the fire. I'm kind of smart, which, given my grammar school attendance record, is another phenomenon. Still, no boyfriend. Grant doesn't even want to be friends.

I just want that look from a boy, not the hungry "I want to sleep with you" look. The "I adore everything about you" look. The "I would move mountains for you" look. The one that whispers, *You are my everything*.

As I return to the index of the thick book to find information on women's roles during the Cold War, I catch myself singing "Tonight" from *West Side Story* under my breath. At each of three schools I went to before Laurel Hill, it happened to be the annual theatrical production. I know the songs by heart. I long to duet with someone from the rooftops. A someone who I'm not afraid is going to break my heart, who accepts me, big hands, cheeks, scratchy voice, and all.

About an hour later, Sorel bursts in my room. "Let's go," she says.

"Where?" I ask, not looking up from my homework, finally having found the inspiration for my essay.

"It'll be fun. I promise."

"Where?" I repeat.

"Off campus," she says with a raised eyebrow. She picks up my boots and coat and turns for the door. "Let's go!" she says without leaving me a choice.

Chapter 15

I hustle after Sorel, pulling my boots on as we tromp down the hall. When we get outside, I button up my coat against the wind that blows nearly invisible snowflakes toward the earth. I follow her to a side road that leads to a residential area off campus.

"As far as anyone is concerned, you and I just took a walk," she says warningly.

At the end of the road an Impala waits, its exhaust puffing white clouds in the cold air. Still addled by the smoke from the fire, I cough. Pepper and Grant sit in the back of the car. Seated in the passenger seat, a wispy girl with bright pink hair smiles when we get in.

"What the hell took you so long?" asks the driver, a bulldog of a girl with a shaved head.

"Slowpoke here," Sorel says, elbowing me.

"What's your name, slowpoke?" the driver asks.

"PJ."

"I'm Mags, and this is Chelsea."

Pepper and Sorel are wedged between Grant and me and immediately start making out.

"Get a room," Mags warns, eyeing them in the rearview mirror. They slowly pull apart. "Screw Valentine's Day," Mags says.

Screw it indeed. Though being in the car with Grant brings an interesting change to the night. *Tonight, tonight . . .*

Mags parks on the lawn in front of a mustard-colored ranch-style house. Silhouettes of a trailer, some old chairs, and other debris dot the yard. She leads us to a side door. Loud music plays audibly from inside.

A haze of smoke clings to the ceiling, and three guys with shaved heads, two punk girls, and one kid with stringy, long hair hang out in the kitchen. I trail Sorel to the living room, where there are more people my age, much like the first group, and one guy with sparse facial hair, who looks to be in his twenties.

"Hey, Sorel," the guy says.

"What's up, Mitch?" she asks, taking a seat on the edge of the love seat he sits on.

I notice he has a tattoo of a caged bird and another of a dagger as he raises his hand to shake mine.

"This is PJ," Sorel says.

He looks at me thirstily, but then someone hollers for him from the kitchen.

Pepper appears, carefully balancing three cups of beer in his hands, and lands in the vacant chair, pulling Sorel to his side. "It's Valentine's Day, baby, and you and I are in the love seat."

Sorel rolls her eyes. "You all right to slum it tonight?" she asks as she hands me a cup.

Her comment pinches me. The mustard-colored house is actually a step up from most of the places I've lived, at least in recent years, never mind the parties I often went to or tried to sleep through.

"Who's the one slumming it?" I ask, but she and Pepper are already practicing mouth-to-mouth.

I leave the two of them and wander into the kitchen. I pass Grant, our arms brushing, as he trots down the basement stairs, where I hear pool balls clacking.

Mitch leans on the door frame, with one arm raised above his head and a cigarette burning low between his fingers. "So, you from that fancy school too?" he asks.

I turn my head, realizing he's talking to me.

"What? Oh yeah," I say, nodding.

He rubs his thumb across his lower lip. The kitchen empties as the music from the living room grows louder. Mitch steps toward me, taking one last drag from his butt. "Sorel said she'd bring some friends, but I never thought she meant someone so foxy." He steps toward me again, and like a choreographed move, I take a step backward toward the counter.

Sensible thoughts, about how this is a situation I don't want to be in, catch themselves in a net in my mind.

His bleary eyes barely conceal his craving.

I fill my discomfort with a stupid question. "So, um, is this your place?"

"Yep. Want to see Spidey?" He puts his hand on my waist.

I wriggle to the side, away from him. There have to be twenty people in the house; why isn't anyone in the kitchen? People are always in the kitchen at parties.

"A spider? They kind of freak—" Before I can say anything else, his lips are too close to mine. I jerk away, with my hand over my mouth. He leaves me with the odor of burned rubber and stale cigarettes. My jaw moves to speak, but the words stick in the net in my mind.

Grant appears.

Mitch turns to a bottle of Jack Daniel's on the counter and unscrews the cap as if he just came in the kitchen for a drink.

I take a gulp of the beer, if only to wash the taste of him off my lips.

"PJ, want to play pool?" Grant asks.

Grateful for the excuse, I follow Grant to the basement, even though I want to head for the door.

"Lame party, huh?" he asks.

I want him to ask me to run away with him. Far from this stupid house and free from Sorel and her confusing possessiveness over Grant yet encouragement for me to hang out with him. Sometimes I think she wants me to like him so she can assert her power and try to break us apart. The riddle of the birthday card from Grant and his inconsistent behavior are far more favorable, at least they have their rewards.

With a crack of irritation at this whole mess, I break the neatly arranged balls on the green felt tabletop. The white one rolls to the floor. Grant and I both bend over to get it, knocking our heads together as we stand up.

"Sorry," he says. "Want me to show you—"

"Yeah," I say before he can finish.

"Are you a righty?" he asks. His voice is like a warm blanket and lazy mornings spent in bed.

"Uh-huh."

He takes my hands and places them accordingly on the cue. My pulse quickens. Our hair brushes together as we pull back the wooden stick in tandem. In one swift motion, the white ball barrels toward the number five. The places where our skin touches light me like a candle. He seems to hesitate as he releases the cue to me, our eyes meeting before I gaze down at the floor.

Between blundering and sinking the white ball in the pockets more than the striped ones, I sip my beer. My tongue loosens. We chat between turns. Grant eggs me on. Finally, he sinks the eight ball.

"Victory," he says, raising his cue overhead.

"I'm so not a worthy opponent," I say.

"Rematch? I'll go grab us each a refill. Be right back," he says.

I watch the Three Stooges on a silent black-and-white TV in the corner, waiting for him to return. The band the Stooges plays loudly from a room above. Hearing footsteps on the stairs, I turn, giddy to see Grant, but instead there's a tattooed arm, with a caged bird, on the railing.

"What are you doing down here all by yourself?" Mitch asks. His eyes have gone swirly from the whiskey. He grabs a pool cue and strokes it as he approaches.

I back away.

"Can we try again?" He presses his hips against mine.

A cold sweat washes from the top of my head down. "Listen, Mitch, I'm—"

"She's with me. And it's time for us to go. Come on, PJ," Grant says from the foot of the stairs. He's granite, craggy, a geology-made man.

"Sorry, I didn't know," Mitch slurs apologetically, holding his arms up feebly like a cactus.

I rush up the stairs. Grant ducks into the living room and whispers in Pepper's ear. Then he ushers me out the door we came in.

Chapter 16

It's snowing more steadily; the flakes, each containing a million possibilities, land on the ground, piling in layers. I take a deep breath. "Thanks," I say to Grant.

"Sleazy fu—" The rest of the word disappears in a grunt as he picks up a handful of snow and throws it, hard, against the house as we walk away.

"He—" I stutter. For some reason I want to apologize on Mitch's behalf, just as I always had when my mother did something wrong when she was under the influence. *Denial.* "He was just drunk."

"Drunk enough to try to take advantage of you. No effin' way."

I pause in the middle of the road.

Realizing I'm no longer beside him, Grant turns around and takes a couple of long strides back to me. Snowflakes melt on my cheeks as tears trail their way along my jaw.

Grant's eyes and lips crimp intensely. With his thumbs, he wipes the space below my eyes. "You are beautiful; of course he wanted to get in your pants. Half the guys on campus do. But you're—" He holds my face, my gaze, not letting me look away. "You're worth more than that.

You have this rare, raw beauty, and I don't want anyone's hands on you but m—" He looks down, shakes his head, and starts walking again.

I stand under the streetlight, the snow whirling in the wind like little frozen stars drifting to the ground.

His hands on me, his gaze, the tension freezing between us, makes me daring. I follow Grant's footprints as they track away from me. I spin around in front of him, blocking his path. My eyes say what my voice cannot: *Please finish what you were saying.*

He looks at me more softly this time. "I mean it, PJ," he says. The force behind his anger is gone.

I look into his dark blue eyes. I unbutton his wool coat, slide my hands into the warmth surrounding him, and rest my cheek against his chest. He holds me until drifts of snow cover our boots.

As we walk, our conversation gradually thaws out, starting with how annoying Pepper and Sorel are, with their bickering and kissing. Then we talk about Grant's brother, who is moving to New York City for a new job, and what we're each thinking of studying in college. Six months ago, college wasn't even on my radar. It's a strange future for me to consider, but Justine, my advisor, assures me not only is it possible, with financial aid and scholarships, but I owe it to academia. I gratefully tucked the compliment in my back pocket to take out the next time I bomb a test.

"What I want to study isn't what my father wants me to do, so there's that. A story as old as the father-son relationship. *Don't do that. Do this.* I keep exploring a new thing, hoping it will interest me and satisfy him, but inevitably, I just don't care enough to commit my life to it. I've gone through anthropology, biology, chemistry, economics, international affairs . . ."

"It sounds like you're working your way through the entire academic catalog. You're on the letter *I*, so what's next?"

"Independent study . . ."

"That one comes before international affairs, if it's alphabetical. And anyway, you have another year," I say encouragingly.

"Not according to my father. I had until, oh, about last year to make *my* choice," Grant says.

"Is he pressuring you?"

"If by *pressuring* you mean threatening, yes. He doesn't get me. He wants me to cut my hair, join the student senate or the football team. We don't even have football in Scotland. Soccer, yeah, and I'm happy with that. Soccer is about as natural to me as walking, but he associates it with hooligans fighting after matches, disorder, drunkenness . . . The only thing he approves of is the fact that I lost my accent," Grant says in a very strong Scottish accent, surprising me. It's sexy, with little crags in all the right places.

"He only found that out when he overheard me talking on the phone with Pepper over the break, but it's not really gone, it's just easier to blend in without it, I suppose," Grant says. "It's like he thinks that by getting rid of anything remotely Scottish, and trying to make me as straitlaced, American pie, and Stars and Stripes as possible, I'll get ahead in life. But I can't deny who I am."

"No, none of us can. The truth always comes out. So, what do you really want to do?"

Grant thinks about this for a minute as giant flakes whip up around us in a gust. I glance back, and our tracks are already almost completely covered.

"Aside from playing pro soccer, I think I'd like to study English or journalism . . . My father wants me to be a lawyer or doctor or something prestigious. He rants, 'I haven't spent a fortune on your education in the United States just so you can kick a ball and write poetry all day.' No, he sent me here so he wouldn't have to deal with me and the fact that I remind him of my mother. It's like he hopes that one day I'll just appear all grown-up, in a cookie-cutter business suit, with a yacht and a BMW, married with a couple of kids, and a few million in the bank. Mission accomplished."

"So what about your mom? What does she think?"

"My mom? She's gone," he says sharply and then clears his throat. "She left about five years ago. Said she needed to get her head together. Apparently that doesn't involve me."

I slip my hand in Grant's; neither one of us has gloves. I want us to curl up together inside a giant mitten until the storm of high school passes. "I'm sorry." And I am. Even though my mother has been around, the sleepwalking trance she exists in is often as good as gone. I swallow what feels like a golf ball in my throat. I haven't spoken to her since the summer. Her words of not being able to live without me echo hauntingly.

We walk for about a half hour, along unfamiliar back roads, snowy arteries leading us back to campus, before I think I recognize where we are. I shiver.

"Cold?" he asks. The snow continues to fall, making the world disorienting and beautiful. "We're almost there."

By the time the campus lights come into view, Grant and I are laughing about ten kinds of delight and nonsense. Vampires versus werewolves, whether toilets flush in the opposite direction in the Southern Hemisphere, tattoos, if we bite or lick lollipops, and the paper-or-plastic conundrum.

Despite the cold, the awkward ice between us cracks. He and I playfully romp in the snow and toss it at each other with shaking fingers. We both crumple to the ground at the top of the hill leading down to the classroom buildings. My leg rests on top of his, and he drops his head back in the pillowy snow. I rest against his chest, so we're face-to-face. I dreamed about this on the lanai in Florida, though it was far warmer.

"You do realize that we've been talking. And doing things friends do. I thought—"

A sad smile spills from his eyes to his lips.

"Are you OK?" I ask.

Grant sniffs and starts to get up.

"Yeah." He pauses and snaps to his feet. "Wait here." He disappears behind one of the maintenance-work sheds I didn't notice. I don't have time to consider what just happened, because he returns seconds later with a floppy-looking piece of cardboard coated in duct tape.

"Where did you—what is that?"

"Sometimes I sneak out of my dorm too," he says, winking. "Hop on."

Grant wraps his arms around me and secures me between his long legs. I grip the sides of the makeshift sled as we careen down the hill, snow flying in our faces, both of us whooping loudly. At the bottom of the hill, we lie in a heap on the fresh snow, once again, both out of breath and laughing wildly.

"That rocked," I say.

"Want to go again?"

We take a couple more rides, and our hands are red and sore before we realize dorm closing quickly approaches. Grant walks me to the porch of Viv Brooks, and we stand there expectantly.

"If this had been my old life, which it wouldn't be, but if it was, I'd invite you in. My mom wouldn't care, but then who knew what crazy thing she'd do or who she'd be with so, no, it probably wouldn't happen. She wasn't the parent that would make sure there was a solid foot of space between a boy and me on the couch—if there was a couch—while we watched *Brady Bunch* reruns."

"That's something you'd tell a friend," he says.

"Is that what we are?" I ask.

Grant looks at me shyly, yet intently; his eyes are soft with remnants of the sadness from before. His long hair peeks out from beneath his dark blue hat. I start up the stairs, but then step down and timidly kiss him on the cheek, my lips reluctant to leave his skin, like this is a do-over on our terms, the beginning of us, of everything.

"I had fun tonight," I say, our eyes meeting again.

"Me too," he answers, and all traces of melancholy are gone. He starts to walk away, then calls, "I still don't want to talk or be friends." But his laugh tells me that's not true.

Then we rush to each other, our lips colliding, and kiss under the falling snow until dorm closing.

Chapter 17

Inside the warm dorm, I stomp the snow off my boots and keep my eyes out for Sorel. I go down the hall and find Connie talking in a hushed tone with Terran, by the check-in desk. The latter flashes me a dirty look. Typical.

"I see," Connie says, eyeing me, chilled and wet in the entryway.

Terran crosses her arms in front of her chest, and her mouth pinches smugly.

"PJ, I'd like to have a word with you," Connie says in an even tone.

"Sure," I say. The lingering thrill of the last hours with Grant does the job of helping me ignore Terran's warning look.

With a quick appraisal of my soaked outerwear, she says, "Terran claims one of her necklaces went missing last week. It had a star on it, filled with diamonds. She put up a sign on the bulletin board, but it hasn't turned up. Any idea where it might be?"

"Oh yeah, I saw the sign. Sorry, Terran, I haven't seen it," I say helpfully, craning toward Terran over Connie's shoulder.

"We're going to have to do a mandatory dorm room search if it isn't returned by tomorrow morning," Connie says pointedly. "She thinks someone took it."

Then it becomes clear. My breath catches. Terran probably hid it in my room to get me in trouble. She promised revenge. I can practically hear her unraveling a web of lies to get back at me for interfering with Charmindy and Brett or for being poor and vulnerable to someone with a scrap of power.

I square my shoulders and lift my chin, determined that she will not get the better of me. "Is that all?" I look into Connie's eyes. I have nothing to hide.

I turn and walk down the hall until I'm out of sight, then tear up the stairs. The bubbles from the night with Grant burst and pop. I proceed to rip apart my room, looking for a necklace, which, apparently, is silver with a star pendant.

Charmindy comes in minutes later, glowing from head to toe. She starts to exclaim about what a wonderful night she had, but she interrupts herself at the sight of me, frenzied and flushed. "What are you doing?"

I flip my mattress. I pull out drawers. I riffle through clothes. I'm not sure how to explain. "Looking for that necklace Terran said she lost," I say from under my bed, running my hand over the dark floor.

"Oh, that? She probably lost it."

I've looked everywhere, when someone knocks on the door. It's nearly lights-out. Charmindy answers, and there stands Connie.

"Listen," Connie says to me, "I want to give you an opportunity to give me the necklace now so there isn't a big scene. Terran said you took it."

Once more I meet her eyes. "I didn't take it."

Connie surveys the disaster resulting from my search. "Why is it such a mess in here? Clean-room review is this Sunday. I hope you get this tidied up, PJ. Charmindy, is she usually like this?"

"No." Charmindy looks at me, confusion flashing across her brow, but quickly puts the pieces together. "Her side of the room is usually very neat. Connie, PJ wouldn't do something like that. Take something that isn't hers, I mean."

"I sure hope not. We do not tolerate that kind of behavior at Laurel Hill. If it doesn't turn up, we *will* have to look for it." She leaves, closing the door firmly behind her.

"Thanks," I say to Charmindy before quietly pulling off my boots, pants, and sweatshirt and falling into bed. I'm not particularly tired, but want to forget the last twenty minutes and bring myself back to the moments shared with Grant. I can't stay focused as I try to replicate his smile and the sound of his laugh or read between the lines of what he'd tried to say. Memories of thefts intrude, smashing like icy snowballs, with the one of my mom and me rushing out of a store with a cartload of stuff smacking me right in the face.

On Monday morning, I sleepily shuffle downstairs. I'm dully aware Terran closes in on me like prey as I enter the common room for a dorm meeting. Her eyes sweep me as if the suspected missing necklace is around my neck and she's ready to choke me with it.

As part of her usual greeting, Connie opens up the floor for messages and announcements. After a reminder that the ski-trip fees are due and a thank-you to everyone who helped with the Valentine's dance, Terran raises her hand. She promptly takes the floor.

"As all of you are well aware, a necklace that was very special to me has gone missing. It had a star with diamonds in the center. I think I know who took it, and I suggest she give it back." She looks directly at me, and several other eyes land on my face. I fight against turning red, because obviously I didn't take it. "Connie said a dorm search will be conducted if it isn't returned."

My color deepens, but my lips refuse to stay shut. "Are you sure you didn't misplace it?" I ask, instantly regretting throwing myself into the ring as she glares at me.

Her eyes narrow. "Yes, PJ, I'm certain."

"I can't imagine anyone in this dorm taking anything," I say pointedly.

"I can. Some people admire fine jewelry, especially when they don't have any of their own."

Feeling pushed too far, I say, "If you're accusing me of taking something, come out and say it." Denser, sharper words want to pour out of my mouth, but I hold back.

Her expression suggests that she didn't count on me standing up for myself. I hadn't either.

"Girls," Connie says delicately, "that's enough. If she says she didn't take it, we have to give her the benefit of the doubt. Sorry about the mistake, PJ."

Terran's gaze locks on mine. "Did you fill your roommate in? Huh? Do the other girls in the dorm know?" She looks out at the faces of the girls, some shocked, others intrigued.

Before I take refuge in staring at my hands, I suffer beneath Charmindy's questioning expression. Of course she doesn't know.

"No, you didn't, because it's humiliating. It's humiliating to be the offspring of a scandalous drug addict, famous for failure, a washed-up has-been wannabe. That's who Pearl's mother is—Janet Jaeger. Not even worth the couple of one-hit-wonder songs she made." She meets the eyes of the girls gathered around her and lands on me, leveling me with her glare.

A hush falls over everyone in the room. I feel as though arrows, one for every set of eyes, have struck me. In the gush of my dissolving composure, I doubt anyone remembers JJ, except for the news article after the fire. It certainly made the rounds.

Terran smiles wickedly. "Oh, and if the name Janet Jaeger sounds familiar to some of you, that's because the infamous JJ made headlines recently. The newspapers and tabloids read, 'Former wealthy rock star nearly kills a hundred homeless, including her own daughter, while using drugs in a shelter, *where they lived.*' Not favorable press, if you ask me."

"Nobody asked you," I mutter. Catching Charmindy's disappointed expression, I awkwardly make my way through the gathered crowd seated cross-legged on the floor and the furniture.

When I reach the door, Connie claps her hands together, breaking the hold of mortification. I expect her to come to my aid, give me the benefit of the doubt, as she said about the necklace. Instead, she moves on. "Girls, we need to discuss the problem with the toilet on the first floor."

As the voices fade behind me, my disappointment rests with me, more than with Connie's silence, for not standing up to Terran myself.

I try to forget about the necklace incident and Terran maligning me in front of my entire dorm. But since she wasn't wrong on one of two accounts, I wonder if, like fire, word will soon spread across campus.

Sure enough, the girls in Viv Brooks give me a wide berth in the hall, and their whispers catch in their throats when I enter the common room. For the first couple of days, Charmindy says fewer words than Shale; mostly he just grunts disapprovingly over my shoulder. But that's typical for him. The image I'm begging to appear in my mind to transfer to canvas for my self-portrait gets dimmer and more distant as Terran's ugly words repeat in my memory.

Toward the end of the week, Sorel catches up with me after spending more days than necessary in the health center with the flu. I happen to know she was avoiding an essay for American Lit.

"I'm not sure if I should start with what went down in the common room or at the party. Don't listen to what Terran the Terror says about your mom. Whatever, right? JJ seems awesome. I mean, your mom's a rock star. Badass. So tell me what happened last weekend with Grant," she asks with a nasally voice.

I'm stuck on how my mother being a rock star is less badass and more bad. I want to tell Sorel how my mom's just forgotten about me, how she hasn't responded to my letters or called. How she missed Christmas and about all the times she wasn't there or, if she was, she hardly knew her name or what day it was.

We walk in the woods, along a dirty path worn through the white snow. When we arrive at the clearing, Grant, Pepper, and a reedy guy named Mark have already lit up. I've only seen him a few times; he's not a usual visitor to the smoking section bordering Laurel Hill.

"What, you can't wait for the ladies?" Sorel asks accusingly.

Pepper gives her a big kiss, reminding me of a slobbering dog. Walking away from them, I approach Grant, my feet cold and my thin jacket not warm enough. I let out a pathetic cough, my insides still charred from the fire. Mark stands at attention. His sharp eyes remind me too much of Terran's, like he's on the prowl. I want him to blow away.

Grant's smile makes his eyes twinkle. He holds the cigarette pack out.

"Hi, guys," I say uneasily.

Mark eagerly leans closer, as if the bait is set and he's ready to slap cuffs on my wrist and ring the sirens. Nausea sinks my stomach. My head feels heavy. Maybe Sorel's flu already circulated around the dorm, and I've caught it. Or maybe it's instinct warning me away. "Nah, I'm good," I say, declining the cigarette offer.

Grant tilts his head toward me. I want to take him by the hand and lead him far from here, hemming ourselves back into Friday night, but my fingers shake, and I'm not very good at sewing; sketching is more my talent.

"Then why'd you come here?" Mark asks as he exhales smoke with a cough. I smell hostility and Terran's citrus perfume.

I don't trust my tongue to answer. I will my face blank. "I don't know. I just walked Sorel here. I'm leaving," I say dumbly. If he's here to get me in trouble, I'm not giving him a reason. I turn to go, slipping on invisible patches of ice in the clearing. When I make it to the path, Grant catches up to me.

"You just got here. Are you all right?"

"I think maybe I'm getting that flu going around." I don't feel well—that's not a lie—but it has less to do with my immune system and more to do with my intuition.

"Where are you going?" he asks.

"I don't know where I'm going," I say. Inexplicably, tears pierce the edges of my eyes. I dodge the reminder of Shale's assignment, the snowy lawn like the blank canvas I've been staring at for weeks.

He leans closer. "Let's go there together," he says as soft as a snowflake. Then softer still, "I want to be with you, wherever you go." The ocean ripples in his eyes, and I'm the tide, ebbing to a distant shore.

"I thought you didn't want to be friends," I say.

He looks afraid and then like he is casting about for courage. "I don't know what I want except you."

I crunch my way along the path toward the campus, weak all over. I want nothing more than to lie down in the snow, will the sun to come out, and melt along with it, if only to make the sharp and forbidding feeling in my chest disappear.

Grant grabs the arm of my coat, halting me. He smiles at me hopefully, gently, his eyes still twinkling. "If we're not going to be friends and if we're not going to talk, then let's—" Echoing the card, he leans in.

I sniffle, pulling away. "You don't want me," I say, shaking my head and continuing up the path to my dorm. "You heard about my mom, the Shrapnels . . ." My voice is as thin and brittle as a twig.

"Yeah. I know of them," he says with a shrug like it's not as big a deal as Terran had hoped. Where there's usually judgment, I don't sense him measuring who I am in relation to her fame or her fall, if I have rock star credibility or connections, or whether I have a sizeable trust fund.

Instead, his eyes dissolve into the same pools of sadness I saw the night we went sledding. He rushes to me, about to speak, but I talk first.

"Confusion doesn't come close to the number of feelings ricocheting inside me. Raw, blazing, aching. I want to be with you, but you made it clear, you don't want to do anything more than kiss," I say as if denying myself everything good that's coming my way.

"I'm just afraid," he whispers.

"And I'm tainted, stained." I blurt out the details of how Terran exposed my mother, humiliating me in front of everyone, and how my roommate only answers me with nods and shakes of the head.

"Stains, they tell a story, they're a memory of moments gone by."

"Ugly, painful moments." This truth swarms and stings no matter if I stay still or swat at it. "There is too much in my past that haunts me, making me incapable of being normal, of liking or loving or being the person I should be."

His eyes fill as if he's looking at the stars for the first time and the beauty he finds there is bittersweet, because as suddenly as something stunning and whole appears, it's just as likely to vanish back into the darkness.

"I'm afraid if I get too close to you, it might burn. Painfully like the spark of a dying sun. And if you get too close to me, we'll disappear into a black hole. That's what I meant about not being friends and not talking and not—I want us to be close, but safe from each other," he says. "I'm afraid to care about someone because I'm afraid I'll lose them. But if we know that, we can make it work, right?"

I slowly shake my head. I want to wrap my arms around his chest, nestle into that warmth transporting me far away from fear and doubt. Instead, I silently walk away, letting his words drift and fall between us. I glance over my shoulder. Grant stands there, stalled, before he plods down the path toward his dorm, the sadness that mimics my own pulling on his limbs.

I reach for the doorknob to Viv Brooks, but it won't turn. Through the glass window, Terran and a few other girls standing at the end of the hallway, simpering grins stretched on their faces. Locked out. I stare back. I close my eyes to keep the tears away, and when I open them, the girls have vanished, and Connie peers at me through the glass before she pulls open the door.

Without tattling or offering an explanation, I dash to my room and cry for a solid twenty minutes. I didn't know words, even ones spoken with so much promise, could wound me. *I want to be with you.* He shouldn't want to know me. My body racks with unnamed pain, spreading through my veins, coursing through the circuits that run from my fingers to my toes and every cell in between. It wrecks me. My chest aches. Grant wants to be with me. I want to be with Grant. There shouldn't be a problem. For months, he's lingered somewhere in my thoughts, and yet nothing has ever hurt as much as pushing him away.

Chapter 18

I commit myself to studying as a worthy excuse to avoid Connie, Sorel, and Grant. Basically everyone—not an easy feat on a private school campus, and especially not when Terran and some of the other girls have it in for me.

Their list of abuses grows: I set my laundry bag outside my door for pickup and later find it in the trash; twice, my towel, hanging from the hook outside the shower, went missing. I had to use the shower curtain. When I sat down in my usual spot for a dorm meeting, I almost landed in a bowl of soggy ashes. Not to mention the sneers, whispers, and general looks of caution.

I hole up with Shale in the studio, poring over thick art books, illuminating the lives and methods of the greats, thumbing through tomes on color, line, shape, texture until my body hums with a glossary filled with terms, historic dates, and everything that doesn't lead me to bring the brush to canvas.

"You want to learn the rules so you can break the rules, yes?" Shale asks.

"That's what you taught us."

He shakes his head as if I've missed a crucial point. "Fine. But a true artist makes her own rules."

"And what are yours?" I counterpoint.

"Mine?" He makes a guttural sound that might be a laugh. "You want to know my rules? You think I am an artist? Yes?" He gruffly takes my arm and leads me to the office at the back of the room.

"You think a man like me makes art?" He shuffles through a rack of canvases, pulling out dozens and letting them fall to the floor. They're brilliant. Nimbus and cumulous clouds fold over each other in waves of grays and blues and purples; thunderheads dance and collide. He captured how the clouds move across the sky. He snorts. "Maybe I did once. Not today. Not yesterday. This is garbage."

"No, it's treasure," I whisper.

He shakes his head. "At its core being an artist isn't a method or something you can study from a book. Then you are just learning about art. Not how to be an artist. What an artist does comes from here." He pounds his chest. "It is a feeling. It is a fire igniting within until it burns its way out. It is passion. It is not an option but a need. It is your own personal truth. And mine, since you asked, I'm a work in progress. I'm still unlearning."

My eyes dampen, and I storm from the building.

The weekend brings a fully recovered Sorel to my dorm room. She reclines on my bed, kicking up her boots on top of my sage blanket. I hunch at my desk, trying to parse out an extra-credit assignment for math. I'm barely scraping by.

"You're so boring. Let's do something huge."

"Good to hear that you're breathing clearly once again . . . and ready to stir up trouble." Or as is usually the case, get very close to trouble but then snake out of its way.

She flicks pushpins from my corkboard across the room.

I get up and retrieve them from Charmindy's floor, bed, and bureau.

Sorel rolls her eyes. "Can you get an overnight note?" she asks.

"Where?"

"Not where. Why?" Her signature grin stretches broadly as she chucks a sock ball at the ceiling.

"What are you up to?" I ask, snapping the socks from her.

"I still owe you a birthday present," Sorel says enticingly.

"Don't be silly. You don't. Plus that was forever ago."

"Do you have a passport?"

I nod, recalling one of JJ's moments of delusional grandeur. She thought she'd tour Europe as a solo act, with me in tow. But that plan was quickly swallowed with a bottle of pills when her former record company said no. At least I got a passport out of it.

"Get a note," Sorel says matter-of-factly.

I haven't ever needed an overnight note, mostly because I've never had anywhere to go, but the request comes with a glitch. I don't have anyone to write one or, as it goes at Laurel Hill, anyone to email, fax, or otherwise electronically transmit one to my dorm head.

"That might be a problem," I say to Sorel.

"Make it not a problem," she says and slips into the hall.

Leaving school for a weekend and escaping the dorm-wide ridicule that quickly reached the rest of the campus plays at me all afternoon with an alluring melody. I'm entering the computer lab to print out an essay due for English when an idea comes to me. I quickly grab a seat and open up a browser on the desktop. I fill in the requested information to create an email account, entering Janet Jaeger in the name box. In the subject heading I write, *Weekend permission*, then hastily type.

Dear Connie,

My daughter will be visiting me this weekend at home in New York. She has permission to leave the campus and take the bus. She will return Sunday by dorm closing.

Thank you.
Sincerely,
Janet Jaeger

P.S. Please disregard the rumors circulating regarding our family. As you can imagine, someone in my position is easily slandered, but I know Pearl takes it to heart, so a little mom-daughter time is in order.

As if.

My mother would never sign her name *Janet* or say thank you, but then again, she probably doesn't even know how to use the Internet, no less how to write an email. She's broken, sold, or lost every electronic device she's ever owned. I look up faculty email addresses listed on a sheet on the wall. Genius.

When I hit "Send," there's a metallic ting in my chest, leaving me with an ache. After the hard time my mother gave me about going away to school, she still hasn't gotten in touch with me. Over six months have passed. I've become a footnote.

Excitement for the weekend replaces thoughts of abandonment when I intercept Sorel outside her chemistry class at the end of the day.

"Done," I say.

"No way? Really? I figured you'd flake out. Cool."

"So where are we going?" I ask.

"You, my friend, are going on an adventure of a lifetime. Pack"—she taps her finger on her burgundy-stained lips—"warm clothing and something you'd go out in. But fit it all in a backpack. 'K? And don't worry about bringing any cash. This weekend is on me. I really didn't think you'd do it. You've been so bookish and boring, like all the time," she says scornfully.

Her words are like a dare.

Later, as I pack, I wonder if she invited Grant. Our foursome consists of a variant of six degrees of separation, only minus two degrees or something. If there is Sorel, there is Pepper, and if there is Pepper, Grant is often nearby. The deficits in my character that bothered me last week dim. I envision trying again with him; maybe we could make it work. Maybe not being friends or talking or kissing will lead us to being more than friends and doing more than talking. Living on the same small campus, sharing a class and friends, has made it hard for us to completely ignore each other. The skittish and protective shell of my interior tells me I want to, but I can't quite deny that he's planted a seed inside my heart and it's struggling to grow and push its way out of the darkness.

I slip the money Erica gave me into my jeans pocket, just in case. I slide on my slouchy engineer boots and pull my black fuzzy coat over a restructured vintage tee with the printed words *I vote for vodka*, and a knit gray cardigan. I wrap a scarf around my neck and sling my backpack over my shoulder. I slink down to Sorel's room, hoping not to encounter Connie or Terran.

"We're totally breaking you out of here," she says, nodding at me approvingly. "Meet me at the bus station."

"The bus station?" I whisper.

"Don't worry, the walls aren't listening," she jokes.

"If you grew up with my mother's brand of paranoia, you'd think differently."

"You're so sketchy."

My brow wrinkles.

"We can't have anyone seeing us leaving together. Part of the fun is in the escape."

"Who's sketchy?" I ask rhetorically.

She actually sticks her tongue out at me.

"You have lipstick on your teeth," I say and walk out of the room.

Chapter 19

Various shades of winter drab tint the campus. I plod almost a mile through the slush to the bus station, or, more accurately, a dingy café at risk of floating away on grease. There's no waiting area, so I loiter in the entryway, already occupied by a smarmy-looking guy leaning against the wall. Feeling his eyes on me as his tongue wrestles with a toothpick, I move toward the window, watching for Sorel but unsure what to look for.

A full hour later, a Volvo wagon as old as me pulls up with Sorel behind the wheel. Pepper rides shotgun, and Grant is in the back. A smile spreads on my face. A breakout indeed.

"This is my fabulous, early graduation present. My dad offered to buy me a new one—" Sorel says, tapping her hand against the steering wheel.

"He did buy you a new one, a BMW, in fact," Pepper interrupts.

Sorel glares at him.

"I would have gone with it, just saying."

"Well, anyway, I will be driving this baby cross-country when I start school next fall, and I figured we'd take it out for a maiden voyage," Sorel says proudly.

"I thought we weren't allowed to have cars on campus," I say, dismissing her temporary stamp of approval on my cool scorecard by forging a note and instead stating the obvious.

"We're not. I arranged for it to be parked at Mitch's so I could use it whenever I want," she says, self-satisfied.

"Seriously, I would have opted for the BMW," Pepper says.

"No one asked you," Sorel snipes.

I glean she doesn't want to be associated with her family's wealth, and not because of humility. The image Sorel wants to portray by dressing secondhand, slumming it, and driving a car that doesn't shout "I'm rich" is all part of unglossing herself from the gold and silver stored in the family vault. She gravitates toward the punk style that the kids favor on Saint Mark's Place, back in the city, and doesn't want to be mistaken for having a trust fund. When you don't have two dimes to rub together, secondhand is the only brand, and slumming it is your reality, being a rich kid seems appealing.

"For the record, I would have gone with the BMW too, but really any car with wheels and an engine would do, if I knew how to drive," I say.

Grant doesn't suppress his smile.

A song about a girl brushing her hair in a burning room fills the space where Sorel would ordinarily toss out a snarky retort. I flash to last summer, my heart hiccups, and then I remind myself where I am and where we're going.

Sorel navigates onto the highway, heading north, and cranks up the stereo. The speakers make the doors tremble. I settle into the backseat, the music too loud for conversation, but steal a glance at Grant. He's intent on the scenery passing by. His dark blond hair has grown since the beginning of the year. I want to run my fingers through it, letting them catch on the strands like sticky webs. I want to feel his cheek against mine, our lips pressing together, and let the infinite swallow us whole. At least there my past wouldn't matter.

The song changes, leaving me with a moment of silence to snap my head back into its proper orbit. I wonder if Grant knew I'd be joining them when he signed up for Sorel's mystery weekend. I wonder if he still wants to be with me. I don't hate myself as much today.

About an hour into the trip, Sorel stops for gas. Mercifully, the car quiets when she turns off the ignition. Pepper fills the tank, and she goes into the convenience store. The space between Grant and me pulses with words unsaid.

If I were the type to pick a daisy, I imagine it would land on the he-loves-me-not petal, just to spite me. Then again, I don't put much stock in games like that. But no one has ever given me flowers, so maybe the gesture would change my opinion. I gaze out the window, trying to erase the maelstrom of feelings for him. Lust and loss tug and tear at me.

As if sensing my inner battle, fingers reach across the leather seat between us, and he grasps my hand.

"OK?" he asks.

I nod, letting our fingers mend that ugly afternoon when I pushed him away.

I swallow hard. I worry my skin might singe him, like he might suddenly flinch and retract his fingers. Then I recall the kiss I gave him on the porch of Viv Brooks, how sweet it felt, like I'd regained some of my innocence. The frightened beast within tells me to withhold, to shrink away from Grant. Liking or loving or being sweet costs too much.

Yes. No. Yes.

Splat. Confusion.

It tells me that it might be easier if it just isn't.

But he doesn't let go. The warmth in his fingers melts the icicles jabbing the place in the middle of my chest. The stabbing pangs release. He grips my hand harder, unwilling to let me let go. I chance a look at his eyes, rippling blue like peace, like promises.

Thinking about him when we're not together feels safe, like a fantasy. There's nothing precious on the line. No chance I'll face humiliation or hurt him. As I let in the immensity of what could be, of crossing out his request not to be friends, not to talk, but to kiss, and then inviting his request to be more, the clawed thing inside works very hard to shut the idea out. I squeeze my eyes closed, trying to see where it went, what it's up to. But within, there is just shadows and darkness. All I hear are the whispers that I don't deserve anyone.

Grant's hair shags around his face, his expression distant, caught up in his own thoughts. But his hand still clings to mine as miles pass. I try to like him less, because the truth is he causes the pain in the center of my chest that burns like frigid poison, and yet he possesses the elixir too.

"It's complicated," his words echo. Yes, it is.

Up front, Sorel digs into a bag filled with chips, soda, and an assortment of baked goods that would hold their shape under nuclear attack. There's a lot of crunching and glugging going on. Pepper tosses a bag of Doritos back to us. The crinkly bag lands on the seat between Grant and me and remains there, untouched. I don't know about him, but I'm not letting go of his hand, not even for food. He doesn't either.

We venture farther north as snowy pines whip past the speeding car.

Sorel quizzes me through a mouthful of crumbs. "Figure out where we're going yet?"

"It isn't so much where we're going, but what we are doing that has me guessing," I say.

Grant chuckles.

"*Eenh,*" Sorel says loudly like a game show buzzer. "Try again."

"I dunno, Canada."

She laughs and bumps up the music once more. The sun sinks behind the evergreen trees that line the interstate as the afternoon relaxes into evening.

Sure enough, we pull up next to a large cement building marking the US–Canada border. After a friendly guard welcomes us in French and English, we show our IDs, he asks a few questions, and then Sorel whisks the Volvo through to Canada.

"Holy shit, we're in Canada," Pepper says.

*"Bien-ven-*frickin'*-ue!"* Sorel screams.

I take a deep breath and let a large smile cross my face, feeling an incredible sense of lightness, like velvet snow. Boldly, I chance a look at Grant. He returns my smile, and it reaches right up to the corners of his eyes.

Chapter 20

"Let's never go back!" Pepper shouts. He laughs. "Good-bye, USA. Ha! Those suckers back at Laurel Hill have no frickin' idea!"

"Don't get carried away there, farm boy," Sorel says, as usual trying to control Pepper with her verbal dimmer switch. "But let's have a frickin' riot while we're here," she yells as she pumps up the volume on the stereo and tears away from the border.

About an hour later, the turbid waters of the Saint Lawrence welcome us to Montreal. Pepper guides Sorel to a parking garage next to a towering hotel.

"Welcome home, boys and girls," Sorel says as we enter the swanky lobby.

A mahogany-paneled drop ceiling runs the length of the space, with clear orbs hanging like giant soap bubbles. A red carpet cushions the area between several long gray couches with matching red pillows, where the guys and I wait. With practiced skill, Sorel approaches the reception desk. I watch her carefully, seeing the quizzical look on my face reflected in the mirrored columns.

Pepper smirks. "She's loaded, PJ. Her dad's like a millionaire, and she has him wrapped around her finger. I guess she caught him cheating on her mom, and now she gets whatever she wants, just to keep her quiet. She wasn't like this a year ago. Nope, she played her ace card. Seems to be working out pretty well too," he finishes as Sorel returns.

We ride to the fifth floor and then follow Sorel down a long hallway to the end. She hands me a key card for the room opposite as she opens door 528.

"Have fun, kids." She winks and disappears inside.

A mixture of panic and appeal courses through me. If I look at Grant, I'll be acknowledging what the single key means, but being far from Laurel Hill helps cast aside the boundaries I constructed to hold my place there. Off campus, I slip easily back into my reckless and feckless self.

I lean forward to slide the key card into the door, leaving an impossibly small amount of space between Grant and me. Another inch and I could crash into him.

In the center of the spacious room, a king-size bed rests expectantly alongside a large window. The modern decor of blue and gray hues contrasts with the white linens. Grant downs a complimentary bottle of water, while I let my gaze skip over the peaks of the buildings dotting the skyline. The northern city light reflects off the mirrored windows that cascade toward the river. The snow glows on a postage stamp–shaped park far below.

Grant clears his throat, breaking the silence that keeps us both safe from the possibility that anything more between us isn't a good idea. I'm like a tempest that will destroy us both. I want to explain how dangerous liking me could be, all the while reminding myself that the inverse is probably also true. Hearts are fragile.

"I'm sorry I—"

"You don't have to apologize. Sometimes things get complicated," he says.

It's true.

I want to cry, but I'm not sure how that will show him that I'm the rogue to all his sweetness and excellence. I want to rip open my chest and show him everything ugly and beautiful that lives there. All the hurt. All the loneliness. All my desires and dreams. I lack one thing, and that is courage.

"Grant, I exist in the wreckage of my mother's life, and I don't want to involve you in that. It's too messy. Sometimes I just get so sad. Other times I feel almost blissful, but mostly I just tell myself it's easier not to feel."

Grant steps closer. The polite boyishness of Laurel Hill doesn't seem to have followed him into Canada. He seems sure of himself, not at all shy. The set of his jaw and the confidence on his lips tell me we both mold to life on campus.

"But I think you do feel. A lot. More than you'd admit."

Tears continue to threaten.

He lifts a hand as if he wants to stroke my arm and comfort me. Instead, he speaks. "As far as I understand it, that's life. What would happen if you did let yourself feel?"

I want to warn him that he doesn't understand. Flimsy bandages hide the open wounds underneath. My voice creaks like cracks forming in a frozen pond.

"There's a tether that connects me all the way back to Manhattan or Chicago or wherever my mother is. I can't run or fly from it, hide from it, or pretend it isn't there. I don't know what to do with all the shit that gets in the way of me getting close enough to someone to shatter the pain and wipe it away—" Making me incapable of painting an image of myself on a stupid canvas in a stupid art studio. Making me unlovable.

Grant joins me at the window, enveloping me in his arms. He presses into my back as if promising that there's glue strong enough to hold us together.

Yet, I'm confused. I worry that if I push him away, I might fall apart.

"I'm afraid too," he says and holds me until I stop trembling and the threat of tears disappears and, at least temporarily, so does my fear.

"What do you suppose Pepper and Sorel are up to?" I ask foolishly, knowing very well what they're doing. I look at the king-size bed in our room, and a quiet question forms in my mind, likely in Grant's too. I wander into the bathroom, trying out the moisturizer and silently admiring the posh amenities.

Grant leans in the doorway. His eyes sparkle.

"One time I was in a hotel like this after my mom had met this guy, Taylor. He was in an opening band, huge tour—I forget the name, the Veins, or something—at Madison Square Garden. They never quite made it all the way. Anyway, somehow my mom hooked up with him." I roll my eyes. "We were freshly kicked out of our apartment, so she brought me to this luxury hotel overlooking Central Park, where he was staying. We were perched high above the city, and I gazed out the window for hours, like a princess surveying her kingdom. Then I discovered a cable TV lay hidden in a cabinet. I quickly caught up on all the pop culture I'd missed after the cable was shut off at our old place."

I flop onto the bed, tumbling back in time. "We stayed there for like four nights, but then the guy moved on. Never saw him again, but we did make off with some plush towels." I laugh at the memory. "I guess my mother thought the view, the TV, and the full mini fridge were a good enough babysitter for an eight-year-old."

Grant looks at me with such a deep sadness I feel like I need to comfort him. He softly says, "Like I said, that's life. Sometimes it gets complicated."

"No, Grant, that's not what I call life."

"We can talk," he says. "The card, what I said about not being friends, not talking . . ."

"Trying to figure me out would make you crazy. I know, because I've already tried."

He's undaunted. "Want to take a walk?" he asks instead.

"I'll do anything to get away from that memory, every memory I have except one." I think of us that night in the snow, playing, kissing, and liberating ourselves.

On our way out, we stop by room 528. Sorel answers, looking perturbed and wearing the same white bathrobe I found hanging on the back of the door in our room.

"We're taking a walk," Grant says.

She rolls her eyes. "I got you a king-size bed and you're leaving?" She looks at me with pity. "Meet us on the corner of Saint Laurent at eleven."

"That robe, it's a good look on you," I say, mocking her typical punk style, before turning and marching down the hall.

Once in the fresh air, on the broad streets of Montreal, I feel freer still. The city awakens me. I could soar into the sky, erupting from the pressure of the rural confines of Laurel Hill and my past like a long-dormant volcano.

"Are you hungry?" Grant asks.

"I'm alive." I laugh, practically skipping.

Grant lights up a cigarette and holds it in one hand and catches my hand in the other as we walk in the urban darkness, neon signs beckoning us, menus waving in our direction, and strangers pressing invitations to clubs and parties, on little cards, into our hands. The world rushes by as Grant and I sweep along the sidewalk, hand in hand. Maybe he and I could work if we moved as far away as possible from the past. I glide as if I have little wings on my feet, buoyed by hope instead of bound by my own personal history.

In the middle of the busy sidewalk, Grant stops abruptly, midstride, and turns to face me. I wait, expecting him to say he forgot something or that we should try the Moroccan restaurant opposite where we stand.

The spices and garlic make my mouth water. Instead, he takes my head in his hands and kisses me, a melting, magic-filled kiss that blurs the lights around me, thrusting me deep into myself, with nowhere to land but my heart. Slowly, like forever taking its time, we return to our place on the sidewalk. "You're all I think about," Grant whispers.

People wearing their heavy winter coats brush by us, a crowd claps for a street performer on the corner, and the two of us, connected by a long-desired kiss, look for something as simple as food. *Yes, Sorel, we're going to take a walk.*

Grant and I eat at a cozy Indian place with whitewashed walls and colorful tapestries, sequined pillows, and candlelight. We may as well be on the subcontinent; I feel so far from the whispers of the past, the gaunt and haunting tremors in my mother's face, and the pervasive deficiency that constantly wells inside me. Our conversation is easy, spanning colorful vinyl records to penguins in New Zealand to the luxury of going barefoot.

At ten thirty, we wander toward Saint Laurent, not in any rush to join our rowdy benefactor and her pushover boyfriend. I'd prefer to roam the streets all night with Grant as my companion rather than go to a loud club or party.

Sure enough, Sorel brings us to an underground punk show and pulls me to the front of the crowd. After an hour of head-pounding music and shouting, I seek out Grant. His eyes swim with amusement.

"What's so funny?" I ask.

"People."

I cock my head. There doesn't seem to be much funny about an array of rainbow-colored heads in tattered and pinned-together clothing, bobbing their heads to the discordant music.

He whisper-yells in my ear, "This isn't my scene. Let's go." Again, he seizes control, as if he left the boy burdened by pleasing his father behind, at Laurel Hill. This version of Grant knows exactly what he wants. A tiny light, like a match, glows with the feeling that he still wants me. But there's a difference between him telling me and me accepting and believing it.

I pick Sorel and Pepper out of the crowd. They're red faced, and their postures reflect a recent argument.

"See you in the morning," I say, instead of telling her we're leaving.

I don't have anything to prove to Sorel, but the well-behaved PJ, the girl Sorel knows, is the by-product of Laurel Hill. It was the rule-abiding cleverness of necessity. And like the shy version of Grant, she was left behind and really only created to maintain my place there. The side of me that would run through the city streets until the sun came up, floating everywhere and nowhere with my friends, is reborn, rediscovered, away from books and guidelines. This life, the smoky bars, drinking, rebellion, isn't quite Sorel's size, but, for better or worse, it fits me perfectly.

"Have fun, City Girl," she calls after me.

The cold night air urges a sharpening of my senses, but the rush of freedom slurs and blurs my surroundings.

When Grant and I return to the hotel, the unexpressed suggestion of intimacy causes fear and loathing to grasp at me with starving fingers. I don't want to believe he could really want *me*, maybe just my body. Desire wakes inside him as surely as it has in every other boy that's looked at me hungrily, imagined me without clothing. But I want to be close, to be loved, so much that I have the impulse to trick us both.

Instead, I click shut the glass shower door to wash away the smoke and city grime. The unwelcome memories the bed in the room brought to mind rub against me like sandpaper.

Through a smoky haze that seems to color most of my memories, I recall a threadbare couch, scratchy against my backside. There was a boy with dark hair that fell into his eyes and nothing but my T-shirt between us. It seems like ages ago or maybe even another lifetime. It meant nothing, and yet it does. It was my first time. Miraculously, it was my only time. I fooled around with boys in grungy apartments, guys at parties, and in secret places known only to street kids. Either the opportunity for a proper bed had never presented itself or I avoided it because that first time left me feeling as if I gave away something that I could never get back.

But Grant and I are magnetic. Something sparks between us that tells me he's different. I want to believe that he is honest and pure. Then, just as soon as the thought ignites hope, my confidence washes down the drain along with the grungy water. I waver. Something inside me contracts like a band wrapped around my chest, tightening with each breath. No, no, no, I plead. I want Grant, I do. Then like a key in a lock, I feel finality, like I will never let us be. I fear that if I let him in, I'll need him, like my mother needs her fix, and, at the same time, turn into someone I won't want to recognize. I hold my face under the water. After a few moments, I gasp for air, and as I blink my eyes open, Grant stands before me, handing me my towel.

His eyes swim toward me, reaching out, pulling me in like a rip current. He takes me in his arms and holds me. I fight my way out of the small, impenetrable emotional cage and burst forth into Grant's arms. I wrap myself around him, feeling our bodies pressing together.

"I'm afraid of becoming addicted to you," I whisper.

"I'm not a drug," he replies.

I'm not entirely sure I believe that.

Grant and I tumble into the bed, my skin still warm and moist from the shower. We each lie on our sides, facing one another. Grant traces a line from my shoulder down to my thigh.

"You're so beautiful," he says. His sincere eyes tell the story of amazement as I lie before him. I laugh softly, deflecting his compliment. "I'm serious," he insists. "You know those little moments, when I'm not thinking, you're there, in them. When I'm dreaming, you're there, waking me up. When I zone out, I see you. Every moment, moments between moments, there you are, radiant and brave, wild, like starlight."

A part of me knows he means it. As I skate along the spectrum from feeling worthless and lost inside my own labyrinthine heart, afraid of what might happen if I let him in, I somehow find myself on the other side. With Grant, I know, for the briefest moment, how real and true he is. I hold on to it as we melt into each other, passionately and softly.

Chapter 21

When the sky hints at lightening, Grant and I doze off, his arms protectively around me. His cheek rests in the crook of my neck; the backs of my legs nestle against the fronts of his. Sometime later, a loud knock on the door wakes me. I hear Sorel's voice from the other side, teasing. "Lovebirds, time to get up. Come on, can't sleep the day away."

For someone who probably had a later night than I did, she bursts with energy. We eat crepes from a little café before hitting the underground mall. Also, for a girl who rocks the punk look, Sorel loves to shop. She buys a new pair of Doc Martens, a couple of hoodies, a tourist's share of trinkets, and a skateboard for Pepper, who rides it through the mall until security prohibits him, shouting, *"Arrêtez, arrêtez."*

We emerge onto the street once again, and after depositing her loot back in the hotel, Sorel pulls a bottle out of her ever-present messenger bag. "Come on," she says, ushering us into a discreet alleyway.

As Sorel passes the bottle of whiskey to me, I chase it with a drag off Grant's cigarette. With each sip, we get silly and brave, shedding our cool exteriors and trading them in for a thrill and exposing the ways we dodge vulnerability. I lead the group up a fire escape, where we spit and drop wads of chewing gum to the ground, narrowly missing passersby.

It's surprisingly difficult to time. Pepper spray paints *God Save the Queen* on a Dumpster, and we heckle a lady wearing a fur coat. Pepper ganks some stickers from a music shop, and we plaster a car. Sorel jumps up and down on the hood of the car and then dances on the roof, denting it with her boots. She flashes no less than a dozen people, her nipples freezing in the cold. Sorel's cackle is the sound track.

The whiskey makes us feral.

We find ourselves in front of a tattoo parlor advertising that it's open twenty-four hours. In the amber glow of incandescent light, bad ideas wait to happen.

"Let's go, kids; Mama's going to get us inked," Sorel says, her eyes frenzied.

Pepper follows her eagerly and selects no less than a dozen images from the wall before settling on a Jolly Roger—the black pirate flag complete with skull and crossbones.

Sorel sidles up to me. "Happy birthday."

"You don't have to do this, Sorel. I'm not used to gifts, so thanks for bringing me here to begin with."

"I knew you just had to let loose. Get off that oppressive campus, away from the books. Live a little."

If Sorel had a motto, this would be it: *Live a little.*

"Hell yeah," I say, summoning enthusiasm. But sometimes I wonder what it would be like to live a lot.

She points out the tribal image she's getting. The tattoo gun hums in the background, and she's off, watching someone else be tattooed, psyching herself up.

I decide to get a smattering of black swallows on my shoulder and just below my collarbone. I describe to Grant the delicate yet strong balance I want from the lines shading the image and the inner area. I wonder what Shale would say about the composition.

"There's this old sailor story, that if you ever get lost, the swallows will guide you back home," he says.

The words sound familiar, as if I've heard them before or they're from a dream.

Grant flips through a portfolio.

"What're you thinking about getting?" I ask, leaning over his shoulder and smelling the soap from our shower the night before.

"I've always wanted a tattoo, but my dad . . . his plans. Eff it." He may have just added a couple of inches to his height. "My grandfather's this burly Scotsman, a fisherman. I spent a lot of summers with him when I was a lad." Grant's voice deepens with hints of his native accent as he speaks. "Being there by the ocean, the fresh salt air, the heartiness of the people. It was a romantic but hard life. People like my grandfather really worked, you know? And after a long day on the water, the simplicity of a steaming bowl of fish stew and a mug of ale was just the thing. My father wanted nothing more than to break away from it all. That's what he wants for me—to put miles and conformity between me and our heritage, where we came from."

For me, that doesn't sound like a bad idea.

Grant goes on, impassioned. "Anyway, my grandfather was always telling stories about mermaids and other folktales. I think I'd like to get a mermaid." He beams. "He has one on his arm. Why not follow in the old guy's footsteps?"

The owner and another artist summon Sorel and Pepper to a couple of booths toward the back of the shop. Grant and I sneak off for a smoke and a kiss.

The chilly air blends our breath and the cigarette smoke into fog as we stand close together outside the tattoo shop. I wish more than anything the night would never end. I feel free of fear, free of a mother whose drug addiction taints so many of my memories, and free of the possibility that I'll break us both if I let Grant get too close.

Later, after the artist etches the clean lines of the inky swallows in my skin, Grant's upper arm reveals the outline of a mermaid. As the form takes shape, I notice she has blond hair, just the shade of mine. Grant proffers his sad smile, like he knows we're both just a fantasy.

After the artist scratches the last scale, he takes a group shot with an instant camera. Sorel gives it to me, since this is my birthday celebration.

"You guys up for the night?" the artist asks.

"Shit, yeah," Sorel says, edging toward rowdiness as the bottle of whiskey empties.

"There's a bar called the Tin Tin. I think you'll like it."

After Sorel pays, we sweep back into the night, all of us forgetting we belong to Laurel Hill.

After midnight, we pop into a pub for some grub. Sorel is now over eighteen, and for this reason, Pepper has a fake ID. When the waitress asks for Grant's and my ID's, we act like hapless friends.

Sorel slurs, "They lost their luggage while flying in from Seattle. They've been wearing the same clothes for days . . ." Her tongue curls around the stupid lies, elaborating as if to see how far she can push them. In short order, with our late-night meal, we all put back a couple of beers on top of the whiskey.

"See, lying isn't hard," Sorel says as she pays.

No, it isn't, unless you're lying to yourself or someone you love.

Afterward, navigating the streets to the Tin Tin takes on a carnival-like quality. The lights spin and blur, music from clubs spills into the street, distracting us, and Sorel blisters with increasing irritation. We pass the same office building, where a bunch of people our age crowd on the stone stairs, drinking and smoking, three times.

"Hey, you guys know where the Tin Tin is?" Sorel calls, her voice muddy from all the alcohol.

One of the girls laughs sharply and then speaks in rapid French.

"Fuckin' Canucks," Sorel says loudly, flashing her middle finger. "This country sucks!"

As we walk away, an empty aluminum can sails by me, and before I can shout for Sorel to duck, it hits her in the back of the head. She whirls around. The French-speaking girl, no bigger than Sorel, with narrow eyes and permanently downturned lips, a girl I recognize as ready for a fight, stands coiled just a few feet away.

"What'd you say?" she asks in perfect English.

Sorel's smile oozes nasty. "What did I say?" she asks as if puzzled. "Fuckin' Canuckin'? Fuck the Canucks," Sorel slurs in a singsong voice. "You have a problem with that?" She laughs.

"I thought that's what you said. Yeah, I do have a problem." There's no anticipation or time for warning. Without skipping a beat, she punches Sorel square in the face. Laughter echoes from the shadows.

Pepper catches his girlfriend as she pitches backward.

My muscles tense, and my pulse quickens.

"Contrary to the stereotype, not all of us 'Canucks' are so friendly and easygoing. Remember that," the girl says, turning back to her group.

Pepper mutters to calm Sorel down.

I bring her a tissue. "Come on, Sorel. We ran into the wrong person. Let's find the Tin Tin," I say.

When the girl settles back on the steps, I relax. They heckle us, but of course, we can't understand.

Sorel dabs her swollen lip.

"Come on, baby, I'll kiss it and make it better," Pepper says. She shrugs him away.

Sorel cowers under the tough-girl's glare and then cruises down the sidewalk. A few blocks later, I pop into a tobacco shop with Grant to ask for directions to the Tin Tin.

"I swear you growled back there," he says, laughing.

"Growled?"

"I thought you were going to rip that girl's head off. Or maybe Sorel's."

I laugh, recalling his comment about me looking like I was raised by wolves. "No, that was Sorel's fight," I say smartly.

"Sure was. Pepper told me her dad is from Canada."

"I guess that explains her intense reaction."

"We Scots are a ballsy lot, but she had no business saying that shit."

"None," I agree. "I'm not bailing her out because she's ignorant or angry at Daddy."

"Definitely not as tough as she looks," he adds smugly as we step back outside.

We make our way to the Tin Tin and meet a much mellower vibe compared to the punk club the night before. Sorel and Pepper do their usual thing, and Grant and I talk about music, which shifts into talking about my mom's band, and then our futures. When college comes up, I say, "Whoa. Wait a second. We're on vacation. Let's talk about something else."

"You're right, we are on vacation. Fancy that. Hey, Sorel," Grant calls, interrupting the kissy-faced couple. Maybe their constant kissing means that they don't have much to talk about. Despite Grant's original request not to talk, we have tons to say to each other. "Thanks for taking us on vacation."

We raise our glasses.

"To Sorel, our sugar mama and the proud owner of her first tattoo!" We toss accolades over at her, forgiving her stupidity earlier, indulging her generosity and this taste of freedom.

Chapter 22

Back at the hotel, Grant and I are sloppy drunk. I paw at him like an untamed animal, as if I don't need anything in the world except his body against mine. Every spot he touches ignites with wild and earthen passion. Maybe I am part wolf.

I want to stay there forever, in that room, in that bed, with Grant. It's like a dream, but the morning brings a gray sky. The ride back to Laurel Hill with Sorel hangs over me like the thick clouds above.

The four of us are trudging along the sleepy streets of Montreal, looking for breakfast, when I notice the same office building from the night before and recall the scuffle. Sorel's lip nearly looks normal, painted with her burgundy lipstick. An invisible outline of the street kids clings to the vacant steps littered with empty bottles.

We enter a diner and take up a corner booth. As Sorel complains about her tattoo feeling itchy, she looks over my shoulder and turns a gasp into a yawn. I spot the girl who punched her. Sorel's face goes red. Her bark is loud, but last night proved there's no bite.

"Damn." She shades her head under her hand. "I don't want any trouble," she says. "It's bad enough my lip is, like, doubled in size."

"It isn't so bad," I say.

When the waitress arrives for our drink order, Sorel asks for a beer. "Hair of the dog," she explains.

"Yeah, but you have to drive," I remind her.

"I'll be fine by the time we leave."

I guess she intends for the beer to lubricate her tongue, in case the girl from the night before gets rowdy again. Sure enough, after Sorel's bottle arrives, along with three coffees, the girl saunters over to us with a couple of friends.

"Well, well, well. Looks like we have the Canadian hater," she says loudly. "How's your lip?"

"Hey, guys. She was drunk. She didn't mean it," Pepper says in Sorel's defense.

"I don't freaking care what she was."

I quietly hope Sorel will keep her mouth shut. I don't want to be ejected from Canada or, worse, arrested. As our return to reality nears, as far as anyone at Laurel Hill is concerned, I'm supposed to be in New York City, visiting my mom.

The girl leans toward Sorel. "Did you learn your lesson? Looks like you're already drinking this morning. Are you going to say shit like that again?"

"No, she's not," I say sternly.

Sorel takes a swig of beer. "Thank you for your hospitality in this fine country. God bless Canada," she says flatly.

"That's what I thought," the girl snaps.

Just then, the waitress brings our food, and the girl disappears. Sorel, with her head bowed, devours her meal and all of Pepper's toast.

When we return to the hotel to gather our gear, Grant and I delay our departure in the king-size bed, as the digital clock counts down the minutes.

Afterward, while we wait in the lobby for Sorel and Pepper, our faces flush with the knowledge that we are quite possibly the center of the universe. I lean languorously against Grant on the sofa, comfortably close now, uninhibited by my own sense of inadequacy and fear. Our interlaced hands rest on his thigh. I feel dreamy, blissful, like we could float away.

Sorel blusters over to the desk to check out.

Pepper cautiously trots over to us. "She's on the warpath," he warns.

"What's up?" I ask.

He shakes his head. "Everything and nothing."

Sorel's bad mood keeps us in silence as she throws her bags around, slams doors, and simmers. When she starts the car, she cranks the music until the melody and words blend indistinctly, forcing us into silence.

After we cross back into the United States, she fires up. "After all I've done for you, I really thought you guys would have stuck up for me back there."

"Baby, I'm sorry," Pepper hedges. "I just thought it was best we avoided a situation."

"I thought at least you, City Girl, would've had my back."

"If it came to that. It was a dumb thing to say, Sorel."

"I thought you were all tough. But that girl punched me last night, and this morning she would have tried to kick my ass again. You could have at least done something."

"Sorel, what you said last night really wasn't cool," Grant interjects.

"Sticking up for your girlfriend, Grant?" Sorel spits.

"No, calling you out," he retorts angrily.

"You two think you're just so perfect. All smoochy-smooch and kissy-kiss. It's just so precious. So glad you finally got together. Has it occurred to you that you have me to thank? PJ, you would have just studied all weekend, your nose buried in your books, too apathetic to have any fun. And, Grant, you would have sulked in your dorm room, pining away for her. But look, I got the two of you off the campus and up to Canada, dammit. And what do I get in return? Silence from my friends when I needed them. If that was you last night, PJ, I would have messed that girl up."

"I doubt that," I mutter.

Before she can respond, Grant says, "Sorel, if you hadn't made that idiot comment, nothing would have happened."

"I bet you're too scared to fight," she says, laying into me. "Whatever cushy little condo you live in probably has a doorman and a driver always waiting outside to bring you wherever you need to go. You're no city girl. Mommy, Daddy, and their money probably shelter you from everything."

The snow-white clouds bleed red. She has no idea. "Sorel, pull over," I say in a husky echo of my mother's voice.

"Or what? Are you going to walk back to Laurel Hill? I wonder what Terran will say."

"Pull the car over. I'll show you where I come from and how we do."

She triggers the cold reality of what my life back in Manhattan was like. I'm tired of being reminded, of having to prove myself one way or the other. I know what I'm made of, and if she wants a taste, I'll give it to her.

"Come on, Sorel. Let it go," Pepper says in a small voice. "You know we all would have had your back. We're boarding school kids, not—"

"Speak for yourself. I'm not kidding. You have no clue where I come from. Stop the car. I'll give you a couple of black eyes to go with your lip." I glimpse my stony face in the rearview mirror. In my reflection, I see JJ, combative, belligerent, at her worst. I twitch.

Sorel pulls over, but doesn't get out of the car. I push the door open as quickly as I can, if only to get away from her ignorance, hotheadedness, and my own rage. I slide down the embankment off the shoulder of the highway and shout up to her. So what if she pulls away. I've been in far worse situations.

A few minutes pass. The car idles above. A door slams.

Grant bounds down the embankment. He pushes my hair behind my shoulders. "I'm sorry," he says simply.

"Sorry because Sorel is being a jerk and I flipped out, or sorry because you've discerned that my entire life up until this weekend has been a disaster?" I look up at him, tears in my eyes.

Sadness tugs his lips down. "Let's go." He leads me back up to the car.

Sorel and her music are quiet for the rest of the ride. She drops Grant and me off at the bus stop without so much as a good-bye. We go into the little café, and Grant buys us each a coffee. I chew the grinds up as I swallow hard. "I'm not sure I want to go back to campus."

"Me neither, but since Mom had a little breakdown on our vacation, maybe we're better off," he says as he sips from the paper cup. He hasn't shaved the entire weekend, and scruff grows in around his jawline and mouth.

A smile pierces my reluctance. "At least she took us somewhere cool."

We chuckle as we shuffle back to campus. The wild child retreats within me with the reassuring reminder that I have a place to live, food to eat, and Grant. I have assignments waiting and a portrait to paint. I don't know who it's of, but it isn't the girl I saw this weekend.

Outside my dorm, Grant gives me a shy kiss, his boyish student demeanor returning once back on school grounds. He and I are both quiet, not saying a word, because good-bye is too permanent.

Chapter 23

The only reminders of the weekend in Canada are the tattoo emblazoned above my heart and Sorel's silence as I pour myself back in my studies. I breeze by a couple of girls whose chatter stops when I pass. Then, at my back, I hear the hiss of their whispers, no doubt about me.

I wait in the common room for a girl from English to give me a study sheet the teacher forgot to pass out earlier. Terran approaches me, her shoulders pitched forward as if she's resisting the urge to charge like a bull. "I know where you went last weekend." She smiles, but there is no mirth in her laugh.

I raise an eyebrow. I won't let her take it away from me. "You do?" I challenge, getting to my feet and standing taller.

"You went somewhere with Sorel and a couple of boys. Mark said he saw you get in a car. You didn't get on the bus to New York like you told Connie, Pearl Jaeger." The way she says my name reminds me how much she detests me.

"Is Mark watching—"

She cuts me off. "Mark only confirmed what I already believed. Along with an interesting call. You see, Saturday evening the dorm phone rang . . ." She punctuates each word with suspense. "'Hello,' I answered.

"'Pearl?' the caller asked."

Terran's voice drops in what could only be an imitation of my mother's smoky tone. "'Pearl. This is your motherfucking mother. Where the hell are you? I bet you're not really at that fucking special school. Why don't you call me? Why don't you visit me? Pearl? Pearly-Pearl-Pearl. What the fuck do you think you're doing, leaving me?' Then she started singing, if you could call it that, 'I've met someone, his name is crack, and he ain't ever goin' to do me wrong. Do you want to meet him, Pearl? I bet you do.'"

My stomach twists into knots, because although it's Terran speaking and not Janet, the expression on Terran's lips ensnares me, the echo of the familiar words morphing me into a rag doll.

"The monologue went on and on. The caller talked at me for a solid five minutes, using coarse language we don't tolerate here in Vivian Brookwood Dormitory and certainly not at the esteemed Laurel Hill." Terran's voice drips with elite authority. "Here, we're educated in order to broaden our vocabulary so that we may express ourselves effectively and eloquently." She leans in close. "Last I checked the *F*-word wasn't on any syllabus here at Laurel Hill. Any idea who the caller could have been, Pearly-Pearl-Pearl?" Terran asks.

The sinking feeling gives way to the reality that my mother finally tried to reach me; it almost doesn't matter what she said. Compared to finally hearing from my mother, despite the extremely questionable content of her phone call, Terran's accusation takes second place. Fibers turn back into bone, and I stand on solid ground again. "Did you get a callback number?"

For a moment, she looks surprised by my lack of defense, but her pitiless mask quickly returns. "Unfortunately, no. But I'm sure Connie will be happy to help you with that."

Just then, Connie's apartment door, a fire hazard plastered with flyers, cards, and dorm reminders, opens.

"I was just going to find you, Connie," Terran says, her words circling me, taunting me, ready to go in for the kill.

Connie looks wearily from Terran to me, as if afraid, and possibly tired, of the former. "Yes, what is it?"

"I have good reason to believe Pearl wasn't at her mother's last weekend. Janet Jaeger called here Saturday night, looking for Pearl."

Connie looks back and forth between us. "Terran, that's another weighty claim. Do you have proof? What do you say, PJ?" Connie's kind expression invites me to tell the truth, but survival trumps honesty.

"There was a mix-up. I spent the first night at my dad's, then I was supposed to go to her house, but when I got there she hadn't gotten home yet, and I forgot my key, so she called the only number she had, trying to let me know she was home. We connected later. No worries," I say. The lies slip easily off my silver tongue.

Terran's glare sinks into my skin like rows of teeth. "That's not true," she says. "Pearl is lying."

Connie takes a deep breath.

"I spoke to her mother," Terran says.

"Correction. I thought you said she spoke *at* you," I say curtly.

"Semantics. You wouldn't believe the things she said to me, Connie. She used words that would burn your mind with their obscenity. She called me a mother . . ." she whispers, gazing at the floor, the picture of innocence.

Connie flinches.

Terran gives one final push, but flounders. "She was talking about crack, the illegal drug."

Connie's face scrunches. "You shouldn't believe rumors. I doubt PJ's mother would say things like that."

I shrug my shoulders, because she would say that and worse, but for Connie's benefit, my shrug means that I don't know what's going on.

Then my spinnerets weave wonders. "She was at a wedding shower for her friend Carrie *Crack*ett. She probably had a bit too much to drink. I apologize if she offended you, Terran." I try a smile, but the way her lips pucker and fold into her mouth wipes it from my face.

Connie edges toward the door. "Thank you, PJ. That was very nice of you. Be sure to solidify your plans better with your mother next time, OK?"

By some act of mercy, she believes me. However, Terran doesn't. After Connie steps about a yard toward the door, she whispers, "Pearl, I'm going to get you one way or another, Pearly-Pearl-Pearl," she sing-songs, imitating my mother. "You're going down."

I start to walk away but stop. "Terran, the thing is, being down here, where I already am, there's really nowhere else to fall. You, on the other hand, you'd have a long way to go, and I promise the landing will hurt." Before she has a chance to get in the last word, I fly up the stairs.

As soon as I escape her seething, the density of the phone call and the ease with which I lied hit me square in the gut like a boulder.

Without proof, Terran can do little aside from harass me. My skin is thick. I can handle it, I tell myself. However, my mother presents another matter. Experience has taught me that JJ can be a menace, not only to herself but also to everyone that she encounters. A chill trickles down my skin until my toes feel frostbit. The threat of what JJ might do this time freezes me with ragged little breaths. I feel small, a helpless child in the shadow of an unpredictable danger. Terran exposed Janet Jaeger as my mother, and it sucks, but the humiliation JJ would cause if she came to Laurel Hill would be permanent. *Could she find her way to Viv Brooks? Am I safe? Is she?*

The next day, I pass on Terran's warning, along with Mark's observation, to Grant, suggesting he tell Pepper, who will most certainly tell Sorel, telephone style. I hope that nothing is lost in translation. I don't leave time to acknowledge what happened in Canada or the electricity that crackles between us. Now, back at Laurel Hill, we've both withdrawn to our respective corners. *What could be* is too big for either of us to scale, because our fragile hearts are afraid of the stakes. Like I told Terran, down here where I am is easier, safer.

To Grant I add, "Sorel and I haven't spoken since we returned. I don't feel the need to say sorry, but it seems the absence of an apology has kept her distant." Conveniently, just as I leave to go to the library, and Grant heads to his dorm, she and Pepper walk up the path to Viv Brooks.

I don't involve myself in awkward silence. "I was just telling Grant that Terran said Mark told her he saw me getting into your car. She has it in for me."

"That's not my problem," Sorel says. Her eyes are heavy, and the bosky scent of pot hangs faintly in the air.

"It's not, but you should know Mark isn't someone to be trusted, especially if you're smoking with him in the woods."

That gets her tongue. "Oh."

"About the ride back, I was out of line yelling at you." I waver about whether to plow ahead, filling in the gaps in her assumptions about my past. Terran shared enough info for anyone curious to search JJ on the Internet. "I, uh, really am a city girl. A street kid. Whatever. What Terran said was true. We were living in a homeless shelter. My mother started a fire. I almost died. I've got nothing. Nothing to prove, no home, no family, nothing," I say sadly, my heart bleeding with the truth.

There's no shock or sympathy. "Don't worry about it," Sorel says. In fact, based on her score book of cool or whatever, her nod of approval suggests I moved up a rank, not that it matters.

Chapter 24

I don't trust the spring. It's fickle like me, and I definitely don't trust myself. Not with Grant, not with behaving, not with the temptation of the cache of pills hidden in my room. The spring months are likely to jump into league with winter, dumping heaps of snow on the newly sprouted crocuses or cloaking the sunshine just to provide people puddles to splash in. I'm not a conservative person, but I don't agree with what the whimsical, you-only-live-once types say—splashing in filthy puddles is gross.

That's exactly what Terran does when she passes me on the path back to the dorm, soaking me with frigid, dirty water.

I shiver when I enter Viv Brooks, eager for a warm shower. "PJ?" Connie says, intercepting me before I have a chance to rush upstairs. I expect her to say something about the necklace, the weekend escapade, or some other misdeed, but instead she leads me into the small office that divides her apartment from the rest of the dorm. A man I don't recognize sits in a chair beside the desk. I fold into the other, wrapping my arms around my chest.

"Pearl, this is Dr. Greenbrae," Connie says.

Did they find the pills? Maybe Mark and Terran provided proof of the trip to Canada. Beads of cold sweat dot my forehead.

Connie takes a deep breath, looking from the doctor to me. She soundlessly opens and closes her jaw, as if she wants words to come out of her mouth but her lips and tongue won't cooperate.

The doctor clears his throat. "Pearl, I'm sorry to be the one to tell you this, but your mother has passed away," Dr. Greenbrae says.

I hear the words, the sounds Connie couldn't make, reach my ears, trying to find a way past the fog in my brain.

The room starts to spin, and the walls feel like they're collapsing in on me. My body sinks deeply into the chair, and my stomach, ever faithful to nerves, convulses into knots. Weakness paralyzes my legs. With one crippling sentence, my entire body dismantles into its raw parts. Connie puts her hand on what used to be my arm. I pull it away.

There's only one possibility. *Overdose* lands in my mind with a thud, but I can't think about the how right now. I only want to scream, *Why?*

Instead, someone in the room says the words "No. No. No." Then I realize it's me. I repeat them again, slowly shaking my head. My mother is invincible. She could stay up for days. She's immortal. Nothing touched her except alcoholism, addiction, poverty, and abuse. But she survived it all. She couldn't have—but I can't even let myself think of that final word to complete the sentence.

"Everything will be all right," the doctor and Connie alternatingly assure me. They say they're there for me, but I have never felt more alone.

I'm actually alone.

I suck air, but am not sure I still want to breathe. Despite what they say, I won't be all right, not for a long time.

"Pearl, I want you to come to my office in the health center tomorrow. In the meantime, is there anyone you'd like to call?" Dr. Greenbrae asks.

Who told them this? How did they find out? I don't understand, but like Connie, I can't get the words to form on my lips. They say more, but I don't hear anything but thunder in my ears, a storm brewing in my belly and lightning flashing behind my eyes, striking me over and over and over.

It's dark by the time they reluctantly let me leave the claustrophobic office. As I walk through the familiar hall, the posters and signs on the walls look abstract, like I'm in a museum of my former life.

Instead of going upstairs to my room, I walk out the door and through the puddles and melting snow, which reveal bits of grass on the sloping lawn in front of the dorm. I stand in the center, gaze upward into the clear night sky, the stars like pinprick diamonds mocking me with their beauty, and shout, "Why?"

Then the tears come, slowly at first, like an engine building steam, then so rapidly one doesn't have a chance to slip down my cheek before the other one collides into it. Quickly, my face is wet, and I shiver in the cold. My body spasms with a cough, a reminder of my life going up in flames.

I hear crunching in the snow. I dread Connie or Dr. Whatever trying to console me again, but instead of Connie's sweet perfume, I smell tobacco. Sorel, Pepper, and Grant appear. Arms wrap around me. Sorel asks me what's wrong, but only shuddering sobs come out of my body. I don't care that they see me like this. I don't care about anything.

Grant puts one strong arm around me. Sorel flanks me on the other side. Pepper is somewhere in the mix, and they herd me back toward the dorm. The boys come as far as the foyer. Grant kisses my cold, wet cheek.

Sorel helps me up the stairs and into my bed. I hear her whispering to someone else in the room. I close my eyes against the dim desk light. Scanning the darkness within, I see nothing but the chasm of my broken heart.

As I lie in the twin bed, in room twenty-two, in Vivian Brookwood Dormitory, at Laurel Hill Preparatory School, I no longer feel a sense of gratitude. In its place is emptiness, a desolate vacuum of nothingness. There's no chime of hope on the wind that my life will be different. The smell of ash fills my nose. I should have died in the fire; it would have spared me this pain. My body aches as if the train wreck of Janet's life has struck me full on. I'll never be the same.

I wake in the midafternoon, the quiet of the dorm revealing the time of day. I sneak to the bathroom for some water. When I return, I peel back a pair of heavy socks, neatly folded together, and extract the pills from my hiding place. I pop two in my mouth, swallow the rest of the water, and get back in bed. *Sorry, Dr. Greenbrae, I'll be treating this on my own.*

As I settle back into bed, an unbidden reel of images of my mother streams through my head.

There was the time she tried curling her hair, but it turned out looking like the paper fans I used to make to cool myself off on hot summer nights.

I see her wearing a hospital gown when I visited her in the psychiatric ward. Her cheeks fuller and her skin clear. I remember how buoyant I felt that day; she seemed so happy to see me.

I remember the disaster and the ensuing laughter when we tried to make cookies from the government-issued peanut butter and other dry goods doled out for Thanksgiving one year. She'd used salt instead of sugar, but we ate them anyway.

I recall how when she was high, after I'd go to bed, she'd check on me incessantly to make sure I still breathed. Although I'd feign sleep, I could smell her musky scent and sharp breath as she leaned over me, a warped version of a mother tucking in her child. It wasn't normal, but still, I'd give almost anything if my door opened and her head poked in right at this moment. Sober or high, I'd take it.

I recall her passing me on Delancey Street, looking right at me, or possibly right through me, and not acknowledging me or maybe not wanting me to recognize her, as strung out as she was.

Tears drop from my eyes, pooling on my pillow. Continuously, my mind recalls moments, snippets of memories of my mother and me. After some time, the memories become heavier, like the images move through something as viscous as the past.

My body feels like jelly, spread thin upon the bed. I drift away from memories of my mother and toward Grant. I try to claw my way back to her. I find myself in a boat, but then as I struggle to get to shore, it capsizes, and I sink deeper and deeper into the internal ickiness that swells inside of me. I float further within and then drift to sleep.

Someone rubs my shoulder. I blink open my eyes and see Sorel holding a tray on her lap as she sits on the edge of my bed.

"I brought you something to eat. How're you doing?"

I roll over, putting my back to her. I don't want Sorel. I want my mother. I want her to console me. To assure me everything will be fine. I want her to rub my back, brush my hair, and hold me, hold me, hold me forever and never let me go.

I hear Sorel slide the tray onto my desk. She kneels beside the bed and says softly, "Grant wanted me to read this to you. It's Robert Frost." She clears her throat and recites a familiar poem.

Then, in the darkness, I hear the door open and close.

Deep in the night, my comforter lifts and a whoosh of cold prickles my skin. Grant's long body slides in behind me, quietly breathing in my hair. He holds me. The familiar smell of pine and tobacco, mint and devotion, wafts to my nose, then a hand gropes for mine, and I know, someday, some distant day, I might be fine. But first, I have miles to go.

Chapter 25

After the third day, Connie appears in my room, catching me awake. She launches right into what must have been a carefully scripted speech. "I'm so very sorry for your loss. I wish I'd have met your mother, PJ."

"No, you don't," I mumble.

"Dr. Greenbrae would like you to go to his office today. He just wants to talk to you." She forces a smile. "He'll be expecting you at one, OK?" She gives another awkward smile and leaves.

My body coils, and my jaw clenches. I want to yell at her, but I don't have the strength to shoot the messenger. I slump back in bed, close my eyes, and will the world to still itself, just so I never have to move again.

Charmindy pops in after lunch. "PJ, are you awake?"

I open my eyes halfway.

"How are you doing? Sorry, dumb question. I'm so sorry, sorry about all of it. If you want to talk . . ."

I don't answer.

"Connie mentioned you have an appointment. I just thought I'd offer to help you get dressed and find the office."

She gets a pair of jeans and a sweatshirt out of my closet. I painstakingly get dressed. The tray of food from the other night still rests on my desk, notebooks and texts stacked around it, punctuating life before and after.

I slide on my boots and trudge listlessly at Charmindy's heels toward the health center.

"I have to get to French. See you later," Charmindy says, leaving me in front of a door bearing a rectangular brown sign that reads *Dr. Greenbrae, PhD.*

I stand outside, my hand on the doorknob, disinclined to enter.

The first time I saw a therapist was part of one of Janet's various rehabilitation programs. The hazy memory of therapy involves puppets and playacting. During the second stint, the doctor asked me questions about my interests and friends. I was all too happy to comply; no one ever seemed to have much interest in me specifically. Though later I understood the questions were to get me comfortable, so she could ask about my relationship with my mom.

The most recent time I had to see a shrink was because, in a delusion, Janet convinced herself I had something wrong with me mentally. Anxiety met anger as I worried maybe she was right, Mother knows best and all that. But *she* had the issues. She fried her brain on drugs. It wasn't fair of her to make that my problem. Perhaps she didn't remember the emotional difficulties of puberty from her own teenage years, but I acted like a normal teenager—confused by the hormonal changes going on in my body and dealing with the lifestyle choices Janet imposed upon me. How's that for psychoanalysis? That'll be thirty dollars, thank you.

Fueled by my memories of this injustice, I stand mutinously outside the door. It opens, and I'm face-to-face with the balding doctor. It's as if he sensed my readiness to bolt.

"Pearl, so glad you came," he says with a practiced joviality.

I stand on the threshold, my hard eyes fixed on nothing in particular.

"Come on in, have a seat, make yourself comfortable." He returns to his leather swivel chair.

I scan the room. A wooden bookshelf spans the wall, stuffed with thick texts with titles like *Managing the Anxious Mind* and *Listen to What Your Teens Don't Say*. Behind the doctor's desk, a window with dusty mini blinds lets in minimal light and a droopy plant wilts in a plastic pot on the sill. On the front of his desk, folders and papers wait for filing, and three plastic toys filled with water and colored gel that drips slowly when you turn them upside down invite curiosity. When I was younger, toys like that fascinated me with how slowly and uniquely the gel oozed. The wooden chair for patients gets nothing more than my insolence.

"I know you're having a tough time, but I'm here to help you. I just want to talk. I also spoke to your uncle and have some things to tell you."

I cross into the office, but don't sit down.

"Come on, just a little farther, take a seat. I won't bite."

No, but I do, I think childishly. Nothing he can say can comfort me. I was wrong when I told Terran about being so low, so broken, rock bottom, about not being able to fall any further. I'm on a permanent descent, spiraling down, down, down.

Impatiently, he continues. "I know this is a really hard time. Loss is never easy. Grief is even harder. But there are things that can help. I can offer you tools to deal with your sadness. We can get through this together."

I don't want anything from him. Understanding my pain would necessitate relating my life story. I'm not willing to relive it; he of all people should know that if I look back, there's no chance of me moving forward.

"What did my uncle say?" I ask.

"Funeral arrangements have been made for next weekend. He'll send a car. He says he expects you to continue classes until then, and you can stay at the hotel with them."

My shoulders creep up to my ears. My body tightens. Cut and dried, *so* Uncle Gary. No *sorry you lost your mother.* No card or flowers. *What am I? Worthless? Do I matter to anyone?* Anger ignites like a swiped match. "I have to go."

Dr. Greenbrae stands up. "Pearl, in order for you to stay here at Laurel Hill, you have to go to classes. You missed a few days, and while those are excused, you'll have to resume on Monday, until you leave for New York. Do you understand?"

I nod.

"You could really use some help. I'd like you to come back tomorrow after class. Can you do that?"

I shrug. "Do I have to?"

His temple twitches. "No, you don't have to, unless you skip any more classes or I hear from your head of dorm or uncle that you're causing problems."

The anger explodes and rockets through me. "Is that what this offer to help is all about, to prevent me from becoming a *problem?*" I turn to leave.

"Despite what you may think, I'm here to help," he calls after me.

I don't entertain that as a possibility. As I march back to the dorm, I struggle to draw a deep breath. The taut balloon of my fury deflates with the reminder of the fire, of how sometimes it's so hard to simply breathe.

I get back into bed, and sadness curls under the sheets with me. I glance up at the poster of Frida, wondering what I'd look like if she painted a portrait of me. Shattered. Fragmented. Crushed. I stay in bed through the afternoon and dusk, losing myself in Frida's gaze, missing dinner and study hall. Grant once again creeps in beside me late at night. He doesn't say a word, just holds me steady, and I crawl into the ticking of his heart.

Charmindy's alarm clock, alerting her she has to get ready for a theater rehearsal, returns me to consciousness. I roll over and breathe deeply into the pillow where Grant's head rested just hours before, smelling faint traces of his shampoo. The sun, streaming in through the window, for all its effort, surprises me with its unceasing quiet, a reminder that not even the brightest star can call me back from the depths of loss I've reached.

Saturday is lonely. On the other side of the door, I alternatingly hear ordinary life and snippets of laughter and long breaths of silence. That evening, I slip out of bed to take another pill and discover it's the last one. I scroll through my memory of Dr. Greenbrae's office to see if there's any evidence of him being a psychologist or a psychiatrist, the latter able to dole out prescriptions. My mother was a champ at getting pills for various aches and ailments. It can't be that hard to score some more.

I toss back the remaining chalky white pill. As I sweep away from my body, my mind switches sluggishly from painful memories of my mother to pleasant ones of Grant. I feel caught between two tides, one pushing and one pulling, and I can't gain enough purchase to move in one direction or the other.

In my mind's eye, my mother lies fast asleep beside me. As I roll over to get warmer, her bare arm reveals the crook of her elbow, covered with red pricks and bruises. I sit up, alarmed, and watch her chest subtly rise and fall. On the floor beside her loops a belt next to a syringe.

I see an image of Grant: Snow falling all around him, dusting his hair, as though he's in a snow globe. He reaches for my hand. I am warm and safe.

My mind flashes to my mother: A knock at the door wakes me from sleep. She answers it, and the police take her away in handcuffs.

Grant returns: Across the room in the library, head bent over a book, his hand scratching over a sheaf of white notebook paper, a wisp of hair chasing the pencil. He looks up and smiles at me.

My mother appears again: indifferent as to whether or not I go to school, indifferent to whether or not I have friends, indifferent to my existence.

Then there's Sorel's voice, and she's shaking my shoulder. "Wake up, sleepyhead."

My eyes open heavily and then drop closed like a thick curtain. "Wait, I'm not done." I didn't get back to Grant. I try to dive back into the pill-induced semiconscious, but Sorel interferes. I groan.

"What the heck, PJ, are you on something?" she whispers.

"Let me go back," I hear myself say.

"Go where?" she asks, confused.

Reality stubbornly tries to snap itself back into place. I take a breath. "I must have been dreaming," I say evasively, opening my eyes partially.

"Bullshit. What did you take? Did that doctor give you something? Want to share?"

I shake my head as I prop myself upright.

She stares at me intently, eagerly.

"I had some leftover pills from the fire and some I snagged from Christmas vacation. Whatever," I say dully. "I just took the last one." A feeble voice tells me that I should pause and forget about it, but instead I add, "Know where I can get more?"

"What were they?"

I shrug. "Some kind of codeine."

Her eyes light up. "Mitch."

Hell no. But when I remember I have to go to the funeral, I don't disagree.

"Get dressed; we'll go see what he's got. But I get half."

"Whatever you say, Sugar Mama."

Still in pajama bottoms, I stumble downstairs.

Terran sits imperiously upon a chair in the common room, decorating a poster for one of her causes. She scales down her nasty sneer to just a dirty look.

Connie appears in the doorway to her apartment. "I see you're feeling better, Pearl," she says sweetly.

"Hardly," I murmur.

Sorel puts on a big, fake grin. "I just thought she could use some fresh air. Get her out, stretch her legs a little. We'll be back in a bit," she says in a faux chipper voice, as if I'm not there, but I may as well not be. I feel myself a few steps away from another fall, but where I'll go this time, I have no idea.

Chapter 26

The landscape sloshes and slops with early spring in the northern reaches of New England. The slush on the ground as we approach Mitch's house chills my feet. By a shed toward the side of the yard, Sorel's Volvo waits for her. She knocks loudly on the door.

Through the slatted blinds, Mitch's mouth spreads wide, revealing a missing tooth. "Well, well, well, look who we have here," he says, opening the door.

The house smells of stale beer and an indistinct rankness, like the underside of a mat of moldering leaves in the woods.

"Hey, Mitch, how's it going?" Sorel gives him a hug, then takes off her coat.

He shrugs. "Better now that I've got company."

From the living room, I hear the television set, riddled with gunfire and shouting. He opens the fridge and tosses Sorel a beer. "Who's your friend?" he asks.

Even through the mud that has been the last week of my life, I certainly remember him. Maybe he really had been too drunk to know what he was doing on Valentine's Day.

"This is PJ. She came with me to a party you had a while back."

"Oh yeah, I remember you now. Red lips. You're that pretty girl. Still going out with that tall kid?"

I nod vaguely. *Am I? Where is Grant? I only feel his presence by night. How is he sneaking into my room anyway? Am I imagining it?*

"Want a beer?" Mitch asks.

"Sure."

Sorel lights a cigarette. I take one from her pack without asking. The pills are better, but the beer and nicotine soften the sharp edges of agony. I sit down on the couch. The TV hypnotizes.

Mitch asks, "So what brings you here today? Checking on your car? Don't worry, I won't sell the junker. I still think you're crazy for trading in that new BMW."

"I did that so you wouldn't be tempted to go for a joyride," Sorel jokes. "We were just taking a walk and thought we'd stop in and say hello." She glances at me, slouching on the couch. "PJ just got some bad news, and I thought getting off campus would cheer her up. Change of scenery, y'know?"

"What happened to Miss Cherry Pie?"

I take a long sip from the can.

"She found out her mom passed away."

I know what Sorel plays at. I may be sitting here quietly, but that is what I always do during these transactions. I keep quiet and let Mama do her thing.

"Ah, man, I'm so sorry." For the first time Mitch looks genuine. "That sucks. Was she old? Sick?" he asks.

Sorel looks to me, truly not knowing the depth of the answer. Even after the trouble with Terran, I never fully admitted or announced that the woman on the Shrapnels poster was my mom. Sorel can find her way to a fraction of the truth, the glitzy, punk rock version, but she doesn't understand what it meant to live with JJ and, now, endure the aftermath.

"I dunno," I say softly.

Their heads dip and bob as if trying to make sense of what I said.

"I hadn't seen or heard from her since last summer. Yeah, I suppose she was sick." After all, therapists and doctors classify alcohol and drug addiction as a disease.

"Well, Miss Cherry Pie, if there is anything I can do, you let me know."

Sorel glances at me out of the corner of her eye. "Actually, do you have anything?"

Mitch leans back in his easy chair, stretches his arms overhead, and puts his ankle up on his knee. "You came to the right place. Come with me." He gets up, and we follow him down a dark hallway to a room at the end. The smell that I've tried to ignore since arriving grows stronger. When he opens the door, a greenish glow emits from the room. A large glass tank stands against one wall.

"Spidey, I brought company," Mitch says to a tarantula creeping along a branch behind the glass. "Sorry about the smell. I need to clean her tank." Mitch crosses the room and rustles among some boxes and bags on top of a dresser.

Sorel turns to the glass and baby talks to the spider. "Isn't she just the cutest thing?"

Creep city.

Mitch sits down on the mattress that rests on the floor and dumps a bunch of little bags out on the bed. In his hand, he has a large baggie half-filled with medium-sized blue pills.

"You only need one of these at a time, but they'll do the trick," he says with a gap in his smile. He fills two of the smaller baggies with the pills and puts everything away, and we return to the living room. I finish my beer. Mitch and Sorel settle back on the couch, and per drug-deal etiquette, we pretend our purpose is more than to score. I want to leave.

"Wanna split a joint?" Mitch asks as if we plan to stay all afternoon. He lights one up, and as Sorel passes it, thoughts of Grant overwhelm me. I close my eyes as I take a hit, thinking of the king-size bed, of walking hand in hand, of the kiss. Mitch's voice cracks me back to the present as I pass the spliff back to him.

His voice is mellow when he says, "Tell us about your mom."

No, not that. I don't want to think about her. Not right now. When I'm alone and in my wonderful world of pharmaceuticals—they buffer the blow from being too direct—but not right now. Not in this smelly house with some loser guy who keeps calling me Miss Cherry Pie. I blink my eyes open against the gravity of the question and the pulp of the weed.

"Yeah, tell us what she was like," Sorel says in a dreamy voice as she pulls her legs in toward her chest and tilts toward me on the couch.

There's nothing to say.

"I don't feel good. I better get back." But there will be no going back. Ever. Instead, I dash to the bathroom and dry heave until I throw up some of the beer. My head spins as I rest it on the dingy tile.

"PJ, you OK?" Sorel calls. I wipe my mouth and look past myself in the mirror. I feel hollow inside. Completely empty, but not hungry. I slowly open the door, and the smell of the spider's tank nauseates me once more.

"I just need some fresh air," I say.

"How about something to eat?" Mitch asks. He pulls out a bag of chips and takes a handful. Sorel does the same.

"When was the last time you ate?" Sorel asks.

I shrug.

Mitch scours the cupboards. "Sorry, Miss Cherry Pie, all I got is chips."

I crunch the orange chip; it tastes like dry cardboard in my mouth.

After Sorel finishes her second beer, she asks, "What do I owe ya?"

"Grocery money." Mitch laughs.

Sorel smiles indulgently.

"Next time you girls come over, I want to be able to give you some proper food. OK?"

Sorel hands him two hundred-dollar bills, which I know is generous for what he gave us, but then again, she's filthy with money.

Once back outside, my stomach instantly feels better, but my head and heart are far, far worse. As I think about swallowing one of the pills, mass times density rushes back like a smashing wave. I slosh through a slushy puddle.

"See, Mitch isn't so bad," Sorel says.

I snort.

"He's a good person to know," she follows up.

I pocket my half of the pills, thank Sorel, and disappear upstairs.

In my room, the Shrapnels poster above my bed signals sorrow, quickly reminding me why I want to dissolve. *Oblivion.* I swallow the blue pill and get into bed, urgently hoping to find a cloud to carry me away.

This pill causes more fitfulness than the others, but at least it dulls my inner world to a bearable grit. I descend into memory once more, my mother always the star.

As the effects of the blue pill hit a plateau, I feel marooned, as if stranded on an island with a guidebook to my childhood and I have to read and reread every painful detail. I want to dive into the water around the island, with the promise that it will caress me and wash away my feelings, but there's just a dull, numb awareness of every atom, cell, and tissue fissuring in my body. I want that drifting, easy feeling like the other pills gave me. Maybe one isn't enough.

The next morning, I prepare for classes, bracing myself for Shale's wrath. However, today, instead of standing blankly in front of my canvas, I gather paints in blue black, lampblack, and charcoal, along with a muted tone of red. In broad brushstrokes, I paint myself, spilling blood, leaving plenty of negative space.

Shale grunts over my shoulder, and the next day I repeat the exercise, a spare rendition of my image in the darkest, most empty colors.

Again, at the end of class Shale grunts and dismisses everyone but me. "Pearl, this is indulging an idea; you're doing yourself a disservice. What you've painted here is merely a sketch. An outline. To see who you are, you must go deeper."

I want to shout at him, but I keep my voice steady as I pack up my bag. "You have no idea how deep I've gone."

"No. I don't. All I know is that you need to go further."

I throw my bag to the floor. "Further? There's nowhere left to go. My mother just died. I am alone. I have nothing. I am—" I close my eyes, and there I see myself, tears streaming down my face, shaking. I go over to the oils, fill my palette, and get an assortment of brushes.

"I will write you a note for your next class," Shale says and takes his post over my shoulder.

Each day, I wake to unwelcome, bright morning light filling the dorm room, courtesy of Charmindy, who opens the blinds before she leaves. Sloughing off the hangover from the pills I took the night before doesn't get easier. I follow this routine until Friday. The only thing getting me out of the dorm is the possibility that the girl I'm painting in the studio will start to look like me.

Chapter 27

The black sedan retraces the same route that carried me away from my old life and my mother, so many months ago.

As I approach Manhattan, the glare of the setting sun makes it so I can see my reflection in the car window. I'm imprinted on the skyline, but the girl doesn't look quite like me. Once a person visits New York City, the pulse, the chaos, the characters never leave; maybe I'll find myself there. A single tear drops from my eye, running down the inside of the door like a raindrop, then disappearing.

The car leaves me in front of the Saint Regis. Apparently, my uncle wanted to avoid media involvement at his home if word got out, so he has us staying in a hotel.

I take a deep breath of the city air, diesel and charred pretzels, steam from the vents in the sidewalk, and the aromatic scent of perfumed spring blossoms. It smells like home, and for a minute, I consider bolting. I could make it here. I always have. I could find a job. If my mother found places to stay, so can I.

Before I move, my aunt's unmistakable, shrill voice carries over the city's song of honking cars and chattering passersby. "Pearl, Pearl." She teeters on heels at the entrance to the hotel, her hand impatiently on her hip. She gives me an awkward hug. A thought buzzes from the back of my mind. *Why didn't anyone call me this week?* The dorm has phones. They all have phones. Yes, Janet was Gary's sister, but she was my mother. I am the daughter of the deceased. I have no one to lean on.

"So glad you're here," she pipes.

Surely, she means the opposite. I've always had the impression the Jaegers consider me an annoying extension of my mother. Someone they have to tolerate and take responsibility for, because Janet failed and left them with the mess to clean up.

When we enter the lobby, my uncle stands stiffly beside fronded plants and a sectional where my cousins wait, eyes glued to their phones.

"Hi, Pearl," Erica says softly when I approach.

Uncle Gary and his duplicate, Logan, allow her singular greeting to speak for the group.

After the elevator dings for the ninth floor, I walk a few paces behind them. My aunt whispers to my uncle, "Those are not the garments I sent her in the fall."

I'm used to her passive insults, but as tough as I can be on the exterior, JJ's death has disarmed me, leaving me soft and vulnerable like cartilage. It isn't so much what Aunt Beverly says, but how she says it. I hear in her voice that I'm not good enough and never will be.

"We're going to the wake and then out for something to eat. Freshen up," Uncle Gary orders when we arrive at the suite with an adjoining room for Erica and Logan.

"Looks like she could use a bath. She should wash her hair while she's at it. It's so stringy," my aunt mutters.

I welcome the city sounds to penetrate the quiet in the car that brings us directly from the hotel to the funeral home. As we cross town, I call upon a memory or moment of significance from nearly every block we pass. I yearn to jump out of the car, throw myself on the familiar pavement, crawl away, and lick my wounds.

Pearl

The eerie quiet of the funeral home, even with the conciliatory music emanating from somewhere unseen, troubles me. Or maybe it's just the peculiar stillness of death.

Lilies decorate the small viewing room, and lines of empty chairs lead to my mother's long ebony casket. I choke on tears. The hinges are closed. I half expected it to be open. I almost want it to be. I want to see her one last time. To see the scar that was sure to have formed by her eye—thanks to Darren. To see her eyebrows, which she religiously plucked. To count the earrings that reached up her ear. I want to hold her hand. To hold her hand one last time. My body racks with soundless sobs.

My uncle barks, "Don't be so dramatic, Pearl."

My legs grow weak. I slump in a chair opposite the aisle where everyone else sits. I don't appreciate the tattoo of judgment written on my uncle's and aunt's faces.

In front of the casket, I kneel and tilt my head up. Beyond the ceiling, I imagine the sky. For a second I think the world holds its breath, but it's me. From deep within, I let out a howl. The sound of an animal. The cry of loss.

Sadness continues to flood me, then like a boomerang, it whips back on itself, and anger takes its place. *Why did she have to ruin her life and mine?* The question isn't rhetorical; it's indignation. Then sadness returns. The two emotions struggle with each other, each battling for my attention as the room and people behind me disappear. Only my mother and all my feelings remain, as they so often have.

A hand grips my shoulder. "Time to go," a man in a gray suit says.

A black awning attached to the brownstone protects everyone from the drizzle as they get into the awaiting sedan. I step to the edge of the outdoor carpet that lies beneath the awning and then out into the rain. I let its cold darts fall upon me, joining my tears.

"Come on, Pearl," my uncle calls.

187

Back at the hotel, after a shower, I riffle through my aunt's toiletry bag, looking for anything that will ameliorate the weekend. I strike gold when I find a ziplock bag filled with aspirin, allergy pills, and a slew of drugs for those perpetually craving more, better, bigger, along with a bottle of painkillers. It's full and nearing the expiration date, but I don't care. *Oblivion.*

The next morning the digital clock reads six when I hear my uncle in the bathroom. I roll over, hoping to doze back off, but they're early risers, and Beverly will surely have something to say about how lazy I am if I don't look lively. I dress and ask my aunt if she minds if I take a walk. She looks uncertain.

"We used to live just down the street. I know my way around. I'll be back in a little while."

"We have to go collect some of your mother's things this morning, and then we have the burial after lunch. There's a meeting late this afternoon that you must attend, and then dinner tonight, of course." She lists these items like a travel itinerary. "Be back before noon," she says as if I won't be missed.

It occurs to me that when word gets out JJ of the Shrapnels passed away, superfans might crawl out of the woodwork, lighting candles and leaving notes like they did when Nell died. I assume Uncle Gary wants to make quick work of this to avoid media attention—and probably get on with his life. It isn't lost on me, the burden she's caused. Part of me hates him for this, and another part feels relieved. I don't want to share my grief with strangers who adored the stage JJ. It's hard enough sorting through the versions of her that I knew.

I throw on my coat, grab my backpack, and scoot out the door before anyone can say otherwise.

The unique vibe present at nearly every other time of day lies tucked away behind concrete and glass in the secret early morning world of Manhattan. The air and light speak of hope and promise. If I squint my eyes toward the horizon, I might just believe anything is possible; it is, after all, the city of dreams. I want it to fill me, to soak it in, to know that the city hasn't given up on me.

I wander past the hotel with no specific destination in mind. I want to be alone with the sidewalks, my memories, and sadness.

I walk briskly down Fifth Avenue, keeping my eyes off the display windows, feeling out of place along this stretch of road. I need to be somewhere more honest and raw, if for nothing more than to play against the deceit of my family.

Ahead, I see the New York Public Library and recall the hours, days, and what may as well have amounted to years spent within its gilded walls. The reason why I sought refuge in its vast quantities of fiction and art and costume permeates another layer of sadness and anger. I fled my mother and her antics when she smoked crack, cocaine, or heroin, going to the quiet of the library, a symbol of normalcy.

Janet never picked up more than a magazine—one of my *Vogues*. She chucked it at me because I didn't hear her ask me to take out the trash. As much as I want her back, countless reasons and occasions during which I retreated from her and wished her away deluge my consciousness.

Janet was like a roller coaster ride, thrilling and dangerous, up and down. When the tracks leveled out at the end of the day or week or month and I realized I'd made it, I found myself laughing with relief. But the ride has come to a sudden end, and the tracks and cars wrap into a knot of confusion in my mind.

The green of Bryant Park presents itself, and after a stampede of moms pass, pushing strollers, I plop down on a bench. A single leaf blows across the toes of my boots, then catches in the low fence that surrounds a patch of grass. A bum rests on another bench about twenty feet away. A jogger skirts the outside perimeter, heading toward Sixth Avenue. I usually coexist with the city and people, but today I feel disconnected, like there's no dial tone and nothing to say anyway.

I look out across the lawn, and the silhouette of an indie film festival shines from the summer, just days before we fled to the battered women's shelter. I'd gone with some friends; their nearly forgotten faces slide one by one into the viewfinder of my mind.

Gino and Ali, Turner, Wyatt, Adriana, and me. Our picnic consisted of cheap wine we drank out of plastic soda bottles. All around, sophisticated groups of young people and old sipped iced Arnold Palmers, enjoyed trays of cheese and smoked meats, crackers, and grapes. We got rowdy, then shushed until someone complained and security told us to leave. Later, we found a hot tub party and then danced and danced until we were dry. It was one of those magical New York nights when nothing could dim the light of the moon except the rising sun.

I circle the park, my mother more present than in real life as the city recalls my memories. As I walk back to the hotel, she follows me, a devil on each shoulder, whispering both good times and bad in my ears, teasing me to chase thrills and reexperience the emotional details as a way to preserve the past. These recycled feelings insult the crushing pain I already endure.

I'm a few hours later than my aunt said I should be back. I knock on the solid wooden door of the hotel room, and my uncle answers it with a stormy look on his face.

"Where've you been, Janet?"

"I took a—" I stop, realizing he mistakenly called me Janet. My mother. The blunder drives home the point that in many ways, in the collective mind of my family of origin, she and I are one and the same. "My name is Pearl."

His eyes cast around darkly, as if I'm to blame for being me.

I take a shower and contemplate popping one of the shiny red pills from the stash in the travel bag, but resist; it will be better to be lucid when we lay my mother to rest and for the meeting. *I can wait just a little longer*, I assure my sullen heart.

Chapter 28

After an uninspired lunch, the long black hearse leads our depressing two-car procession out of the city to the cemetery.

My mother had long since dispensed with what one might call friends. She certainly had enemies and hangers-on, people she partied with, but in one way or another, she'd burned everyone she ever knew. My uncle would not have the inclination to let any of those people know she died. But it's only a matter of time before the press gets wind that former rock star Janet Jaeger overdosed on drugs, at least that's what I assume. I can see the TV segment now, a glossy montage of photos, JJ equal parts a spotlight darling and irreverently flipping off the cameras.

As if pressing the brakes and screeching to a halt, I suddenly wonder who found her. *Who was she with when it happened? Or was she alone? Who was the last person to see her take a breath?* Tears fall freely from my eyes as we cross the bridge; the skyline rises away from us like a glassy, geometric wave at our backs.

At the cemetery, I stagger across the path, putting distance between the group and myself. The cloud-smudged sky, rows and rows of granite headstones, and my ashen heart are like a black-and-white photo, a snapshot captured during some other lifetime.

At the family plot, where my grandparents were laid to rest years ago, the box containing my mother is a blemish. This is all wrong. I want to throw myself on top of the casket, bang my fists, and shout, "Wake up. We weren't done here." But as if stapled to that old photograph, I'm frozen in time, unmoving, the contrast between then and now.

I toss a single lily on top of the ebony casket as they lower it into the earth. As the casket alights, I shake with grief, drop to my knees in the soggy grass, and sob. The men in the family singe me with looks of disgust. They'll never understand. They haven't survived the battlefield of her life. Aunt Beverly avoids looking at me altogether. I turn away, but then a pair of arms grips me, pulling me to my feet, and Erica hugs me, her muffled sob echoing my own.

Overhead, the laden clouds burst with rain as if exhausted by the sheer effort of trying to hold back their reservoir of grief. Enormous droplets thrust themselves toward the ground, painting everything wet like tears.

The rain and her absence, a character cut from the play of my life, further mute the ride back into the city. *What caused her to drop away? Was there one pivotal moment that turned her forever?* She wasn't a bad person, not really; she just made bad choices. I want to believe that. Buried deep under years of resentment, dishonesty, and anger, the answers hide, lost forever. I rest my head against the seat and close my eyes. As usual, my mother waits for me behind my lids.

Grainy slide-like memories of my mother looking past me with dark, unblinking eyes, her face twisted and gray, when she appeared at my elementary school on drugs and incoherent. I still feel the humiliation in my bones like fractured rock. When I look up, disoriented, like waking from a bad dream, we pass the very same school. A carved sign fixed upon its brick facade reads *P.S. 7*, and crushes me beneath its weight.

The car stops in front of a towering glass office building. Uncle Gary gets out, beckons me, and waves his family away, which can only mean one thing: I'm the subject of the meeting my aunt mentioned.

On the sixteenth floor, I follow my uncle down a long corridor that ends with a door bearing the names *Lawrence, Sanders, Sloan, and Associates, Attorneys at Law.*

In the silence of a small conference room, a slight man, with a ring of dark hair above his ears, wearing a suit and tie, takes a seat at the head of the table. He and Uncle Gary greet each other with a handshake.

"I'm Brandt Sanders," he says in a monotone as he opens a folder. "Alrighty, this should be simple enough. I see the deceased, Ms. Janet Jaeger, did not have a will or any bequests. She had no property, assets, or savings." He glances at my uncle, perhaps to let this fact settle or invite a correction.

"She did receive a quarterly royalty check." Brandt tilts his head, reading. "It isn't much, but it will be transferred to Miss Pearl Jaeger, the deceased's daughter." He looks around the room as if it could be anyone but me. He angles his pen in my direction. "That's you?"

I nod.

"Alrighty." Brandt flips through more papers. "However, you will not be able to receive the monies from these quarterly checks until you are eighteen. They will accumulate in an account set up by your uncle, Gary Jaeger, until that time comes, which is—" He looks at the papers again. "In approximately eight months. Until then there is also the matter of your custody."

My uncle clears his throat. "I am willing to continue funding her high school education at Laurel Hill Preparatory School as long as she remains on the honor roll and stays out of trouble." He directs this at the lawyer, not looking at me.

"Very generous of you. Do you understand, Miss Jaeger?"

"Yes." My voice squeaks from disuse.

"As for the summer and vacations, where will she reside?" Brandt asks.

"This summer she may go to a summer school program that I will also fund as long as my conditions continue to be met."

"Is this clear?" Brandt asks me.

I nod.

"Will you also be providing her with transportation to and from Laurel Hill Preparatory School?"

"Yes." My uncle nods.

"As for holiday vacations?" Brandt adds notes to his file.

"Primarily she will remain on campus when that is an option, or my house," my uncle says as if I'm not in the room.

"Alrighty," Brandt says. He scribbles on a notepad. "Let me see, anything else?"

A wailing siren stories below pierces the silence in the room.

Brandt passes me a pen. "This first document you will be signing acknowledges the royalty checks. It also indicates your uncle will provide you with a monthly allowance of one hundred dollars to use at your discretion, but intended for school supplies, clothing, and other necessities. Initial here, here, and here." He gestures impatiently on the form.

"This next document is an acknowledgment that you understand your uncle's parameters for funding the remainder of your high school education, including summer school and any other education or enrichment programs you pursue between now and June of next year.

"Finally, these last papers are custody documents," he says, sliding the papers across the table. "These will become null and void on Miss Jaeger's eighteenth birthday, when she becomes a legal adult; however, the education stipulations will remain in effect until the following June, upon her graduation." After signing, he shuffles the papers into a neat pile and says, "Alrighty. That's done. Enjoy the rest of your day."

The silence we carry through the building as we leave follows us into the car, quietly punctuating how I hardly exist. And yet, my uncle offered to pay for my education. *Where was he all those times I really needed him?* Like when I had the flu and we stayed in Janet's friend's apartment without leaving for three days, until a stray bullet came through the wall. Or the time, while drunk, Janet fell down the cement stairs in the subway. *Why didn't he intervene before the worst-case scenario became reality?*

However, reasoning with Janet was useless. She couldn't distinguish between the truth and the stories she told herself—that she was a victim, that everyone was out to get her, that everything was someone else's fault, that no one was to be trusted.

Then another thought jolts me. I was just a kid, an innocent bystander, the monkey in her show. Now when it's too late and she's dead, he has finally gotten involved. *Does my uncle harbor guilt? Does he feel sorry for me? Is he just doing what he thinks is right? Does he actually hold on to hope for my future?*

I flounder in a sea of unasked and unanswered questions until I feel like I might drown. I sink and sink, giving in to what-ifs until the door opens and light from the marquee of an upscale restaurant floods the dark interior of the car.

In a dimly lit restaurant, with lots of linen and bits of food arranged like architecture projects gone awry, a server fills my glass. The menu doesn't interest me. I haven't been hungry for weeks. Nonetheless, I order pasta primavera. The meal takes on an asphyxiating quality when Uncle Gary and Logan discuss the lineup for the Yankees. My aunt studies the wine list, commenting on a bottle of sauvignon blanc to no one in particular.

Forks and knives clatter on the dishware. I close my eyes, as if by not seeing them, I won't be able to hear them talking about something pointless while my world implodes.

I clear my throat. "So how did it happen?"

My uncle shovels steak into his mouth. My aunt takes a liberal sip of wine. Logan cuts a chunk from his steak. Erica stares at her plate.

"I'd like to know how my mother died," I say more loudly.

A fork rattles.

"Not over dinner," Aunt Beverly says.

My uncle shakes his head harshly. "No, she ought to know." His tone stabs the air like the knife in Logan's hand. He looks pasty and foul.

"Janet was found in an abandoned building down in the Bowery. She had a needle sticking out of her arm. She was lying in a pile of her own filth. The autopsy report stated that she overdosed. She also had HIV, and her liver was failing. In the last few months, records show an arrest for drunken and disorderly conduct. She'd been admitted to the emergency rooms of no less than three city hospitals, requesting pain medication. Janet had been in a house where cops found two kilos of cocaine. She had been on suicide watch at a psych ward, and a passenger in a stolen car." He pauses, nearly out of breath, his face blotchy and the color of eggplant. "That's what happened. That was your mother's life, Pearl. That is your inheritance."

A tear trickles down my face as I recall the last conversation she and I had before I left. She'd begged me not to go away to school. She promised sobriety and a new life, that we'd have an apartment of our own again. *If I hadn't left, would she still be alive? Would I have been able to protect her from herself?*

As soon as we get back to the hotel, I swallow one of the red pills. I'll do anything to escape the pain of the burial, the trip to the lawyer's office, the scene in the restaurant, and the truth. I want to cancel today, yesterday, and this entire year. I'd like to grab an eraser and, with nice, clean sweeps, brush everything away, leaving nothing but satisfying puffs of chalk dust. Instead, I curl into a ball and quietly cry until the pill forces sleep.

The next morning I wake up to my uncle in the bathroom again. I'd rather be in my bed at Laurel Hill. After I get dressed, I tell my aunt I'm going to grab a coffee.

"We're having breakfast downstairs at nine sharp." Her pallor suggests all the wine she drank gave her a hangover, and the set of her mouth lists somewhere near regret, but probably more from having to be here with me than the alcohol.

I bolt out the door. I want New York to myself one more time. I hail a cab and direct the driver to take me to the Bowery district.

I stand on the sidewalk among the still-shuttered stores. A garbage truck belches smoke and chugs along the street as men in orange vests toss black trash bags into the cavernous maw of the vehicle. I want to clear my head. I want my lump of confusing thoughts to be as easily disposed of as the trash.

I look from brick to stone to wood and concrete, wondering which building it was and who found her. *Was it the police? Someone she used drugs with?* I exhale the unanswerable questions and flag down another cab.

After breakfast, back at the hotel, Erica says, "I have something to give you." Tourists and businesspeople shuttle past as we wait for the elevator.

Up in the room, she hands me a paper shopping bag. "Here, these were your mom's things," she says. "Aunt Janet was really funny. She always made me laugh, well, when I was younger. I'm sorry, Pearl."

I grip Erica in a hug, belatedly realizing that she's the only family I have left who'd return the embrace.

I don't dare look in the bag just then. I stuff it in my backpack and rush out to the car waiting to ferry me back to school.

As the city falls away, I outline what I learned will be my life for the next year and a half. Stay in school, get good grades, stay out of trouble, and receive a monthly stipend. Go to summer school and back to Laurel Hill. It seems straightforward enough. Far better than the streets, but I already miss the freedom of my old life, being able to come and go as I please; spontaneously roaming from apartment to parties, basements, clubs, or rooftops with my friends; and having something like a mother to return to.

I tell myself to stay focused. Beyond graduation, the future flies in the wind like a kite. I have no option other than to keep aloft, because now there's something to lose and a legacy I have no interest in fulfilling. Yet, there's an ache, a weight inside, anchoring me to the ground and I'm afraid of sinking, sinking, sinking.

Chapter 29

Back in my dorm room, I drop my backpack by the door. I open the paper bag and pull out a pair of sunglasses; my mother was fanatical about wearing them. She sat on, lost, or otherwise broke every pair she owned or stole. I slide them on my face, and the room darkens.

I reach into the bag again, and my fingers rest on a slim silver ring, which I gave her back in kindergarten. Actually, it was pewter, which we found out when the guy behind the counter at a pawnshop said he'd give her fifty cents for it. It was worth two dollars at the little Christmas bazaar my elementary school held as a fund-raiser. After a yearlong drug binge, she'd lost so much weight the ring fell off her finger. From then on, she wore it around her neck. I take it off the chain and slide it on my ring finger, but it doesn't fit. I try my middle finger, then my pointer, and finally my thumb, where it stays put after I push it over the knuckle.

I pull out a CD with a familiar album cover, a miniature version of JJ's favorite LP, *Pearl*. I laugh. Janet upgraded to compact discs. She'd only ever listened to vinyl, claiming it was more authentic. I cross the room to Charmindy's stereo and slide it in.

At the bottom of the bag are two envelopes bound in a rubber band, a couple of the letters I'd written to her when I started at Laurel

Hill. She must have lost or not received the others. On the top, there's an ID, a savings card for a discount liquor store, and a wrinkled photo of me with a six-year-old smile, missing teeth, and bangs. I would like to paint it, as if by capturing some of that blissful innocence and letting it dry on canvas, I can reclaim it for my own. The child's smile tells me she's unaware of how her mom will crash, how she'll be the only remaining visitor to the world JJ left in ruin, and how, because of that, she won't even recognize herself.

I smooth the fringe on my forehead. A deep gouge rends the center of my chest as I gaze at that picture, Janis's smoky voice singing "Cry Baby" from across the room. Tears, impossibly hot and heavy, drop from my eyes. With desperate hands, I take one of the red pills. *Oblivion.* I curl up on the bed, clutching the bundle to my chest, and the last thing I remember is "Tell Mama" playing from the stereo.

Buds emerge from the branches on trees, daffodils poke through the fragrant mud, and the suddenly lively student body suggests spring fever wafts close in the air. For me it feels like the longest, darkest season has just begun. I avoid eye contact and small talk. I bury my nose in books, the inky lines blurring together. I gaze at my shoes and the remaining mounds of melting snow bleeding into the cracks in the cement.

I avoid facing Charmindy in the dorm, which isn't hard because she's so busy. But while trudging to Painting IV one morning, she catches up with me. "Listen, I know I've been giving you the cold shoulder. I can't imagine what you're going through. What you went through. When Terran said all those things about you and your mom, I was upset, but not about that. Of course not." She shrugs. "You couldn't control anything she did, any better than we can convince Shale to give us passing grades. But I was disappointed you didn't tell me about your mom. It's kind of a big deal, you know? You could probably navigate the streets of Chennai with all the stories I've told you. It stung that you never shared parts of your life with me. That's what friends do."

I feel a drip, drip, drip as part of me thaws. I don't smile, but have the memory of one. Stopping midstride, I wrap my arms around her, holding tight, thankful for once, finally, to sorta be understood.

When I pull away, she lifts one eyebrow. "Wow, a hug from you. That's a good start." But beneath her no-nonsense exterior, I know she squeezed just as hard.

In Shale's tardiness to Painting IV that day, the students gum up the courage to chat. I talk with Charmindy about how, since my aunt and uncle want to send me to summer school, I've been filling out applications. I'm only applying to the ones in New York City.

"I hoped to do this art program at Parsons. It's hard to get in, though, plus I don't think my aunt and uncle would approve. It wasn't on their list."

"At least they don't want you to be a doctor."

"No, they probably think I need to see one, though." I'm sticking out my tongue and rolling my eyes, making a funny face, when I realize the room is silent. There's a grunt at my shoulder, and I get back to work, painting my six-year-old self from memory.

After class, Charmindy says, "I have no idea how you get away with not painting, then doing a really shoddy version of the assignment, then painting the most depressing self-portrait I've ever seen, and now, copying that photo of yourself you hide in your desk drawer."

I'm surprised she noticed.

"The assignment is to do a self-portrait. Plain and simple. He didn't say anything about reinterpreting the term *self-portrait*," she adds.

I remember him commenting on how he doesn't adhere to any rules. Perhaps in a sly way, he's pushing us to see if we'll bend our assumption of what he meant and arrive at the liberating frontier of no rules with a blank canvas. Freedom to let our artistic selves shine through. Either that or he pities me, the moody orphan girl.

In the following weeks, I put in the minimal amount of effort to maintain my grades, Charmindy urging me along. Sorel, Pepper, and Grant make their appearances, but still shrouded beneath grief, confusion, and an assortment of pills, I pour what little energy I have into studying, if only to stay in Uncle Gary's favor.

In early May, Charmindy becomes a relative stranger, caught up with studying and Brett, and, I'll admit, maybe it's because when I'm in our room, I'm knit into my bed and Janis's album plays on repeat in her CD player. I don't blame her. Otherwise, I'm in the studio, emptying the tubes of oil and pigment.

Dr. Greenbrae calls me into his office several times, but the pills keep me in a constant daze, and I remain unbothered by little more than my own infinite sadness and the lines of paint I can't seem to wash from beneath my nails.

Sorel catches me in the library one afternoon. "Pearl."

"Yeah," I say, rereading the sentence she interrupted.

"Frickin' look at me, will ya?" she hisses.

I slowly lift my head; it feels full of the fluffy seeds of a thousand dandelions.

"Prom is in a couple weeks, then graduation," she starts.

The word *prom*, coming out of her mouth, does not elicit the response I assume she'd hoped for.

She clears her throat. "And, well, we miss hanging out with you." She shifts in her chair. "I, uh, I'm not sure what's going on."

Exactly everything and nothing at all are *going on*.

Sore exhales sharply when I don't respond. "We never see you anymore; you don't come to breakfast, lunch, or dinner. You're, like, wasting away."

I shrug. I sense her interest waning. I want the comfort of her presence, but quietly, like holding hands. Conversation risks the reminder that I'm still here and Janet isn't.

"Anyway, I picked out a dress for prom, Pepper's my date," she says. I imagine the smirk outlining her lips, like it would have been any other way.

Her chair squeaks across the floor as if she's moving to get up. I'm losing her.

Without looking up from my book, I say, "You're going to prom? I pegged you for an anti-prom crusader." I think of my anti–Valentine's day idea. It seems like a million years ago, when dinosaurs roamed the earth.

I glance up. Sorel's grown rounder than I remember her being, or maybe that's because I'm disappearing like a balloon; snip the string, and I'll float away.

"Just this once," she says. "Anyway, my dress is black. I want you to see it."

"Of course." I rest my head in my hand, hardly able to hold it up.

"Pepper says Grant's been mopey lately. He misses you."

"I miss me," I say, closing my eyes.

Sorel snorts. "Graduation is soon. Good-bye, Laurel Hill." She pauses and fiddles with the snap of a leather cuff around her wrist. "Hey, what are you doing this summer?"

I blink open my eyes, realizing I still haven't received acceptance letters to summer school. My uncle probably intercepted them, and a car will appear and chauffeur me to an unknown destination. "I don't really know."

"You should visit me in Seattle."

"Not likely. I'm in my uncle's custody now. Straight As or—" I search my mind for the *or*, then look down at an image in my textbook. "The guillotine."

Sorel laughs. "Will you come to my grad party?"

"If I can."

"I'll sort the details." She winks, and her mischievous smile suggests it'll happen. "Oh, and do Grant a favor and let him know you're still alive. OK?"

Chapter 30

I remain conscious for final-exam week, again, my stash of pills dwindling. I'm not sure how I function with them, but can't imagine having to deal without them. Charmindy lingers in the room more frequently than usual, her nose tucked in a book, studying like mad. Even though all I hear are the rustle of pages and the click clack of keys on her laptop, her neck bent with tension and her back to me, her presence reminds me I'm not as alone as I think I am. I wonder if it's because she noticed I'm sort of becoming translucent and she's concerned. Or maybe someone said to keep watch over me so I don't straight up disappear.

Shale gives us until six in the evening to hand in the self-portrait. I have eight to choose from. As I climb the stairs to the studio, I consider whether I'll give him one of the sparse images—really just slashes of blue paint on the white canvas—one from the darkest time of my despair, the six-year-old version of me, or one done more recently, which almost looks like I'm fading into the paint.

I flip on the studio light, then spot Shale, sitting under his desk lamp, immersed in a book. He doesn't look up when I haul out my canvases, inspecting each one.

He grunts over my shoulder. "I thought you told me you were here to paint honestly."

"This is one version of the truth."

If I didn't know better, I'd think his lips twitched with amusement. "You'll pass, but barely."

I jerk my head around. "What? Just barely pass? No one else painted eight portraits. That should count for something."

"No one else is you, Pearl Jaeger." He strokes his beard as he studies each painting. "You haven't pushed your boundaries yet. You can do better."

"I put everything into those. I . . . I . . . it was tormenting. Could you possibly try to understand what I've been going through this semester?"

"I want to see who you are, not who you think you are. This—" He shakes his head. "This isn't you."

"How would you know? You don't know me."

"Yes and no." He tilts his head like he's weighing his words. "I know you are moody, confused, that you are sensitive and kind. I know that you've endured more than most, but less than some."

His pause is long. "I know you because you are me. I am you. We are the same. Almost. The only difference is I accept this"—he gestures to himself, patting his chest with the tips of his fingers—"this messiness, this uneasiness, the uncertainty, and even on some days, the goodness here." He shrugs as if what he means is obvious.

I want the static in my head to quiet. He has no idea who I am. He has no right to insult my work.

"You make art. You make good art, Pearl. Someday you will make great art, I believe. But that is only if you are willing to compose it from your blood, sweat, tears, from ugliness and beauty, freely, without boundaries and expectations and ego."

He pauses, as though letting each word saturate me. "How do you do that? It's simple really. The only enemy you have is yourself. Stay there, with her, until you aren't enemies anymore."

All I hear is rhetoric, hyperbole, nonsense. "I have no idea what you're talking about."

"I hope you will."

I suddenly feel like Shale is too close, not in the way Mitch was but close to me in another way. I need to be outside or in my dorm or fading away, numb from images and imaginings of the truth. I gather up my dumped bag, and the Parsons catalog refuses to go back in. I'm not sure I want to go to the design program in New York anymore. I'm afraid. It's too risky. There's too much there that could undo me. My pulse throbs in my ears, and I feel flighty, like the ground slips away beneath me. I start to leave.

"Should I be pleased to know whether you got in?" He nods at my backpack, at the catalog.

"Yeah. But uh—" I want to race away, far away, but I don't know where to go, other than the place the pills bring me.

"I spoke with one of my friends, a professor there. She was impressed with your sketches, but I think your home is with oils."

"I don't know where my home is, but I'm not sure it's the city, and it's not—" I back toward the door, away from his gray eyes, away from so many reflections, versions of myself.

He interrupts, pointing at the array of paintings. "Which one do you want to pass in?"

I glance back. "None of them."

"I can't give you a grade if you do not give me one."

I don't answer. I'll take the fail, because right now I feel like I'm falling again and the only safe place to land is in my bed.

I toss a pill in my mouth, hoping to fade away. Too many of Shale's words jumble and repeat in my thoughts. I can't escape the sharp smell of turpentine piercing my nose. My breath is shallow as I curl into a ball and then stretch out and then toss onto my back. I want away, away, away, but all I can do is stay, burdened by pills and words and gravity.

I have no idea how much time has passed, when, near the foot of my bed, Sorel stuffs clothing into my backpack.

"What are you doing?" I ask. My tongue is thick.

"Breaking you outta here. Graduation. Tomorrow. Yeehaw!"

"But my uncle." I roll onto my side.

"Not to worry, been taken care of. I got their address from Connie and sent them a sparkly little graduation party invitation with flowers on it."

"And?"

"It had the RSVP info, and your aunt, well, she's got something up her ass, but after some sweet schoolgirl charm, she consented to have you go to the weekend fiesta at my family's lake house in the mountains, then return to my parents' house in Virginia for the remainder of the week, until you go to summer school. That's option *one* anyway."

I raise my eyebrows. The plan has my attention. I admire her moxie. I sit up. "There's another option?" I ask, unused to choices as of late.

"Two, actually," she says mischievously.

"They are?"

"You could go back to their place and hang with what sounds like the tightest couple of people on the planet, and that's saying something. Wait until you meet my parents. Or—" She pauses for dramatic effect. "You can remember me always as your nearest and dearest friend and go stay with Grant and his brother for the rest of the week in New York City. But, of course, no one needs to know that."

"Sorel, I don't understand, how did—? What did—" But I can't say any more; my eyes mist, and my lips tremble.

"Don't cry, PJ. Was it the wrong thing to do?" Sorel asks with an uncharacteristic gentleness in her voice.

I cover my face.

"PJ, I can call them back, if—" She interrupts herself. "Did something happen between you and Grant? I just thought it would be fun after everything you've been through."

I sweep my arms around her. I cry into what looks like the beginning of dreadlocks in her raven-dark hair. She hugs me stiffly in return, as if she isn't used to the exchange of affection, from me anyway.

"Sorel," I say between sobs, "that's the nicest, most thoughtful thing anyone has ever done for me."

She looks taken aback. "Really? You're that easy? A phone call and a fuck and you're driven to tears," she says brashly.

"Really." I swallow hard and wipe my eyes. "I've been going it alone for most of my life. I mean like *alone* alone. No sweetness, y'know?"

"Yeah, well, money isn't always good company either."

"Sappiness aside, that was really nice of you, and yeah, they suck," I say, referring to my aunt and uncle.

"No more sulking. I mean, mope if you really want to, but after I snag that diploma tomorrow, you and I are on our way to freedom." She cheers. "But get packing, because the Volvo doesn't wait for late arrivals. Oh, but first you'll need to endure lunch with my parents," she says sardonically.

A sliver of hope, borne on the kindness of a friend, creeps into the muddy, darkened corners of my mind.

After Sorel leaves, I try to pull myself fully out of the depths of mental muck. I idly fold my clothing and pack up the few incidental items I've accumulated. I reach up to the shelf in my closet for the cardboard box and return my magazine collection, trinkets, and the stuffed bear. I roll up the Shrapnels poster and tuck Frida away.

When the sun takes its leave for the day, I wander down to the common room and find Charmindy gathered with a bunch of other girls from the dorm; they're talking over a movie and eating popcorn. The room quiets when I enter. Charmindy brightens. "Want some popcorn?" She holds out the bowl.

I can almost hear the boos and feel the rotten tomatoes sailing my way from the audience. But no one says anything, which is almost worse. Then I catch a few flickering smiles and not the insulting, surly kind.

My lips turn up. "Thanks," I say, belatedly answering Charmindy. I take a handful of the popcorn and settle on the arm of one of the couches.

Along with most of the other girls, I wear flannel pajama bottoms and a T-shirt, but our similarities end there. They all seem comfortable with one another, swapping stories and laughter like they belong. Via Charmindy, I have a visa to their world, but I feel like I'll never be a citizen.

On one level, I connect with Sorel, Charmindy on another, the kids from back in the city too, and then Grant, wonderful Grant. Even if he doesn't understand me, it's like he accepts me without question. That's rare and maybe special. Part of me wants a place in this room full of normal girls, with their braids and lip gloss. Molly talks about how much she loves Charmindy's thick, lush hair, while Rhodesia bubbles with delight about a boy.

The untamed side of me, the one raised by wolves, regards their chatter as so trivial I almost feel embarrassed for them.

Despite this, Viv Brooks is the best place I've ever lived, with its reliable electricity and warm running water. It's safe and clean. The people are mostly kind, except Terran and her cohorts. She sits across the room, pretentious and glaring, but she'll graduate tomorrow. It isn't likely I'll ever see her again. I take in the pendant in the shape of a star around her neck, glittering in the lambent light of the TV screen. The necklace she'd claimed had gone missing. I suppose lost things have a way of turning up.

I slide onto the couch I've been perched on and help myself to another handful of popcorn. I half listen to the conversation, half watch the movie, and at least from the outside, it might look like I belong.

Later, I forgo a pill, but sleep proves elusive. My mind repeatedly crash-lands on memories. The kernels of popcorn roll and burst in my otherwise empty stomach. The ridges of my hips press into the mattress beneath me. I recall my mother's near-skeletal body, bone thin and skin sagging.

I hear a whisper; maybe it's my heart. *I belong with me.* I almost instantly forget it, but like a seed planted in fertile earth, those words dig down, preparing the ground to help me reclaim my mind, heart, and body. What little I have amounts to those three things, and they are mine and mine alone.

Chapter 31

The sun streams in, warming me, and I recall my turbulent night: the jostle of stale thoughts, the currents of uncertainty, and the velocity of time moving me forward when I haven't let go, creating drag.

After a shower, I pull on a pair of ruby-striped leggings, a belted minidress, and boots, along with my denim jacket, an appropriate-enough outfit for graduation day. I swipe on my *Diva* red lipstick and blink under my curtain of bangs and brows, suddenly afraid of the girl I see in the mirror.

I step out into the morning sun. Crystalline fragments of light sprinkle the dewy leaves of the trees like jewels. The new day brings a semi-clear mind. Or maybe it's the lack of a pill coursing through my system that's untangled my thoughts. I'll go to the dining hall. I'll eat breakfast. Maybe I'll even interact with humanity. Simple. Straightforward.

I settle into a corner table with a bowl of oatmeal, a banana, and a coffee. As I take a sip, I watch parents and students, grandparents, and siblings wander in and out of the dining hall, eating omelets made-to-order, homemade coffee cake, pancakes, and waffles. The syrupy smell invites a kind of nostalgia I've never had before.

Grant saunters through the wooden double doors. It's been a while since I've seen him properly. Of course, there's the back of his head in math, but otherwise I've steered clear, afraid of what he'll see if he gazes too long at me. Since the news of my mother, I haven't looked much beyond the sidewalk, books, and homework, or my internal longings.

He towers several inches taller than most of the people in the room, but he hides behind his long hair. He wears jeans and a slate-colored sweatshirt and carries a book. I watch him dispense cereal, select a banana out of the basket, and pour himself a cup of coffee.

He subtly scans the dining hall, not scowling but not smiling either. When his eyes find me, they sparkle, and he quickly strides in my direction.

Just a few feet away, his sad smile slides across his face as if I'm a mirage that might vanish if he comes any closer. It's the same smile from the night we collapsed in the snow, our laughter whirling in the wind.

"Can I sit here?" he asks.

"Of course," I say, taking another sip of coffee.

"Good to see you," he says as he settles in, confident now that I'm real.

"You too."

"Ready for summer?" he asks.

"I guess so. You?"

"Back to Scotland for a couple of months, but first I'm going to spend a week in New York City with my brother. Maybe we could hang out while I'm there."

Sorel hasn't told him her plans. *What if it doesn't work out? Where will I stay? But what if it does work out?* My hands start to sweat next to the warmth of the coffee cup. Maybe she saved it as a surprise. He watches me, expectantly.

"That'd be great. I'll be at summer school there, so yeah." My lips feel like turning up at the corners.

Grant and I easily slip in and out of conversation. We exchange measured shyness, as though we're meeting for the first time all over again. I finish my coffee and set the mug on the tray. My eyes linger on him. He hasn't shaved in a while, the scruff coming in, just as I noticed when we left Montreal. His hand drums softly on the table. I recall those fingers trailing my shoulder, my neck, my cheek. I crave him and his touch.

"Sticking around to watch Sorel in her cap and gown?" he asks, looking up between bites, innocently unaware of my thoughts.

"I am." I look up, and there she is, wearing her usual uniform, a tatty combination of a black skirt, fishnet tights, and a shirt sticking out from beneath a snug sweater. "Speak of the devil," I say.

She flashes a mock look of anger at my comment. Pepper gets her breakfast like her own personal waiter. "I'm your angel, remember," she says, looking at me meaningfully, then at Grant. "So kids, after I tear off down the aisle with my diploma, we're going to have a fancy-shmancy lunch with my lovely and pleasant parents. You'll have to be on your best behavior. Easy on the swears, and no mention of parties, piracy, or any other high seas adventures. You catch?"

Grant raises his eyebrows, perhaps realizing we'll be sharing another meal together later.

Then Sorel says, "Kidding. I don't care what the frick you do." Her voice is louder than the polite dining hall chatter surrounding us. Pepper places a plate of eggs, sausage, and toast in front of Sorel. "We are going to have one kick-ass weekend," she declares as she jabs a slippery sausage with her fork.

I sit between Grant and Pepper on the bleachers relegated for students, while the parents and families sit in chairs on the lawn behind the graduating class. Amid cheering and clapping, my awareness pulls me to the warmth of Grant's leg leaning absently against mine. *How did I let all those months slip away from me?*

Grant still must like me; Sorel wouldn't have arranged the party otherwise, but worry creases my forehead. It's been months since we've had a meaningful conversation, since I've done more than simply exist. Maybe he doesn't want to be friends or talk. Maybe he just wants to . . . I'd settle for that too. But I wouldn't blame him; I don't always want to be friends with myself.

After Sorel makes a triumphant bound across the stage, doubt continues to niggle at me. When we return to the lawn a few golden-rod graduation programs scatter on the grass, lonely and abandoned. An abundance of hugging, crying, and shoulder slapping occupies the groups and pairs around me. I scan the crowd for Sorel to congratulate her, but Grant catches my attention. He's talking to a girl named Suzy from my Spanish class. I can't see his expression, but she grins flirta-tiously. I didn't know they knew each other, but then again, I haven't noticed much all spring. She laughs at something he says. A lump forms in my throat. Sorel said Grant used to hang around with a lot of girls; maybe Suzy was one of them.

I take a risk and slip my arm around Grant's back, grasping his side beneath my fingers. I could melt there, against him. I count the heartbeats hammering in my chest.

"Hey," he says like something he'd lost finally found its way back to him. He slides his arm over my shoulder. His smile is irrepressible.

I tilt my head up and flash him a question in the form of a smile, the first in a while. The world generously offers us a moment that is entirely our own. My surroundings fade away. Suzy's bouncy voice qui-ets, and it's just the two of us. His eyes are as blue as the sky and burn away every doubt, fear, and concern I've ever had in my life. It lasts mere seconds, but my heart records it forever.

Suzy clears her throat and flips her hair, reminding us she's there.

Sounds, smells, and activity return me to the sweeping field at Laurel Hill and this glorious day.

She looks impatiently at Grant. "So, will you think about it? We'll be there all weekend." Her gum snaps and pops.

"Uh," he mumbles, then turns back to me, his eyes twinkling like he's entranced.

"Have you seen Sorel?" I ask.

He doesn't speak, but his eyes say that he's seen *me*.

Suzy studies her manicure. She couldn't have known we were together, because up until that point, neither did I. She couldn't have known that the gesture, with my arm across Grant's back, my hip against his, and the smiles we exchanged act like adhesive. Grant had been waiting for me all this time, patiently, diligently, and wordlessly.

Chapter 32

Sorel honks for me outside Viv Brooks. Charmindy left the day before. We talked about sharing a room together senior year. I leave my suitcase and boxes in a neat pile next to hers in the center of the empty room, labeled with my name for storage. I close the door behind me.

Amped, Sorel bobs her head to a punk song.

I slide into the backseat next to Grant.

Sorel shouts, "Good riddance, Laurel Hill," followed by a cackle, and cranks the stereo higher.

We cruise for about a half hour before pulling into the parking lot of a white colonial building, the restaurant where we'll meet her parents. Flags and flowers decorate the front porch.

"The fun gets paused here, folks." Sorel becomes subdued, fussing with her lipstick and hair in the visor mirror.

Inside, the classical music playing in the background contrasts with the punk anthem I have stuck in my head. The four of us look out of place, but somehow I feel like I belong with this pod of misfits, Grant with his long hair, Pepper with his piercings, and Sorel with her boot-kicking attitude.

Sorel introduces us to Blake and Sheila.

"Mr. and Mrs. Randall," her father corrects.

"Blake and Sheila," she says firmly, with a thin, insincere smile.

I can't imagine how she got the name Sorel. Mrs. Randall, a delicate woman, wears a taupe suit with matching stockings and pumps. Mr. Randall, also in a suit and tie, which won't stay put over his paunch, has thinning hair. The Randalls are bland, beige, soggy breakfast cereal. Never mind her name; how did Sorel come from this pair?

The meal, fraught with tension and oblique animosity, resembles the many meals I've shared with any given combination of the Jaegers. No stranger to trying to make things as swift and painless as possible, I sacrifice myself as a buffer, making light comments and asking Mr. and Mrs. Randall friendly and polite questions. Not wanting to endure the discomfort any longer than necessary, in no time we're back in the Volvo. Quickest lunch, ever.

"Your parents are such stiffs," Pepper remarks.

"Tell me about it. But that is the second to last time I'll need to interact with Blake and Sheila," she says with a smile marked by scorn. "Just a couple of days back at their house, packing up, and then we hit the road."

"You're going cross-country with Sorel, Pepper?" I ask.

He grins. "Just me and Sweet Potato on the open road."

Sorel shoots him a look. Grant stifles a laugh.

"While we're on the topic of summer plans," she says over her shoulder, "Grant, are you excited about a week in New York City with Gavin?"

"Totally. I haven't seen my brother in ages. It'll be nice before I have to go deal with my father."

"Would you like company?" she asks.

Grant looks confused. "What do you mean?"

"PJ was supposed to head out west with me, but Pooky Pooky got permission from Mommy and Daddy to come with, and I think she's heard enough of the cutesy-wootsy, so now she's all on her wee lonesome." Pepper's ears are fuchsia, and Sorel plows on. "What would you think if she stayed with you and Gavin?"

Grant wears that same sad smile, like maybe I'll say no. "I mean, yeah, would you want to?" he asks.

I edge closer to him in my seat. I tell myself not to be afraid. "I'd love to." Now I'm pink.

I hear him exhale. "I think I should ask Gav—wait, Sorel, how did you know my brother's name?"

I can practically hear her smiling. I didn't peg her as someone with warmth in her heart, as cool as her exterior is, but I've learned she occasionally surprises with generosity.

"He and I had a conversation," she says in a terrible Scottish accent.

"Huh?"

"Pepper found his phone number in your things, and I called him for you, asked if it would be OK if you brought a special friend. I didn't mention how hot you thought she was and how the two of you would keep him up all night with your moaning and groaning." She laughs. "He thought it was a great idea. He doesn't know what he's getting into. It's settled. You can thank me anytime." She vibrates with how masterfully her plan has worked out.

Grant and I stare out the windshield, both of us wearing buoyant smiles.

"You're like Cupid, a matchmaker, my sweet potato," Pepper coos.

"Shut it," Sorel says and turns up the volume on the stereo.

After driving for hours, we wind up on a long wooded road before the cement turns into gravel, then into dirt. Sorel pulls up the emergency brake in the sloping driveway. A log cabin perches on top of a hill with a panoramic view of the valley below.

"This is where I spent summers. Welcome to the Randall Family Forest, Boring-burg. But for our purposes, it's perfect." We bring our luggage, following Sorel inside. "You guys get the room down here," she says, pointing down the wood-paneled hall. "We get the master suite." Sorel flashes Pepper a lusty look, and they disappear.

Grant and I find the bedroom with a queen bed in the center, topped with a quaint pink-and-green patchwork quilt. The decor in the house bespeaks rustic comfort.

Grant sets his bag down and steps toward me. "I missed you."

Our cheeks brush. "I missed me." I press my face into his neck, inhaling deeply as he presses against me.

"I wanted to make all your pain go away, but there's not enough poetry or dinners or sneaking around to dislodge that kind of grief. I'm so sorry." His pause is long enough for him to lean back and take the remains of me in.

I don't waver under his gaze. If there's anything valuable left, I want him to see it, to snatch it before it disappears, to help me return to myself.

"I want to take it from you, bury it somewhere far away, make you OK. I didn't know what else to do, other than hold your place here." He puts his hand over his chest.

My own heart swells. We enter a secret place where time no longer matters. It's just us. I am gone. I am his. He cups my jaw in his hands and draws my face close. I set hungrily into his lips for a long-overdue kiss. His pants and my leggings hit the floor. Our tops follow. He undoes my bra, and I sink onto the bed. Our legs intertwine. I leave the fire of the last year behind as we melt into each other.

When Grant and I emerge from our room on the first floor, someone has painted the sky a pastel watercolor, reminding me vaguely of Charmindy's work in Painting IV. We join Sorel and Pepper out on the back deck to watch the sun disappear behind the distant hills. They each have a beer, and Pepper goes inside to get more.

I close my eyes, and for an instant, everything is right in the world. Memories of my mother are lifetimes, or at least miles, away. I forget my disappointment in myself for replacing living with pills. Just the setting sun, the fresh mountain air, Grant, a couple of good friends, and I remain. It's better than oblivion.

"OK. That was nice, but it is time to get this party started," Sorel says, interrupting the moment of serenity and lighting up a cigarette. She claps her hands together and goes inside. After a moment, the speakers blare abrasive punk, and Sorel reappears.

"My parents were just here, so they stocked the fridge. Minus the beer, which I acquired thanks to my pal Mitch. You're welcome," she says, shooting us a sarcastic smile. "If you're hungry, get something to eat. If you're thirsty, grab a beer. There's more in the car, among other select beverages. If you want to get wet, jump in the hot tub or lake, and if you wanna get high, come see me." Sorel smiles mischievously.

After she tosses her cigarette off the deck, she pulls a joint out of her pocket. When it comes to me, I hesitate, but then it's only pot; I tell myself that it's no big deal. Our laughter echoes off the mountainside as we joke about life at Laurel Hill and tear apart nearly every student on campus.

"There's the girl with the really long nose, what's her name?" Sorel asks.

"Morgan?" Pepper answers.

"I swear if she lifted her lip like a millimeter, she could touch the tip of that thing."

We all try to touch our lips to our noses to hilarious effect.

"I can touch my tongue to my nose," Sorel adds, demonstrating.

"You can do a lot of things with your tongue, babe," Pepper says. She swats him. "Then there's the girl who was homeschooled up until Laurel Hill," he adds.

"She was in my chemistry class. She's so painfully awkward, but she doesn't have a clue," Sorel says. "She once explained that argon was the element used in some fantasy book she's crazy about. She said it made the characters in the story magical. I don't even know. What a geek." She shakes her head. "Oh, and there was this other kid in chemistry who had such bad acne I'd get distracted and want to squeeze his zits. I was totally like, dude, let's go to town and pop those suckers."

"Or maybe brew up some kind of potion made with argon to make them go away," Pepper interjects.

They make fun of everyone, from the jocks and popular girls, especially Terran—Pepper does an ace imitation of her orating at an assembly—to the nerds who fully embraced their status and probably would have laughed right along with us.

"We're such douches," Grant declares, high and hysterical with laughter.

"Need. Food. Now," Sorel says. She disappears inside and then bangs on the sliding glass door. We all turn, and she's bare chested, pressing her boobs against the glass. "Come on," she shouts.

We go inside to get something to eat, littering the kitchen table with an assortment of bags and boxes of junk food that her parents left. She makes a soda cocktail, opening five different bottles, and then spikes it with Jack Daniel's. We all refuse to try it, so she guzzles it.

Grant gathers vegetables from the drawers in the fridge and proceeds to boil water for pasta. Proper cooking is a relatively foreign sight to me. With my mouth full of chips, I ask, "What's he doing?"

"Chef Grant!" Pepper cheers, taking notice.

Grant smirks.

"Chef Grant appears when he's had just enough weed to be hungry, but not so much he doesn't know what he's doing. I trade him weed for dinner. It's quite romantic. But you should know that it's a fine balance between him being self-conscious because he likes to cook, but not giving a shit because he's high." Pepper chants, "Chef Grant, Chef Grant, Chef Grant."

He commentates on Grant's every movement. "Now our culinary master slices an onion wafer thin. What will he do with it? No one knows—"

Sorel sulks, the attention off her. "He can't actually cook. I bet it'll be gross." She finishes the soda.

Before I know it, a plate of pasta primavera, sprinkled with parmesan cheese, appears in front of me.

"What, none for us?" Sorel asks.

"PJ was the only one who didn't pick on me," Grant says.

Sorel grabs another beer from the fridge. "Yeah and maybe because she's gotten so skinny," she says under her breath.

I lower my gaze, hiding beneath my bangs and my thick brows. Just as I have for the last months, once more I want to disappear. Apparently, I'm nearly there. Instead, I dig into the plate of pasta.

The song on the stereo ends, leaving the room too quiet for a minute. Sorel staggers to her feet, presumably to put on more music, but flips on the TV instead.

Grant sits down with me, and we eat while the other two stay in the living room. He tells me all his favorite dishes and how his next endeavor is mastering baklava. "Or really anything involving phyllo dough. Doesn't the word sound like it tastes good? Phyllo," he says. "Phyllo, phyllo," he repeats. I could listen to him say it all day, but then he laughs and says, "Actually, maybe it sounds like dirty feet."

I bring my empty plate to the sink. Sorel slouches on the couch to the clash of a battle scene on *Buffy*. Grant and I clean up the kitchen, then go back outside and sit on the deck railing.

"That went from high to low," I comment.

"That's Sorel," Grant says, lighting a cigarette. "But it'll be weird next year without her."

"Just me and the boys." I laugh. Or maybe just one boy and me. In the near darkness, the end of Grant's cigarette glows each time he inhales. His eyes sparkle. The stars shining above seem endless. I wonder if Janet is up there somewhere, riding a meteor or glittering like a diamond.

"Thanks for the pasta. It was really good," I say, meaning to distill any lingering tension caused by Sorel's mood swing and quell the sadness inviting its way in at the thought of my mother.

"So you and me and NYC?" Grant asks.

"Yeah, that's something, huh?" I say, knowing Sorel reentered the conversation.

"That was really thoughtful of her. I mean, a lot of the time she's like this, but other times she can be sweet," Grant says.

"A sweet potato," I add.

At that, we both laugh and move in for a kiss. I can't get enough. We shuffle back inside, the TV dark, and Grant and I fall together onto the bed.

Chapter 33

A symphony of birdsong wakes me early in the morning. When I open my eyes, Grant looks up from the tattoo of the swallows on my shoulder.

"Good morning," he says. His voice is gruff and sleepy.

Waking up next to Grant is better than pills, drugs, or alcohol. He runs the fingers of his inked arm over mine. I study the mermaid.

"I've been thinking about getting another one," he says. "Maybe we can go when we're in New York."

I caress his upper arm, and then put my hand on his chest, then my lips on his, and we remain in the bed long after the birds have finished their breakfast.

After we eat, the house still quiet, Grant suggests we take a hike. We follow the driveway down until there's a marked trail. The humid air hums with bugs, but gaps in the stands of birch, oak, and pines climbing toward the blue sky offer beautiful vistas. Instead of returning to the hard, man-made elements of Manhattan, I think about planting myself here. The fresh air smells virgin. The clouds are transient. A lake appears in the distance. We continue toward it, all the while picking up and leaving off conversation as we wander through the woods.

"Favorite candy?" I ask.

"Smarties," he says, explaining they're different from the chalky ones we have here in the States. "You?"

"Twizzlers."

"Favorite color?" he says.

"Blue," we say at the same time. I knew that.

We toss coffee shops, novels, and photographers back and forth as we walk.

At the water's edge, Grant searches for flat rocks and skips stones.

"That's one thing I miss," he says. "The water. In Scotland, you're never far from it. This might sound weird, but when I'm near water— the ocean, a river, or lake, I feel sure everything is going to be OK. Y'know?"

I envision a young Sorel visiting this very place during the summer. It contrasts with how I often spent my summers, escaping my mother to the library, trolling the streets, looking for something to eat, or finding trouble. But this summer has gotten off to a perfect start.

When we get back to the house after lunch, Sorel irritably thuds through the kitchen. "Where did you guys go?"

"Took a hike. It's so beautiful here. Thanks for inviting us," I say, hoping to clear the air from last night. She gobbles a croissant and a muffin from clear plastic containers before disappearing upstairs.

Grant flips through some books on a shelf in the living room. We lounge around for the afternoon, the mood dampened by Sorel's pouting. Later, she calls us outside. She holds a joint in one hand and a beer in the other.

"Party time."

We repeat the scene from the night before. Beer, pot, loud music, but this time we splash in the hot tub and watch the sun set. Grant hops out to get us each a beer refill, but Sorel shouts, "Bring me a Jack and Coke." After she downs it she announces, "Let's play truth or dare. I go first." Her impish smile looks familiar on her lips, but her glassy eyes betray more than mischief.

"Grant, PJ wasn't your first, was she?"

Already rosy from the hot water, I can't tell if his cheeks have grown redder. "No," he says, looking at me. Again, his sad smile spreads on his lips. I notice he doesn't look at Sorel or Pepper.

"Interesting. Tell us about her, Grant," Sorel says sharply.

"I answered your question. My turn," Grant says.

"Pepper, was it you who clogged the first-floor boys' toilet last spring?" he asks.

Pepper goes indisputably red. "Yes." Then he starts laughing. He looks at Sorel. "I mean no, ew, that's nasty. My turn. Sorel, do you love me?"

She pauses and sighs. "Yes." She says no more. "My turn. PJ, have you ever had a crush on Pepper?" Something about the tone of her voice makes me uncomfortable.

"No." I fumble for what to say next. I don't want to be insulting, but I don't even think of Pepper as attractive. He's her boyfriend. That's always been very clear. "No, just Grant," I follow up, leaning back on his chest.

"Good," she says and takes off her top as she moves to straddle Pepper. Grant and I look away. He makes a gagging face. I suppress a giggle, but an uneasy feeling, reminiscent of that night in Canada, snakes its way to my stomach.

After a minute, she turns back to us, her naked chest hidden under the foamy bubbles. "Everyone wait right here," she says, her usual smile returning. She comes back, still topless but partially concealed behind a tray with more beers and a Jack and Coke for herself. When she gets closer, I also see a baggie filled with pills.

"Drinks for everyone, in case you want to wash one of those down," she says, pointing at the bag and looking at me.

At the sight of the pills, the anxious feeling turns slippery. Part of me wants one, but a bigger part of me wants to coherently experience the night with Grant. Before, I took pills to disappear, and now, I don't want to cloud our time together.

Sorel ignores us and mounts Pepper again, knocking back her drink in one gulp.

Grant motions with his head toward the house. He takes the tray with him. Does he want to get high, just not while the two of them get hot and heavy? An irksome hope threatens me toward a dark chute. I push the thought away, back to Laurel Hill, back to Mitch's house, back to Florida. Away, away, away. I don't need it.

Grant sets the tray on the counter, next to a CD case, with Sorel's old Laurel Hill ID and a rolled-up dollar bill. It looks like she crushed the pills and snorted them.

Grant shakes his head. "That's not good." He takes me by the hand, and together we go to the shower to rinse off.

Sometime in the middle of the night, I wake to Sorel shouting. I sense Grant stirring beside me.

"What's going on?" I ask, not sure if I'm waking from a dream and into a nightmare.

"Sounds like whatever drug-and-alcohol cocktail she had isn't agreeing with her." Grant gropes around in the dark for his pack of cigarettes. "Damn."

"I'll get them," I offer, remembering he left them on the deck railing. I creep out of the room to find Sorel stalking around the kitchen, her face red, her hair wild. She wears only her bathing suit bottom, her appearance uncannily like my mother's. My stomach ties itself into tight knots.

"What are *you* doing up?" she spits.

"Getting Grant his cigarettes," I say, moving toward the sliding glass door.

"I smoked them. Did Grant ever tell you we had sex? Or the time him, Pepper, and I had a threesome." She laughs wildly. "Did he tell you that? Or about his ex? She was a hottie, not a skinny shit like you. How about Suzy? I know they've been hanging out. You're washed up, PJ. It's over," she says with a manic glint in her eyes. In her words, I hear my mother's voice, along with Terran's desire to undo me.

Standing under the bright lights of the kitchen, once more I feel like a helpless child. What *do* I know? I don't even know where I am, never mind who I am. Or who any of them are, not really.

I go outside and find Grant's cigarettes right where I thought they'd be. I pull one out and light it as quiet tears fall.

Moments later, I hear thunderous yelling. "'Eff you!" shouts a fierce Scottish accent. The door whooshes open, and Grant slams it behind him. The cabin shudders. He puts both hands on the railing, taking deep breaths. In a couple of short strides, he kneels in front of me as I sit on the Adirondack chair.

"Don't believe everything she says. She's whacked right now."

I nod.

He rests his hands on my knees. "I heard what she said to you. I shouldn't have let her get me so angry, but she was lying. She shouldn't have been talking to you that way."

"Yeah, I'm learning to question everything."

"No, not everything," he says, looking into my eyes. "Remember when I told you I didn't want to be friends, or talk, or whatever?"

Of course I do.

"I told you that because I'm scared. I had a girlfriend freshman year; we were serious. She cheated on me, dumped me. That, on top of my mom not coming back, it kind of messed me up. I didn't want to commit to anyone. I just wanted to escape, to feel good, physically."

"Yeah, I know what that's like," I mutter.

"I didn't want complications, talking, or being friends, or getting close, because if I did, well, it could hurt. I could get hurt."

"I also know all about that."

He presses five of his fingers against mine and then folds them together. He squeezes gently, as though not willing to let me retreat to the shadows. "When I first saw you, I was afraid you were exactly the kind of girl who could ruin me, wreck me. But I couldn't get you out of my head. Then I got to know you, and I wanted to take the risk." He draws a deep breath. "I want to talk and be friends and kiss and be more than friends."

I lean close to him, my thoughts written on my lips. I kiss him gently. "I do too."

He holds me as the darkness surrounding us crowds me with doubt. I look up at the sky, the stars deeper than a dream.

We sleep in. When Sorel emerges from her cave, midday, she doesn't acknowledge the night before. Half-asleep, she stuffs herself with the remaining muffins, slathering them with irresponsible amounts of butter. She downs a can of Coke. Her mood simmers and foams.

We load into the car; the pep and the punch blow out with the breeze that flips the leaves of the trees over, revealing their pale, veiny undersides.

"Seems like it might rain," Grant says absently.

The ride is quiet except for the electric buzz of Grant's hand in mine.

As the Manhattan skyline comes into view, the rain subsides. Nerves and excitement make my leg jitter. The drive south seems to calm Sorel down, and the pleasant version of her joins us once more. She drops us off in front of Gavin's brick building in Brooklyn.

"Home again, home again. You have to come visit me in Seattle, City Girl. I'll call with my info when I get settled in," Sorel says. We exchange a hug.

"Thanks for everything. You know where to find me," I say.

Something lacking in our good-bye tells me we might never see each other again.

Pepper and Grant bump fists.

"See ya in the fall, dude," Pepper says.

We watch them pull away. I let out a loud breath and then deeply inhale the balmy city air, a mixture of summer sweat, hot dogs from a street vendor, and ginkgo trees.

Chapter 34

Grant and I trot up the four flights of stairs to his brother's apartment. Gavin lives in one of Brooklyn's gentrified neighborhoods, but elevators are in short supply.

The brothers exchange a hearty hug, and Grant introduces me.

Gavin's eyes light up. "Well, little brother," he says, winking at me sweetly and roughing up Grant's long hair. "Da's gonna make you cut that, you know," Gavin says with his thick accent, unlike Grant who's abandoned his, except when he bellowed at Sorel the night before. I've also noticed when we're making out his words are accented and seductive. My temperature increases a degree or two and not because it's warm in the apartment.

"Nah, I'm keeping it," Grant says. "I'm hoping you'll style it for me while I'm here."

The guys roughhouse for a minute. Then Gavin says, "If you want to get out on the field, never mind out of the house, he's gonna hack, hack, hack." He moves his first two fingers up and down like scissors.

They talk about Gavin's job and life in the United States and about things back home, all the while guiding me across the topography of their shared life: the characters, relations, and social politics of their island world far across the Atlantic.

"Let's go get a brew," Gavin suggests.

"This is America, Gav. I'm not twenty-one and certainly don't know the local barkeep."

"Right. Well, let's go watch some football anyway. There's bound to be a match on telly."

Grant looks at me. "Do you mind pub food and soccer?" he asks, clarifying. In his brother's presence, his accent returns, like the sound of the rolling sea, the sky, all of it for me.

I've never been more enthusiastic about sports and food in my life. Grant and Gavin are endearing. Brothers. Family. The mature but good-natured Grant from Montreal has once again replaced the young, timid Grant from Laurel Hill, but he's more spirited, lighter. It is like when I put my arm around him on the lawn at Laurel Hill, he suddenly knew with certainty who he was and what he wanted.

The days start with Grant and me kissing and lounging and kissing some more on the couch in the small apartment after Gavin leaves for work. Then the train delivers us into the city, and we pretend we're tourists, visiting the museums, historical buildings, and Times Square—places Grant has never been.

Sadness filters through my glee as we walk hand in hand down Broome Street, looking for a tattoo shop Grant heard about. When I see the block letters spelling *Bowery* against the reflective green of the street sign, I stop.

"What's the matter?" Grant asks, looking around.

Tears run down my cheeks.

"That's where she was found," I croak.

"Who?"

"My mom."

He instantly pulls me to his chest. If he weren't holding me up, I'd collapse to the filthy sidewalk.

"I don't know if it'll ever get easier." As minutes dissolve into the drumming of Grant's heartbeat, I realize maybe it will.

We turn into a café and get in line for coffee. The barista looks familiar, with thick, dark hair and cinnamon-colored skin. "Gino?" I ask when we reach the counter.

"Pearl?" Gino is thinner than when I saw him last. His crooked teeth need flossing. I wonder when he last looked in a mirror. "Pearl! Hey, what's up?"

"This is Grant. Grant, Gino. We used to hang out," I say, making introductions.

"Oh man, did we ever," Gino says. "Remember the time we met Downey? Iron Man, right?! Crazy night. I got arrested later. Did Ali tell you? Man. That bitch is cracked. Watch out for her. She got pregnant, so you probably won't see her around anyway. You back in the city, or what? I heard you went to juvie or something." He doesn't let me answer as he strings his questions together like the long line of customers forming behind me.

"Yeah, I'm good. Back for the summer."

Gino's coworker hands us our order.

"I'll, uh, see you," I say, the crowd shuffling me out of earshot. I hastily stuff a dollar in the tip jar.

"Sounds like my old friends are thick in it," I say to Grant when we're outside. My relief surprises me, knowing I would not have been immune to whatever trouble they've gotten into if I hadn't gone to Laurel Hill. "I have an idea. How about I show you *my* city?"

Grant lifts a quizzical eyebrow. I want him to see Manhattan through my lens, not just the tourist spots. Like a living photo album, I relay some of the less sordid stories revealed only to me by street corners, buildings, and shops. It feels good to chase away the darker memories of my mother and fill the vacancies with tales of free popcorn and art galleries, designer knockoffs, and days spent playing hooky.

"You lived some life. I don't know if I could keep up." Grant bites his lip.

"I think you're keeping up just fine," I say, my lips landing on his. With sore feet, we take the train back to Brooklyn.

Grant pops open an amber lager once settled at the apartment. "Gavin left a note, he's at soccer practice with a league he joined, and invited us to watch." He holds up the beer. "Instead, we could finish these off." But before we do, our lips meet, our clothes are off, and we're both thankful we don't have to follow the rules at Laurel Hill.

Later, when Gavin comes in, I stir, wrapped snuggly in Grant's arms. I hear a chuckle, and then the bathroom door closes. I lie on the sofa, gazing up through the window, the moonlight meeting the city light in a rosy glow. I never want to be anywhere but in Grant's arms. There, I feel safe, cared for, and like an integral part of myself isn't missing.

Nevertheless, as soon as I catch the thin strand of happiness, Sorel's comments slither into my mind. *Have they really slept together? Am I just some stupid, washed-up girl?* The picture of my mother cheating on one boyfriend with another guy knocks around with my doubts. *Who am I to be so lucky to rest in Grant's arms?* I imagine it all slipping away. Good things never stay.

I roll over, disturbing the blanket and stirring up Grant's scent, a mixture of tobacco, mint, and clean. Comfort washes over me, rinsing away the dirty memories and doleful thoughts.

The next day we locate the tattoo parlor and sit for hours while fierce ocean waves color in the space around Grant's mermaid. I think of Shale and his paintings. Their rolling wildness contrasts with the mermaid's ecstatic smile. Above the waves, the artist adds the night sky, lit with stars. The piece covers Grant's entire upper arm. He gives me his sad smile as I study the rushing waves kissing the shimmering stars.

"Do you like it?" he asks.

"It's beautiful." As I look more closely, the mermaid's features mirror my own. If only it were possible for me ever to be that happy.

The last night before Grant's flight breezes by bittersweetly. I lament the nearly three months apart, coming so soon after I finally snuck away from grief and said yes to life and Grant.

"I'm staying at my family's cottage to get away from my dad. It's doubtful I'll make it back to Laurel Hill in one piece if we're in Glasgow all summer together. The thing is, there's no phone service. Do you like to write?" Grant asks while we watch our clothes tumble clean in the basement of Gavin's building.

"Of course." I want to capture the magic of these shared moments, saving them so that when we return to Laurel Hill, nothing between us is lost. "It'll be like the old days. We can pine for each other from afar . . ."

"I'll be pining for sure, my lady," Grant says, bowing regally.

After we watch Gavin's soccer match that evening, he goes out to celebrate with his teammates, and Grant and I return to the apartment.

Before going inside, we climb to the roof. The night cues summer, with a warm breeze, and the full moon triumphs over the city lights. Sitting on a cement outcropping, our legs dangling in space, Grant smokes a cigarette. I take one too, ignoring how my lungs sting.

He tells me about how his mom loved collecting wildflowers and seashells. He goes on. "When I remember her I think of the color purple, the shade that hovers over the ocean at sunrise." His voice quavers, and as if to stop the tears I know to be coming, he turns and gives me a soft kiss. After a time he speaks again. "I fumbled for your heart all year. You were all I thought about, and then it was like you disappeared, even though you were still there. I don't want to lose you again."

I take his hand in mine in answer as we look out over the city.

Long after he falls asleep, I lie awake, worrying. I don't want us to end. I wake him with a kiss. Fingers clutch hair, lips discover eddies and pools, legs tangle, and hands grasp skin with desperation as the night fades to dawn.

I hold it together as Grant gets into his cab and I in mine. I don't cry until I cross the bridge back into Manhattan. Suddenly it feels like my mother's shadow, in Grant's absence, threatens to devour me alive.

Chapter 35

I wipe my eyes as I enter the appointed building to register for summer school. The decor, bright and bold, patterned and geometric, distracts me from the glut of memories and sweeps me up in creative passion. Throughout the airy room, large, artfully designed panels covered in swatches of fabric—printed with portraits of famous alumni who had proudly attended Parsons School of Design—garner my attention.

A spry second-year student, with spiky black hair and a dramatic shirt with buttons running up the side and a collar sweeping across the chest, guides me to my dorm. She wears designer jeans and boots similar to mine. She waves to several points of interest, and we discuss some of the more notable graduates and their recent projects.

I settle into my dorm room and unpack, but wait to select a bunk until my roommate arrives. I hear voices in the hall, and a statuesque girl, my age, with an Afro that hardly fits through the door, comes in, singing.

"You must be Pearl," she says, her voice like polished silver bells. It's beautiful.

"PJ," I reply.

"I'm Dominique. But everyone calls me Kiki." She looks me up and down. "Top or bottom?" Her long lashes flutter. "I always go for the top," she says, winking and tossing a bag onto the upper mattress.

I make my bed while she tells me about her family, her school in Atlanta, and her dreams of making fashion history. She is one of the most cheerful people I've ever met, but has a wicked sense of humor and a tongue to match. "You and I are going to have fun this summer," she says, squeezing my shoulder.

The kaleidoscope of art students behave themselves during the new-student orientation, but at the dinner afterward, we turn up the volume. I sit with Kiki, Roxie, and Reesa, two sassy girls we met earlier. Kiki, with her sweet yet confident southern accent, has the ability to make everyone feel welcome, as if we've been going to the same summer camp all our lives. Yet, the old, familiar feeling of being the odd girl out skids into my mind.

"Earth to PJ. Girl, I'm talking to you," Kiki says.

I snap to attention.

"I brought some SoCo from home. You mind if these girls hang out in our room tonight?"

"Maybe you and I have more in common than I thought . . ." Because a drink sounds like the best way to chase away the emptiness of being in Manhattan without Grant and deep in memories of my mother.

The lax rules at Parsons allow students to smoke openly on the veranda adjacent to the third floor. We can come and go as we please, but have to check in by midnight. I can't imagine how this passed my aunt's scrutiny. Based on our brief interaction at the hotel, maybe Erica, along with Shale, put in a good word for me.

Kiki mixes cranberry juice and soda with the Southern Comfort and passes around a hodgepodge of coffee mugs and glasses. She raises hers. "To a fabulous summer of design, decadence, and debauchery." Everyone hoots.

There aren't many guys in the program, but a male's head peeks around the corner of our door. "Room for one more?"

"Haruki!" Kiki squeals. "Of course. Come in. Our official gay. Come join us, honey!"

Haruki doesn't look any older than fifteen and has the energy of a five-year-old. Like an accordion, he fits himself right between Roxie and me. Each time Kiki refills our glasses, the conversation tilts toward laughter. As the night gets older, we get sloppy and senseless. Eventually I doze off, sitting on the floor, leaning my head against the bed frame.

I nod forward, and with a jerk, I open my eyes to see the apparition of Kiki and Roxie making out. I crawl up to my bunk, imagine Grant's arms around me, and pass out.

I wake to the first day of classes, slightly hungover; a bagel and coffee seem like the antidote. I rush to the textile lab as Kiki bounces along beside me, gushing about the impromptu party.

"Damn, that was fun. You passed out early."

"I didn't sleep much the night before," I admit.

"No?" she asks, hinting at the truth. "Someone special?"

I nod, unable to suppress a grin.

"Spill."

I tell her about Grant and the long, lonely summer before returning to Laurel Hill. "Will you distract me so in a blink we're back together?"

"Abso-freakin-lutely." She laughs.

The first week at Parsons flies by on the air of keen excitement. I don't have to slog through math and history, English and Spanish. The classes on design, fashion media, sewing, and techniques hold my attention with the kind of interest Shale would envy from his students. Despite my love for all things Kahlo, I'm relieved there's no painting, or grunting over my shoulder, involved. I build my portfolio, and although my outlook for college remains uncertain, for once, I feel hopeful about my future.

Not overloaded with homework, Kiki, the others, and I gab, get containers of takeout, stroll around the Village, and, by night, share cocktails and stories.

Each day, when I wake up, I long for Grant with a physical ache that draws my muscles tight and clouds my head like a drug. As the day bowls on, I swap it for grief over my mother. It doesn't help that my classes take me on numerous jaunts around the city, where it's as if Janet haunts each street and avenue. I don't know where my memories of her stop, or if they do.

On a field trip for History of Fashion Industry, one of my classes, I notice a brand-new high-rise erected in place of the stretch of dilapidated row houses where I once lived with JJ. She's inescapable, at least in Manhattan. Or maybe she's like the row houses—gone, replaced with something newer, shinier, straighter. I clutch my chest, tears threatening; I have to learn to live with her or, rather, with my painful memories of her.

At our next stop, amid students taking notes, I stand on Washington Place in the shade of the Brown Building, the location of the Triangle Shirtwaist Factory fire many years ago. Police sirens blare from somewhere behind me. I instinctively glance over my shoulder. The edifice of a familiar dust-colored building looms behind me.

My thoughts crash back through time, and I slouch down a cement wall, landing with my knees pulled into my chest.

Kiki squats next to me as the teacher continues. "You all right?" she whispers. "My head pounded this morning until I had some caffeine. I never thought I'd say there's such a thing as too much SoCo. Want to split and grab a cup of coffee or something?"

Now would be a great opportunity to lie down in my bed, nap the day away, but the truth is, aside from the memories, I welcome the tour through parts of New York I never knew and replacing the stories JJ wrote. I press up to my feet. "Thanks. I'll, uh, be fine."

I try to shake off the flashback as the teacher leads us to the next point of interest. I cannot outrun or outlive the memories and the accompanying dread they introduce to my days. They keep pace with me, no matter what I do or what I tell myself. I can't imagine living a life where I have to constantly straddle the line between the present and past.

Later that night, Kiki, Roxie, Reesa, and Haruki pass around crushed-up pills, spread into thin lines, on top of my sketchbooks. The night at the cabin with Sorel and so many other sordid memories run like lines of static, dizzying and relentless. Behind my eyes, Sorel's there with her palm out. Charmindy's wagging her finger. My mother stares blankly. I should say no, but as my sketchbook makes its way around the circle, white noise rushes in my ears, and the feeling of defeat crushes me. I will never escape her. Tired of fighting with my own frightened mind, I take a sniff and drop into the void.

Only it isn't a void at all. Everything moves at the speed of light, like when taillights on the parkway blur into one long streak of vivid color. I brim with ideas and creativity. I have stories to tell and adventures to take. And it all has to happen right now and now and now.

We climb to the roof. Someone brings music, and we dance. We move and groove. We watch the sun come up and do it all over again and again and again. We are on fire. We live out loud. We are unstoppable.

When I crash, I come down hard. Starved for sleep, I drop into my bed after classes and close my eyes. My mother waits, impatiently, her leg jiggling, and then Grant appears. A blizzard makes a loud shushing noise as it fills my head, burying us all. Those two always show up when the distractions run out. My past and future, vying for my attention, for my emotions, but I have nothing to give. I've spent every ounce of energy on white pills crushed to powder. I finally drift off and later wake to Kiki snoring sweetly above me.

As I lie there, my vision of Grant wins, temporarily. I think back to us on the quilted bed in the log cabin, running my hands over his chest. I think of his lips on my belly and thighs. I miss him with an ache that feels like withdrawal.

Chapter 36

The summer school version of midterms subdues us. Everyone buckles down and studies. Sort of. I imbibe copious amounts of caffeine, trying to stay sharp, but the absence of amusement brings out the grouchiest, grumpiest, and most irritable in all of us. In a moment of coherence, I recall that my uncle pays for the funfest. If I fail, that would mean— what? I'm not exactly sure, but the show would be over. No more partying. No more Parsons School of Design and certainly no more Grant at Laurel Hill. No future. With the devastation of that final thought as my strongest motivation, I focus and make sure I know my contour methods and my Jeannes from my Jeans.

When we troop out of the testing room, Kiki announces, "Let's celebrate. How about we all get dressed up and go *out* to dinner for a change. I know just the place." Her smile reminds me of the adventurous and generous side of Sorel, the girl I miss. I imagine her and Pepper in Seattle, falling in love all over again.

Back at the dorm, Kiki says, "Let me style you, pretty please?"

"You don't even need to say please. I've been wearing the same clothes—"

She doesn't let me finish. "Check these out," she says, holding up a pair of skintight vintage gold short shorts. They look like something my mother would have worn before I came along. I wonder if all the old photos and magazine clippings of her posing and playing with her band are in a landfill somewhere. There's no photographic evidence of my childhood, other than the picture in the paper bag from Erica; I'm like a ghost.

"You've got the legs for those shorts; damn, they go on for miles," Kiki says, rooting me back to the present. She pairs them with a sheer black top and a long pair of earrings. Kiki also does my makeup, with smoky eyes and red lips, her specialty. And thanks to Reesa, on one overwrought night involving a mixture of substances, my bangs are freshly trimmed and miraculously the same length.

"I know you don't wear much makeup, but usually this is a no-no. The rule is heavy on the eyes, light on the lips or vice versa, but we're going out. We'll make an exception. Your eyebrows should have their own insurance policy. I never want to see you pluck them."

I glance at the place by my bunk where there should be a poster of Frida Kahlo, but I left everything except my clothes in campus storage for the summer. *What would Frida say?* She was no stranger to the party lifestyle, or pain, or the need, not just the desire, to create art. *And Shale?* He doesn't seem to be the group-activities type. Although I can imagine him downing a bottle of scotch or whatever it is old masters drink to stop themselves from shaking.

"You look straight off the runway. Damn, I'm good," Kiki says when she's pleased with her creation.

She tries on no less than a dozen outfits before settling on a short lime-green halter dress, enormous gold hoops, and black heels that make her taller than me.

"You're the one with the legs," I say, complimenting her.

She cocks her hip, and we take a selfie with her phone.

Our group assembles in the hall.

"Everyone looks too good tonight. You may *not* do the usual elevator scramble of seeing how fast we can all undress and redress," Kiki orders, referencing a game we've been playing that involves us stripping down as we ride up to our floor in the elevator and switching clothes before the doors open.

"At least not yet," Roxie answers, laughing.

Haruki waves around a bottle of tequila when we get in the elevator. "But I have this. Take a healthy sip, ladies," he says. "Prepare yourself for anything tonight, including the runway, fame and fortune, fashion history." The bottle goes around, and the contents decrease by half.

Full of sass and brass, we pile into a cab and then parade down Eighth Avenue, arriving at Bite. Kiki assures us it's the perfect venue to see and be seen, with crimson lighting and red velvet seats.

Looking like a pack of models, not counting diminutive Haruki, we find an empty table.

Kiki explains that her cousin is a promoter for Bite and that they serve tapas, little plates of food to share and taste. "She's out of town, Miami. But none of that is the point," she goes on, "the point is to get noticed and get your drink on." Without hesitation, she asks the server to bring us a round of cosmopolitans.

"My treat," Kiki says, flicking her credit card to the server. "Open a tab, please."

"The girl from hot-lanta brought the heat to New York City," Haruki chants, toasting Kiki.

I cringe at the cost of drinks. Good thing she's buying.

We blend in with the crowd seated around us and mobbing the bar. Kiki keeps an eye on the room at large, but also an ear on us, occasionally chiming in. I'm discussing with Reesa the test we took earlier, when Kiki interrupts. "That sounds fascinating and all, but we're not in the classroom anymore, and anyway, that guy over there keeps trying to get your attention." She discreetly points at a guy who is sure to be male-model material, with dark, tousled hair and brown eyes. I smile shyly from beneath my bangs and then look away.

Moments later, a round of shot glasses arrives at our table, and the server indicates they're compliments of the hot-model guy. Everyone cheers as we knock them back.

"Go thank him," Kiki insists, giving me a nudge.

I shake my head, frozen. "I'm not good with guys, plus there's Grant." Then for a moment, suspended from time and place, I picture Grant's twinkling eyes, his smile, and everything about him—from head to toe—that makes me melt.

"Yeah, you should really go thank him," Haruki says.

"You go thank him, you're the one who thinks he's cute," I tease.

"I'm not gonna lie, he's F-I-N-E fine."

More laughter, and for a moment I forget about the lure of the cute model across the room. We've hardly nibbled at the food we ordered, when another round of drinks appears. This time a refill of our cosmos.

"Another gift from that tasty-looking mouthful over there and his friends," the waitress informs us.

"That's what I call Sexy McSexpants. You have to go over there, PJ," Roxie urges me. She wears a thin macramé band tied over her straightened black hair and a sleeveless tank and leather pants.

"You're the hot one, you do it," I reply.

Kiki shakes her head disapprovingly. "Come on, I'll go with you. But first, a trip to the bathroom." She winks at me.

I wonder where the pills and the booze come from, knowing she hints at sneaking away for a line of whatever she has stashed in her bag. Before we can shuffle out of the crescent-shaped booth, Sexy McSexpants and one of his companions come over.

"Hi," he says with a slight accent. "I'm Matteo, and this is Dante. We're going to a party in a little while and are wondering if you want to join us." He looks at me, sexy oozing from every inch of his skin.

I wait a beat too long to answer, so Kiki replies for me. "Yeah, she, I mean we, would love to."

"Nice." He sits down after Haruki—practically swooning—scoots over.

"What are your names?" Dante asks, not taking his eyes from Kiki.

She introduces us. "I'm Kiki, and this is PJ. And that's Reesa, Roxie, and Haruki. We're design students at Parsons," she says, omitting the tag word *junior*, which would reveal we're just high school age.

"Nice to meet you," Dante says.

Matteo smiles at me while sipping his gin and tonic. The strong curve of his jaw and his intense eyes tell me I've probably seen him in a sultry magazine ad.

"We were just going to the ladies' room. Excuse us," Kiki says, pulling me along. I follow her to the bathroom, and she closes the unisex door behind me.

"Look alive, woman," she hisses. "Those two might be a ticket to meeting some important people in the fashion industry. If you learn anything from me this summer, realize it's all about networking, networking, networking. Three-quarters of success is who you know, and the other quarter is who you party with. Let's get it started tonight." Her enthusiasm and convincing smile draw me directly in. She pulls out a couple of pills, crushes them flat with her credit card, and then feathers them into lines. She tightly rolls up a bill.

"Your turn," she says.

I breathe deep.

"You're my roommate, we're in this together. This is our time. Come on, PJ." She winks as we strut out of the bathroom, affectionately putting her arm around my shoulders.

Back at the table, Kiki stuffs me into the booth next to Matteo. My bare arm presses up against his. Warmth. Touch. It's thrilling and dangerous.

Five minutes later, I'm invincible. Kiki's words echo in my mind, this *is* our time.

Our voices climb as we exchange stories, losing track of how many drinks we've had. The guys assimilate seamlessly into our group, with teasing and flirtatious smiles. The vodka and tequila adequately lubricate us, and nothing else matters.

Matteo looks at his watch and announces, "Time to go. You in?" He looks at me again with his caramel-colored eyes, and I nod, the pills replacing my uncertainty.

Outside, Matteo saunters over to a motorcycle and hands me a helmet. Dante does the same with Kiki. "We ride," he says.

I've never been on a motorcycle before. I climb on behind him, pressing my chest against his back, and wrap my arms around his waist. So much of me touches so much of him. As we dodge yellow lights, the speed of the bike matches the rush that licks me from within. I want to go faster and climb higher.

Matteo parks beside Dante on East Seventy-Ninth Street. I can just make out the lights edging Central Park. All this time back in the city, and I still haven't set foot there. The others meet us in a cab.

We march into a swanky building with a door attendant, who doesn't flinch when our crowd strides by him, then up to the top floor.

Models, a few actors I recognize, and designers populate the penthouse. Clusters of dangling pendant lights illuminate the high ceiling. In the center of the room, a U-shaped couch faces a stone fireplace where candles burn softly. A multicolored glass sculpture that looks like melting wax in the center of the square coffee table contrasts with the otherwise neutral palette in the room. The floor-to-ceiling windows open up onto a broad terrace with a pool and a vista of the city.

"This is Augusta Santos's place," Matteo whispers in my ear as Dante ushers Kiki away. My other friends huddle together, starstruck. Augusta Santos, an up-and-coming designer, made money during the Internet boom and expanded into fashion: rubbing elbows with all the names that matter and rumored to be the next big thing.

Kiki and Dante bring over drinks. She gives me a look that reads something along the lines of *Holy shit, I can't believe this is really happening, but I am playing it so cool right now.* After Matteo introduces me to several faces I recognize from various issues of *Vogue*, he leads me outside. I'm wobbly and giggly when we take a seat in a little nook.

"You're a student?" he asks.

"Yeah," I say blandly, afraid if I say more my words will come out in a slur.

"But you could be a model."

"Very funny."

"No, really. You should come by my shoot on Friday. I can introduce you to my agent. She'd be upset if I kept a face like yours all to myself," he says, flattering me.

"That's very sweet of you, but—" I shake my head, disbelieving. I think of all the ways I do not look like a model, my face, my hands, and the awkwardness I feel inside my skin.

"You belong here," he says, spreading his arm wide and gesturing toward the party. Then he nods his head as he leans closer. His breath is icy. Another inch and our lips will meet. I can't think quickly enough. I freeze and then pull my shirt off as I rise to my feet. Matteo's eyes widen.

"Come on," I say, pulling him by the arm. My laughter drowns the lingering anxiety floating in my subconscious. "Let's go for a swim." At the pool's edge, I strip entirely naked and then jump in. When I surface, Matteo's figure appears even more perfectly sculpted when undressed.

Before I know it, Kiki wades in the pool too. "Just watch the hair," she warns anyone in earshot.

Several others jump in the pool. I hear someone shout, "Incoming," and two guys toss Haruki in. We splash and laugh as bottles of champagne make their way into my hands and out. Matteo pulls me toward him and wraps my legs around his waist. I feel every toned part of him touching me.

"Where were we?" he asks. His lips search for mine. The party noise fades away. I imagine I'm going to kiss Grant, pressing up against his trim body, and his arms closing around me. But realizing the truth, I let go and slide under the water. I hold my breath for a moment. I shut my eyes, wishing myself away from the chaos and confusion. I come up for air, the party as loud as ever. Matteo treads water by my side, his flirtatious smile fox-like.

I panic. "I should probably leave. I—" The need feels urgent yet undefinable. There is an easy way to explain: Grant. I can't say his name, not after what just happened. I press myself up on the pool deck, grab a towel from a stack, and rush inside with my clothing.

I dress and dash out the door. The elevator dispenses me into the night. I don't have enough money for a cab, so I walk toward the park up ahead. Although I know it's foolish to go in at this time of night, it offers refuge from the light and blare of the city. I need to get my head straight. The only place I can think of where that might happen is Laurel Hill. Since that requires me to travel over the river and through the woods, I opt for the nearest patch of grass and the shelter of trees.

I slip into the park. My gold shorts shine in the yellow light cast by the wrought iron lamps. I follow the path south, my heels clicking on the cement. At a fountain, I take them off. I root around in my bag for a penny, toss it in, and make a wish. I long to wipe my near-mistake from memory and savor Grant there instead. He drew me into his heart, and I almost ruined it.

I emerge on East Fifty-Ninth Street, replace my shoes, and plod on. Before I know it, I walk down Fifth Avenue, remembering the weekend of the funeral. This time the windows win my attention. The displays could pass Anna Wintour's meticulous attention to detail. I stroll past the block that makes up Saks, studying the life-size dioramas, brightly lit, transporting me to the glossy pages of *Vogue*, my refuge. It's like they point toward possibility, like I might just make it out of this madness.

I recollect accompanying my mother down this same avenue at Christmastime. Before the lights seemed to go out in her eyes permanently, she'd have brief moments of parenting clarity, like taking me for a walk to look at the store windows, then over to see the tree at Rockefeller Center, or listening to me read her a picture book. Her missteps were uneven then, not yet gelled into constant chaos. Even so, I had an undercurrent of fear, as I waited for a good day to quickly spiral into a bad one. Experience taught me, like repeating vocabulary on a chalkboard, *this moment of happiness is fleeting; someone will take it from me.*

I trace the outline of my reflection in a window. My damp hair hangs limply to my shoulders, my long legs balanced on top of heels and my thin frame distorted by the glass. I am no more than a replica of my mother. This is not the self-portrait I want to paint. Tears spill from my eyes as cars rush by.

As I continue south, the wind dries my eyes, and I shiver. Part of me regrets leaving the party. Just when I felt like I fit in, Matteo even telling me I belonged, I ran away. It's like I'm so accustomed to bad outcomes that I create them.

Farther along the sidewalk, a group of guys gathers in front of a convenience store, sipping out of bottles in paper bags. As I click closer, their eyes land on me in my gold shorts and barely there tank, my hair a mess. I'm the picture of vulnerability. I wrap my arms around my chest.

One guys whistles. Another says, "Meow." A third calls, "Hey, baby, you lookin' for a good time tonight?"

My eyes fix on the cement in front of me. Just as I pass them, a hand paws at my waist. I jerk away.

"Come on, I'm as gentle as a pussycat. Here, kitty kitty, here," the guy calls.

I hustle toward the subway entrance behind the library—where I spent so much time when I was younger. Patience and Fortitude, the lion statues, stand sentry as if they've been waiting for me. I imagine them scaring off the guys who catcalled me. Then a memory tumbles into focus. My mother had left me in some room, with some creepy dude. I'd fallen asleep, and I woke to him tugging my pants down. I hate her. I hate her so much I want her back, want to lash out at her, to shake her, and to have her witness and bear my rage.

I shout into the dark subway tunnel, "Get out of my head. Leave me alone."

Minutes later, I choke on tears as the doors seal me in the train car. I cry openly on the subway, sobbing as the train rushes below the city where it all began. A shadow crosses into the flickering light of the carriage. I look up. A bum hovers over me, wearing a tattered jacket down to his knees and a hat with holes in it.

"You OK, miss?" he asks in a kind voice.

I search his eyes. He's as lost as I am. *How do I find my way when I was given the wrong directions?* I wonder if he was raised by a crack addict or if he is one. Was he abused and used until he was left with nothing? I'm off course, without a map or a compass. My tears dwindle. I'm literally in a dark tunnel.

And somewhere, I hope, there's a light at the end of it.

A crackly voice announces my stop.

"I'll be OK. Thanks," I say, hoping that we both will.

I slip into the dorm just before midnight. Moments later, laughter tumbles down the hall and Kiki stumbles in, half her afro damp and her eyes glassy. I hear the others shouting for her. Then Roxie's voice rings, "Come on, you can sleep when you're dead!"

Kiki stops short when she spots me. "What happened to you?"

"Didn't feel good."

"You missed the rest of the part-ay. They invited us out next weekend. A new club. Dante is pretty hot, huh?" she adds, but her voice softens as she looks me up and down.

"And Matteo, damn right delicious," Roxie says.

Yet there's Grant.

After I get into bed, I pull out a letter he wrote me when he arrived in Scotland. I've read it at least a dozen times. It tells of the trouble with his dad and the relief of escaping to his family's cottage out of the city. He describes the kind of quiet only the sea offers, in words that make me feel the ripples of placid water after a storm. I read the last sentence over and over: *I wish you were here.*

Chapter 37

As recollections of my childhood amass like ranks of soldiers ready to open fire, I hurry through the week, determined to dodge the bullets in my mind come the weekend. I want to let go, to feel young, wild, and free, unburdened by the past.

On Saturday, Kiki and I get ready again. "You have to wear this," she says, passing me her favorite strappy black dress, topping it with a faux-fur vest—much like one my mother had—and tall black boots.

"Are you sure?" I ask.

"Of course." She surveys my attire. "Smoky eyes," she says. "But we'll go with a light gloss on your lips this time."

"You're like my own personal stylist and fashion guru." I think of my mother before her designer clothes slowly disappeared from her closet as she sold them off. "You're like a sister, Kiki," I say, giving her a squeeze.

"Sister from another mister. I always wanted one. Instead, I have three brothers. Although, they come to me now when they want to go out and look good for the ladies."

She dons a studded miniskirt, a cappuccino-colored tank with lace down the front, her signature gold hoops, and strappy heels.

With our crew assembled, we hail a taxi, which delivers us to the Meatpacking District and another trendy club housed in a converted old warehouse—places I imagine my mother used to frequent with her celeb status.

Dante appears, followed by Matteo, wearing a V-neck and jeans that make him look delectable. "What happened to you the other night?" Matteo asks, twisting a piece of my hair in his fingers.

"I didn't feel well," I say. "Too much to drink."

As he ushers us past the bouncers, he whispers, "I have something better for tonight." We pass the pumping dance floor, and Matteo leads us upstairs to a private VIP room with a sweeping view of the club and DJ.

Kiki passes around champagne. "Pop, fizz, cheers," she calls. "Let's start this party."

After we dance and down two bottles, Matteo pulls me onto his lap and kisses my neck, nibbles my ear, and whispers how beautiful I am. "I want to kiss you inside and out. I want to lick you, to taste you, tickle you . . ." He slides me onto the leather banquette and pulls a baggie out of his pocket. He pours white powder, which I'm sure isn't crushed pills, onto the glass table and divides it into long, thin lines. He takes a long sniff and passes a rolled bill to me.

I'm effervescent from the champagne, and I don't think twice. I inhale deeply and feel a tingling sensation. My teeth go numb, and a smile identical to Sorel's parts my lips. I start laughing as if I own the night, this club, like nothing can stop me. I stand up and dance on the banquette. Matteo joins me as the others vulture the remaining lines on the glass table.

My body moves in time with the music. When the DJ mixes one song seamlessly into the next, I don't stop. Instead of thunder, there's laughter in my ears, and I feel as light as a feather. A few other friends of Matteo's enter the area, two girls, also unmistakably models, accompanied by three other guys. I twirl and turn to the heavy beat.

When my champagne glass is empty, Matteo takes the opportunity to pull me close; a long kiss wets my lips. I never want him to stop. Everywhere he touches my body ignites with energy that doesn't belong to me. There's momentum and velocity to my delight; everything that does and doesn't matter tumbles swiftly away from me. The music, the flashing lights, and the trickery of my own mind possess me.

"I know who you remind me of now," he says.

"Who's that?" I ask.

"Kate Moss. Dante, doesn't she look like Kate Moss?" he shouts to his friend.

Dante lifts his face from Kiki's neck, where he kissed her delicately. "She does." He nods affirmatively.

I feel desirable and dazzling.

"We'll start calling you KM instead of PJ," Kiki jokes. "Do you have any more of that stuff?" she asks unabashedly.

Matteo takes the baggie out of his pocket and says, "I thought you'd never ask."

Another line and another jolt of energy charges through my body.

Kiki pulls me up to dance with her on the table. She unzips the back of my dress as she kicks off her shoes. She unbuttons her shirt to reveal a black lace bra. She slides her hands on my shoulders from behind and breathes in the sloping curve of my neck, then licks it with her tongue. She and I dance in a rhythmic, sexy way, forgetting ourselves, the world—everything but the two inches of space that close between us. I'm not sure where my body ends and hers begins. She pulls me toward her and plants her lips on mine, soft, sensual, a woman's kiss. She pulls away, and we continue to dance, her bare skin brushing against mine and our lips meeting from time to time until the song ends.

When we step down, Matteo kisses my tattoos, my shoulder, and my lips. Dante cuts another line on the table, and Kiki, topless, kneels by his side. Matteo draws me over to the table.

"One more?" he asks. We each take another hit.

I lift my arms overhead and spin, losing track of Matteo and what day it is, what happened last week and the year before that. History erases itself, and I am free.

I join Kiki, Dante, Haruki, Reesa, and Roxie on the banquette, and rapid-fire conversation pings from person to person. We hardly listen to anything but the sound of our own self-important words. My pulse throbs in my ears when, across the room, I spot Matteo making out with one of the girls who came in earlier.

Seeing Matteo and the girl kissing cuts through me with a deep reminder of betrayal. The moment comes crashing down. I don't feel glamorous anymore. I feel used. Sorel's coarse words rip into my mind: "You're washed up." They sting all over again. Doubly so with thoughts of Grant.

Fueled by drugs and crushed by rejection, I slide my feet back into Kiki's boots and storm out, rudely bumping into Matteo as I exit. Kiki and the others rush after me.

Once on the relatively quiet street, Kiki bursts out, "Come on, PJ, that's what happens, it's no big deal."

I don't answer, consumed by how meaningless it all is. I peer into the endless darkness formed by the long corridor of buildings.

"Plus I thought you had a boyfriend anyway," she says pointedly.

Grant bursts into my distorted mind. Grant. Oh dear, Grant. "What have I done?" I put my fingers to my lips, still tasting like champagne and Matteo.

Haruki interrupts my fretting. "Actually, sweetie, that was perfect timing, we have exactly twenty minutes to get our asses back to the dorm."

Back at Parsons, too wired to contemplate sleep, we climb to the roof. Kiki pulls out some powder from Dante, and I do another line, once more seeking that feeling of lightness, that erasure of being. My body strains to keep up with my mind and my mind with my body. I teeter to the edge of the roof and look down. Cars and taxis whiz by, shouting drifts up from below, and laughter crackles from behind me.

I feel alone. I am a girl on the edge, on the edge of the past, present, and future, on the edge of love and lust, on the edge of truth and deceit. I tilt forward and back, wavering on heels and inebriation. I look down and then up. Falling is terrifying, but so is flying. A shooting star races through the sky. Just before it disappears, I make a wish and step away.

Chapter 38

We retreat to the patio, chain-smoking and going over our night, avoiding the tender issue of Matteo kissing another girl and me kissing Matteo. None of it matters, except for one reason, Grant. I admonish myself for being under the influence of my own stupidity and struggle with whether or not to tell him.

"That dance was H-O-T hot, ladies," Haruki says as he exhales a plume of smoke.

"You're gay," Kiki says.

"So are you," he counters.

"Bi," she says, correcting him.

"Whatevs," he says, rolling his eyes.

"But our PJ most certainly is not," Kiki says.

She wrests my attention. "What?" I ask, confused.

"You're not gay. In case you ever wondered. Not even bi," Kiki remarks.

"What are you talking about?"

"It was a sweet kiss, but you didn't quite put your heart in it," she says, referring to her lips on mine.

Everyone laughs.

"No," I whisper. "Because my heart belongs to someone else." The kiss with Mateo stains my mind. I wonder if, like Shale said, I can layer a coat of paint over it, hiding the mistake.

A chorus of "Oohs" brings me back to the conversation.

"He's patient and kind. I would give anything to be with him right now." I look up at the black canvas of night sky and wonder if the stars will ever return, if Shale ever saw them again, if I will.

"You should call him. What's the time difference?" Haruki says wistfully, as if he too would like the guy I described.

"Yeah, why don't you ever talk on the phone?" Kiki asks.

"He doesn't have a phone where he's staying for the summer," I say. The dark night presses me toward sleep. I close my eyes, listening for Grant's voice. I imagine the conversation, but before I can follow the thread of thought across the sea, I blink my eyes open and the sun has come up.

A sparrow pecks at a crumb next to a cracked terra-cotta planter. Haruki and Kiki snooze on a lounge chair, back-to-back, Haruki's eyeglasses askew. I close my eyes again, hoping the summer ends soon.

With just under a month left in New York, the weeks speed by like an accelerated three-ring circus. In the center, the ringmaster, Kiki, doles out potions for all of us eagerly awaiting performers: Haruki, Reesa, Roxie, and me. We entertain her with outrageous stories and dance until the sun pierces the night.

Then, still wired, we go to class, thinking we're everyone's gift to witty and enlightening conversation, creativity, and amusement. Afterward, we crash until the sun sets and then repeat: drinks, drugs, dancing, and rooftop mischief.

When the deadline for our final projects approaches, I'm spent and unstable, like I'm eroding, pieces of me falling away in sandy clumps, revealing guilt over the night with Matteo. Insecurity and inadequacy duel within me. I have a stack of half-finished letters, each starting *Dear Grant,* but the rest of the words come out in a tangle.

Creatively bereft, all the ideas I came up with for my final during the hours of gabbing prove elusive, as if I can't quite snatch what made them so brilliant to begin with. I push my notebook away.

Kiki chews on the end of her pen and complains that her project isn't coming along as well as she hoped either. "What we need . . ." she says with a wink. "Come on, I know where we can go."

"Not Dante's?"

"Nope. This will be fresh and direct," she says knowingly.

The cab brings us deep into the East Village, and the streets look too familiar, like the buildings whisper and try to lure me into the channels of the past. I hold my breath. I hesitate, with one hand on the door.

"What's the matter, PJ? This is where Dante and I went. It's fine." Kiki leads me up the cement steps of a building that looks greenish in the streetlights. The strata of graffiti color the wall in the vestibule. The old building smells like rotted wood, ashes, and boiled cabbage. Kiki rings a buzzer, and we climb to the third floor. She gestures in the direction of the peephole, and the door opens after the clicking sound of a series of locks.

We enter a clean apartment where a toddler, wearing nothing but a diaper, rides on a toy that looks like a little fire engine.

"Sawyer will be right with you," says the woman who answered the door, and then she excuses herself. Kiki crouches down and entertains the toddler. I try to blend in with the wallpaper, having the oddest feeling that I've been here before, but that could just be my brain warping stale memories with my present reality.

Shortly after, an older man emerges from a back room, wearing striped pajama bottoms and what looks like a brand-new white T-shirt; the folds from the package run down the front like tiles.

"Junior, it's almost time for ni-night," he says sweetly to the little boy.

Kiki stands up and smiles at Sawyer. "I came by here the other day with Dante," she says.

"I remember you; no one could forget you, that hair and your beautiful smile. You light up the whole room." He doesn't say this in a sleazy way; he actually seems like a sincere and gentle person.

When he turns to me, it's with unmistakable recognition. "JJ, is that you?" He steps closer.

I shrink into the ancient wallpaper.

"I haven't seen you in ages; in fact, you haven't aged. I thought you and I decided you were finished with this stuff," he says.

The room spins. I press myself against the wall.

"This is PJ," Kiki says, correcting him. "Don't worry, she's cool. A good friend."

He studies me a moment longer, then says, "My mistake. You look just like someone I used to know a long time ago."

I need to leave, but, familiar with these transactions, I know I have to be careful. I swallow hard and feign a smile. "Yeah, I get that a lot. It's nice to meet you. Do you mind if I use your bathroom?" The afternoon with Mitch and Sorel careens into my mind. I feel sick all over again.

I close the door, thick with layers of peeling paint. Sudsy bath toys linger in the bottom of the tub, and the clean scent of bubbles fills the air. I don't dare look in the mirror. I won't let myself cry. But I need to breathe, because my life is on rewind and fast-forward at the same time, preventing me from simply inhaling and exhaling.

When I come out, Kiki says, "Ready?

She buzzes as she hails a cab. "That guy is getting old; he thought you were someone named JJ, that's weird, huh?"

"No, it's not."

Kiki looks at me as if I'm not right in the head.

Pearl

"JJ was my mom." The city blurs by through the rain-soaked window.

"Strange coincidence," she says, apparently not realizing the truth, probably unable to conceive that someone's mom—my mom—would go to a dealer's house to get drugs. She probably imagines they were high school buddies or on the same tennis team. Her mom sends weekly care packages filled with snacks, soap, and other goodies.

Back at the dorm, I want nothing more than to forget the exchange at Sawyer's. I want to escape planet JJ-PJ and the possibility that there really is no difference between the two of us.

I do a line and start to sketch out my project, but concentration shuns me. Kiki takes a hit of pot because she complains about the same thing. Before long, my sketchbook, a mess of black lines and wrinkled paper, harasses me with failed attempts.

"This sucks," I say, gripping my head in my hands.

Kiki passes me the bowl confettied with pot. "You need to balance it out, the ups and downs," she says knowledgeably.

I take a hopeful inhale. I lean back in my chair, and with that, the room starts to close in on me. With open eyes, I see darkness all around. I feel myself getting very small, in danger of actually disappearing. A pinprick of light shines in the distance, and I continue to fade.

The chair is no longer underneath me. My lips are frozen. My body is bound and heavy, as if it withers and sinks at the same time. I want to get up, but can't. I want to speak, but words refuse to come out of my mouth. My head spins, and I'm nauseous and helpless, infantile, riddled with the possibility that I'm returning to the very beginning, crawling, mumbling, goo-ing and gah-ing, becoming nothing more than a thought. The string that holds me fast to solid earth spins away from me.

Cold hands press against my forehead. Kiki leans over me. Reesa and Roxie enter the room, amorphous figures I can't focus on.

"You're going to be all right," voices reassure me.

263

"You just had too much."

"Stay with us."

"Breathe."

"That's a girl. Come on, PJ."

A muffled song plays repeatedly on a loop. I want it to be quiet, to stop or change, but can't convey the thought. I am out of rhythm with it and the beat of my heart and the movement of my breath. I have no awareness of time, but I'm very far away from where that matters and yet keenly aware of the density and immobility of my body. And the beat plays over and over and over in the background.

I blink my eyes, drifting in and out of focus. More vague words of encouragement. They mean to be soothing, but I sense fear overlaid with my own.

Everything that composes me, atoms, molecules, blood, bone, it all gets still, quiet, as if waiting for my decision. My mind hushes. There's nothing left to listen to except for the slow, expectant beating of my heart. One. Two. Three. When I get to sixty, I draw a deep breath.

I don't want this. I wish to feel and touch and taste my life. I'm not ready to leave.

My lids are heavy, reluctant. I'm not sure what I'll see when I open them. I count breaths this time. Inhale. Exhale. I blink. I wriggle my fingers and toes. Very slowly, my vision clears, showing the desk and chair exactly as they were before. Kiki and the others sit next to me on the floor. I lift my head and drop it back. I feel like I went away and only parts of me returned. My mouth is dry. "Water," I rasp.

"You OK?" Kiki asks, putting a bottle in my hand.

I don't answer.

"That was freaky," she says too soon.

"Yeah." Shakily, I get to my feet and stumble to the bathroom, leaving the others stunned and motionless.

My brain moves slowly, as if pieces of it haven't yet rejoined the parts that brought me to the shower, got me undressed, and remembered how to turn on the faucet.

I let the water trickle overhead and lean against the wall, still shaken up. I don't try to figure out what happened; I want to avoid replaying it in my head.

All I know is that I never want it to happen again.

The shower stall fills with billowy clouds. I let them envelop me until the water runs cool. When the steam clears, I am sure of one thing: as free and loose as I felt at the club, as much fun as I've been having in the dorm, I won't find salvation in a mixture of cocaine, alcohol, and pot.

I'm not JJ. It was nothing more than a detour, a foolish one, what turned out to be a scary one, but I know well enough how toxic it is. I knew the singular outcome vicariously through my mother, and after tonight, whatever close brush I had, I now know it firsthand. I danced too close to the inevitable. I have to be my own heroine. I'm all I have, and I'm not ready to say good-bye.

When I return to the dorm room, Kiki's head rests on her desk, passed out, her breathing loud and nasal. The same ambient beat that played when I lost consciousness continues. I turn it off, and for the first time ever, I welcome silence. I climb onto my bunk, draw the sheet up, and fall into a dreamless sleep.

Chapter 39

I'm sluggish, as if I haven't quite recovered from whatever happened the night before. My body and brain conduct a mutiny for all the damage I've done. I go through the motions of class, spacing out, my thoughts creeping from fear to the strength of my resolve.

As I continue to struggle with my final project, genuine inspiration eludes me. Then I realize I haven't done something that throughout my life I've spent a better part of days and weeks doing. I grab a fresh sketchpad and leave the dorm, solo.

Over the summer, I became so accustomed to traveling in a pack it feels odd going out alone, but the streets hum with the fondness of home and the familiarity of being on my own. It's like I have new eyes, but with the comfort of the old, as my fingers curl around the contours of the sketchpad and pencil.

I venture toward Union Square, but stop at a café first. I think back to my week with Grant in Brooklyn. The center of my chest feels like it melts with longing, and the one person who can make it solid and satisfied writes me letters from across the Atlantic. He's not kissing some guy or girl, dancing on tables, or using drugs. Guilt sweeps through me like a frozen northern wind. There's howling in my ears, reminding me of my deception. I glance skyward, as though the guiding light of stars will burn brighter than the daytime sun. Instead, a woman leaning heavily on a shopping cart, a young man playing the guitar, and a mother with a small child toddling along beside her usher me forward. I cross into the park. The leaves on the horseshoe of trees dance and shimmy. With that, I let lust, drugs, and Matteo gust away.

Grant is my ocean, moon, and stars. He is my poet, my athlete, the sweetness in my life. Together, we are everything I believe in, and yet I've been unfaithful.

I stir my coffee. A truth swirls around the edges of my consciousness, taunting me, daring me to see it. It emerges as I bathe my face in the bright morning sun. I've been unfaithful to myself. I've disavowed what I know is right. I've been doing the things that I hated about my mother. Then a pitiful voice tells me I'm just a teenager, having fun. I make excuses, telling myself if it becomes a lifestyle, it would be worse than bad, but I'm not going to do that. I know better. I *thought* I knew better.

I find a vacant bench, watch people, and then sketch, streaking graphite onto the paper, slicing through the past and present; clean lines form armor, art, wild ensembles made for hiding secrets and telling stories. Like the stone Grant tossed in the lake, my mind skips from one painful memory to the next. In between, I watch the ripples spread in concentric circles, one thought blending into another. Strangely, there is enough space between each that I don't feel a desperate need to flee. They're just thoughts, just memories.

Midday, my stomach growls. I wander over to the falafel place I used to frequent. For once, I have enough money to pay. The cashier doesn't recognize me; they practically have a new one each week, but from behind the grill, the owner smiles.

"Haven't seen you in a long time. You look different," he calls over the sizzle of frying onions.

"Better or worse?" I ask.

"Just different." He isn't being insulting, but a lot has changed since I was here last summer, before Laurel Hill, before Grant, before Janet died. I glance at the squares of baklava on the counter and remember Grant and me laughing about the word *phyllo*.

I sit outside on a gum-stained stoop and dig into my pita. The falafel inside is even better than I remember. The tahini sauce dribbles down my chin.

The woman from earlier, the one with the shopping cart, wobbles by. She's dressed in layers of rags and dirty cloth, even in the summer heat. Garbage bags fill the basket, but wound on the metal frame are colorful ribbons, breezing alongside her home on wheels with each step. Like a bird, she wound pieces of thread and scraps of cloth to form a nest.

I've longed for a home to return to and realize it's just north in a small town, with an even smaller campus, in a dorm room I'd like to decorate with ribbons.

I begin sketching, first a nest, and then a woman dressed in a robin's egg–blue gown, rising from the nest, spun from gold. When I'm done, I get to my feet, searching for the woman, crossing streets, feeling frenzied I might not find her.

When I near the dorm at Parsons, I spot her cart, parked between two newspaper boxes, and opposite, on a stoop of her own, she rests, her eyes closed. I tuck the sketch under her hand and hope when she wakes up, she smiles.

When I return to the dorm, there's a note tacked on my door. *Grant called 11:53* and a number.

I try calling, but with each unanswered ring, my disloyalty and mistakes push him further out of my reach.

My unoccupied dorm room gives me the uninterrupted opportunity to put pieces of my project together. It has to represent what I learned over the summer and what fashion means to me and present a unique ensemble using at least three of the techniques I've studied.

The broad assignment requires refinement, and as clarity returns to my mind, I finally formulate a plan.

I've lost track of time when Kiki waltzes in the room. "Feeling better?" she asks.

"Much."

"You scared the devil outta hell last night. Glad you're OK," she says. Her accent makes the sentence sound like it's coated in sugar even though it was just the opposite.

"Yeah, me too," I answer quietly, not ready to lose the thread of inspiration as I hunch over my desk.

She reclines on her bunk and in minutes is snoring sweetly.

The last three days of classes consist of presentations. Everyone has to give a speech about his or her project and explain in detail what each component represents. Looking back, I never thought I would spend a summer studying fashion—my long-held dream—and nearly sabotage the entire thing.

By the time the final person stands and speaks for a half hour, my leg jiggles up and down, antsy. Kiki examines her fingernails, and Roxie's eyes droop. At the end, a round of applause jolts us all from our distractions.

"Everyone meet here at six a.m. sharp for our final field trip to the pre–Fashion Week event," the teacher says, dismissing us.

Kiki catches up with me in the hall. "Before we head back to the dorm and start packing and partying, you and I have some business."

I freeze, worrying that maybe she wants to charge me retroactively for all the money she's spent on booze and pills. She pulls me outside, hails a cab, and directs it to the Metropolitan Museum of Art.

Dumbfounded I ask, "What are we doing here?"

"I think the teachers were holding out on us. I have a surprise for you, and, well, me," she says.

The cab leaves us off in front of the vast steps of what has to be my favorite museum in the world.

"Really?" I ask in disbelief. We visited loads of galleries, museums, and boutiques over the summer, except, strangely enough, this one.

We stand in front of a sign announcing the largest costume collection on display, dating from classic Broadway to the beginning of color cinema and beyond.

"It's just opened today, and I got us tickets. Wish I could have sprung for the others too, but I knew you'd appreciate it the most," Kiki says.

I caught rare glimpses of the real Kiki over the summer, not the spitfire party girl present most of the time, but the genuine girl with a big heart. At times, she reminds me of Sorel, minus the grim adventures to the dark side.

We admire costumes from *Singin' in the Rain* to *Gone with the Wind* to *The Great Gatsby* and get lost in conversation about style and technique until the docent announces it's time to leave.

"That was the best last-day-of-summer-school, back-to-school-not-shopping-but-looking-at-clothes trip a girl could ever take," I say. "I'm not sorry I ever missed out."

"What? I mean, I'm glad you liked it, but back-to-school shopping, that's like a rite of passage. What do you mean, you missed out?"

"JJ," I whisper quietly. "Sawyer, that night—" I say, not really wanting to remember. "At some point he must have sold to my mother. She overdosed last spring."

Kiki's lips form a large O, and she pulls me close. "Like I told you, sister from another mister. Better late than never. Come to Atlanta, my mom will adopt you for sure. And we can play dress-up anytime."

"Thank you," I say with a smile.

The next day we hurtle through a whirlwind of tents at the pre–Fashion Week event, getting a behind-the-scenes glimpse of what goes into the production. Fashion, at its core, is an art form, beautiful in its own right, but also meant to adorn, enhance, shock, and express the inner life externally. I miss thumbing through my favorite copies of

Vogue, but even more than that, I long for the smooth glide of paint on canvas, colors bleeding together or standing independently, and oil drying like tears.

Pulled in one direction and then another, we conclude the summer program with a banquet that night.

Once back in the dorm room, Kiki pulls out a bottle of Southern Comfort. "We end how we began, a handful of girls and a gay," she says, looking at Haruki and the rest of us with a grin.

"You girls are so beautiful," he says. "I'm sad to say good-bye."

Me too, mostly.

Chapter 40

As the sun burns through early morning haze, I say good-bye to Manhattan, and with tremendous amounts of anticipation, the black sedan carries me north.

Half of me hopes Grant will be waiting in front of Vivian Brookwood and we'll race across the lawn to meet each other. He'll sweep me up into his arms and twirl me around like a scene out of a movie.

My backpack slips lower on my shoulders when I approach the vacant porch. Maybe Grant hasn't arrived yet. As I enter, Connie greets students along with a different senior dorm assistant this year: Charmindy.

"Welcome, welcome," Connie says, overly cheerful, as if truly pleased to see me.

Charmindy says, "Surprise!" then passes me a Sharpie and name tag. "You know the drill." But before I can scribble the letters to my name, she gives me a squeeze. I linger there, breathing in her spicy scent, not realizing how much I missed her.

Connie gives Charmindy a withering look. "I know you're friends, but you have to greet everyone the same. Vivian Brookwood etiquette."

Shocked, I say, "I want to know why my *friend* didn't tell me she was going to be senior dorm assistant, meaning *she'll* have a single and I'll have a new roommate, since we'd planned to share again." Despite my disappointment, I can't resist a smile.

"You'll be in room seventeen, Sorel's old room," Charmindy says.

"With?" I say with more impatience than I mean.

"Me!" Charmindy replies.

When I enter room seventeen, the smell of a fresh coat of paint fails to erase Sorel's essence: nag champa incense, strictly forbidden in the dorm, but she burned it anyway. I deposit my suitcase and backpack and am turning to leave, to see if I can find Grant, when Charmindy appears.

"Long time no see!" she says brightly and pulls me into another hug. Her freshly cut hair grazes her shoulders. Her parents, Mr. and Mrs. Rajasekhara, appear, chattering about Charmindy's class schedule. After cordial greetings, Mrs. Rajasekhara asks me about my classes and then tells me I look healthier than last year. She promises to send us care packages more often—sweetly crediting my improved appearance to the goodies she'd sent.

Charmindy's dad gazes out the window, reminding me of Sorel's after-hours exit and entry to the room, courtesy of the bulkhead that rests just below his line of sight. I look forward to putting it to use. I'm not sure what Charmindy will think if late-night rendezvous with Grant become a regular thing, especially with her role as senior dorm assistant. Now that a continent doesn't separate us, I ache, more than ever, for his touch, for his honesty and smile. I'm turning to leave a second time when a dolly stacked with boxes appears and a staff person peers out from behind.

"Pearl Jaeger?" he asks.

"That's me."

"Great, just sign here that you received these."

I do as asked and instead of leaving as I intended to, I make quick work of unpacking so I can return the boxes before he leaves the building.

A rumpus of flying Frisbees and blaring music in front of the boys' dorm contrasts with the orderliness of Viv Brooks. As I pick my way up the stone steps, avoiding abandoned boxes and suitcases, a thought marches into my mind: *What version of myself did I take with me this time? Manhattan Pearl? JJ's daughter? An exemplary Laurel Hill student? The girl in the self-portraits?*

Pepper lounges in the entry room. "Hey," he says, lengthening out the word by at least a dozen *Y*s.

"How was the adventure to Washington?" I ask.

"Memorable." He smirks.

"Will I hear about it?"

"Most of it," he says devilishly.

"I can't imagine what life will be like here without Sorel."

"Yeah, me neither," he says, turning instantly glum at the reminder. "I'm going out to see her Thanksgiving, Christmas, spring break, my sweet potato sugar mama. Don't tell her I said that. We're going the distance, long distance, but we promised to stick together; it's just one year. I'm applying to schools out there."

"Cool," I say, offering a smile to conceal my doubt. Sorel dances to her own drummer, and if Pepper isn't around, she'll find someone else to keep the beat for her. I scan the room. "Grant here yet?"

"Nope, haven't seen him."

The breath in my chest stutters. "Could you let him know I stopped by?"

I plod back to my dorm. I've anticipated our reunion with such intensity I haven't considered anything postponing it. Perhaps he had flight trouble or his dad accompanied him, which might explain the delay. My steps hitch as I consider going back and waiting, but I still haven't decided if I'll tell him all the details about my summer. I cheated, but a voice in my head whines, *We didn't exactly set the parameters of our relationship like Sorel and Pepper.* I seesaw back and forth between truth and lies.

I finish unpacking as the shadows of the trees lengthen. Far across the lawn, the sun bathes the maple leaves in a peachy glow, obscuring Grant's dorm.

I wander into the common room, looking for Charmindy. She probably had to go comfort an already-homesick freshman. Surrounded by students and families, once again, I feel alone. The chatter and laugher reminds me of the power of family to provide a sense of belonging, a frame of reference, and the lingering hug that says they're just a phone call away.

My arms are wrapped around my chest when Charmindy enters, sans parents or puffy-faced, teary freshman. "My parents just left, we got here yesterday for dorm-assistant orientation. Settled in?" she asks.

"Sure," I say.

"What do you think of our new room?" she asks.

"Already feels like home," I answer.

"I'm glad I don't have to live in Terran's old single. Bad vibes in there. Oh hey, did you hear her necklace turned up, just before the end of school last spring? Crazy, huh. I guess it fell behind her dresser or something."

"Yep, crazy," I reply, recalling seeing it around her neck before graduation. "What's the story with the other DA? I thought it was supposed to be Abbie, right?"

"I'm sorry I didn't tell you. I applied, but yeah, they selected Abbie Friedman. Then over the summer, I got a call asking if I was still interested; I guess I was the next pick. Her parents divorced, and it looks like she's not coming back. I sent you a few emails, but you never replied. I didn't know how else to get in touch with you."

During the rush of months in New York, I never thought to check my Laurel Hill student email. I'm essentially the only person on the planet without a phone, so it's not surprising we fell out of touch. I feel like a jerk because all I've been thinking about is myself. Now, with Charmindy before me, I sense she's changed. Aside from having generally stretched out and cutting her hair shorter, it's like she's sharper, more mature, and edgier, as though she left the lavender and perfumed veil of innocence in India.

"Are you going to dinner?" she asks.

Although I'm sure Grant would have stopped by my dorm before going to the dining hall, I hope he'll arrive hungry, find me out of my dorm, and appear, wrapping his arms around me.

Charmindy and I fill our trays with lasagna and garlic bread and sit at a small table for two. "Tell me all about Parsons," she says.

I wouldn't have shared the extent of the craziness before, but now that she's dorm assistant, an authority figure, I guard the secrets more closely. "Parsons, epic design program, mostly I focused on fashion. And Manhattan, loads of history, great restaurants and museums . . ." I say carefully, unsure if I have a Laurel Hill version of an FBI file with notes to keep watch over me. "You?"

Charmindy's eyes flicker, her eyebrow lifts, then she says, "I sweated my ass off in Chennai. Obeyed my parents' every whim, studied, and volunteered," she says with candor. "In a word, my summer was *shit*."

Water nearly comes gushing out my nose. I grab my napkin and try to stifle a great, snorting laugh. "I've never heard you swear, the most you've ever said was *darn* if you stubbed your toe. What—?"

She suppresses a grin, but says, "Listen, according to my test scores I'm more intelligent than ninety-seven percent of the students here, but there is another kind of smart you might not expect me to have. Despite the fact that I come from a wealthy family, am wrapped up in my studies and achievement, I'm not stupid or blind. I know you had a hard time last year. I know you were generous with the pills prescribed for your cough or whatever. I know you snuck out and partied with

Sorel . . . And I turned the doorknob to let Grant in when you needed him by your side."

I don't know what to say. The boisterous greetings of returning students, the shushing of the dishwasher behind the wall, the rushing in my ears, it all goes quiet, because I realize Charmindy didn't turn her back on me; in fact, she may have been watching out for me all along. Warmth spreads across my skin like a hug, but I'm still not sure how to respond to this kind, bighearted, understanding, and forgiving friend of mine. A real, true friend.

"So your summer was shit? Your poise and academic accomplishments don't suggest the word *shit* is part of your vocabulary. I never expected you to say that. Junior ambassador to the UN or something, but not shit, that's my territory."

"Wait, I wasn't done. And your big, bad I-don't-give-a-shit attitude suggests that you actually do care, a lot. Plus, as senior dorm assistant, my first point of business was enacting equal opportunity vocabulary usage."

We burst into laughter.

"There are probably a lot of things about me that would surprise you," she says, straight-faced, but a smile hints at the corners of her mouth. "I also know there's more to your story, but first I'll tell you about mine. Back to the shit . . . I volunteered for a charity organization this summer, back home, and saw some real-life *shit*. It made parts of me harder but softened others. It made me clearer on who I am, and what I want to do during this lifetime, and it isn't turning my back on people, especially people I care about."

"Thanks for not getting me in trouble last year."

"I probably should have been more available to you."

"No worries, Char. The fact that you were there at all speaks volumes."

Back at Vivian Brookwood, with still no sign of Grant, along with the other girls, I crowd into the common room for Connie's welcome spiel. My mind and heart scale the possibility that Grant isn't coming. I plummet into fears of a dark and lonesome senior year without him. Pepper and I can start a lonely hearts club.

Charmindy's deliberate voice cuts through my thoughts. "I'm Charmindy, the senior dorm assistant. If anyone has any questions, needs someone to talk to as you get used to boarding school life, please don't hesitate to ask. My door is always open."

Usually senior dorm assistants get a single. Did she opt to stay with me, or did Connie want to keep the single open in case Abbie returned? I wonder if Charmindy can assist me with how to fill a growing sense of emptiness or how to survive without Grant.

Later on, Charmindy paces the floor in our dorm, wringing her hands. She stops, levels me with her gaze, and then drops the news that Brett Fairfax visited her for a week. "I left that part out, huh?"

Once more, she leaves me nearly speechless. "He visited you in India?"

She gushes. "I don't know how you keep things from me. I was about to explode if I didn't tell you. I'd mentioned the charity program to him last spring, and he signed up. It was a big surprise to see him standing there at the first meeting. He was the only one smiling and holding a box of chocolates. It was sweet. We shared them with these little kids who'd never eaten anything like that before. We were in Mumbai together for a week." Her cheeks blossom pink. As the minutes tick by, punctuated by Brett this and Brett that, my heart feels exposed by my own uncertainty.

Lights-out casts me into nervous worry. I contemplate sharing the situation with Charmindy, but still jet-lagged and exhausted from her new role, she's already breathing deeply across the room.

Tension spreads through my neck and shoulders. I toss in bed, feeling insecure and abandoned. Moonlight illuminates the Frida Kahlo poster over my bed; only, I don't feel like she's watching me anymore, but rather, watching over me.

I rub my neck, and under the heel of my hand, I feel the slightly raised tattoo of the swallows. I trust they won't lead me anywhere but to the home in my heart. Shale's words, rusty, from before the summer come back, bit by bit, in his clipped yet clear accented English. "The only enemy you have is yourself. Stay there, with her, until you aren't enemies anymore." Fear. Rejection. Abandonment. The triumvirate makes me brittle. When I connect the dots, obviously, my perception of inadequacy carries over to my relationship with Grant. Shale would tell me that I have to forget the what-ifs and think about what is. I stay *there*, with the script of all the things that could go wrong, the wildly ridiculous scenarios that have been playing in the background of my mind all day, until one by one they slowly start to dissolve.

I roll over and stretch my legs, pleased that there are enough brain cells remaining in my head to arrive at a reasonable response to the very strong fear that everything is about to suck.

Chapter 41

As I summon sleep, a tapping sound merges with my predreams. I ignore the old building's creepy shifting noises for a moment and focus on the source of the tapping.

I go to the window. My heart skips a beat. Grant, tall and smiling, with notably shorter hair, peers up at me, illuminated by the full moon. I slide over the sash and touch lightly down on the bulkhead before bounding onto the grass and into his arms. I feel him smiling as his cheek presses against mine. I put my hands on either side of his neck and draw my lips to his. I purr with excitement, relief, and joy.

The frogs and crickets chirp loudly from the woods. Hand in hand, we scoot back to his dorm room. The campus is quiet, and I'd almost rather stay outside under the stars, but it's too risky. Pepper snores loudly and rolls over when we pass.

Grant and I lie down, facing each other on his bed.

Anticipation hums in my cells, causing my words to vibrate. "Where have you been? What happened?" I want to add that I missed him, but the words weld themselves to the roof of my mouth.

Pearl

"My father. It's a long story that involved going to Gavin's, watching a soccer match, among other things. Do you want to hear about it now or later?"

I reach my lips to his by way of answer and feel myself melting into him, closing the space wrought by time and the Atlantic. He feels so right. His hand skims the small of my back as we press into one another. Our breath gets heavy. Then an alarming thought slices through the moment. Matteo. The last lips that touched mine belonged to Matteo. The last person who touched my bare skin was Matteo. Guilt and an avalanche of uncertainty crash down on me. I retract.

"What's the matter?" Grant asks.

I hesitate; in my head, honesty smiles dutifully, telling me to do the right thing. Excuses, demanding that I not tell him the truth, throw a tantrum like a petulant child.

"You go first," I say, postponing my decision.

"For one, my hair." He rubs his hand through his short, messy hair, then tiredly over his face.

"Why'd you cut it?"

"From the moment my plane landed in Glasgow, my father lectured me about everything from my appearance to my future. He started in with a carefully laid plan of feigned patience and appealing to what he thought interested me, but when I didn't agree with his ideas, he did a one eighty. We fought, but like I'd planned, I went to the summer cottage, alone. When I went back to Glasgow for a few days before my flight here, he was like a madman. He came at me with scissors and cut off a hunk of it. Who does that?" His voice tremors and then he goes on, solid rock once more." Then, after a few days, I couldn't stand it anymore. I left, changed my ticket, and went to Gavin's. I tried calling."

I recall the note on my door.

"He doesn't understand me. He has this idea of who he wants me to be, based on who he never became, like he wants me to make up for his shortcomings. And the idea of who I want to be—" He pauses and takes a breath. "Is the person he isn't. Does that make sense?" His accent nips at the words.

"Yeah," I whisper. "You want to pursue your own dreams. If you live your father's version of a life, it would be a lie and will make you unhappy. That's what matters, right? That you're happy?" Inside, I wither.

"Exactly. My brother more or less satisfied him, but he wants more, me. Gav has a cushy job, is clean-cut, and is making a good name for himself. We knew his scientific mind would take him places, but I'm almost the opposite, or the other half, physical and artistic, like our mother—" He runs out of words.

I'm reminded there isn't anyone who has expectations of me.

After a thoughtful moment, he continues. "Then my dad appeared in New York—sorry, I don't mean to go on about this. I'm spoiling our first time back together."

"You aren't." *My* confession is about to royally mess things up. I lift my chin to kiss him one more time. Part of me fears it might be the last.

He brushes my bangs from my eyes, and my heavy eyebrows scrunch together. "Tell me about your summer," he says.

"At Parsons—" It's as if I have sand in my mouth. "My roommate, Kiki, she sort of reminded me of Sorel, if Sorel was basically the opposite of the way she is and—" I'm not making sense. What I did doesn't make sense. "We partied a lot. It got kinda heavy, Grant. Sort of outta control."

He moves back from me a fraction as if he senses what's coming.

"I didn't mean for it to. It was just there, and I overdid it." Each word brings me closer to loss.

"What are you saying?" he asks plainly.

"At a party, I kind of kissed someone. Well, he kissed me. I was pretty high and drunk. It didn't mean anything, and I realized what was happening and stopped it."

The words, reluctant before, can't come fast enough. I want him to hear my apology before he pushes me away. I want him to understand and forgive me. "We kissed again, but it was really messed up. Kiki, she kinda kissed me too. The whole thing, it was the worst mistake ever." I start to cry. "I'm so sorry, Grant. I am so, so, so sorry."

He stiffens and pulls his arm from around me. "So, what you're saying is you were with someone else?"

"We didn't have sex. It was just kissing," I say pleadingly. Tears spill from my eyes.

"You said you kind of kissed someone. You either did or didn't."

I can't look at him, and that is enough of a response.

"You were effed-up on what?"

"Kiki had all kinds of alcohol and pills, and then those guys gave us coke. I didn't mean to, it was just there, and I missed you and—" Whatever words I try, I know they won't suffice.

"She made you take these drugs, and then somehow your lips just ended up on someone else's?" he asks sarcastically, straining not to raise his voice, but the Scottish accent clips his words. "No, PJ, you made a choice. You took the drugs or the booze or whatever, and you were with someone else?" He sits up. His elbows rest on his knees, and his hands run through his hair. "I don't understand why. What about—?"

"I know it was wrong. I missed you, and being back in New York with all the memories was so hard. I just wanted to escape it all. I just wanted to have fun and forget everything."

"Including me, huh?"

"No, not you. That's why I wanted to tell you. I don't want secrets between us. I want to be honest with you. I wanted—I—" Words of substance to replace my flimsy excuses and irrelevant reasoning fail me. "I messed up." I position myself beside him, but already see the gulf forming between us. I don't want to leave. I'm not ready to let go of the one good relationship I've ever had.

Grant sniffles. "PJ." He whispers as though he's trying to keep himself from falling apart. "That's shite." It's the voice of hurt. We're mere inches apart, but he may as well be miles away, back across the ocean. "I think you need to leave."

"I don't want to. I don't want to give you up. I don't want to hurt you. This hurts me too, to know I failed myself, that I failed us. It was so wrong. It was foolish, and I would never do it again."

His silence is like a dry riverbed. Then he says, "That's right. You won't." His tears are gone, his voice desolate.

"Grant, please. I'll—"

The vacancy in his eyes tells me words are useless. I'll never do it again because there will be no us. The finality with which he spoke disgraces me. I slowly sit up.

"I'm so sorry. If you'll ever forgive me, please—" I whisper, but I say no more. My head feels like it's clamped in a vise, with the threat of releasing in a fit of hysterical crying. I have to be quiet, or I risk getting us both in trouble on top of everything else. I force one leg in front of the other as I creep past Pepper, fast asleep, probably dreaming of Sorel, to the window.

When I make it back to my bed, I bury my head in the pillow and cry, a muffled, pathetic sound. I cry for what I've done wrong. I cry for loss. I cry for my heart. My mother broke it once, and now I've done the dirty job of breaking it again, along with Grant's. I think about Janet and the innumerable boyfriends whose hearts she crushed. How am I any different? *Why should it matter? Be young, wild, free; do what you want*, a loathsome voice in my head hedges. I disgust myself. I want to escape myself. I want . . . *No, Pearl. Stay where you are. It will pass*, another voice says, unbidden, sounding like a Norwegian translation.

The racing in my head stops. My mind quiets to the beat of my heart and the sound of my breath, like the breath of the sea inside a conch shell.

I remain in a place of lucid questioning. I listen and wait. The sky starts to lighten. A story, written in invisible ink, based on the script from my childhood, slowly reveals its letters. Pieces of it start to fall into place as Charmindy stirs across the room. I'm not ready to leave this magical and mystifying place where I've discovered what I thought was true isn't fixed in place.

Grabbing a pair of jeans, my boots, and a sweatshirt, I quietly steal out of the room. I need to continue to think. I doubt anyone will miss me if I don't appear at the Head of School Welcoming Ceremony.

The campus, still tucked in under warm blankets and sleepy light, doesn't betray me as I sneak to the wooded path leading to the clearing. This time, I'm not there to smoke. The space affords me a quiet refuge where beliefs cut, shuffle, and rearrange themselves.

I slouch down against the large rock in the middle and look up toward the sky above. A bird flits across the opening in the canopy of trees. I close my eyes and lean my head against the rock.

What is my story?

My mother didn't have an operating manual for her own life or mine. So she made do with the belief that there weren't consequences, that she wasn't crushing hearts beneath her heel, yet she denied that many of the things that happened to her were a result of her actions. It was all just fear. She was afraid of what would happen to her if she didn't escape her emotions, but there's no escape. No magic pill.

I'll live through this. Without drugs. Without escaping.

The sun shines almost colorless through a pocket in the leaves and branches. It's the color of hope.

A voice deep inside asks, *What'll it be, Pearl? It's your choice, life or death, a future or drugs, friends and love or unendurable loneliness?*

I stay there awhile longer, letting all my thoughts filter down and settle like sediment so a new foundation can take the place of the old. A fresh kind of peace settles over me. I no longer feel myself running and kicking and screaming. There's no pull to be somewhere else. There's no chance I'll be mistaken for anyone else.

I close my eyes, listening to the hum of my breath, the birds singing, and the gentle rustle of the leaves.

Eventually, everything will be all right. And until it is, I'll be OK.

As I leave the woods by the trail that I walked countless times last year, it's like my feet have never touched this path before. Maybe I can't be free of my mother or the past, but I'm not going to let it trap me or lead me places I don't want to go. And for anyone who thinks I can't, I shout, "Watch me!" My voice echoes off the walls of the hills.

Chapter 42

Back at Viv Brooks, it's quiet until the students return in pairs and groups. Showered and dressed, I act as if I've been there all along.

Charmindy raises her eyebrow as we gather in the common room. "Where were you?"

Words tumble out of my mouth before I can stop them. "I was having a revolution."

She looks fearlessly into my eyes, not dodging my intensity. For once, I'm steadfast and hold her gaze. A smile as subtle as the *Mona Lisa*'s appears. "You mean a revelation?"

"Yeah, sure," I answer.

I can't say more because she has to lead some of the mandatory activities in the dorm and then peer group and sports sign-ups.

In the student center, a table displays information about a term abroad. My Spanish teacher had mentioned last year that some of us would be candidates for the program.

"*Hola,*" says one of the girls at the booth.

"*Hola,*" I say faintly.

"Are you a candidate for a term abroad in *España*?"

"Maybe?"

"Who's your *profesor*?" she asks, pronouncing the last word in Spanish.

"Senora Azuelos. I'm Pearl Jaeger."

She looks at a sheet of paper.

"You're on here. If you'd like to take some information, you can consider the trip to Spain next semester. There will be two sessions for applying. The dates and times are on that sheet," she says, indicating a red flyer.

As I leave the student center, I spot Grant on the sidewalk by the gym. Everything about him attracts me like a bee to nectar; even his short hair somehow suits him. Before opening the door, he looks over his shoulder, then quickly away, as if he's seen something he doesn't want to.

I instantly feel wretched. I disgust myself. I hate myself. I may as well skip college, because I've already earned a degree in stupidity, with a minor in selfishness.

Charmindy is sitting on the steps when I return to the dorm, as though she was waiting for me. With one sharp look, she lifts her eyebrow, then says, "Let's walk." Once away from the dorm, she asks, "There's still a missing scene from your summer. What aren't you telling me?"

I clear my throat. *Where to start?* "I did something, ten notches past dumb. I hurt someone I—" My heart confirms my thoughts. I try again. "I hurt someone I love. And I think it hurt me, if not as much, possibly more than it hurt him."

"In other words, you screwed up."

"That's the sum of it."

"And you want to make it right?"

"I want to make *me* right. Not right like I didn't do anything wrong. I did. But right as in I wouldn't do something so damaging again. That I'll take care in making decisions. That I won't be so afraid of love." The words sting as they come out of my mouth.

"I see." She pauses on the sidewalk. "I know about a lot of things, not love so much. But there is one thing I am sure of, you can't give up. You can't annihilate your emotions. You need to feel them."

"Yeah, and it sucks."

"Sometimes to get through something—have you ever heard the saying 'The only way out is through?' No shortcuts. No escaping. No avoiding. Do you understand?" she asks with her patented lifted eyebrow. Her dark eyes penetrate mine. I don't doubt the possibility that she can read in my mind the belief I held for so many years that I am tainted, damaged goods and that something is wrong with me. But I also see in those dark pools resting in her face, gleaming with honesty, that she doesn't believe a word of it.

"You can heal and move on. You have to believe that," Charmindy says wisely. "I believe that."

We walk a bit farther in contemplative silence.

"There's something else I know, though it's probably one of the hardest things a person can ever do. It's another *F* word."

I raise my eyebrows this time, racking my mind.

"Forgive," she says as though the letters are sacred.

"I think you misunderstood. Grant needs to forgive me, not the other way around."

Before she can say more, we've looped back to the dorm. A group of first-year students draws her over in a chorus of questions about schedules, leaving me with more of my own.

My schedule waits for me on the corkboard in the dorm. I pull it down and scan the top few classes, AP English, humanities, Spanish . . . then my last period says *Art V: Independent Study*. The teacher's name in the adjacent box reads *Rasmus Shale*.

"I didn't sign up for another class with Shale . . ." I say aloud, earning a frightened look from a passing freshman.

I plunge into classes the next day, stopping by the administration building during my break to see Justine, my advisor. She's busy and distracted, with a line of students requesting transfers, but when she sees me, she smiles.

"I figured you'd be in. Not thrilled about Art V?"

"I didn't—"

"No, but since you passed Painting IV with an A-plus and Shale tested you out of the other art classes, we figured this was your only option, unless, of course, you don't want to take any art electives." Her smile suggests pride.

"I passed? But—"

She shuffles papers impatiently. "PJ, I have students waiting, you need to make your decision or come back later."

"No, it's fine. I'll take it, I guess. Thanks," I say hastily.

Although I find plenty of time to think about Grant, only in AP English do I actually have to see him in person. He refuses to look at me, but I can't tear my eyes from him while I should be taking notes on rhetorical strategies. His entire arm reveals fresh tattoos. They must have been part of his rebellion. Or a way to prove that he isn't his father's puppet. Or maybe just a genuine tribute to his grandfather.

Sure enough, Mr. Nichols tears me from my thoughts. "PJ, care to elaborate on chiasmus?"

My eyes freeze on Grant's arm. There are a pair of swallows, much like mine, sitting on a branch that stretches up along his forearm, then transitions into a nautical rope that runs along the frothing sea surrounding the mermaid.

In my embarrassed silence, Grant lifts his arm to answer the question, revealing an anchor inked on the inside of his bicep, along with other fresh tattoos. I wonder if they're pieces of his grandfather's stories or souvenirs collected during his months in Scotland. I missed so much of his life over the summer, my own life too.

As my thoughts cling to Grant, Mr. Nichols has us discuss the essays we had to prepare for the first day of class from our summer reading. I can't help but glance in Grant's direction what feels like every few seconds.

His face is a blank canvas, filling me with self-loathing. I'm unacceptable.

During our five-minute break halfway through the period, I follow Grant out of the classroom and down the hall. Before I can get his attention or figure out what I'm going to say, he enters the boys' bathroom.

"Grant?" I call after him as the door swishes closed. I wait for longer than it would take him to use the toilet. I wait some more. Finally, I look both ways down the hall, and then I nudge the door open. He rests a hand on each side of the white porcelain sink, looking into the drain.

"I'm going to transfer out of the class," he says, not looking at me.

"No, I will," I say quickly, dreading having to go back to Justine's office. "Or maybe neither one of us has to. You can just pretend I'm not even there." Tears fill my eyes. For my entire life, everyone, including myself, has been pretending that I'm not even there. It aches.

"I've been trying to, but I can't," he says, his voice tight.

The swallows inked on my chest practically flutter. I step toward him. I speak softly, barely above a whisper. "Do you hear me when I say I'm sorry? I am so, so, so sorry. I have a lot of things that I'm working out, things that have prevented me from being true to myself, no less you."

He looks up and pierces me with a hard stare. "I'm sorry I had to get in the way of you working out your crap," he says, brushing by me toward the door.

My throat tightens. I realize I sounded like my mother with her empty promises. "No, you didn't. I got in my own way." Tears drop from my cheeks.

He studies me, and his lips part as if he's about to speak, but he exits to the hall, leaving me with nothing but the agony of my own tears.

Chapter 43

I march up to the third floor of the art building armed with questions I transform into demands, but when I get to the studio, Shale stands at an easel with his back to the door. His wrist moves smoothly as the brush conducts an orchestra of color. He's painting.

I step carefully across the creaky floor and take up a post at his shoulder. Instead of clouds, he smears an angry sea; waves crash on a stormy shore.

When the clock indicates the period is over and the faint bell from another nearby classroom building chimes, I sling my backpack over my shoulder, wondering if Art V is a waste of time, if I should do homework at one of the benches, or if Shale is actually going to teach me anything.

When I'm nearly through the door, Shale calls, "See you tomorrow, Pearl."

The days pass with college fairs and classes, notably English, where I study Grant, looking for a loophole, a way back in, when I should be studying great works of literary merit. His off-campus manner, strong and sure of his every step and word, has consistently replaced the shy, timid on-campus one from last year. He moves differently, steady but also edgy, like he might break loose and bolt at any moment. His face reflects the confidence that his long hair used to conceal. He's grown-up. Grant knows what he wants, and it's no longer me.

Then there's art, where I've taken to watching Shale paint. I'm not sure what the administration has in mind for independent studies with fusty, old art teachers, but I don't think this is it. Nonetheless, we pass the hour in companionable silence, while I watch entire worlds take form on canvas. He's completed several ocean scenes; in each one I notice the strokes become finer, the sea calmer.

Charmindy calls to me from the hall one Sunday. My stomach reflexively sinks as I worry that I'm in trouble. "Phone call," she says.

I go to the bank of phones at the end of the hallway.

"Pearl? Gary Jaeger," my uncle says stiffly, as if any other Gary would be calling me.

"Hi." I pause, not knowing who should fill the silence on the line. "School is good. The summer was"—I hesitate—"quite the learning experience. Thank you for your assistance," I say formally.

"I've been keeping track of your academics. I'm impressed, except for math. I want you to get a tutor. But I'm calling to suggest you apply to colleges. As before, I will continue to provide funding if you continue to excel." There's no warmth in his voice, but the opportunity makes me feel the heat of a hundred golden suns.

I started the college-application process with Justine at the end of junior year, because everyone in the privileged bubble at Laurel Hill assumes that if you go to prep school, you'll go to college. I had no idea whether I'd be able to carry off supporting myself and paying for school. I'd thought about taking a year off, getting a job and saving, or trying community college.

"Thank you," I sputter. "Oh, and um—"

"Yes?" he asks, impatiently.

"There's a term abroad to Spain being offered this winter. My advisor suggested I apply. She said it looks favorable on applications.

I wonder if I was accepted, if you might be able to help out with the cost?" I ask awkwardly.

"Send me the information. Pearl, remember to stay focused on your grades, nothing else."

"Thank you," I answer.

With no distractions like Sorel or Grant, parties off campus, or tragedies, other than the ones I carry around like old bags of bricks, I study with Charmindy. My uncle would view her as the perfect influence. She has a 4.2 GPA, early acceptance to Harvard, and an impressive roster of accomplishments, both academic and extracurricular. She doesn't go to crazy parties on the weekends, meet up with boys, or sneak off to the woods to smoke. That is, until I see her padding out from the familiar path.

As I gaze forlornly out my window, like a corseted character in one of the classics I analyze for AP English, Charmindy emerges from the woods with a boy I've seen dunking a basketball when we have to go in the gym because of rain during cross-country practice. My mouth drops open. They amble up the lawn. I return to my text and then turn to the window again to confirm what I saw, but instead of Charmindy and the tall guy, Grant materializes from the pathway. My heart sinks.

That night, during study hour, thinking about Charmindy and the mystery guy keeps me reading question forty-seven in my Spanish text repeatedly.

I lean on her desk, where she has a tidy array of colored sticky notes next to her notebook. "Will you help me with something?" I ask.

"What can I do?"

"Well, I saw something that I'm curious about and wasn't sure who I should talk to."

"Go on," she says, one brow lifted, as ever.

"A well-respected and important member of our student body emerged from the woods today with a tall, handsome young man and—" I can't keep a straight face.

She blanches.

"Out of character much? Breaking rules? And what about Brett?" I ask.

"It was nothing. Jamar and I are just friends." Her cheeks burst pink. "We went there because he—" She can't say it.

I wait.

"He—" But she shakes her head.

"He smokes cigarettes?" I whisper.

She doesn't reply.

"That's the only reason to go to that clearing." *And to think deeply about the direction of one's life and resolve to take a new path.*

"I don't know what I'm doing. He just—I mean, I really, really like Brett. He's actually perfect. But sometimes too perfect. I know it's stupid, but already there's so much pressure. Too much. I couldn't sneak any art classes into my course load, and my grade from Shale wasn't exactly pleasing. Going to the woods with him took the edge off in a way. I did something on my terms for once." Her forehead wrinkles. "I know it's silly, but if I don't keep my grades up, my parents will reject me. If I don't achieve academic excellence, they'll cut me off. I'll become an outcast. But having to keep that up constantly, I almost can't imagine doing it for the entire year, for the next six or eight years until I graduate from college."

"That sounds familiar in a roundabout kind of way."

She shakes her head. "No, you wouldn't understand."

"Charmindy, I do. Even though our parents are on the opposite ends of the spectrum, mine absent—my mother didn't set the bar very high . . . actually, there was no bar except the kind you order a beer from. There were no expectations from her, so I didn't really have any for myself. On the other hand, it sounds like your parents have set them so high it sometimes feels like an impossible reach, never mind trying to have a life outside of that. In both cases, it's like they created something for us that doesn't fit, doesn't work. Y'know?" I pause, not sure if I'm making sense. "I want to believe anything is possible. Maybe you could talk to them, figure out a way to do something you like. I've been thinking about a term abroad, something like that . . ."

She smiles warmly. "Thanks," she says. "I can't leave because of dorm-assistant duties, but yeah, yeah," she repeats as if her brilliant mind has already figured out a solution. "And Brett, of course. I don't want to mess up—"

"No, definitely don't pull a PJ," I say self-deprecatingly, thinking about how I let myself down over the summer, how I let Grant down, and how more than anything I don't want to be someone I'm ashamed to look at in the mirror, or paint.

Charmindy's eyes turn soft. "Hey, no one has ever said anything like that to me before. Usually it's just 'work harder, do better.' Sometimes in those messages I hear that I'm not good enough."

"That, I completely understand." I pause, but my thoughts quickly shift. "So, um, when you were in the clearing, did you see Grant?"

"Yeah, he was there, but that brings me to another issue: do I fulfill my duties as a senior dorm assistant and report what I, um, witnessed?"

I shake my head. "No, no. That's crazy. What about—what's his name—Jamar?" I say, panicking, not wanting Grant to get in trouble.

"Yes"

"You don't want to get him in trouble."

"No, but I'm torn. I'm breaking rules. He's breaking rules."

Wearing Sorel's patented mischievous smirk, I say, "How about this? We trade. I'll be a rule-abiding student and not step a toe out of line, and you can claim a couple of broken rules for me."

We break down in laughter.

"Deal."

I never expected to have a friendship with someone like Charmindy. I only ever equated myself to being friends with the burnouts and outsiders. But as this bond forms with her, I know there isn't something so wrong with me that I can't have better, truer friends too. The fine line between doing well in school because it was a haven when I was growing up and doing well at Laurel Hill to appease my uncle begins to shift to doing well simply for me. Maybe I'm worth the effort.

I attend one of the informational meetings for the trip to Spain and apply, along with a group of other hopefuls. I also seal and stamp my applications to Parsons, FIT, RISD, UCLA, and Pratt. Justine asks if I want to try any safeties.

"Despite my, um, wild summer," I say, clearing my throat and not holding back or apologizing for who I am, "fashion design lives in my veins."

"You seem confident, then."

"Confidence balanced on top of a delicate emotional house of cards that I've recently constructed out of my very bones," I say, glancing up at the paintings of women on her wall, the strength of sisters being strong for each other throughout history staring down at me.

Her mouth quirks into a smile as if she knows exactly what I'm talking about or has no idea and thinks I'll drool on her or bark, like I'm not quite all there, if she disagrees.

The growing order inside of me allows some of the past to slip away like a bad dream, with one exception. I hang on to Grant, in my heart, every time I see him in classes, on the soccer field, around campus, and in my mind as I fall asleep. As the weeks pass, I cling to the dwindling hope that somehow I will be able to change his mind.

During Art V, while I sketch on my pad, Shale steps back from the easel, crosses his arms in front of his chest, and exhales. The ocean on the canvas is placid; the blues almost blend with the sky. It's a triumph.

"Your turn," he says.

"What do you mean?"

"Get a canvas. It's time."

"Class is almost over."

"Art doesn't account for time or schedules," he says, ignoring my protests.

"I don't know what you want or expect from me. I was just put in this class. Apparently, you wanted me here. What do you want me to do?" I say, exasperated. Also, I haven't touched a brush to canvas since my self-portrait, and although the shape slowly takes form, I'm still not exactly sure what I look like.

"Don't worry about my expectations. You need to raise yours." He strokes his beard, studying me intently.

I look toward the window, the easels, anywhere but him. "I don't have any."

Shale shakes his head. "Pearl, read the quote on the wall, there." He points, his voice like a spotlight.

"'Students are responsible for cleaning their tools and materials.'"

His eyes narrow. "The other one."

"'Creativity takes courage.'"

"Tattoo it on your face, on your soul if you have to."

"What does that have to do with—?"

"Here's another: 'We understand the history of humanity through art.' And therefore ourselves. We understand our own personal histories through art. I do not believe in forgetting the past, but living with it, day to day, takes courage. The kind that casts aside fear and tells us to keep going, despite the troubles that threaten to ruin us. Pearl, you are an artist. You have a history. You are courageous. Mix them up like paint. This class is meant for you to see what happens next. What happens after not giving up." He says this so clearly it's like I suddenly understand Norwegian, or maybe it's just the common language of art.

I huff, but once more, his comment about being my own enemy resounds like the bell in the distance signaling the end of class and the start of something new, something that doesn't resemble JJ. I select a canvas, paints, and brushes. I begin the outline of a girl. I fill her in until she almost looks like me as the sun casts copal light in the fading day.

Chapter 44

Instead of staying at Laurel Hill for Thanksgiving, Charmindy invites me to her sister Poesy's apartment. Her sister is a junior at Columbia. She promises a whirlwind visit, in part because she claims she and Poesy are the polar opposite and because she has to return to Viv Brooks a few days early for a dorm-assistant training session related to bullying.

As we drive into Manhattan, twilight cloaks the city in pink and gray. My insides slosh with intrusive memories. I try to cast them aside as we ride to Poesy's apartment on the Upper West Side.

"Char! Nice to meet you, PJ," Poesy says in cheerful greeting, giving us both hugs. She's nearly identical to Charmindy, but four years older and, from the looks of the glass of wine in her hand, four years more relaxed.

"These are the rules: no spilling wine on the sofa, what happens in New York stays in New York, and, most of all, have fun. Pearl, you look like you know how to do that, please teach my sister. In the meantime, I have to run, but whatever you need, *mi casa* is *tu casa*." In a cloud of perfume and with the click of her heels, Poesy rushes out into the evening.

The next day we shop—or rather, I browse, admiring a beautiful gold dress. I can't help but think of my mother and her rock-and-roll rags, the way she wore high fashion in an irreverent way, but that's what made her so badass: she wore the clothes, not the other way around.

We have dinner at Morimoto, and as expected, the sushi is delicious. Afterward, Poesy meets some friends for drinks. The taxi Charmindy and I take back to the Upper West Side detours because of construction. We edge in traffic to a part of the city I know well.

I clear my throat. "That's one of the places I used to live," I say, pointing up at a nondescript building bordered by graffiti and a twenty-four-hour pawnshop. "Charmindy, I'm not like you or most of the students at Laurel Hill."

She looks at me thoughtfully before answering. "You're exactly like most of the students at Laurel Hill, and more importantly, you are exactly yourself."

I've always wanted someone to tell me I'm smart and pretty and not just because they want something from me. To congratulate me on a job well done, to tell me they knew I'd succeed. To post a scribbly picture I drew on the fridge and tell me it was beautiful. To kiss my boo-boos, brush me off, and tell me to hop back on my bicycle. I've looked into eyes, seeking a promise that the person they belonged to believed in me, that I was worth believing in. And the most unsuspecting of friends said it all in so few words, and somehow, unbelievably, I feel like I already knew it, deep down, hidden away. I start to cry tears that don't burn or come from a place of sadness and emptiness.

Charmindy's eyebrows quiver with concern.

I smile. "You're right."

We spend Thanksgiving in an apartment overlooking the Macy's parade, sipping wine, and eating a combination of flavorful Indian cuisine and traditional American fare. The following days we watch movies, go to an art museum, shop some more, hang out with Poesy's friends, and indulge in rosy-cheeked laughter.

The night before we return to school, Charmindy and I pop the cork on a bottle of red and wax poetic about life, strange and beautiful. She leads me down faraway lanes spiced with curry and kissed by the sun. I take her through some of the highlights of my wasted years.

"So how do you rebel or—" My thoughts are thick like syrup. "Or break free from your parents? How do you establish who you are, separate from them? I mean, you, for instance; they want you to go the traditional route of success and all that. Grant's too. But what if your parents," I slur, "correction, *parent* was so screwed up, blew it, and there are no expectations?"

I ramble on. "Or do I just conform? Just give in and settle for worthless?" I shake my head as if trying to get the words to come out right.

Before Charmindy can reply, I barrel on, fueled by how the wine lights the thoughts burning inside me. "Charmindy, all my life I've felt like I'm skirting the edge of disaster, attack, loss, and pain or falling directly into it. How do I break the cycle?"

She looks at me with sadness in her eyes but hope written on her wine-stained lips. "You do better," she says strongly, holding my gaze. "We're not our parents. Whatever they have planned for us or not planned, as the case may be, it's just a blueprint, a single possibility among millions. What you described isn't written in your blood, it's like poisonous air you were forced to breathe. Breathe it out, it's gone. Now you choose. *You do better.*"

That night, I dream that I hold a baby. I gaze lovingly into her blue eyes as I stroke her milky face. She morphs into a toddler, with glowing cheeks and blond hair. I hold her tight, and we smile at each other. Then she's a girl with long legs and hair in braids. We clasp hands. She continues to grow, but she remains in my arms, close to my chest. Her blond hair grows over her shoulders. She wears a familiar shirt with a rainbow on it. She's heavy in my arms, all elbows and knees. I look into her eyes, hold her hand, and keep her close. I hold fast until she is me. I look at myself and hug and hold. I don't let go.

I won't ever let go.

"You are safe with me," I whisper.

"I will take care of you," I promise.

My eyes blink open. Dappled light fills the living room. A bird alights on the windowsill and seems, for a moment, to look in with one bead-like eye before flying away again.

Chapter 45

Glad to be back on campus after the quick and tasty holiday, I pass Pepper in the language-studies building on my way to Spanish class.

"Hey," he says awkwardly.

"How's it going?"

He shrugs.

"Did you see Sorel over break?"

"Nah. It didn't work out. She was busy or something. But I'm going out there for Christmas," he says with half a smile.

"Cool. Tell her I say hi."

"Happy birthday." He looks like he wants to say something else, but then continues down the hall. I didn't realize he was sentimental.

Senora Azuelos begins the class by reminding those of us who applied that we'll find out the following week who has been selected for the trip to Spain. I hope my name appears on the list, if for no other reason than not having to endure breaking into a thousand pieces once a day during English class when I see Grant, then carefully reassembling the fragments of myself afterward.

In AP English I take my usual seat out of his line of vision, but keep him in mine. I bolster myself, ready to fracture like glass. I've memorized how he relaxes his legs under the table and how he rests his head in his hand about three-quarters of the way through Mr. Nichols's lecture.

When the bell signals the end of class, I wait to exit behind a slow-moving crowd, and Grant stands by my side, the closest we've been since the night in his dorm. I notice the scar by his chin. His deep blue eyes. Words don't come, but he offers a sad smile, says, "Happy birthday," and then strides away.

The girls in the dorm surprise me with a birthday cake, no doubt orchestrated by Charmindy. Since Terran and most of her crowd graduated, the other girls are generally nicer to me. Again, no doubt Charmindy's doing. Before I take a bite, the phone rings down the hall, and someone calls, "PJ, it's for you."

I don't imagine it's Uncle Gary calling to wish me a happy birthday or to celebrate my emancipation.

"Hey, City Girl."

"Sorel?" I answer, surprised.

"Happy eighteenth birthday." She sounds different, slower, far away. Her voice lacks its usual crackling fire. "It's so freakin' awesome out here. You should visit. I'm having the time of my life. Twenty-four-hour party."

She doesn't convince me. I've been at the twenty-four-hour party, and it's overrated. "Cool. Pepper misses you."

"Ugh. Pepper."

I'm not sure what she means, but it almost sounds like she's referring to an annoying little brother.

"I hear you and Grant broke up. Sorry."

I take a stilted breath. "Yeah." It was over before it started. "So whatcha been up to? How are classes?"

"Y'know. Have you seen Mitch? I'm sure he'd love if you visited him now that you're single." Her words are barbed and not just because she mentions Mitch. "Like I told you, he's a good person to know. You could have whatever you wanted whenever you wanted." She laughs. Voices and vices call in the background. "Shit, I gotta go. Happy birthday," she says, and the line goes dead.

I don't return to the common room right away, but sit, glued to the chair. Sorel's words prick me all over. I remember when we first met, how cavalier and bossy she was, our trip to Montreal, then the family cabin, her mood swings, and all the little moments in between. Something about our exchange doesn't line up with those memories. She was distant and not just because of the miles.

During study hour that night, Charmindy closes the door. "My sister and I got you a special birthday present." She hands me a large and heavy gift bag.

I unwrap the gold-threaded dress I tried on when we shopped in Manhattan. It's sparkly and fitted in all the right places.

"This is beautiful. Thank you," I say, awestruck. I run my hand over the contours of the fabric, and then Charmindy indicates there's more. Inside, I find a bottle of red wine.

Charmindy puts her finger to her lips, hushing me. "You only turn eighteen once," she whispers, procuring two glasses. After she pours, she raises hers. "To Pearl, who, like her sisters in the ocean, is beginning to emerge as a beautiful treasure, a gift to herself and a gift to us all."

Tears catch on the outsides of my eyes. We clink.

Charmindy and I dutifully try to study as we sip the wine, aptly called "The Red Pearl."

I turn to the index in the biology book on Charmindy's bookshelf and find the P section. I read that unwanted material infiltrates an oyster, and instead of somehow getting rid of the undesirable sand or dirt or whatever else, the mighty and courageous mollusk transforms it into a thing of beauty, a pearl.

Later, as I lie in bed, unable to sleep despite the wine, Grant steps into my mind. We dance in the snow. Then there's Sorel, wishing me happy birthday, but my mother's voice splices my thoughts. Mother of Pearl.

In a rare moment of sobriety, she spoke at an AA meeting that we went to, sharing the wise quote "If you love something, let it go; if it comes back to you, it is yours. If it doesn't, it was never meant to be."

She wasn't a candidate to give advice, but perhaps this applies to Grant and me. I don't want to let him go, but sometimes what I don't want to do is exactly what I need to do. Like beads on a necklace, I count each emotion that ties me to him, love, loss, regret, anger, frustration, disappointment, and insecurity. Then I count one bead for his smile, his eyes, his tattoos, his hands, his power on the soccer field, his kindness and sincerity, his intelligence, his body mingling with mine, his quiet assurance as I grieved my mother, and the fun we've had and laughs we've shared. I continue, counting each one and letting them go until I drift to sleep.

Shale has become my nemesis. I learned to tolerate him standing over my shoulder last year, watching me paint, grunting in disapproval, but the independent study, with me wasting canvases and oils trying to create an image of myself that feels true, is pointless. When I think I've landed on what I look like, I get a grunt or a groan, and the worst part is I know he's right. He said I was courageous. I'm not sure he knows me, despite what he said about us being one and the same.

I get one of these grunts after adding the final lines around my eyes, and immediately throw the canvas in the trash.

"It isn't what you look like. It's what you feel. Dig deeper. I want to see you engage with the resistance and push against it. Do not give in. Do not give up." Beads of sweat form along his forehead, as if he's fighting for more than indignation, last words, or ego.

I feel like smashing the palette in his face like a pie.

"Pearl, you feel stress, pressure. Good. It means you care. It means you know you haven't met your potential. Your friend Charmindy, she was not particularly artistic, but she committed. She showed up until the class fulfilled its purpose for her. You must do the same. I will keep pushing you."

"Pushing until I break," I mumble.

"If I have to, yes."

I didn't think he'd heard me. I don't wash my brushes or clean up, but instead rush out the door, tears threatening to push past my anger.

Senora Azuelos announces that six students in her class, including me, along with six others from the other advanced-level Spanish class, will be going abroad during winter term. I careen through finals on a raft of excitement and trepidation for the trip, but the undercurrent of missing Grant and regretting what I did carries my thoughts downstream.

That evening, as I leave the dining hall, I spot him and Suzy sitting together. She's a hazy figure from Spanish last year, Sorel's graduation day, and occasionally walking with Grant between classes. She rests her hand on his tattooed arm as it sits on the table between them. Jealousy is like mucus in my throat.

Charmindy places her hand on my shoulder. She looks at me in her firm and determined way. I relax, and although slow to change, I'm ready to leave behind the eighteen-year battle that has been my life.

On the last day of classes before holiday break, I plod into the studio for the first time since I walked out.

I almost see a smile in the fuzz of Shale's beard when I appear in the doorway with snow dusting my shoulders. He wears his favorite sweater, with the black-and-white Nordic pattern and chunky fasteners down the front.

"I'm sorry I left like that. I've been thinking. Actually, that's a lie. I haven't been thinking. I just found myself here, in the building. I don't know what you want from me. I'm not an artist. I don't have anything to give." I pause to take a breath. "I'm dropping this class, even if I don't get credit or you fail me."

Shale passes through various shades of gray. He clears his throat. "If that's your decision." He strokes his beard and walks across the creaky floor toward his office.

I turn to go but stop, magnetized to the room.

The creaking floor goes quiet. "Pearl, before you go. I have something for you—" The creaks get closer. I turn, and he passes me a large, flat wrapped package.

I take it in my hands and glance toward the door.

"Please open it now."

I draw a breath, pluck the bow off the front, and tear the paper. A swath of blue and gray paint appears, swirling like the ocean and sky meeting, like the paintings he'd worked on for the first months of the semester. I pull the rest of the paper off, and I'm gazing at my image, a blend of air and water like I'm dissolving or appearing from the depths. I have no words. It's beautiful and sad at the same time. My eyes mist, and when I look up at Shale, his do too. His intentions become clear. He's pushing me because he cares.

I swallow hard, whispering, "I'm sorry about what I said." His accented words about how it's good that I feel pressure because it means I care remain in the air. I suppose in his own chilly way, he really does too.

"Take some time to think, Pearl. I'll be here." He turns and walks back across the creaky floor.

Later that night, I tell Charmindy about our exchange.

"Shale's an iceberg," Charmindy says. "All his emotions are hidden underneath that white shock of his frosty exterior."

"You mean his hair?"

She chuckles. "Although I only managed to scrape by in Painting IV, I happen to believe Shale used tough love because we, you especially, matter to him."

"Yeah, I know. I guess I'm not used to it."

"Get there, Pearl. It's a nice place to be."

Chapter 46

The days before Christmas slosh drearily with memories and resentment. A rainy and humid week spent in Florida does nothing to bring me Christmas cheer, with the exception of Erica's brief stay. She and I baked and decorated cookies and went to the movies before she flew back to New York to be with her boyfriend.

When I board the plane for Spain, I'm more than ready to take flight. Senora Azuelos and Senor Robbins, the other Spanish teacher, directed the twelve students, including me, to assemble in Madrid for orientation. Then, in pairs, they'll assign us to a school somewhere in any one of Spain's cities for our exchange program. There, we'll attend classes for about six weeks, then regroup and travel together for several weeks to various points of interest. The highlight for me is the Guggenheim Bilbao, with a traveling exhibit of selected works by Frida Kahlo. All the while, we'll have assignments and projects, just as we would back at Laurel Hill, but completely in *Español.*

The still-bright afternoon light welcomes my arrival as I take the metro into the center and find my way to the hotel address indicated on my itinerary. I lift my bags up a crescent-shaped set of stone steps with red geraniums clustered around the entryway into an older but classic stucco building.

At the front desk, the concierge gives directions, and voices beckon from down a long corridor.

Across from the entryway, a grand piano stands in front of large windows with gauzy drapes billowing in the light breeze. A couple of groups of familiar faces, along with the teachers, gather. Then the chatter in the room falls away. My legs won't move me farther.

To my right, joking with another student, Grant leans on the arm of a sofa. My heart skips a beat. No, ten. I don't know what to do or where to look as Senora Azuelos greets me. Heat builds in my cheeks. She keeps me occupied for several minutes with chatter, in Spanish, of course, and then the arrival of another student pulls her away.

We have to speak Spanish for the duration of our stay, so I make idle talk with Rory, a petite girl with brown hair and a slight lisp. I'm so keenly aware of Grant, just a few yards away, I can hardly concentrate on what she says, never mind translate it. My mind floats in a million directions, chasing memories, possibilities, doubts . . .

"Grant," a bubbly voice calls from the entry. Suzy struts into the room. Hope evaporates on a whiff of her cloying perfume. She beelines for Grant, but Senor Robbins intercepts her with a greeting.

I stew while the teachers review our travel plans, give us a rundown of the rules, tell us what we can expect from our weeks with our host schools, and go over generalities about the work, projects, and assignments. They emphasize words like *multiculturalism* and *diversity*, explaining that life might feel very different from back at Laurel Hill.

We do group icebreaker games, and then Senora Azuelos calls out our names to divide us into the pairs that we'll have for the duration of the six weeks at the various host schools. Grant, Suzy, a stubby boy named Wilson, and I remain. Then it's just Grant and me.

"*Excelente,*" Senora Azuelos pronounces. "*Ahora conversaréis sobre sus actividades favoritas y que quieres hacer durante el semestre.*"

I'm certain Grant doesn't want to talk to me about his favorite activities, or anything else, for that matter. I lean against a pillar on the far side of the room.

His hands are deep in his pockets as he paces in front of me.

We're far enough away from everyone that no one will overhear, and since my brain isn't working optimally, I speak English. "Do you want to see if they can give us different partners?"

He stops and looks at me sharply as he takes a breath. His cheeks fill with his exhale, then he lets it out. He rubs his hands through his dark blond hair. I'm not sure if he's aggravated or flustered.

With wobbly legs, I stand myself upright to go talk to the teacher. I stop midstride as she explains to the group that arrangements have already been set in stone. *"Nadie pueden cambiar."*

Suzy's cheeks burn red as she slinks away from Senora Azuelos and glances sideways at Wilson, then to Grant and me.

"That answers that," I mumble. "I'm sorry you can't be with Suzy."

Through the window, the umber buildings blur as my eyes fill with tears. I walk out the way I came, to find a bathroom. The escape, a break from campus, from struggling with my feelings for Grant, sours. Strong fingers close around my wrist.

"Wait," Grant says.

I slowly turn around, afraid if I move too fast, I'll get dizzy.

"I think we can try this."

"Try what?" I ask, confused.

"Try being partners."

"Oh."

"What did you think I meant?" he asks.

Shock gives way to a hesitant smile. "I don't know what I thought you meant, but certainly not that." I brush my bangs flat against my forehead, then run my hand down the side of my face. "I thought I would be the last person on earth you'd tolerate being in the same room with for six weeks. English class was hard enough."

A sad smile flips on and off his lips, quick as a blink. He starts to say something, but the teachers assign us rooms for the night.

I listen for my name. *"Suzy, Rory, y Pearl están conjuntas."*

Suzy pulls cosmetics out of a Hello Kitty backpack, which goes right along with the cutesy style she has going on. I notice a preponderance of syrupy pink.

"I can't believe we're already here. I knew I'd get in. It's going to be crazy awesome," she says in her high up-speak Valley-girl voice. She pauses with a makeup brush in her hand and turns to me. "I'm so sorry if having *us* here together makes you uncomfortable."

"Huh?" I ask, looking up from the guidebook on my lap.

"Grant and I, duh," she says with a simpering grin.

I close my eyes and grind my teeth together.

"You know, you shouldn't have let him get away. He's such a great kisser and—" She looks up at the ceiling as if in reverie.

It's her face or the nearest breakable object. The guidebook hits the wall with a thud, and the pages flutter as it drops to the floor. But I'm more angry with myself for messing up than I am about her stupid comments. I assume she knows what I did. Matteo wasn't worth it.

Before I slam the door behind me, Suzy says, "Gosh, what's her problem?"

I dash down the steps of the hotel and onto the street. They kissed? The image of his lips on hers, glitter and gloss sticking to his skin, and her fingers in his hair flicks through my mind like a never-ending flip book.

I turn down a side street. I have the sense this is karma. I'm so parched tears won't come. I spot a café with white wrought iron tables and chairs outside.

I scan the menu.

Coffee, wine, beer, water.

Wine, beer, water.

Beer, water.

If caught drinking beer, surely I'll find a return plane ticket in my hands. I'm not willing to give Suzy the satisfaction. Nor do I want to ruin this opportunity abroad, not to mention my life. Plus, Frida is just weeks away.

"Una agua, por favor," I tell the man behind the counter.

I settle on a chair outside and sip the water. My gaze weaves between the buildings, toward the sky. I've made it to Spain. That's something. Grant said we'd try being partners. That's something more. I dig deeper to figure out why Suzy bothers me so much. She isn't after my boyfriend, because Grant is no longer my anything. I have to *let him go.*

I catch these stray nibbles of thoughts as pigeons peck at the ground. A few tables away a dark-haired couple kisses. I'm jealous. Not of the couple, not really—of love. I want to be Grant's good morning and good night, to be his fountain of happiness, to call him home, our affections for each other to be soft, there to be a future in some hidden café in another country where we can kiss and kiss and kiss. Geez, those two are really going to town. I turn back to the pigeons.

I want Grant's love, but in order to receive it, I have to give love. I failed. Somewhere nearby church bells ring, reminding me that there's something I do have, at least for the next few weeks—time.

I hardly taste the lavish meal as the fourteen members of our group, including the teachers, eat at the hotel restaurant. Instead, resentment and confusion bite my tongue. I say my *por favor*s and *gracias*es, but watching Suzy flirt with Grant at the far end of the table curdles my interest in remaining in my chair.

I bump the table when I get up, and for a moment, all eyes are on me. I excuse myself, feigning exhaustion from jet lag, then go up to the room, but I catch his glance, lingering on me, and I melt all over again.

I step onto the balcony overlooking the city. I think of New York, my city. I think of my mom. If only she could see me now. Each of my thoughts matches a star, blooming in the sky. I've made it this far out of the confines of the life she'd created, but I've also made a mess. I'm drifting back and forth between empowerment and helplessness, when someone knocks on the door to the hotel room, interrupting the parade of thoughts clanging and banging through my head.

Suzy probably locked herself out. I grumble as I open the door a crack. Grant leans on the door frame, staring at his shoes. When he looks up at me, he bites his lip. "Can we talk?" he asks.

I let him in, ignoring the school rules, still applicable abroad. My reasoning, Grant and I aren't strangers to hotel rooms, and at eighteen, we're officially adults, whether I've grown up or not. He follows me onto the small balcony, and we each lean against opposite ends of the abutment that divides it from the neighboring one. Technically, we're outside, so the no-boys-in-your-room rule doesn't apply; Sorel advised me of this ambiguity in the school guidebook last year. Our legs and feet are inches apart. He digs in his pocket and pulls out a pack of cigarettes. He lights us both one. This, on the other hand, is a Laurel Hill offense.

"Haven't had one of these in a while. I thought I'd quit," he says. "When in Rome or wherever."

"I haven't had one since last summer," I say, taking a drag and coughing, my lungs unforgiving.

"No?" Grant asks.

I shake my head.

"That's good. I mean, you know, for your health."

I stub it out. "Yeah," I say with an unsteady voice. In fact, my entire body feels like the earth moves beneath it. Like something deep under the surface burns and shifts slowly like magma.

"I saw you rush out earlier."

I croak out, "Yeah."

"I'm sorry." As he says this, I know these should be the words coming out of my mouth. He gazes up at the stars. "This is just about the same sky I looked at all summer, wondering where you were, what you were doing. Missing you like hell—" His voice cracks.

I look up at the twinkling place where he gazes, my vision blurred by the tears running from the corners of my eyes.

"Missing you still," he adds.

His words melt me further in the slow-motion quaking of my world. Then there's the aftershock.

"I was wondering if, at least for now, we could try to be friends. For real. No pretense, no games."

I'll never forget the message in the birthday card from last year. We've kissed. We've talked. We've been more than friends.

I clear my throat. "Yeah, sure. Let's be friends." Fate has us meeting each other backward.

Chapter 47

I lie awake until the sun tints the buildings outside my window earthen shades of clay. We pass the next few days in Madrid as the teachers immerse us in the culture and customs.

On New Year's Eve, Grant and I board a crowded train for Barcelona, along with Rory and her partner, Henry. Suzy's expression is tart as she watches us leave. A lifetime ago, I would have stuck out my tongue or flipped her off. Instead, I watch the locals and tourists shuffle around. I wonder where we all came from, where we're going, and how we ended up here, together, in this moment.

Grant and I squish into a couple of vacant seats in a crowded railcar. I wish comfort would replace the tension of uncertainty that vibrates between us. I'm not sure how to be friends after we specifically weren't friends, turned into more than friends, and then weren't friends at all.

After we're under way, he casually asks, "What colleges did you apply to?"

I list them off.

"UCLA? Me too. My soccer coach seems to think I'll get a scholarship. The scouts have been nosing around, so that's promising."

"What will you study?" I ask, testing out this new territory, the middle ground of just being friends.

"English lit," he answers.

"How'd your dad take it?" I push the conversation past casual and into the realm of known, intimate details. I can't take the words or truth of it back.

He rubs his hand through his hair, as though he still isn't used to its short length, or maybe it's become a nervous habit. "He didn't. An athletic scholarship will help. If he's not paying, he has no say. It'll be all right. I'll be OK."

My heart stutters as his words remind me of my own. "That's good, right?"

He nods.

I quickly run out of things to say that don't involve our shared past. I watch the scenery change from urban to rural as leafy fields of potatoes and beans spread toward the horizon.

After a while I ask, "How's your brother?" The fact that we were once more than friends strains against anything I try to say. I want to get silly with him like I used to, reference memories and moments, or at least talk about things we have in common.

"He's great. He asked about you when he met me at the airport." His sad smile appears for a moment. "The real reason I was late to school was we went to see a soccer match—US Men's National, it was good. Then my dad caught up with us . . ."

"Cheating on me with soccer, huh?" I immediately realize the ramifications of what I thought of as just a joke. The blood drains from my face, my palms are suddenly clammy, and my stomach does a somersault.

He turns sharply away and looks out the window.

"I'm sorry. I don't know why I said that. It was just a joke. It wasn't funny. I'm sorry, Grant."

He abruptly shifts in his seat to face me, and our knees knock together in the narrow space. He pulls his jacket off, revealing the tattoos on his arm. "Do you have any clue how much you hurt me? I believed what we had was something so different from any kind of connection I thought possible, like it was cosmic or something. I have you tattooed on my arm." He points, his fingers trembling, his breath coming heavily. "I wanted to be with you always."

He brandishes his tattoos at me. The mermaid stares me down; her eyes, filled with wonder, stun me with guilt. "I can never forget you now. Every day reminds me of the shite you made out of our relationship, out of me. I thought you were different. I thought because you had experienced so much pain, you'd know better than to do that to someone else. I wanted us to be forever. To be honest. To be true. Why, Pearl?" His face vanishes behind his hand. Then his fingers grip his hair, and he turns back away.

I slump in my seat, crushed by the weight of his words. I want to disappear. I want to escape. I want his voice to stop ringing in my ears. The snapshot of his face, torn between anger and anguish, burns. Then Charmindy's words flit through my mind, "The only way out is through." I catch the strand of thought like a bird catches a worm with its beak and swallow hard.

"I take responsibility for what I did. I chose a night of partying over you. I chose drugs and drinking over us. I'll never do anything like that again to anyone. The path I started out on wasn't an easy one. I'm not blaming that, but it was as if I was tuned to a certain frequency, and I had to get louder to change. I didn't know until recently that love is showing up, love is honesty, it's listening, and love is comfortable and safe. But I know now. I promise." This is one promise I know, deep down, without a doubt, that I'll keep.

Grant sits like a statue as the train rumbles on. Nothing about his expression helps me discern what he's thinking. But I feel good about finally singing the truth, even if it was only for me to hear. He turns to the window, leaving me to my thoughts.

In the Jaeger family, promises proved dangerous. My mother made me promises that she repeatedly broke, and each one sent a deeper fissure through my heart. But the feelings of wanting to flee the situation with Grant have dissipated. I'm right where I am, in this seat next to him. I poured myself out. I have no craving for the oblivion I once sought in drugs or alcohol. I'm extremely conscious of what a slippery slope that is for someone like me, my mother, or Sorel even. I've decided that oblivion isn't for me; I want to live guided by courage.

Relief and hope wash over me. If I ever have another chance at love with Grant or anyone else in my life, I'll handle it with utmost care, like a treasure, like a pearl.

I realize in that moment I have, like the proverb from the AA meeting, let Grant go. I look at the swallows inked on his arm, the ones that match mine, and the lightness I now feel suggests they're all flying home. The train rocks me to sleep like a lullaby.

The four of us, Rory, Henry, Grant, and I, enter a *Soto Cerro Barcelona* dorm suite, with a kitchenette, a small communal area, a bathroom, and two bedrooms, presumably one for the girls and one for the guys. It's basically the equivalent of Laurel Hill, but means *Thicket Hill*, and apparently, they're more comfortable with coed living quarters compared to their sister school in New England. Go figure. We can't hide our surprise at the arrangement, except for Grant, who immediately disappears with his luggage into one of the bedrooms.

Dismissing Spanish and the strictly enforced rules of gender separation at Laurel Hill, Rory asks, "So, do the teachers, like, know?"

Henry and I shrug.

"Do they check on us?" she asks with disbelief.

"They'll be spending a couple of days in Barcelona; I think they said the second week? Just to make sure everything is OK. But, dude,

I think we're on our own," Henry says, hooting and throwing himself over the back of the couch and then reclining, with his shoes still on. "My mom would freak."

Rory does a victory dance, then falls over the back of the couch and into Henry's arms.

Amused, I'm quite sure I'm witnessing the beginning of an experiment in freedom. Rory and Henry look like the train ride helped them discover their shared chemistry. I walk over to the window, a habit when I enter new places. I think of life back in the States. This is an experiment of another sort for me, with Grant in such close proximity.

I go out the window onto the fire escape and whoop at the top of my lungs. As the wind blows through my hair, it carries away with it shreds of my past like autumn leaves on the breeze.

The window rattles as Grant comes out. The hint of a smile crosses his face. He bites his lip and lights up a cigarette. We're both quiet until the embers fade, along with the tension in his shoulders.

"About before . . . We're OK," he says. "We can do this. Friends?" he asks.

"Friends," I answer.

That night, New Year's Eve, the four of us go out for dinner, forgetting dinnertime is much later than in the United States. We end up getting grilled sandwiches to go from a little café. The counter person takes pity on us uninformed student travelers and slips us a few beers. He winks and wishes us *Un prospero año nuevo.* We take our food and beer toward the port and find a park festively illuminated. Strings of lights line the rigging and rails on the sailboats and yachts. I shiver against the wind coming off the water, but the weather is mild for January, at least compared to what we're used to back in the States.

After dinner, as fireworks boom over our heads, Grant slips next to me. Our arms brush, just as they did in the clearing in the woods, warming me with a blend of vibrancy and comfort. I look at the sky above, recalling the shooting star last summer. I turn my head toward him, his eyes reflecting the colors blinking in the sky. Then he tilts his gaze down to meet mine. All it takes is one breath. Our lips meet, and the explosions continue into the night.

After settling in at our exchange school, our first weekend arrives, and Rory and Henry have become a goofy and giddy new couple. A twinge of jealousy shoots through me, just as it did when I saw the couple kissing back in Madrid. Grant and I wrap and stow away the kiss we shared on New Year's Eve. We haven't exchanged more than a smile since. I want that closeness, the affection, and romance. However, on the flip side, taking into consideration my situation with him only a couple of weeks prior, being friends, seeing his smile, and laughing together are vast improvements.

"You guys want to go out later?" Rory asks from the table where she finishes her homework.

"What did you have in mind?" Grant asks.

"Diego and Martina, in our social studies class, said they and a bunch of other people are going to a club tonight."

"Yeah, sure," he answers, glancing at me.

I don't disagree.

I pick through my enormous backpack and find a pair of gray skinny jeans with sequins running like raindrops from the waist down to the bottom of the pockets. I pair them with a black fitted tank, a shrug, heels, and a swipe of my favorite red lipstick.

"You look good," Grant says when I come out of the room. I fight against the thought that he's taking a long sip of me, all dressed up. The two little lines between my eyebrows move closer together in confusion. Then I remind myself Kiki would have said the same thing. We're just friends.

"You're such a fashionista," Rory chimes, tugging on her sweatshirt and stretch pants. "Please, help me get dressed. I'm so style challenged."

Rory looks far more cosmopolitan in a pair of jeans, black boots, a simple white shirt, and a Pashmina scarf from my bag than in anything from the limited selection from her luggage. Grant, Henry, and I follow her to the restaurant to meet Diego and Martina.

My stomach drops as we enter a tapas bar. Thoughts of my summer escapades that started when I met Matteo in a similar establishment flood me with dread and regret. Then the events in the VIP room at the club coast into my mind as Martina tells us where she wants to take us later. As we settle around a cozy table, Grant gives me a wide smile, chasing my fears away.

I try to enjoy the food and conversation, but each sip of my drink reminds me of that fateful night. I want to remain lucid and in control, but notice Grant works on his third beer by the time the bill comes.

Once out on the street, we walk in pairs along the sidewalk to the club Martina raved about. Grant carelessly slings his arm over my shoulder. "That was good, huh? I'll have to get ahold of some saffron while we're here. I haven't cooked in a while." I detect the slightest slur in his voice.

"Yeah," I say, removing his arm. "Friends?"

His steps slow. "What—" He starts. "Oh." Maybe the beer made him forget the restrictions he set on our relationship. Perhaps he experiences the same inner conflict I do.

As soon as we enter the club, Rory pumps herself up along with the music and dances with Henry and the others. To her, partying and freedom are new, but I've done this before, and it's lost its luster. It feels punishingly like a repeat of the night I badly want to forget.

Grant emerges from a crowd by the bar and hands me a shot. "To us," he says. His behavior baffles me, but I wordlessly tap my glass against his and swallow. Adequately buzzed, I let Rory pull me onto the dance floor. When the song changes, Grant twirls me around a few times. I let myself fall into rhythm with him. I'm buoyant in his arms. He pulls me in, and our bodies are closer together than they are apart. I completely forget myself. Grant and I move and sway, and it doesn't feel like things have ever been different.

Chapter 48

The four of us stumble back to the dorm, the streets quiet except for Rory and Henry laughing and tripping lightly in front of us. They disappear into our room, and Rory closes the door. With one glance, I follow Grant to the fire escape.

We share a bottle of water. Sobriety slowly returns as the sky lightens. He leans on the rail and studies me. I don't look away.

"Let's not be friends." He pauses. "I want to be your boyfriend. I want to hold your hand and listen to you talk. I want to explore this city and remind each other of the Spanish words we forget. I want to share a cup of coffee, a bed, a dream. I want to be yours—"

"Yes." I don't let him finish because in that moment our worlds collide. Instead of exploding, splintering into fragments, there's a stillness, a cohesion like when raindrops join together on glass. Yet this feels like sunshine and maybe somewhere there's a rainbow. With my trembling hand, I take his and lead him to the bedroom.

He slips my top over my head and rubs his hands over my shoulders and down my sides. "Tell me when you want me to stop."

"I can't. That would be a lie," I say. "And I promised I will always be honest with you."

I lean toward him, feeling the electricity of my bare skin against his. I can't hold back the tears that spill from my heart; they're quiet, settled, the happy kind.

Grant wipes my eyes.

Our chests press together as we fall onto the bed, kissing each other madly, wildly. My skin holds the memory of his touch, my mouth his tongue. It's exhilarating and relaxing at the same time. I feel awake and asleep. I feel the sun and the moon. Afterward, he wraps his arms around me like a promise never to let go.

We wake to the sound of breakfast out in the kitchenette. Grant stretches beside me. I roll over, and that familiar, sad smile appears.

"Why do you still look sad and happy at the same time?" I ask, brushing my index finger from his top lip to his bottom. He closes his eyes. Then, when he blinks them open, he searches mine.

"Ever since our conversation on the train, I've been thinking about us. I almost feel like I'm giving you a loaded weapon when I say this, but I'm crazy about you. I say *crazy* because I tried *not* to forgive you for what you did. Part of me thinks it's crazy to want to be with someone who hurt me. I tried to hold on to my anger. I tried to hang around with Suzy." He looks perplexed when he says her name. "But it's always you. I think about you when I wake up in the morning and when I go to sleep and every second in between." Tears dance at the corners of his eyes and mine.

"So maybe I look happy and sad because I'm happy to be with you, but so afraid you might disappear or get so caught up in drugs, another guy, or some nonsense that you won't be you anymore."

I smile through my tears, letting them run freely. No one has ever wanted me for me before. For this gift, I am willing to love myself and, in turn, be able to love him fully. I'm willing to be my best for us, just for the honor of having an *us* to love.

"I never want to let you go. I never want to see you fade. I just want to watch you glow," he says.

We kiss and kiss and kiss.

Grant and I let the minutes drift by as the Sunday morning unfolds on the other side of the door. Everything that I need exists right where I lie. We snuggle, face-to-face, just a light sheet draping us, and talk about Barcelona while Grant absently twists a piece of my hair. We discuss going to a *fútbol* match as I trace the inky lines on his arm.

"I love you," he says sweetly.

This time his smile emanates pure happiness.

"I love you too," I answer.

For the remainder of our stay at the school, Grant and I are two student tourists exploring the city and love. During our downtime, we traipse around the ancient streets, cheer and boo at a few soccer games, visit the museums, and admire the parks and architecture. We stumble upon a tattoo studio, and Grant flashes a smile.

"Time to start on the other arm?" I ask.

He considers getting the emblem of his favorite soccer team, but instead the artist adds a pearl to the mermaid's hand, and beneath her, he works an oyster into the design.

Too soon we say good-bye to Diego and Martina and our other new friends, leaving the student exchange behind us. We ride the train to Bilbao to meet up with the rest of our group.

As the scenery passes by, I fall into rhythm with the train, yet my thoughts, for once, don't chase me down the track. Instead there's landscape. Still life. Maybe someday a portrait.

"So, back to life in a horde," Grant says, referencing our group parading around the cities, led by Senora Azuelos and Senor Robbins.

I chuckle. "It seems like it might be different, though." I try to put words to how I feel as I imagine transitioning from life with just Grant and me in Barcelona, and our newly anointed relationship, to what it will be like back in our group, but can't quite define it.

"Things *are* different," he says.

"They are," I agree.

"But that doesn't mean the fun has to end," he adds, winking.

While we wait for the rest of the students to arrive inside the café where we're supposed to meet, Suzy elbows by me. Planting herself in front of Grant, she angles toward me and says, "I think he's had just about enough of you."

Her comment scratches. I can never be anyone except who I am, and I really like the person I'm becoming. Nonetheless, I vacillate between taking the high road and flipping out, screaming some choice words I picked up at the soccer games in Spain; after all, I'm still a work in progress.

"I doubt that," I say with dregs of irritation.

She huffs and places her hands on her hips. Her eyes narrow, glaring at Grant, urging him to come to her defense. "Grant, what is she talking about? I thought there was something going on between us?"

Grant runs his hand through his hair. "I'm sorry if you got the wrong idea, Suzy. Pearl and I were on a break."

"But you said—"

He cuts across her. "I never said anything about Pearl to you. You created this"—he gestures with his hands in frustration—"this thing in your head. I'm sorry, Suzy, but—"

She interrupts him this time. "Now she's Pearl? I thought she was PJ. PJ as in pointless jerk. Grant, when we kissed—" She looks steadily at me, and I can't help but notice that everyone else in the room watches the three of us intently, a real-life soap opera unfolding in the restaurant. "I felt something between us. I thought you felt the same way."

I expect her to be close to tears or have hurt written across her face. She just looks infuriated, as if she's losing a competition or prize. I want to say something, but continue to hold my tongue.

"That's the thing, you *thought*. I never said . . . Suzy, listen, I'm sorry you're upset, but—"

"You led me on. You're the pointless jerk. You—"

"Stop with the name-calling." I interrupt this time. "Enough, both of you," I say. "The truth is I made a mistake, but Grant forgave me."

He takes my face in both of his hands and gives me the juiciest kiss ever. Whooping comes from somewhere in the room.

The next day, our first stop is the Guggenheim Museum. We take a group tour, and all the while, the exhibit room where Frida Kahlo's work hangs on the wall tugs at me to the point of distraction. After a long morning of gallery talks and tours, it's lunchtime. Instead of sitting with the group and tucking into our sandwiches, Grant pulls me down a corridor, with a mischievous grin. I wonder if he wants to make out in the museum, already regretting being back in the supervised group.

"We missed a room," he says, and I know exactly where we're going.

I stand in the entryway, the decades-old oil paint bold and beautiful against the white walls. Frida surrounds me, pulls me into her passionate world. I feel her pulse in the flowers twined in her hair, her steady gaze matching the poster on my wall back at Viv Brooks. The misfortune and victory of her life endure in her lifted chin and the representations of the pain that ran through her chest and along her back to her legs, along with the ache of regret and a troubled heart. I see the skill, the pride, the joy in the detail of her brushstrokes. I recall a quote, her saying how she often painted herself because she was the subject she knew best.

Shale's instruction to sit with the enemy within, to raise my expectations until I am friends with myself, joins my thoughts. I think of the friendships I've lost and gathered along the winding path of my life, and now here I am, surrounded by the work of my favorite artist and standing next to Grant, far, far away from the past.

As I pause and linger in front of each framed painting, there's nothing else. I forget and then remember myself, grateful I have me to come back to.

Chapter 49

The buds on the trees and the scent of mud in the air reveal the arrival of spring at Laurel Hill. Having spent so much time abroad, I expect things and people to be out of place when I return, like I'm a book missing from the shelf. Instead, I find the campus humming with its usual precollege-acceptance drone about small versus large envelopes, along with preparations for the final push before exams.

When I return to Viv Brooks, Charmindy is at her desk, the poster of my mother is on my wall, and I am home.

Charmindy leaps from her chair. "You're glowing. Tell me all about it," she says while I'm still in the doorway.

We hug, and I gush about the trip, the museums, Grant . . . She fills me in on some minor gossip and goings-on in the dorm until Brett calls down the hall for her, boys unable to go past the common room, unlike the dorm in Barcelona.

To my delight, for the first time in my life, I feel OK in the present and excited about the future. Twisted, self-destructive fears don't cause me to worry until I climb the three flights of stairs to the art studio.

Shale's whiskers lift when I enter. "You came back."

"Yes," I reply.

"Ready?"

"No." I get a canvas anyway, gather paint and supplies, find the light, and begin painting. I put down my brush. "It feels all wrong, like I'm using my left hand, or I'm blindfolded." I step back.

Shale grunts. "Your icon, Frida Kahlo? You saw her work while in Bilbao, yes? You think she became prolific, that she gained access to the visual language that allows her to reach through time and pigment and speak to you because sometimes she didn't feel like it? No. She lay in her bed, in unimaginable pain, and painted anyway. She painted because she had to. She had no other choice. It was create art or be swallowed up, devoured by her enemy, herself. When she was broken, shattered, she painted. Ask yourself what art means to you. This is not a rhetorical question." He's nearly out of breath. He stares at me like he's waiting for my reply.

I return to Frida's images in the gallery at the Guggenheim and surround myself with her bougainvillea blooms, birds, lilies, dogs, and dusty Mexican desert. I breathe deeply, and then I trace my way all the way from Manhattan, passing littered streets, broken dreams, starlit nights, and golden light, all the way here to where I am right now, but still, the image begging to be seen on the canvas doesn't translate.

When I don't answer the question, he asks, "How much do you want it? What are you willing to do? Do you want to be a dabbler, a hobbyist, only living half your life? Do you want to be a patron of the arts? We need them too. Or do you want your artistry to help you put yourself back together, brushstroke by brushstroke, rearranging the pieces of you until one day, you put the brush down and at last you feel complete?"

"But I don't know how."

"Yes, you do."

As April rains itself out, college acceptance letters roll in. By the end of the week, I've received acceptance letters from all the schools I applied to except one. The challenge now is choosing.

I'm sitting in the library, completing a research project, when Grant enters looking upset, his hand rubbing his head feverishly. "Will you take a walk with me?"

I quickly put my books away and follow him outside. We quietly cross the lawn together toward the woods. When in the clearing, he lights a cigarette and says, "Sorel." He swallows hard. "She is in the hospital. She was in a car accident." I return to the claustrophobic office where Dr. Greenbrae gave me the news about my mother. Sorel could be worse off.

Nonetheless, his words fix me to the spot where I stand, unable to move or speak. However, my inner terrain has become more familiar and the prospect of how loss might unfold within me less terrifying. In the past, I would have immediately wanted to run, run, run away and escape the pain of memories and the potential for loss. Instead, I feel it slicing through me, white-hot. It doubles back and gives me its worst. I crumble, and then like a phoenix, I do the agonizing work of regenerating. I put my arms around Grant, hoping my newfound strength can help steady him.

"What happened?" I whisper.

Grant takes a drag off his cigarette. "Apparently she was high. She wasn't the driver. I guess she was with a friend, and they had just left some dealer and shot up in the car. It must have been bad."

"Where's Pepper?"

"He left. But he had one foot out the door without her here anyway."

I can't imagine Sorel in a hospital bed and how close she came to being gone from this world. In my mind, I watch her caper around me in the grove, kicking up leaves and cursing at the sky. I hear her voice the last time we spoke, thousands of miles away, and realize what about it had bothered me. Intuitively, I knew she was high. She sounded just as my mother did, indifferent, absent, like she'd already let go of whatever tethered her to life.

A memory of a car accident blends with the image my mind creates of Sorel in the passenger seat, the driver losing control, heads smacking glass, the sound of crushing metal.

I open my eyes and inhale deeply, realizing I've been holding my breath. I talk myself off the edge of the traumatic memory and assure myself with my feet on solid ground.

Grant and I, two figures under the great trees, stand there in shock and disbelief until the last light fades from the sky.

The next day and for several weeks after, Grant and I meet in the clearing almost every evening and, in our own way, say good-bye to Laurel Hill. We pledge not to smoke anymore, a reverse tribute to Sorel as she heals from the crash and slays her demons.

One evening, I bring my old journal with the heart inscribed on the cover. I scribble a memory down about the car accident when I was about five, how I slid across the vinyl seat into the passenger-side door as the car twisted around and around on a bridge exiting the city. The car finally stopped when it wedged under the guardrail, and the front tires spun over the water below.

From this story, I move forward in time, jotting down all the stories, all the fears, traumas, and hurts. I spill them out of myself and into that wooded place, writing intensely, passionately, across the pages. The trees recycle my memories into oxygen, and my heart forms them into pearls. I tell the stories of my childhood, as much as a eulogy for my mother as for me, and my lost years.

Sitting across from me in the dining hall, Grant tosses me a quarter.

"What's this for?"

"The deadline for your decision is tomorrow."

"I can't flip a coin to decide where I'll be for the next four years."

"You've done far crazier things," he says warmly. "It's just an idea."

I study the gritty coin. It's from the year I was born. I take this as a sign. "Heads up, UCLA. Tails, FIT," I say.

Our eyes meet.

"OK, here I go." I watch the coin spin and pirouette before I catch it. "Heads."

Grant hoots. "Now we can be neighbors," he says with a giddy smile.

"I would have picked UCLA even if it was tails. Getting out of New York City seems like the right direction, plus a handsome Scotsman will be there." *Do better.* Charmindy's voice echoes in my mind. "I'll do better," I say aloud as an image forms in my mind. I give Grant a reassuring squeeze and rush off to the art building.

I squeeze a rainbow of color onto my palette: bright reds and marigolds, bold greens and blues. I add tans and a shade that reminds me of eggplant. Then I add a dollop of a color I'd call sunshine. Shale isn't at my shoulder, in his office, or pacing along the creaky floor.

I begin painting, and instead of a girl fading away, I see myself bursting forth, an explosion of color that can only be described as pure wow. I anticipate a grunt over my shoulder, but it doesn't come. When my neck and arm ache, I step back; gaze at the painting, so joyful I can almost hear music in it; and set my brush down.

On a sunny day in late spring, as I roll up the Shrapnels poster, my mother's expression taunts me. It's as if she challenges my resolve to do better. Then Frida, in all her agony, looks at me approvingly, as if to say, *Sister, this is your show. Play it how you like it. You've got this.* I tuck her away and note her voice is louder than JJ's.

Charmindy comes in, almost out of breath, as though she just sprinted across campus. "Quick. Come with me."

As she pulls me by the hand, I ask, "What happened?" imagining accidents or calamities.

She doesn't answer. We arrive at the student center, where students, parents, and alums mill around, drinks in hand, chattering. It's a meet and greet on the eve of graduation. With their backs to me, a layer of people line the wall. I spot Shale talking to a dignified couple. He's smiling, beaming actually.

"What is this?" I ask Charmindy over the din.

"This, my friend, is you."

In a gap between a man wearing a pressed button-down and a woman in a navy cocktail dress, the edge of an oil painting, the edge of me, appears. In a few long strides, I reach the perimeter of the room. If I were to paint myself now, there'd be a girl with her mouth hanging open and beads of salty water brimming from her eyelids.

"Who did this? Why?"

"For you," Shale says, coming up behind me.

I gaze from canvas to canvas, seeing versions of myself in various stages of dissolution, but as I continue around the room, there are images of me constructing a new self, landing brilliantly on the latest self-portrait, titled *Spring*, as if finally, after a long winter, I've come to life.

Shale turns to me. My face glows, and my eyes glisten. "Now, that is the girl I've been waiting to see."

Graduation is a sunny day complete with plastic leis and the tossing of tasseled mortarboards. Beneath my gown, I wear the gold dress Charmindy gave me on my birthday. I'm radiant. I think of JJ at the

Grammys and the times I'd play dress up in her gold gown, grasping at the mother I wanted. But now I have my own dress, my own sparkle.

All around, there's hugging and laughter, tears too. I thank my teachers, Connie, and even Dr. Greenbrae, who seems surprised to see me in attendance.

A car waits for Charmindy, Grant, and me in the exact spot a similar one left me nearly two years ago. The flowers in front of the Laurel Hill sign are different, an array of peonies, orange cosmos, and azaleas.

Charmindy travels with Grant and me to Brooklyn. He and I plan to spend a week with Gavin before going to Scotland for a few weeks and then traveling west for school next fall.

Unbelievably or morbidly, depending on how I look at it, with only one remaining member of the Shrapnels, along with a retrospective on a music channel, there's been an uptick in sales, resulting in a larger than normal royalty check being deposited into my account. That, plus saving my allowance, bought me a ticket.

"You sure you want to cross the bridge?" I ask Charmindy. "It's pretty hot out."

"I promised I'd send Brett a picture of me every day we're apart this summer. It'll be a while before we see each other in Boston for the fall semester."

"But you saw him this morning, before we left."

Charmindy gazes out the window as the skyline comes into view. She opens her mouth, closes it, and then says, "And, y'know, it might be a cool way to part ways, on the Brooklyn Bridge, before you guys go to visit Grant's brother and I go to my sister's. That way, you know you always have family on both sides."

I smile appreciatively. As we enter the city, I think about the triad of accepting and letting go, forgiving, and welcoming the possibility of change and renewal in my life. I think about going to college, about Grant and me, friendships that have become sisterhoods, and family.

Charmindy interrupts my ponderings. "Poesy would love to see you again if we can arrange it before you leave," she says.

"Let's all go out to dinner," I suggest. "I know a great place," I say, thinking of a little hole-in-the-wall pizza shop that serves the most inexpensive, yet authentic Italian pies with fresh mozzarella, roasted tomatoes, garlic, and basil.

The car leaves us off, and we gather our luggage, most of it awaiting our arrival at our respective universities. I breathe in another version of Manhattan air, a mixture of exhaust, river water, and home. Passing to the pedestrian part of the bridge, the cables and granite pillars rise toward the sky as though promising us we too can touch the blue, the sun, each other.

"So, Scotland?" Charmindy asks, breaking the New York City spell.

"Yeah, I have to see my dad," Grant says dryly.

"And visit the family cottage, your grandfather, and see the sights," I add excitedly. The trip was my idea. I knew that if I could mend my shattered self, he could repair his relationship with his dad . . . and selfishly, I want to hear his accent come back.

"Are you *from* Scotland?" Charmindy asks in surprise.

Grant nods.

"Get out! Where's the accent?"

He smirks. "It's here, buried under layers of bitterness," he says in a perfect Scottish burr.

Charmindy raises her eyebrows.

"Just like I have mommy issues, Grant has daddy issues," I say with a laugh.

He playfully nudges me.

"Well, nice for you both. I have mommy *and* daddy issues."

We all laugh.

A peculiar, fuzzy, and sparkly feeling comes over me. Charmindy and Grant have both taught me something that sweeps up the remaining shards of my broken childhood.

I inhale, and the words come on my exhale. "I realize the *F* word, *forgiveness*, has two sides, like a coin. Charmindy, last fall, when we took that walk, you told me the hardest thing a person could do is forgive. At the time, I thought you misunderstood me, thinking I needed to forgive Grant and not the other way around." I pause, afraid for a moment, but he squeezes my hand, listening, urging me on. "Really, I think you meant for me to forgive whatever it was that caused me to hurt someone I care about. I needed to forgive my mother and myself in order to move forward with my life."

I turn to Grant before going on. "By forgiving me, you taught me that forgiveness, even when it seems inconceivable, is possible. It's something I can and must do too, over and over again. This winding road of mistakes, unlikely friends, teachers, and you brought me to this wonderful moment." My smile stretches wide, and it's almost like the wings of the tattooed sparrows flap, keeping the beat of my heart. I realize they've guided me home to the company of my two best friends in the world.

I pause halfway across the bridge, the river and sky and city stretching in every direction, with every possibility. I take out the journal I filled with my life story, and pen the words and whisper, "I forgive you." Each syllable lifts the burdens and weight of the past. I have become so used to carrying its load I only realize its density when I let it go. The inside of my brain is suddenly clear of cobwebs, and my heart fills with sunshine.

I trace my finger around the heart on the cover, thumbing the pages on the tattered journal, a record of the triumphs and tragedies from the past eighteen years that I recorded over these last few weeks. I'm no longer afraid to look back, because all those experiences brought me to where I am now.

I take a deep breath. I toss the journal containing the tired tale of my life with JJ and everything that came after into the water below.

After a moment, I can't quite see it, but I imagine the pages fluttering slowly down toward the river, the water washing away the ink.

"What did you do that for?" Grant asks, aghast, knowing what the journal contained.

"I don't need it anymore. I'm the author of my life." I smile at Charmindy and at Grant. "Thanks, guys," I say.

"For what?" they both ask at the same time.

"For being you and helping me to be me."

And now I know what it means to be free.

Acknowledgments

There are only two words that belong on this page: thank you, but there aren't enough words to express the enormity of what my gratitude means. Warm thank-you hugs filled with the fuzzies to the following:

My family, thank you for cheering me on, cheering me up, and bearing with me while I click, clack, write, and write some more.

My friends, Tamar, Christine, Seana, and Val, your check-ins are like a breath of fresh air.

God, thank you for reminding me daily to flex my wonder muscles. This life is truly awe inspiring.

Cheyanne, I'm glad we get to share and swap stories on this adventure!

My Skyscape team: Courtney, I'm thankful you visited Brooklyn recently and crossed bridges, figuratively and literally; Kelli, your emails are a favorite in my in-box, always; Dennelle, your multitude of skills sure do make a gal feel special; and much, much gratitude to Megan Beatie, and all the people who take my words and make magic.

Readers, it is an honor and a privilege that I get to share these little bits of my heart with you.

Thank you.

Author's Note

At the heart of Pearl's experience was the lesson that she wasn't alone, no matter how often she felt like she was. To some readers, her story might sound extreme, but for those living with domestic violence, addiction, and other forms of abuse, it is very real, scary, and isolating. There is no need to wait for a crisis to get help. Various kinds of assistance are available, from talking to a counselor online, on the phone, or in person, to staging an intervention, to getting out of a dangerous situation. Making a decision to reach out isn't necessarily easy; it takes courage and a leap of faith, but I believe that every person's safety, well-being, and life are worth it. Here are some resources:

Substance Abuse and Mental Health Services Administration: SAMHSA (1-800-662-4357) is a federal agency that provides confidential, free, twenty-four-hour-a-day, 365-days-a-year help in English and Spanish for individuals and their families facing mental health and/or substance-use disorders.

Teen Lifeline: 1-800-248-8336, teenlifeline.org.

National Domestic Violence Hotline: 1-877-799-7233, thehotline.org.

National Council on Alcoholism and Drug Dependence, Inc.: 1-800-622-2255.

Al-Anon and Alateen: Both offer help for people who have, or know someone who has, a drinking problem. 1-800-425-2666.

Kristin Brooks Hope Center: KBHC offers a mental health, depression, suicide help line. 1-800-784-2433, hopeline.com.

National Suicide Prevention Lifeline: 1-800-273-8255, suicidepreventionlifeline.org.

About the Author

Photo © 2015 Lara Farhadi

During her teens, Deirdre Riordan Hall traveled throughout the United States and Europe, developing a love for stories and a desire to connect with worlds—imagined or real—on the page. She has written *Sugar, To the Sea, Surfaced,* and the Follow Your Bliss series. When not spending time with her family, writing, or traveling, Hall is at the beach, pretending to be a mermaid.

DISCARD